All That's Left of Me

ALSO BY JANIS THOMAS

All That's Left of Me

A Novel

Janis Thomas

LAKE UNION
PUBLISHING

Text copyright © 2018 by Janis Thomas
All rights reserved.

No part of this book may be reproduced, or stored in a retrieval system, or transmitted in any form or by any means, electronic, mechanical, photocopying, recording, or otherwise, without express written permission of the publisher.

Published by Lake Union Publishing, Seattle

www.apub.com

Amazon, the Amazon logo, and Lake Union Publishing are trademarks of Amazon.com, Inc., or its affiliates.

ISBN-13: 9781503901148
ISBN-10: 1503901149

Cover design by Rex Bonomelli

Printed in the United States of America

For Linda Coler Fields—
I wouldn't wish for any life that didn't have you in it.

PROLOGUE

Wednesday, June 29

"Charlemagne," Louise Krummund announces. She stands on her porch, cradling a furry, puffy lump, and beckons me to join her. I'm already late for work, but my curiosity leads me to her. "His name is Charlemagne." The name sounds odd coming from Louise, with her thick Brooklyn accent and bright-pink curlers peeking through Clairol-blonde hair. "But we'll call him Charlie."

Then why call him Charlemagne in the first place? I don't want to sound rude, so I keep the question to myself.

"We got him from Paw-Tastic Pets," she says, then turns defensive. "Oh, I know, I know, we should have adopted from one of those rescue places. But we all just fell in love with him as soon as we saw him in the window. And they were having a fantastic Independence Week sale. We couldn't resist."

I reach out to stroke the brown-and-black fuzz of the ridiculously named creature wriggling in Louise's arms. He is cute, this Charlemagne/Charlie, and I allow myself the enjoyment of scratching his ears and stroking his belly. I pull my hand away, and he yaps in protest. I laugh, then submit to his demands, running my fingers through his fur.

"Can I take a picture of him to show Josh?" I ask, as is my habit.

"Here," she says, holding the puppy out to me while grabbing for my phone. "I'll take a picture of the two of you."

Charlemagne/Charlie graces my cheek and mouth and neck with puppy kisses as I hold him in the crook of my arm. His sandpaper tongue tickles my skin. Louise fumbles with my cell phone—she doesn't know how to use the camera app, and I will later find twenty pictures in my photo gallery because she accidentally used the speed setting. The puppy grows restless and starts to gnaw on my fingers with his sharp teeth.

When Louise decides she's taken a good shot, she hands the phone back and reaches for the puppy. I don't want to let him go. But I do.

"Bring Josh by any time to play with little Charlie," she says. "I'll make us a pot of coffee. I get these special Peruvian beans from Amazon. Pricey but worth it. You should definitely come in and try it."

I nod, even though I know I won't. Louise has been asking me over for coffee since we moved in—seven years ago—and I have yet to accept her invitation. I wonder if she'll ever give up.

She cuddles the puppy against her ample breast, then disappears into a house full of children and unwashed laundry and the lingering aroma of bratwurst. I watch the puppy until the door closes.

ONE

The first morning it happens is unremarkable in every other way. The same blade of sunlight slices across my comforter, setting a stripe of faded sunflowers on fire. The familiar aroma of my husband's espresso wafts through the air. The shadow voices of CNN steal their way into my ear from the TV in the kitchen. My eyes are grainy and swollen from a fitful night of sleep.

An unremarkable day. Just another day to face, to endure, to survive. Another morning when my life bears down on me, weighting me like an anchor, dragging me beneath the ambivalent sea. And all I want is to be numbed by the icy current. To give in, give up, let the waves crash over me and drown me into sweet nothingness.

But there are things to be done, people to attend to, responsibilities, duties, motherhood—caretaking included—wifedom, sadistic bosses with their overbearing attitudes and Altoid breath, bitter ex-husbands brandishing threats, leaking faucets and broken banisters, bills in need of payment, and the constant whispered needs of a thousand to-dos, all of them dragging me down but ultimately forcing me to pull myself out of the safety of my bed.

This is my life.

I never imagined I would feel the way I feel now. I want to escape. I finally understand those women—and men—who simply walk away from their lives. Those people who drain their savings and disappear, shuck all their encumbrances and rebirth themselves. But I am glued to my encumbrances. And I have no savings to drain.

Another woman would embrace her life. She would face her challenges with grace, find the positives and focus on them instead of allowing the negatives to overwhelm her. I used to be that woman. I used to smile in the face of adversity and spout Pollyanna platitudes and count my blessings. Until I couldn't anymore.

Shower completed: the first check mark on my list. My husband, Colin, waits for me as I move out of the bathroom. He sits on the end of the bed. His eyes are on the floor, peering at a fleck of something, some *not-supposed-to-be-there* something. A leaf, perhaps, or a shred of paper. A blade of grass. I can't see it without my glasses, so I choose to ignore it.

"I got him up," Colin says, expecting a congratulatory gesture on my part.

"Good." My voice is thick with the remnants of sleep, those that have not been eradicated by the near-boiling water of my shower.

"He's in fine spirits this morning," Colin continues, deciding—I can tell—not to linger on the "something" on the carpet.

"Good." Again with the one-syllable response. I'm not awake enough to offer more.

I glance at Colin and try for a smile. He matches my effort with his own. We are not estranged, my husband and I. We've simply transitioned into that limbo where married couples often find themselves: not lovers, not friends, but two people sharing space because of a commitment they made during a beautiful and *costly* ceremony where countless people showered them with flower petals because rice had been banned by PETA. There was a time I considered that day one of the happiest of my life. Now it's just a memory.

I love Colin, I do. But mostly because he's still here.

"Katie's gone already."

I move to the dresser, turn off the baby monitor, and grab some underwear from the top drawer. I drop the towel, my nakedness exposed. No one's looking.

The digital clock reads seven fifteen. An early departure for my daughter. I try not to think about where she is or who she's with at this hour. Katie is almost seventeen, a year from college. *Time to let her go.* I repeat the mantra to myself often, because this is the phrase a good mother uses, the words a good mother says after years of maternal devotion. The good mother smiles when she says these words, proud that she has managed to nurture and raise another human being. I repeat the mantra without smiling and without pride, because it is a front. Katie lurks in teenage angst and writhes in hormonal upset. If I have nurtured her in the past, here in the present I can find nothing useful to say to her. The less time I spend with her, the better. For her sake, not mine.

Colin leans so far forward, I fear he will topple over. With his long-armed reach, he retrieves the offending something on the carpet. I watch his reflection as he inspects the item, as though it were an intriguing specimen on the tray of a microscope. He stands and tucks whatever it is into his pocket, and I avert my gaze before he can meet it in the mirror.

"I can start the oatmeal," he offers, "if you're running late."

"I'll do it," I snap, then soften. He is only trying to help. "Just let me get dressed."

"I am capable of boiling water." A hint of a grin.

"Are you?" Meant as a joke, but unfunny aloud.

Colin moves slowly across the room, sagging slightly, his slouch a physical reaction to my meanness.

"Colin. Thank you for taking night duty."

He gives me a weary grin. "It was easy. He slept through the night."

Of course he did. He never sleeps through the night when I'm on duty.

Reading my mind, Colin shrugs. "We can bring in someone for nights, Emma."

"We can't afford it, Colin. You know that."

"Well, maybe after the book . . ." His words dry up. He hasn't finished his third book yet. He might never finish the damn thing.

"I'll be right down," I say.

He nods, then steps into the hall.

Only after he closes the door do I notice. Something is wrong. Or not wrong, but not quite right. I don't know what it is, can't put my finger on the not-quite-right thing.

I glance around the room, searching for a telltale sign: a picture listing to the side, a lamp pushed out of place, something missing, or, conversely, something here that shouldn't be. Nothing reveals itself. The room is as always. Threadbare comforter, weary landscapes trapped in dusty frames suspended on drab beige walls that need a fresh coat of paint. Framed photo of my mother on my nightstand beside my digital alarm clock, hand-carved jewelry chest—my one treasure, my lone inheritance—gaping up at me from the scuffed dresser, the tiny ballerina in the back corner of the faded velvet tray forever motionless. Nothing is amiss.

And yet, and yet. That not-right feeling niggles at me, whispers through the hairs on the back of my neck as I pull my graying brown hair into a loose chignon. Pokes at me as I don today's work ensemble of navy skirt, cream blouse, stockings, and toe-crushing pumps.

I've worked at jobs that allowed me to wear comfortable clothes, but not this one. My boss, Richard, demands that his employees adhere to their gender in all manner of appearances. So I carefully zip my skirt and button my blouse and wrestle the hosiery up my legs and ignore the blisters bulging on both of my insteps. And as I do, I think longingly of that bartending gig I had in college where I got to wear jeans and sneakers and T-shirts.

But the not-right thing lingers in my consciousness, begging for attention, dragging me away from my memories.

A few generous swipes of concealer do little to hide the bruiselike crescents beneath my eyes.

What is it? I ask myself.

The brushstrokes of rouge look comedic against the ghostly pallor of my cheeks and I wipe them away with Kleenex.

What is it that isn't?

I choose pale pink for my lips; a shade darker would look clownish and grotesque.

What is the not-right thing?

I reach into the jewelry box for my pearl earrings and slide them into my ears as I stare at my reflection.

I hear the quiet of the morning around me. For the first time in a week, the puppy next door is not barking his head off.

And *that* is the not-right thing.

TWO

I make my way down the stairs, gripping the railing as I always do when I wear pumps. Time is not a woman's friend, and I am approaching the age when a snagged heel can cause a disastrous fall down a flight of stairs that would lead to the ruination of a formerly vibrant life. My life is not vibrant, but it is still my own. My seventy-eight-year-old mother was vibrant. She took aerobic classes three times a week and gardened every day until she tripped off the curb of the community center and broke her hip. I buried her six months later. I am roughly half her age. But my anticipation of the foregone conclusion has begun.

Our staircase is wide, to accommodate the wheelchair lift. The width was one of the features that drew us to the house. The wheelchair platform is already below. As I descend, I gaze absently at the metal track that runs to the second floor. My ears are attuned to every sound around me, none of which is the sound I expect or desire. The quiet disturbs me almost to distraction, and even with my firm grasp on the rail, I feel my ankle turn. I right myself before I can do damage but sit hard on the carpeted step. Pain reverberates through my tailbone. I stand and continue down the steps more slowly.

My mind is elsewhere. I'm thinking about the neighbor's puppy. Charlemagne/Charlie, the adorable little fluff ball whose kisses were coarse and sweet.

I was enchanted by him at first, but my enchantment has been replaced by weary resentment. Little Charlemagne is a yapper. All day and all night. There are periods of quiet, those short blocks of time during which I imagine one of the Krummund children deigns to give the puppy their attention, distracting him with chew toys or games of fetch or roughhousing or rawhide bones. But otherwise, he barks. Bursts of high-pitched staccato yelps that stop only for as long as it takes him to draw breath. The Fourth of July fireworks sent him over the edge. He didn't stop for twenty-four hours straight.

Louise is aware. She smiles guiltily when I catch her outside, on her way in, on my way out, on our simultaneous way to the trash bins.

"You can't put one of those shock collars on a puppy his age," she said a few days ago in lieu of an apology. To which I responded with an ambivalent shrug.

"Oh, and, um, don't worry about collecting our paper next week. We can't go up to the lake. Charlemagne isn't ready for that trip yet." She tried a conciliatory smile. "The barking will stop. I promise. I appreciate you not calling the police for a noise disturbance."

She was kidding. *Ha-ha-ha.* But last night, as I lay in bed hoping, praying, begging for the nothingness of sleep that would erase the hellish day I'd had, Charlemagne, that little ball of fluff, had barked-squealed-yapped with the endurance of an Olympian. A pillow over my head, palms against my ears, Motrin PM—which I can only take when Colin is on night duty—none of these could coax me into REM. And there was Colin beside me, motionless, snoring softly, undisturbed by the canine cacophony next door—even though I knew he would awaken with a start from the slightest hitch in Josh's breathing. And I felt my insides twist and my mind fragment as the moments ticked-dragged-trudged by. And I couldn't stop the thought that screamed through my head just before sleep finally prevailed.

I wish they'd never gotten that godforsaken dog!

As I step onto the first-floor landing, I feel my armpits dampen, despite my antiperspirant.

Perhaps something happened to Charlie/Charlemagne. Maybe he got out of the house and ran into the street and was hit by a car, or he choked on a chew toy, or fell victim to one of the older Krummund boys' version of roughhousing, which ended with a snapped neck. Maybe he got into the rat poison or or or . . .

I stop myself. The puppy is fine. The puppy is not roadkill. He's napping. He's eating. On a walk with Louise, although that's unlikely. Probably she took him to the vet for a checkup. *Yes.* And if something happened to him, God forbid, I will not feel guilty. It will not be my fault just because I held an ugly thought toward him while I desperately clawed my way into sleep.

The puppy is fine. Another mantra. A prayer. Accompanied by an inexplicable prick of dread.

I walk into the kitchen to find that CNN has given way to Disney XD. The raw angles and stark lighting of the news broadcasts upset my son. Animated Phineas and Ferb discovering new ways to pass the summer and exploit their sister, Candace, delights him. He sits in his wheelchair, his head craned to the side, arms stiff and glued to his torso, his hands bent at an unnatural angle, fingers hooked. His tongue lolls out of his mouth, pink and straining as a chuckle escapes him.

He detects my approach, as he always does, and I quicken my step. When Joshua knows I'm near, he wants to see me, and he will twist and turn until I am within his sight line. Nothing causes more heartache to a mother than seeing her child struggle. But I can neither prevent his distress nor my own heartache to any measurable degree, because my son has cerebral palsy and every word he says and every action he performs is an excruciating undertaking.

"Mom," he says when I kneel beside him, although the sound from his lips more closely resembles "Maah." Joshua speaks in a foreign language in which only Colin, Kate, Raina (his caregiver), and I are fluent.

My mother understood him, but theirs was a language without words—a wink, a nod, a slight gesture that communicated novellas.

Josh is fifteen and brilliant and trapped in a body that betrays him every day, every moment. But he is my son, and I love him fiercely, and his steady, blue-eyed gaze warms me.

"Maah, y' af t' sss thi'. Fuh a' Fe bu r'k eeee." *Mom, you have to see this. Phineas and Ferb are building a rocket.*

"Well," I say. "Isn't that amazing." I wish I could build a rocket that would transport me to another dimension, a dimension where cerebral palsy didn't exist.

"He needs you to give him a haircut."

I turn to Colin. He stands at the stove staring down a pot of water. The pot is unfazed.

Josh throws his head back and grimaces. "Aye doe."

"Yes, you do," Colin replies.

My husband is right. Josh is long overdue. His dark-brown hair is starting to curl around the nape of his neck. He has beautiful hair, my son. I grieve the possibility that no woman except me will ever run her fingers through it.

"Dad's right," I say, gaining my feet. "I'll do it on the weekend."

"No," Joshua argues. Josh has trouble pronouncing his *n*'s, but ironically or not, he has no problem with the word *no*. "Aye wah g' t' th baba."

I shake my head as I cross to the stove. I nudge Colin to jolt him from his fixation on the pot of water. "A watched pot never boils."

"Your mom," he says and moves away from me as though my nearness is an affront. But again, he's right. This is my mother's expression. I realize I would sound just like her if my words didn't possess an underlying sense of despair.

"Aye wah g' t' th baba," Joshua repeats. *I want to go to the barber.* He smacks the armrest of his wheelchair for emphasis.

I won't be swayed by his adamancy. I've grown accustomed to the gaping stares, the averted glances, the petty sympathy, and mock empathy my son inspires. But the callousness we received from an unwitting and unwitty patron of the barbershop on our last visit is something I cannot endure again. Joshua is inured to such flagrant insults. But I'm not. I am a host for unthinking cruelty. Every mindless barb against my son is like a sharpened blade thrust into my heart.

"You don't like my haircuts?" I ask as I reach for the carton of oatmeal from the cupboard.

Josh doesn't answer. His eyes are on the TV. He's watching but also avoiding my question.

Colin takes a seat at the table as I stir the oatmeal. He withdraws the pipe from his bathrobe and places the end between his teeth. He used to smoke every morning, filling the bowl with his own blend of sweet-smelling tobacco and savoring each hit while reading his paper. Colin hasn't lit the pipe since his father died of emphysema some six years ago, but neither has he lost the need to feel the beloved mouthpiece on his lips. He bites at it and draws on it, like an adult pacifier. The ritual soothes him, calms him, readies him to face the day. I envy him.

Were there something in my life that would offer me calm, I would take part in it at every opportunity, but I have found nothing. I smoked cigarettes for six months, took yoga for twice as long. I tried meditating every morning for two years, but never reached quiet mind or enlightenment or whatever it is you're supposed to strive for.

Long ago, I found relaxation in books; I read voraciously. But that ended with motherhood. Before then, actually. Kate's was a difficult pregnancy, and I was constantly distracted by the aches in my stomach and the spots of blood in my underwear and the constant worry that I would lose her. I couldn't get through a chapter, a paragraph, a sentence without rereading it a second or third or fourth time, and at last I would give up and lay the book down and instead of reading, I would wallow in the fears of my own making.

And after she was born, perfect and wailing, I still couldn't relax enough to immerse myself in a book. I tried, but it was useless. I purchased whatever novel was popular at the time and sat myself down while Kate slept, hoping to carry myself away with the words of another. But within moments, I would find myself at her crib, obsessively listening to the sound of her breathing, making sure there was no obstruction in her airway.

Josh's pregnancy was easier; I could get through an entire article in a parenting magazine without stopping, and I was heartened. Perhaps, perhaps, I could find my way back to my lovely books. But then I gave birth, and that thing happened, that thing that forever altered the shape of my son's life and my own, and I haven't read a single paragraph since, save for medical instructions and report cards and the fruits of my boss's labors. But those don't count.

"Are you all right?" Colin asks.

I stir brown sugar, heavy cream, and a dash of vanilla into the oatmeal, then pour it into the two awaiting bowls. Then I turn to Colin, who gazes at me expectantly. "Fine. I'm fine."

I carry the bowls to the table and set them in front of Colin and Joshua respectively. I take my place beside Josh to feed him. Katie used to do this, feed her brother, every morning before she left for school. They sat side by side trading insults, which I allowed because of their obvious fondness for each other. She doesn't do this anymore. Not since she met *him*. That boy who she says is *not her boyfriend* but whose every text sends her running to his side, anxious to please him. He is the cause of her angst and the growing discord between us.

I scoop some oatmeal and move the spoon to Josh's lips. He rolls the oatmeal around in his mouth before swallowing.

"Mmm. Goo', Maah."

"Thanks, Josh." I give him a moment to clear the first mouthful. "It's just strange," I say. "You know, not to have that constant barking. I hope Charlemagne's okay."

The air doesn't thin. No lightning strikes. But save for the cartoon on the television, there is silence. As I lift the spoon toward Josh's mouth, I see that he is giving me a strange look. I glance at Colin. His pipe has stilled within his grasp.

"Who's Charlemagne?"

"Shrma wa' th fr emp i Wa Ewru si th cops a th Womuh Umpa." *Charlemagne was the first emperor in Western Europe since the collapse of the Roman Empire.*

My son is a font of information, gleaned from the internet with the aid of his caregiver, Raina, whom we chose because of her extensive work with cerebral palsy patients. He forgets nothing.

"I'm talking about the Krummunds' puppy, Charlemagne," I say. "I told you about him, Josh. I showed you his picture. Brown-and-black fuzz. Remember?"

Again, I am met with confused silence from both sides.

"What puppy?" Colin withdraws the pipe from his lips and pushes his paper aside. Josh's head jerks backward, and his mouth curls into a frown.

Their confusion becomes mine. "The puppy they got a week ago? The one that hasn't shut up for more than three minutes at a stretch? The one you said should have his voice box removed?"

"Maah, thas mea." *Mom, that's mean.*

"I didn't say it, Josh. Your father did."

Colin's brow furrows. He worries the pipe in his hands. "The Krummunds don't have a puppy, Emma."

THREE

"But they do," I insist. I saw him. I touched him. I felt the razor-sharp puppy teeth trying to pierce the flesh of my fingers. *What is going on?* "They got him from Paw-Tastic Pets."

Colin shakes his head. "I have no idea what you're talking about."

"M' eithe." *Me neither.*

"Are you guys kidding?" I glance back and forth between my husband and my son, searching their faces for a hint of amusement or mischief, but I realize they are not playing a joke on me. The not-right feeling returns with greater intensity. I stand and drop the oatmeal onto the table. The spoon clatters against the side of the bowl. I back away from the table, away from Josh's curiosity and Colin's concern.

"Maah?"

"Emma?"

"You saw the dog, Colin," I say sharply. Colin shakes his head slowly, and I mimic his action at triple speed. The kitchen is too bright.

My cell phone. Louise took countless pictures of Charlemagne and me on it. I walk to the kitchen counter on heavy legs. The blisters on my instep throb. I grab my cell phone and swipe it to life. Ignoring the two sets of eyes on me, I scroll through my pictures. Up and up and up through the gallery of photos.

Joshua is homeschooled. Colin and I tried to put him in public school, hoping that such an assimilation would be beneficial to his social growth and awareness, but it was not a good experience for any of us. We looked into private schools, hoping that a sizable monthly tuition would ensure the necessary accommodations. We were disappointed with the choices, but also relieved we wouldn't need to take a second mortgage. We settled for homeschooling. Raina has a degree in education. She is responsible for the daily care of my son, his physical and occupational therapy, and his schooling as well.

He isn't confined to our home, but his outings are limited. So I make a point to visually record any and all things I think he might find interesting, those images that might stimulate him. I think of my cell phone as a conduit to the world at large for Josh.

My hands shake as I scroll backward through the images, the myriad images, the picture I took of a latte from Starbucks when the combination of foam and espresso created an unlikely flower; the shot of Mr. Mosely, the elderly security guard at my firm, wearing a pair of Groucho Marx glasses, holding a fake cigar; the sunrise from two weeks ago on a morning when I couldn't sleep. No puppy. No Charlemagne. Up and down I scroll, back and forth through a sea of images captured for my Josh. No black-and-brown ball of fuzz. I still feel my husband's questioning gaze and my son's skeptical look.

I know I showed Josh the pictures of Charlemagne. I *know* I did.

"I must have accidentally deleted them," I say, more to myself than to them.

"Emma." Colin's voice, steady, calming. "Have some coffee."

I don't want coffee. I want to know what happened to Charlemagne. Charlie. I set the phone down.

"I'm going next door." Resolute, especially for me. I stride to the back door, purposeful, until Colin interrupts me.

"The Krummunds are gone, Emma. They left for the lake on Saturday. We're getting their mail for them."

I don't look at Colin, nor do I glance at Josh. I'm cold all over. Dots of sweat erupt from my forehead, my upper lip. My calves seize. My arms are useless appendages.

I wish they'd never gotten that godforsaken dog!

No. It's not possible. I'm dreaming. I'm asleep thinking I'm awake.

"You had a dream, honey," Colin says. "That the Krummunds got a dog. Must have been a very intense dream, eh? Right, Josh?"

"Tha happeh t' m ah th' tiee," Josh agrees. *That happens to me all the time.*

But it wasn't a dream. This past week of incessant barking was not a dream. The feel of Charlemagne/Charlie's fur through my fingers, his teeth sinking into my flesh, his sandpaper tongue . . . those were not a dream.

"I'll feed Josh," Colin offers. His tone is neutral. It doesn't betray the worry he feels. His wife has gone mad. His wife has conjured puppies from thin air.

Colin. So steady. So clearheaded. A neutron bomb could explode in our living room and my husband would calmly suggest we break out marshmallows for roasting.

"That would be great," I say. I grasp the cell phone so tightly the muscles in my hand ache. "I'd like to get to work on time for a change."

"I'll wait for Raina," Colin replies. His gaze lingers on me for a moment longer, then he scoots his chair around the table toward Josh.

"Ah y' kay, Maah?" *Are you okay, Mom?*

No. I'm insane. I'm having a breakdown.

Appropriate smile. "I'm fine, honey. Just tired. Your dad's right. I had a doozy of a dream." Irreverent chuckle. "But I'm fine."

He may or may not believe me. It's hard to tell with Joshua. He squints at me, then turns his attention to Colin and the spoon moving toward his mouth.

I make my escape without pausing to kiss Josh's head, which I usually do. Panic chases my footsteps. I am unable to sort out the last ten minutes of my life, unable to formulate a coherent thought. I only know I have to move.

What is going on?

I keep walking, through the living room, past the breakfront, the top of which is crowded with family pictures, of the kids at various stages of their lives—Josh always in his wheelchair, Katie always in a striking ensemble. Colin and me, our arms around each other, wearing smiles I barely recognize.

I reach the foyer, my pumps clacking on the cracked tile floor, and grab my jacket and purse from the closet. I head for the back door, then remember I left my car at the curb last night because Kate's un-boyfriend took the liberty of parking in the driveway, barring my access to the garage.

As if he thinks he has a right to my driveway. As if he thinks he has a right to my daughter.

I swallow my resentment and retrace my steps through the house.

As I reach the front door and grasp the doorknob, I hear Josh call out, "Maah?" I pretend I don't hear him, then pretend I don't feel guilty for pretending, and step outside into the sunshine.

I hope the fresh air will give me some kind of clarity, a metaphorical slap in the face that will return me to my senses. It doesn't.

I shuffle down the ramp that leads from the porch to the path and glance past the handicapped van on the right side of our driveway. The Krummunds' house has that look of abandonment. They are gone. No Charlemagne/Charlie. No SUV or trailer. Louise and her tribe have gone to the lake.

A seed of hysteria begins to bloom in my gut.

Our front walkway is made up of redbrick pavers, set down long before Colin and I bought the house. Roots from the oak tree in our yard snake through the lawn and under the pavers, pushing up edges, creating an uneven and often dangerous path to the sidewalk.

The pavers are much more of a threat to me when I'm wearing pumps, but I can't slow my pace. I need to reach my car, to climb behind the wheel, to slam down on the gas pedal and be gone from here. Because I'm not asleep, and it wasn't a dream, and the longer I linger in the absence of barking, the more certain I'll be that I'm losing my mind. But in my haste, I catch my toe on that one paver that protrudes more than most, and over I go, arms flailing unsuccessfully for purchase on thin air, my purse and jacket sailing all the way to the brink of the sidewalk.

My knees take the brunt of the fall and pain bursts from my kneecaps all the way to my hips. The heels of my hands are raw, stinging. I know without looking that my stockings are shredded, but I'll be damned if I'm going back into the house to get another pair. Richard will have to deal with me barelegged today.

The tree roots, gnarled and gray, peek through the pavers. This is not their first triumph. I've fallen dozens of times since we moved in. I have a scar on my shin from landing on an abandoned trowel. For years, I've been asking Colin to remove the tree and the root system. Another husband might see a gushing wound on his wife's leg, or abraded palms or battered knees, and immediately remove the offending item. Not Colin. Another husband whose mother-in-law recently died as a result of a fall might take action, if only for his wife's peace of mind. Not mine. I curse him under my breath as my thoughts race. *Why haven't you done what I asked you to do? How many more times will this happen? I wish you took that damn tree out when we first moved in!*

I crawl to my feet. For the few seconds during my tumble, I'd forgotten about Charlemagne/Charlie. The silence of the morning assaults me with renewed force. My Honda Civic beckons from the curb. I stumble down the remainder of the walkway, my heart pounding, my ears throbbing painfully with nothing to fill them. I carefully step off the curb and circle the car, unlock the door with trembling fingers on bleeding hands. I lower myself behind the wheel, my ruined knees protesting, and yank the door shut behind me. I take deep breaths.

If Charlemagne were barking, I wouldn't be able to hear him within these confines of tempered glass and steel. For a moment, I imagine he is still there, hidden behind the Krummunds' front door, scratching and yelping to get out.

But he isn't.

Deep breaths don't calm me. The seed of hysteria in my stomach has grown to a closed fist; tension radiates outward through my entire body. A flutter of movement in my peripheral vision catches my attention. The curtains in the front window sway slightly. Colin must have been watching me. Not for long. Surely if he'd seen me fall, he would have come outside to help me. But long enough to see me frozen behind the wheel, staring sightlessly through my windshield for several minutes. I can only guess what he must be thinking, wondering.

I put the key in the ignition and slowly pull away from the curb.

FOUR

I live in a town, not a city. A suburban enclave filled with people who prefer less noise, more space, and better educations for their children. It could be anywhere. It could be nowhere. The name is irrelevant, much like my life. A huge metropolis thrives some forty miles away. I used to go there often. Now I only see its tall buildings and neon lights on the television screen.

I drive by rote, not consciously aware of stop signs or pedestrians or the other cars around me. I don't remember the moment I left behind the flower-named streets of my neighborhood and entered downtown, but within ten minutes of starting my car, I'm parked at a meter on Main Street.

Long rows of lovely three-story brown and beige and gold brownstones line both sides of the street. The ground floors are made up mostly of storefronts, while the second and third floors are walk-up apartments. Sometimes I think I'd like to live in one of those apartments. If I didn't have a family, I could. How simple it would be to have only a few rooms to clean, a superintendent to fix things for me, peace and quiet. In another life, perhaps.

My office is five minutes from here. If I head there now, I can make it on time. If I do what I know I must, I will be late.

I shut off the motor and drag myself from the car, leaving my purse behind. I loop my key ring through my fingers and scan the street.

At 8:25 a.m., downtown is coming to life. A stoop-shouldered septuagenarian sets an A-frame sign on the sidewalk in front of his shop. SPECIAL! VEAL CUTLETS $5.99/LB. A few paces down, an Asian woman places a bucket of impossibly purple carnations on a display riser. Beyond her, a pink-aproned girl writes the smoothie of the day on a whiteboard. On the other side of the street, a swarthy middle-aged man rearranges comic books on a wooden rack. A couple of hoodie-wearing teenagers watch him from the nearby stoop, smirking and smoking, even though they can't be old enough to buy cigarettes. A group of schoolchildren from the year-round private academy around the corner is led across the crosswalk by two unsmiling women. The children's plaid skirts, khaki slacks, and white shirts look crisp and starched and too warm for summertime.

No one notices me. No one seems to be affected by the presence of a lunatic, which I *must* be. Perhaps I'm not really here. Perhaps I am as much a fiction as Charlemagne/Charlie. The thought is both frightening and comforting.

The shop I seek is a few stores down, and the closer I get, the more my legs feel like lead.

When I gaze up at the awning, the painted letters of the sign swim in my vision, rearranging themselves into other words: *Let it go. It can get worse. Go now.* I squeeze my eyes shut, then open them.

PAW-TASTIC PETS, GROOMING, AND KENNEL

I approach the front window. The tips of my fingers are numb, my lungs labor to fill, my temples throb with a dull, rhythmic ache. Through the glass I detect chaotic movement—sprightly scampering, blurs of puffy fur and untamable, tangled curls, flashes of teeth and pink tongues, confetti newspaper strewn about in an effort to absorb the bodily functions of half a dozen crapping, peeing creatures.

I stop less than a foot from the window. And there he is, in the center of the frenetic activity, resting on his haunches while his compatriots scurry around him. His small body quivers with canine rage, and he glares at me with wet, chocolate-brown accusation. Charlemagne. Charlie.

My knees buckle, and I am falling. Down the rabbit hole.

~

"Are you okay? Oh my God!"

My surroundings slowly come back into focus. The street, the morning, the pet store.

I am not a fainter. When I was twelve years old, I was watching my neighbor trim the high branches of his tree with a chain saw while his eight-year-old son supervised from the ground. The man lost his grip on the power tool and down it went, buzzing through the boy's forearm. I felt horror and empathy for the boy, even as the blood shot from the remaining ravaged limb. The father fainted dead out of the tree—broke his collarbone in the process. I remained clear-eyed and focused, called for an ambulance, and fashioned a tourniquet out of the long sleeves of my cotton sweatshirt.

But today I fainted over a dog.

The pet shop employee is a girl, eighteen at most, with a shock of bleached-blonde hair and two loud stripes of neon-blue eye shadow decorating her heavy lids.

"I was just changing the puppies' water and I saw you out front looking in, and you were standing one minute, and the next minute you were on the ground." Her accent is Pennsylvania. Her look is South Jersey. Her wide-eyed overenthusiasm is pure teenager.

I battle for my bearings and, with the girl's help, gain my feet.

"Your stockings . . . they're toast. Are you all right?"

I find my voice, buried under the debris of bewilderment and disorientation. "Yes. I'm all right." I have never been so far from all right in my life, not even when my son's diagnosis was announced. I wasn't fine then. I was angry and confused and felt betrayed and wanted to kill myself and my husband and all of the medical staff who had taken part in his birth and were accomplices in that thing that happened to him. But even through the dread and disbelief, I knew who I was and where I was and what my life was and was going to be.

"I didn't eat breakfast this morning," I tell the girl, because she seems genuinely concerned and perhaps worried that her job is in jeopardy because some woman fainted in front of the pet shop on her watch.

"I forget to eat breakfast sometimes," she tells me. "My ma always says that breakfast is the most important meal of the day, that you should never skip it, but all I need is some coffee and a few cigs—" She stops herself. "I mean, you know."

I don't know. I don't know anything.

The girl looks me over and seems to be satisfied that I'm not going to collapse again. She glances into the window, then back to me. "Cute, huh? I tell you, these are the cutest, sweetest batch of pups we've gotten since I started working here. Mixes, all of them. Shepherd-terrier, I think. Won't be too big, good with kids." A sales pitch. "Look! That one likes you."

I don't want to look; I don't want to turn my head. I know what's waiting there for me. I can't help myself.

Charlemagne stands on his hind legs, front paws against the window, staring at me through the glass.

"Isn't he adorable?" the girl coos. "He's my favorite. We had a family come in a couple of weeks ago. I thought they were going to take him, just fell in love. Said they were coming back, but they never did."

I cannot swallow for the lump in my throat.

I wish they'd never gotten that godforsaken dog!

"You know, you still look kind of pale," she tells me. But I'm barely listening. A woman has emerged from the shop next door. She is older than anyone I've ever known, the flesh of her face a mass of grooves and pleats and ridges, with white hair dancing around her cheeks. She is very short and very thin but not emaciated, and neither is she hunched over.

She sets a placard on the sidewalk with nimble grace. This woman does not appear to have suffered at the hands of time.

Her eyes find mine and her smile is quick and full of mischief, and I almost believe she is a product of my imagination.

"That's Dolores," the girl says, disproving my suspicions. "She just opened shop this week."

I nod absently and return my attention to the puppies. Charlemagne has moved away and his sudden disinterest is palliative. Air flows in and out of my lungs with much less effort than before.

"Well. I gotta get back in. You sure you're—"

I put up my hand to stop the girl's words. "Thank you for your help."

She scurries back into the pet shop. My feet move of their own volition toward the shop next door. No thought, no intention, mere action. I gaze into the window and am transported to a Dickensian world. The front display boasts an antique carousel, a Madame Alexander doll, a wind-up monkey—his stuffed digits clasping time-worn cymbals—and a two-story dollhouse.

I stare transfixed at the dollhouse as unease whispers into my ear. The house is familiar. The banister, the porch, the second-story bathroom with the oversize shower stall and padded bathing bench, the twin bed in the third bedroom down the hall, its pink-flowered duvet faded and dull. The exposed beams on the ceilings and the sagging front porch. The house is set on a plank of wood, decorated with fake grass on either side of a black-painted driveway and tiny red bricks that mimic my herringbone walkway, although these are straight and level, unlike my own, because there is no tree in the middle of the yard with roots to corrupt them.

Aside from the absence of the tree, this miniature abode is too similar to my home for it to be coincidence.

Jackhammer heart. Thoughts slamming together creating a maelstrom of noise in my head. Sweat dripping down my back, under my blouse. Hands shaking. I am aware of all these things, and also cognizant of the time, slowly, swiftly passing.

Before I can check the tiny foyer tiles for cracks and the staircase railing for loose screws, the old woman's face appears above the miniature terra-cotta roof tiles. She winks at me and my blood runs icy hot.

A horn blares behind me, jolting me. I tear my gaze from the woman, from the display, from the house that is mine and not mine, and I peer at the watch on my wrist. Eight forty-five.

I'm late for work. Again. The world has changed; reality has become a convoluted entity, the meaning of which I cannot decipher. But I'm still late for work. I hold on to that fact, that simple truth. It brings me to action, to forward motion, and I am thankful, because whatever forces are at play on this bright morning, whatever the outcome of this freakish surreal tangent, I need my job and the paycheck it provides.

FIVE

The PR firm where I work is housed on the first floor of a squat building with mirrored-glass walls and jaundiced ceilings. A takeout deli rents an alcove just off the lobby. A law firm and a family counseling practice take up space on the second floor.

When I walk through the front door, I see that Mr. Mosely is still out sick. A young man dressed in an ill-fitting suit stands behind the security counter in Mosely's stead. I hold up my ID card and the youngster waves at me as though he knows me. I wave back.

In my company, the employees' day begins at nine, but Richard expects me to be at my desk by eight thirty, ready to do his bidding. I am his executive assistant. *Minion, servant, slave.* I've been here six years and should have been promoted at least twice in that time. I have not. I should have my own office and my own accounts. I do not. Richard contends, with his usual priggish buffoonery, that I can't possibly be expected to take on more responsibility at work when I have a full platter of encumbrances at home. Richard is a wellspring of bullshit. I could do his job a thousand times better than he in a quarter of the time it takes him.

I went back to work when Joshua was nine and Kate was eleven. It was a necessity. Colin's second book, a biography of Hemingway, was not well received, and the money we anticipated never materialized.

"Hemingway's overdone," Colin had said without a hint of defensiveness, without the slightest bit of regret that his failure was forcing me to completely realign my life. Colin's life would change not one iota.

Prior to my employment at Canning and Wells, my world revolved around Josh and Kate and the care and nurture of family life. Grueling and demanding, with occasional moments of quiet joy, which were not always overshadowed by weary capitulation.

My first six months at work, I was plagued with guilt over allowing someone other than me to care for my son, to wipe his mouth and wipe his ass and bathe him and feed him and subdue him when the cramping spasms racked his body and soothe him during those times when his own profound sadness would overtake him. Those tasks were my responsibility. I still perform them, after work and through the night and in the mornings, with the help of Colin and every so often Kate. But in the beginning, I couldn't stand not being there. I called home every half hour, whispering questions and concerns and instructions into my cell phone from the bathroom stall of the ladies' room.

Soon, I realized that Joshua was okay without me, possibly better for my absence. Cerebral palsy doesn't allow a person to skip puberty or adolescence, and as he matures, as his body develops, I detect a sense of embarrassment, of dread over the fact that his mother is forced to see him naked on a daily basis. I use clinical detachment when I bathe him, but a mother cannot completely ignore the scarlet splotches of shame on her son's cheeks.

Sometime during that first year, I began to enjoy my time at work, tapping into the well of creative juices that had lain dormant for so long. My first boss, Xander Moss, was kind and without ego. He fostered collaboration and welcomed ideas from anyone, including the janitor on one standout occasion. But then, as though punishment for my sin—my sin of finding undeserved happiness and fulfillment outside my family, my marriage, my children—Xander retired and I was given Richard.

On his final day at Canning and Wells, Xander took me aside. He put his rough, wrinkled hand on my shoulder and gave me a warm, jowly smile. "I've put in a good word for you, Emma," he said. "I was thinking you might take my position when I left, but Bill and Ed think you need a little bit more time. But they are aware. And so is Richard. They'll do right by you. I promise."

That was five years ago. Bill Canning and Edward Wells have not done right by me. They never will. I'm smart and talented and I work hard, but I'm also a woman of a certain age, not a young, leggy blonde, hungry and slavering to make her mark, ready to do whatever it takes to get ahead. I haven't the energy or determination to climb out of the category I've been placed in by the powers that be. They see me as a moderately attractive middle-aged mom, working her ass off to make ends meet. That is what I am. *Executive assistant.* No more, no less.

Richard is seated at his monolithic desk when I arrive, his door open, his expression grim. He is looking/not looking at a report. His head jerks in my direction; the corners of his mouth turn down into a leer.

I removed my panty hose in the car in the parking lot behind the building, tearing them off my legs as though they were on fire. My naked upper thighs rub together as I make my way into his office, iPad in hand. My palms still burn from my fall.

"Emma." He doesn't glance at his watch. He doesn't need to. "I assume you will be staying late this evening."

I don't answer. My mind is elsewhere. In a pet shop downtown.

"Sit," he commands, and like a dog, I obey. I sit in one of the two plush chairs facing his desk, smooth my skirt over my raw knees, and cross my legs at the ankles. I glance at my bare calves and am relieved that they are smooth and hairless this morning, which is atypical since shaving is not a priority.

Colin resents my ambivalence toward self-grooming but disguises it with humor. He rubs his legs against mine under the covers of our bed and jokingly suggests we might start a fire, or asks where the extinguisher is hidden, or feigns alarm that my razor-sharp stubble will tear open his skin. Sometimes I laugh and roll over and spread my legs for him. But more often, I wrap myself in indignation that he would comment on such a trivial matter while our son lies in the next bedroom with useless limbs, unable to get comfortable *ever*, plagued by nightmares, both while he sleeps and while he's awake.

Occasionally, I do neither. I jump from the bed on the heels of Colin's *joke* and storm to the master bath, where I ceremoniously drag the rusted disposable Daisy over my legs, silently but unequivocally making a point. Which is what I did last night. Thank God. With any luck, my boss won't notice my lack of hosiery.

"I need extra effort from you today," he says. Richard Green is a man of points—pointy nose, pointy chin, narrowed eyes, and severe widow's peak. He is fit for fifty, trim, but beneath his clothes I imagine he is a series of sharp angles.

"We have Peters coming at eleven, and I want to buff up this proposal. The language regarding cross-promotion with UltraFit is lacking. Talk to Jack and see what the two of you can do about it."

I nod and make a note on the iPad. My digital handwriting is clumsy.

Canning and Wells doesn't handle celebrities. We are not based in New York or Los Angeles, so we don't attract actors or rock stars or athletes, the kind of stars who want and need face-to-face ego stroking and hand-holding. We work with small business, internet start-ups, restaurants, health clubs, privately owned resorts, a few national chains. We do the occasional nonprofit work for charities and causes, but only enough to look good to the IRS. We have sister firms in Texas and California with whom we partner for our national chains.

Richard oversees the marketing and business acquisition and retention department. We work closely with the other three: social media and web traffic, news and media coverage, and branding. Our social media department is made up of young hipsters who wear band-logo T-shirts and don't comb their hair every day. Our news and media department is filled with middle-aged men who sport too-tight neckties and constant scowls. The branding department is a revolving door for employees—old, young, male, female, gay, straight—largely hired for their individual resemblance to a specific audience we might be targeting at the time.

"And I want to see Ralph in SM as soon as he gets in. The Twitter feed for Mmm Burger looks like a kindergartner wrote it. Check the daily. Your list is sizable today."

Again, I nod mutely. Richard sets down his report and stares at me over his desk.

"Are you okay, Em?"

I despise it when Richard calls me Em. Em is my husband's name for me, my mother's name for me, not his.

"You look tired." He gazes at my face for a few seconds, then his gaze descends to my body. His eyes narrow.

"Are you wearing hosiery today?"

"I was. I'm not now."

"Hmm. And why is that?" He pushes his chair back and stands, then slowly moves around his desk. I smell the familiar, overpowering scent of mint as he approaches. "You know my dress policy, of course. I don't ask a lot of my employees, do I? Panty hose are the proper accessory for ladies, yes?" He takes the seat beside me and inspects my calves. "Most women your age can't get away with bare legs, but you can, Em. You have wonderful legs." The pointy tip of his tongue flicks over his bottom lip, then disappears. "Still, rules are rules. You are an executive assistant, *my* executive assistant, and your position at this firm involves certain . . . obligations. I expect you to remember that and behave accordingly."

Goddamn him.

"I took a fall, Richard. The hose were ruined." I force myself to remain composed, though his proximity makes me uncomfortable.

"That's terrible. Awful." He slowly reaches over and tugs at the hem of my skirt, inching it upward until my bloody knees are exposed. "I'm so sorry. Do they hurt badly?" He glances at the outer office, making sure no other employees have arrived, then gently lowers his palm onto my torn flesh. I don't flinch because he wants me to flinch.

Charlemagne has dominated my thoughts, but the puppy's image suddenly vanishes, replaced by the reality of my boss's cold touch. I stare at his long fingers, swollen knuckles, the coarse dark hair sprouting up between the tumescent veins on the back of his hand.

This is not the first advance Richard has made. I am a safe and appropriate target for his wanton urges. I'm certain he would prefer to approach the twentysomethings with their high bosoms and tight skin, but Richard has his own twisted sense of propriety.

I am ashamed by all the ways I have allowed my boss to sexually harass me. The "playful" pats on the ass, the outstretched arms "accidentally" brushing against my breasts, the slow passes behind me in the break room, his front pressed against my back, his erection full and thick and unmistakable despite the layers of clothing between us. I could take my grievances to a panel of older, right-wing, cigar-smoking men, but the outcome of such a complaint would not benefit me or my job.

Again, the paycheck. Mortgage, bills, medical care, accoutrements of teenage girls, college tuition on the horizon. I cannot rock the precarious boat of my employment. I am forty-one years old. My job possibilities are limited. So I suffer his hands on my knees and his lecherous looks and impossible deadlines and petty grievances. And I check my bank account balance every Friday night to make certain my autopay is in effect.

And yet. If only I had the balls, the self-respect, the emotional resources, the wherewithal—all the things I used to have but lost somewhere along the way. I would expose the bastard if I still had those tools, and how much better would my time within these walls be?

"You look tired," he repeats, only this time his voice is a low whisper and his fingers are sliding up my inner thigh, beneath my skirt. He has never gone this far before. My skin crawls. His Altoid breath nearly suffocates me.

"Richard, I should get to my desk and get started on my daily list."

"Yes," he murmurs. "You should." I can feel the pads of his fingertips on my cotton underpants, pressing against my labia through the fabric. My stomach churns acid. I bite my bottom lip to keep from screaming. He emits a guttural grunt and, with his free hand, reaches for mine. He presses my hand against his hard penis, groans again as he slips his fingers under my panties.

I stand suddenly, clasping my iPad to my chest, and Richard nearly topples to the floor. He struggles to stay in his seat, then looks up at me with unbridled anger. He does not like to be rejected or humiliated. I have done both.

"Good morning, Mr. G-g-green."

Wally Holleran stands at the door of Richard's office. He is a nice man with a severe case of late-onset acne, thick black-rimmed glasses, and a slight stutter. Richard calls him Golly Polly Wally behind his back *and* to his face. He nods at me, giving Richard a chance to paint a condescending smile over his mask of hostility.

"Let me see," Richard says, slowly gaining his feet. "My assistant was twenty-five minutes late this morning, I have a meeting I am ill-prepared for because of the stupidity and complacency of several of my employees, and the first person I see here, other than my tardy assistant, is you, Polly Wally. Does that sound like a g-g-good morning to you?"

My hatred of this man has been simmering below the surface for years, but now it bubbles over into volcanic rage. And the thought careens through my head before I can stop it.

I wish Richard Green had never come to work here. I wish he never existed.

I swallow my contempt. It burns my throat. Richard storms to his desk as I covertly smooth my skirt.

"Is there anything else, Richard?" I ask, my voice steady.

He glares at me and shakes his head curtly. "No. Not for now." A threat, a promise.

I head for the doorway and politely sidestep past Wally and his mortification.

And as I make my way to my desk, Charlemagne/Charlie returns. His shepherd-terrier eyes beseech me. *Why did you wish me away?* As if one reckless sentence formed by a fatigued-and-fractured mind could be the cause of his perpetual imprisonment.

It is madness. I no more have the power to wish a puppy away than I do to erase Richard Green from this firm. My boss has not disappeared in a puff of smoke. He stomps around his office, his erection deflating even as his frustration magnifies. Today will be a misery for everyone on his staff because I didn't let that bastard violate me. Wally slinks by my desk, eyes downcast. I silently apologize to him. He paid for my transgressions by simply offering a well-meant greeting, a mistake he will not repeat.

He doesn't look up.

SIX

The mind is a funny thing. When we have no explanation for something, we create one. Rationalizations, excuses, hypotheses. When there is no alternative other than mental illness, our minds turn fantasy into reality.

While I know—*I know*—that Charlemagne/Charlie's presence in the Krummund household was real, my rational mind recognizes that this is impossible. Therefore, over the course of the next few hours, as I perform my boss's bidding, my subconscious works to create a plausible substitute for what transpired. By the time Colin calls, I almost have myself convinced.

"I just wanted to make sure you're okay," he says.

I crouch behind my computer monitor. If Richard sees me on my cell phone, he'll go ballistic. Luckily, he's in a meeting with social media, but his eyes wander regularly to the outer office.

"I'm fine," I whisper. "Thanks for checking. I can't talk. Richard's on a tear today."

"Oh dear. I'm sorry."

I've never revealed to Colin the brutal nature of the abuse I've received. My husband is not a knight in shining armor with sword raised to battle. He is a philosopher, an educator, an observer. Words are Colin's weapons, and he wields them only moderately well. Still, he knows that my boss is a mean-spirited tyrant who sends me home each evening wounded and defeated.

Another husband might tell me to quit my job. My husband cannot. I earn twice as much as he does. Then again, another husband might not call to make sure I'm okay. I must give Colin credit for his concern.

"I was worried about you," he says. "So was Josh."

"I know. I'm sorry. You were right, though." I force a chuckle. "The Krummunds didn't get a dog. I took a Motrin PM last night, and it must have knocked me for a loop."

My mind has already rewritten the scene from this morning: I awoke sluggish and disoriented from a long and visceral dream about my neighbors and their vociferous new puppy. *Of course it was a dream. What right-minded person names their dog Charlemagne?* And as for the little ball of fluff himself, I now recall that the last time I was downtown for a haircut, I stopped at the window of Paw-Tastic and spied the little devil in the display kennel, which is how he came to dwell in my subconscious and play a starring role in last night's dream. That's what must have happened. And because it *must have happened*, it did.

These imagined scenarios are quickly becoming realities to me; soon they will be indistinguishable from the rest of my memories. Even now, I can scarcely remember the feel of Charlemagne/Charlie's fur between my fingers as I stood on my neighbor's front porch. *Because it didn't really happen.* Sensations feel so vivid in dreams but quickly fade upon waking and then disappear altogether.

Colin chuckles with me, his relief loud in my ear. "I can't imagine Louise Krummund naming a dog Charlemagne."

"I know, right?" *She did, though. No, she didn't. It was a dream.* "I've got to go, Colin." Richard hasn't caught me yet, but my time is running short.

"Okay. See you later. Love you."

"You too," I say, my automatic response. Not *I love you*. Because *I love you* is a bargain, and I'm not sure how much longer I can hold up my end of it. I hang up and tuck my cell phone next to my keyboard. When I glance into Richard's office, my boss is scowling at me through the glass.

~

The rest of the day passes as expected. Richard tirelessly metes out my punishment, adding another dozen tasks to my daily log that need to be completed before I leave. Jack and I are forced to rewrite the Peters copy three times, even though the second draft was perfect. My lunch hour is taken away. I am asked to fetch coffee on numerous occasions, only to be told each time to make a fresh pot, *the old pot is burned*. His glares are frequent, and there is violence behind them as never before. I'm careful to choose my bathroom breaks when I know he is occupied. I have always suffered Richard's advances with disgust and rolling eyes. Today, I am afraid of him.

At four forty-five, when most of the employees of Canning and Wells are shutting down their computers and straightening their desks, Richard strides out of his office and crosses to my desk. He peers down at me as I squint at my monitor. I've been entering data for two hours from an enormous stack of folders Richard bequeathed to me. They are old files, some from decades ago, most regarding clients we no longer have. There is no need to take up precious hard drive space with these files other than to satisfy Richard's sadistic bent. However, I kept my mouth firmly shut when he set them on my desk.

"You'll be here awhile longer, it seems."

"I can finish these tomorrow," I reply, my eyes on the screen.

"No. Today. I need them entered today." His voice belongs to a rodent, a weasel. "You were late this morning, Emma. You can make up the time this evening. I have some other items I need sorted out when you finish with this."

I look up at him. His lips are curled into a salacious sneer.

"I can't stay late tonight, Richard. Joshua has physical therapy."

He nods, then raises his eyebrows. "Yes, well, it seems your son's session has been canceled tonight. While you were on one of your extended ladies' room sojourns, a text came from your husband. I happened to be passing by and retrieved it for you."

Blood rushes to my cheeks. My heart thumps wildly in my chest. Fury, like a living, writhing thing snakes through my veins.

"I took the liberty of texting back for you. I let *Colin* know that you would be staying late. He answered with *X*'s and *O*'s. Very sweet."

I glance at my cell phone, which lies dormant beside my keyboard. I haven't checked it recently. There were no alerts and no flashing lights because Richard *took the liberty* of clearing them.

My coworkers file past. Their workday is done and they head for sweet freedom. The pace at which they walk is twice the speed of their arrival this morning. With each set of feet that passes my desk, my fury morphs into fear. Soon I will be left alone with a monster.

"I can't stay," I say again.

Richard rubs a finger against his lips. "You know, Emma. I have always valued your strong work ethic. But lately, I have sensed . . . how shall I put it? A lowering of one's standards. I mentioned it to Edward last week, and he quite agreed. Perhaps it's time for Canning and Wells to make a change."

His words hang in the air above my head, dark as storm clouds. I lower my eyes and open another file.

~

It happens quickly, my one small mercy.

I've been glued to my desk for the better part of an hour, ignoring the pressing need of my bladder. Richard circles his office like a big game cat, tracking the receding footsteps of my fellow employees until every last one of them is gone. If I can just hold out a few minutes more, the janitor, Bobby Mackenzie, will arrive and I won't be alone with Richard. I glance at my cell phone—6:05. Bobby is late.

When the pressure to relieve myself becomes almost unbearable, my brain seizes upon a historical fact my son imparted to me over the course of a lengthy holiday dinner. My mother was still alive. Katie was less insolent. She hadn't met *that boy* yet.

"Tyka Bra'ay die a' a berse bladuh," Josh had said, sporting his trademark strangled grin while I translated to the rest of the family. *Tycho Brahe died of a burst bladder.* According to Josh—and Wikipedia—the famous alchemist and astronomer did not want to offend his host by excusing himself from the dinner table in the middle of the meal. Josh had then banged his fork on the table and announced he had to pee, and could someone please take him now, and didn't his asking to be excused make him smarter, if not more impolitic, than Tycho Brahe?

I would laugh at the memory if I wasn't worried about wetting myself.

If I were a brave woman, I would allow my bladder to explode, embrace death rather than face what I know awaits me if I leave this chair.

Finally, the pressure becomes fiery pain, and I can no longer hold it. I barely move my head and glance sideways through the glass of Richard's office. He reclines in his desk chair, hands clasped behind his head, eyes closed. Very still, too still, but I can't wait anymore.

Slowly, I stand and back away from my desk, my eyes never leaving my boss's inert form. When I reach the hallway, I run my fingers along the wall as I continue to creep backward, afraid that if I turn away from him for even a second, Richard will suddenly appear behind me, like a ghoul in a slasher flick.

My bruised palm brushes against the door to the ladies' room, and I push it open. I didn't know I was holding my breath until the door closes behind me. I exhale, then suck in huge gulps of air. I engage the bolt on the main door, then head for one of the stalls, squeezing my upper thighs together, hoping I'll make it to the toilet. I'm thankful I don't have to do battle with my panty hose, but I almost have an accident while trying to wrangle a seat cover from the dispenser.

A moment later, sweet relief.

I sit for what feels like a long while. I don't think my urine stream has ever lasted so long. The sound of it echoes off the pale-yellow tile walls. Beneath the echo, I detect another sound, soft, creaky. I squeeze my upper thighs again, cutting off the noise of my pee, but there is only silence. Bending at the waist so that my face is inches from the door of the stall, I peer through the crack.

No movement, no shadow on the floor, no color other than yellow appears in my vision. I must have imagined the creaky sound.

I relax again and finish my business. It takes another moment.

I flush the toilet and turn toward the door of the stall, then reach out to unlatch the lock. I detect a flash of charcoal just beyond the stall. My heart slams against my rib cage as I jerk my fingers to the left, trying to resecure the lock. Too late. The door bursts inward and Richard lunges at me.

Spittle whitens the corners of his mouth as he yanks me to him. His bony fingers press into my shoulders. His lizard tongue flicks into my ear as I struggle to break free of his grasp. His breath is a mixture of Altoids and whiskey.

How did he get in? I bolted the door. Master key. Doesn't matter.

"Richard, no!" I cry. I wedge my hands between our bodies, press my palms against his chest, and shove him backward with all my strength. He barely moves.

"You've been teasing me for five years, Em. I know this is what you want."

I shake my head and try to pull away from him, but there is nowhere for me to go. I kick at his legs and slap him as hard as I can. His cheek goes red even as a serpentine smile spreads across his face. His eyes glow with savagery.

"You like it rough, huh? I had a feeling." He grabs my wrist and twists my arm behind my back. I cry out, and he twists harder. I have no choice but to turn away from him so that he won't tear my arm from its socket. He slams me into the corner of the stall, and my forehead smacks against the tile. For a split second, I think I might pass out, and I pray for unconsciousness, but luck is not with me. The devil is with me. I feel a trickle of warmth slide down my temple as Richard presses his body upon mine. He reaches around my waist and gropes my breasts, digging his fingers into the tender flesh, all the while grinding his vile engorgement against my ass.

"No. No. No no no." I hear the words in my head, but my lips, my mouth, my vocal cords, aren't working right. I feel the toilet handle digging into my hip. Tears stream down my face, mixing with my blood.

This is my life. This. Is. My. Life.

"It's a good thing you didn't wear hosiery today, isn't it, Em?"

He yanks my skirt up—*God, please, no!*—and tears off my underwear, and I experience a brief and incongruous regret that he just destroyed my favorite panties—sky blue with a lace waistband and a small spray of flowers on the front. Reality elbows thoughts of undergarments out of my mind as he shoves his hand between my thighs. I open my mouth to scream as he crams three of his fingers inside me, pushing them up so far that my throat seizes. I strangle on my tears and my hatred.

I reach down and claw at his hand, my nails ripping open trenches on his skin. He squeals with rage and withdraws his fingers, then grabs the back of my head and smashes my cheek against the tile. White-hot pain bursts through my head. Thoughts float; darkness threatens again.

The feel of him entering me, thick and sharp and horrible, brings me back. His breathing comes in short, ragged bursts as he pushes himself farther and farther inside me.

I press my swollen cheek against the tile and close my eyes.

Charlemagne's face appears behind my lids, the puppy I saw in the pet shop window a few weeks ago, then dreamed about last night. I vaguely recall how, for a moment, I believed I wished him away.

If only my wishes really did come true.

SEVEN

I can't let Colin or Josh see my face.

When Richard finishes with me, he disappears from the ladies' room. I stagger to the door and bolt it, even though I know he can get in if he so chooses, then collapse against the wall. My skirt is still bunched up around my waist. I can feel Richard's foul essence seep out of me.

My thoughts are a jumbled mess. I try to think of someone to call, someone who will help me, rescue me from this bathroom. Not one person comes to mind. I don't have friends. I did, a long time ago, back when I enjoyed life rather than endured it. I let those friendships go. After Josh was born, I didn't want to invite anyone into my heartache, didn't want to expose my vulnerabilities, didn't want the responsibility of needing anyone. I need someone now, and I have no one except myself.

I'll get through this. I have no choice. I just need to rest a minute.

The voice in my head chastises me. *This is your fault*, it says. The voice is right. I could have left work on time. I could have stood up to Richard when he told me I had to stay. But I didn't. Because on some very basic level, I invite suffering into my life. I have come to define myself by my suffering.

I don't know how long I sit. The metal screech of the janitor's cart being wrenched from the utility closet brings me out of my stupor and moves me to action. I stand on shaky legs and straighten my skirt as best I can, then approach the mirrors. Every step is agony.

As I gaze at my wretched reflection, my mind reels. For a brief moment, I consider going to the hospital and filing a report but immediately reject the idea. What possible good would that do? Richard would spin it. That's what he does. He'd say I wanted it. *You've been teasing me for five years, Em.* He'd find ten witnesses to testify that I flirted with him, led him on. I'd lose my job, my income. My private life would be ripped open and torn apart, my family laid to waste. And then what?

No. No hospitals. No police. I just have to figure out how to keep this from Colin and Josh.

I could get away with the cut on my forehead, explain it as a mishap with a coworker and the bathroom door. I could get away with the absence of underwear and the bruises blooming on my upper thighs, since neither my husband nor my son can see beneath my skirt. The scrapes on my arms and legs I can blame on my fall this morning. But not my cheek. My cheek is swollen and slowly turning purple. Josh would figure it out. His mind works like that of a crime scene investigator. He'd know that if my hands and knees stopped my fall, I would not have hit my face, at least not nearly as hard as the damage suggests.

I'm not worried about Katie. My daughter doesn't see me anymore. Even if she did, I doubt her thoughts would linger too long on the ramifications of my injuries. But Colin and Josh are different. Colin would be devastated, as much by his inability to exact revenge as by the knowledge of my suffering. Josh would be altered. I am the strong parent, invulnerable in his eyes. He doesn't witness me sobbing in the shower or screaming into my pillow, which I do regularly. I need to keep his image of me intact.

And these are the things that plague me. Not the fact that a loathsome, evil fuck attacked me in the ladies' room, violated and beat me, but the fact that I can't let my son and husband find out.

The door rattles against the bolt, and I jerk with surprise.

"'Lo?" Bobby Mackenzie, the janitor.

My voice cracks when I try to respond. I clear my throat and force a chipper tone. "I'll be right out!"

"Miz Davies? That you?"

I retch into the sink.

"Yes! Hi, Bobby. Just give me a minute, okay?"

"Sure thing, Miz Davies. I'll just start with the men's this time."

"Thanks!"

I splash my face with cold water, cup my hands, and drink. The cut on my forehead has stopped bleeding, but a crust of red remains. I grab some paper towels and wet them, then gently rub at the blood trail on the side of my face. I discard the soiled wad and grab more, repeating the procedure, only this time between my legs. The towels feel as coarse as sandpaper, and I wince with each swipe. My hair is a bird's nest. I reach up and remove the remaining bobby pins, freeing the brown curls from their confinement. I pull a chunk of hair forward, hoping it will cloak my devastated cheek.

I tuck in my blouse. The wrinkled fabric tells a sordid tale. One last look in the mirror. One more handful of wet paper towels to dab against my face. One deep breath. I move slowly to the door, slide the bolt free, and step into the hallway.

Bobby's cart stands at the open men's room door. I hear the janitor inside the bathroom, humming an old Frank Sinatra tune. "It Was a Very Good Year." My throat burns at the irony.

I pass the cart without a word.

~

"Hi, honey."

"Hi. Are you still at work?"

"Yes." No. I'm in a dark little dive at the far edge of downtown. "I'm not sure what time I'm getting out of here. The meeting didn't go well today, and they've given us twenty-four hours to fix our proposal."

"I understand."

"Listen, can you ask Raina to stay late tonight to help you with Josh?" I polish the scarred wooden counter with my index finger.

"Emma, I'm perfectly capable of taking care of Josh by myself." He is, but he won't. He'll ask Raina to stay. He'll shadow her and watch her closely as she carefully sponges Josh before helping him into his pajamas. Colin will never stray, but I have given him every reason to fantasize about other women. Raina is not beautiful, but she'll do.

"I know you are," I tell him. "But an extra set of hands is always helpful."

"I'll talk to her." He pauses. "Em, are you okay? You sound . . . I don't know . . . upset."

"I am upset, Colin. I'm stuck at work with Hitler's apprentice." The lie slides out of my mouth with no difficulty.

He chuckles. "I'm sorry."

So am I, Colin.

"I'll take night duty again," he says. A magnanimous gesture. "So you can sleep. You work too hard, Em. Are you sure there isn't some other job you can find?"

"This is a conversation for another time, Colin. I have to go. Richard is waving at me." The sound of my boss's name from my lips nauseates me. "You'll probably be asleep when I get home." *Please, God, let him be asleep.*

"Unless Josh . . ." Has an episode. He doesn't say it. Doesn't have to.

"Well, if he doesn't, and you're asleep, I'll see you in the morning." *And hopefully the swelling on my cheek will be gone and I can cover the purple with foundation and we can all pretend that everything is perfectly fine.*

"Okay, babe. Don't work too hard or too late. I'll give Josh your love."

The bartender sells every shade of Marlboro—red, gold, silver, blue, and green. A holiday season of cigarettes. I choose the golds because they are familiar and order vodka on the rocks. A double. The bartender gives me a sideways look, his gaze landing on my cheek, but makes no comment or inquiry. I carry the cigarettes and my drink to the small patio outside where smoking—and, apparently, heavy petting—are allowed. A couple sits in the far left corner next to the railing, faces mashed together, murmuring softly as they grope each other beneath the table. They are oblivious to my presence, as if I am invisible, as if I don't exist.

I sit at a table as far from the couple as possible. The summer night air is filled with the aroma of fried onions—a staple of this establishment, and based on the intensity of the smell, ordered frequently.

I try to avert my eyes, but my gaze is inevitably drawn to the lovers across the patio. They remind me of another time in my life, when the world seemed full of possibilities and love was a joy, not a burden. Before Colin, before my ex-husband, I knew a man named Dante. I loved him.

Dante was born and raised in Suffolk County, but he seemed to embody the very essence of Bohemian sensibilities. Perhaps his name, given to him by third-generation Italian parents, required that he be an expert on all things European. He introduced me to wine and cheese and making love at all hours of the day. We talked world politics and read Descartes and Kafka to each other and congratulated ourselves on our forward thinking and progressive attitudes and open hearts.

Dante knew me better than anyone. He held up a mirror and made me look at myself. It ended badly, like most things. It wasn't just his cheating. Sometimes I didn't want to look in the mirror.

I was at the end of my undergraduate studies when he left me. Occasionally I wonder what happened to him. If I had disposable time, I could join Facebook and look him up. If he's still alive, I'm certain he uses social media. Facebook and Twitter would appeal to his pathologically overabundant ego. But I have neither the time nor the inclination to find him. Despite our unfortunate end, Dante remains one of my few precious and treasured memories. The possibility of now-Dante, fat and balding and cursing his bloodthirsty ex-wives and delinquent children, doesn't interest me.

I light a cigarette and inhale deeply. No coughing fit ensues, like in the movies. Perhaps, after what just happened to me, I am hardened to the smoke. Despite the warmth of the July night, I'm shivering. My hand shakes as I lift the glass to my lips. The vodka slides down my throat, and almost immediately the knot in my stomach begins to uncoil.

I don't drink often. I would if I could, but I can't. Not when doom always lurks on the outer edges of my life, threatening to close in on me. If there were an emergency, as there have been countless times over the last fifteen years, I must be sober, in control, ready to take charge. But tonight I need alcohol. I need the protective layer of ambivalence alcohol provides. Josh is safe at home with two responsible people caring for him. So I will drink this vodka and another. I will order a basket of fries and force myself to eat them, even though the thought of food makes me sick. I will get behind the wheel only when I am sober enough and I will go home to a darkened house and steal into my bed and pray that the swelling on my cheek will have gone down by morning.

A bag of ice lands on the table with a thud. Startled, I look up to see the bartender standing beside me. He is tall and heavily muscled, with a tattoo of a large-breasted woman snaking up his biceps. His eyes are kind. He says nothing, just stares at me for a moment. Then he turns and walks back into the bar.

Tears blur my vision. I crush my cigarette into the ashtray, then pick up the bag of ice and press it to my cheek.

~

My plan goes smoothly. The house is dark when I pull into the driveway. As the garage door creaks open, I breathe in through my nostrils.

Richard's stink clings to me. I cannot possibly slide into bed next to my husband unless I bathe. Another complication.

I ease into the garage and alight from the car, then make my way into the house, pressing the button to close the garage door on my way in. I stand for a moment and listen, but there is only quiet. No late-night dishes being done, no television at low volume, and, of course, no barking dog from next door. I remind myself that there never was a barking dog next door as I shuffle into the laundry alcove off the kitchen.

I remove my shoes, skirt, and blouse, and every movement of my arms, my torso, my legs produces varying degrees of pain. My clothing goes directly into the trash bin. I make a mental note to dump the contents of the bin into the barrel outside first thing in the morning. I grab a pair of sweats and a T-shirt from the basket of clean, unfolded laundry then pad to the half bathroom down the hall. I spend a few minutes sponging myself from head to toe, gently in most places, but aggressively where there are no injuries. I realize, as I scrub at my underarms, my calves, my stomach, that I am furious. Not with Richard, not with myself. With God.

So what if I invite suffering into my life? You don't have to accept my invitation. What have I ever done to inspire Your rage?

My fury is short-lived. Because I know I won't get any answers. And I probably wouldn't like them if I did.

The second floor holds the hushed cadence of slumber. At the far end of the hall, Katie's door is closed. Josh's door is open, as always. I can hear his deep, labored breathing from where I stand, and the slight, gravelly snore that indicates he is sleeping soundly. I feel the pull of him, my own need to go into his room and sit beside him and stroke his hair and whisper those loving motherly words. But I resist. I can't take the chance that Colin will hear me. My husband sleeps soundly, but any anomalous noise from Josh's room might wake him.

I tiptoe into the master bedroom and head to the bathroom, passing the monitor and the amplified sound of Josh's snores. I close the door behind me and move to the sink. A night-light flickers from the socket on the wall, offering enough illumination for me to brush my teeth but not enough for me to see my reflection. I don't need to see it. My cheek, eye, and forehead throb in high definition. I grab the Motrin PM from the medicine cabinet and shake three onto my palm. Two is the dosage.

As I pull the door open, my husband calls to me, and I start. "You can turn the light on if you need to."

"That's okay." Normal voice. Calm, relaxed. Everything's-just-fine voice. "Sorry if I woke you."

"You didn't, really," he mumbles. He is half-asleep. I exhale, relieved. "I was having a dream about Josh. He was walking."

My heart shifts painfully in my chest. I've had that dream, too.

"Love you, Em."

"Go back to sleep," I tell him as I make my way to the bed and gently turn back the covers on my side.

He says something without moving his mouth. The next second, he is breathing deeply.

I ease myself down onto the bed and wince. Pain bursts up from my core and spreads through my limbs. My eyelids are suddenly leaden. The Motrin might have been a bad idea. I need to wake up early in order to camouflage my shame. Concealer, yes. And I'll need to feather my hair around my face. Surely Richard won't mind me wearing my hair down in order to keep his sins a secret.

Richard. How can I face him tomorrow? How can I continue to work for that hideous man?

How can I raise a son with cerebral palsy? How can I nurture a daughter who despises me? How can I spend my life with a man who doesn't even strive for mediocrity?

I can because I do. Because I must. Because *this is my life.*

I fumble for the bedside clock and, with great effort, set the alarm. I'm not certain I've set it correctly, but I don't care. I'm asleep by the time I lie down.

EIGHT

Friday, July 8

I sense it before I open my eyes, before the alarm sounds. That not-right feeling.

I bolt up to a seated position, anticipating and dreading the pain that will accompany such an action. I'm shocked when I experience no discomfort whatsoever. I gingerly scoot to the edge of the bed and swing my legs over the side. The bright barbs of agony I expect don't materialize.

The master bedroom is shrouded in shadows. Colin sleeps soundly. Josh's breathing echoes throughout the room from the monitor.

I shut the alarm off, then stand and hurry to the bathroom. Safely hidden behind the closed door, I turn on the light and behold myself in the mirror. I reach up and touch my cheek with my fingertips. My hands are shaking again, not with cold, but with incredulity. The skin beneath my fingernails is neither purple nor ravaged. It is unblemished and pink. The cut on my forehead is gone. I lean into the glass, not trusting my fortysomething eyes. No marks of any kind are evident anywhere on my face.

I look down at my body and immediately scrabble out of my sweat-pants. I sit on the lid of the toilet and explore my inner thighs. The bright blossom of bruising that was so apparent last night has vanished. *But how?* I can still feel Richard's salient fingers thrusting into me, his sharp, rigid tool breaking me apart.

I contract my vaginal muscles. Even the most sedate lovemaking with Colin leaves me sore and chafed, but I am neither. There is not the slightest shred of evidence of Richard's offense.

I should be elated. God has granted me a reprieve. He has healed me expeditiously so that I won't have to offer my husband and son an inane explanation for my wounds. But beneath my gratitude is suspicion. Because I know God doesn't give a whit about me.

What is going on?

I push myself up from the toilet and gaze at my reflection again. Disbelief floods through my system, coupled with anger. Yesterday I was raped, beaten, humiliated. This morning I have nothing to show for it. Last night I took small comfort in knowing that when I faced Richard today, he would be chastened by the irrefutable proof of his handiwork. Now, without my shattered cheek, he can look at me as he always does. With condescension and animosity.

But how . . . how can this be? I'm not a comic book hero with superhealing powers. I am me—housewife, mother, *executive assistant*. I've heard, read, seen on TV stories of people who effect impossible results to futile situations solely with the power of their minds, like the woman who lifted a car off her toddler, and the man who walked away from a parachute malfunction with nary a scratch, and the girl who cured her leukemia with prayer. But those people are *extraordinary*. I am ordinary, average. The only superpower I possess is the ability to convince myself daily that my life is worth living.

The explanation doesn't matter.

I wash my (unbruised) face, and when I lift the toothbrush from the holder, I remember the tattered clothing I discarded in the laundry alcove. After scrubbing my teeth, I sneak through the master bedroom and quietly descend the stairs. Dawn's precursor colors the first floor charcoal, and I make my way to the laundry alcove by sense rather than sight. I feel for the switch by the washing machine, and the sudden illumination from the overhead LED bulb blinds me. I take a breath, then approach the trash bin. My heart pounds inexplicably. Because a part of me already knows what I will find.

Nothing.

The actuality crashes against the expectation. My mind fractures.

I see myself placing my ruined blouse and navy skirt in the bin last night.

The bin is empty.

Several years ago, my appendix burst and Colin rushed me to the hospital, a place with which I am familiar due to Josh's circumstances. But it looked different from the perspective of a patient. The explosive pain in my gut rendered me nearly incoherent, and I was immediately sent to the OR, where a green-scrubbed doctor administered opiates and general anesthesia. As instructed, I counted back from one hundred, only reaching ninety-eight before I was swept away. When consciousness returned, over an hour later, it came with maximum distortion. When I opened my eyes, in response to a strident command from an overly enthusiastic nurse, the world around me was slanted, warped. The lights were too bright, the room too white; the nurse's face wavered and morphed above my head as I struggled to take in my surroundings.

Now, as I gaze into the empty waste bin, I experience a similar permutation of reality.

This cannot be, this cannot be. But it is.

I brace myself against the dryer and spend a full sixty seconds breathing, trying to gain my bearings. When the world around me stops swaying, I race to the stairs and climb them two at a time.

Just as I reach the second floor, I hear my son call to me.

"Maah?"

I need to go to my closet; I need to see, to check, to understand, to *know*, but Joshua's plaintive cry stops me. I go to him, as I always do.

His eyes shine in the darkness, twin beacons lighting my path. I move to his bedside as he crooks his hand toward me.

"Ah y' kay?" *Are you okay?*

My son, with his gnarled hands and twisted limbs and inconsiderate bowels, is asking *me* if *I'm* okay. I do not deserve this boy. I sit beside him, reach over the bed rail, and place my hand on his.

"I'm okay, Josh." The acrid scent of his sweat mixes unpleasantly with the baby powder we apply to his many cracks, creases, and folds. He perspires more than most people because his every movement is an exertion of colossal proportion.

"Don't worry about me," I tell him. *I'm worried enough for both of us.* At least I don't have to hide my cheek, although in the dim light of his room, he wouldn't be able to see it. But I think he would sense it.

"Aye af' t' pe." *I have to pee.*

I nod and reach for the urine bottle on the nightstand. I gently uncover him and help him with this process. When he finishes, I cap the bottle and carry it into the bathroom, then dump the contents into the toilet and flush it down. The bathroom has three doors, one leading to Josh's room, one to the hall, and the third to Katie's room. I rinse the bottle and set it on the counter, then wash my hands.

I open the door to Katie's room, just a crack, and peer in. She sleeps soundly atop her covers, fully dressed. I didn't see her at all yesterday, so I'm not sure whether she fell asleep in her clothes or woke up early, got dressed, and then fell back asleep with the expectation of a pebble thrown at her window to awaken her. I'm aware that she sneaks in and out of the house via the roof and trellis. I care not so much because she is out at all hours with *that boy* but because the roof tiles are worn and cracked and in need of replacement and the trellis is rickety, the wood rotted in places. I've told her many times that one day the wood will splinter and she will likely break her head open on the concrete below. She doesn't listen to me anymore.

"Maah?"

I quickly close the door and return to my son.

"I'm here." I stroke his damp forehead. "What do you need, honey?"

"I wah t' ge' uh." *I want to get up.*

"Josh, it's early. Only six o'clock. You don't have to get up yet."

"I wah t'. I wah loo' s'thi uh." *I want to. I want to look something up.* On the computer.

I refrain from releasing a sigh. I don't want him to see or sense my distress. My urgent need to check my closet for the clothing that should be lining the waste bin downstairs will have to be suppressed. Josh's world is small, made larger only through the images I capture and his time on the internet. If he wants to surf the web to accumulate information, I must comply.

I spend the next twenty minutes on his morning ablutions: sponge bath, toileting, fresh clothing, teeth brushing.

I live my life according to my to-do list and rarely think beyond my circumstances, but every so often I envy the vast majority of moms who have children who are able to do all of these things by themselves. They take their lives for granted, these mothers. They yell at their children to get out of bed, to get in the shower, to change into something without stains, to get to the breakfast table, to hurry hurry hurry up. Their lives are a luxury because their children are capable.

Mostly, I don't begrudge these mothers their normal lives. But this morning, I do. Because this morning, my sanity is a tenuous thing. This morning, my need to verify or invalidate my delirium outweighs my need to care for my son.

But I do it. Of course, I do it.

Colin pokes his head in just as I am heaving Josh into his chair. "You guys are up early."

I muster up a smile as Josh says, "Mo'ee, Daah."

"I'll start the coffee," Colin offers. Coffee meaning his espresso. He makes enough for both of us, but I don't drink it. He doesn't seem to notice.

"Do you have time to set Josh up on the computer?" I ask, keeping my voice light.

"Sure. As soon as I get the coffee going." He steps into the room and ruffles Josh's hair. "I need to do some research, pal." For his new book. The one he's been working on for a while. "Think you can help me with it?"

"I wah loo' s'thi uh."

"Okay. We'll look up your thing first, then my thing. Sound good?"

"Sows goo'." *Sounds good.*

Josh clamps his hand over the joystick of his chair and follows Colin out of the room. I stand there for a moment, listening as Josh's chair wheels onto the lift. The motor hums softly as the lift descends. When I hear the thwack of the lift coming to a halt on the bottom floor, I leave Josh's room and go to the master bedroom.

Shaking hands, again. I reach for the closet door, slide it to the left. Pull the chain attached to the bare bulb on the ceiling of the closet. My wardrobe glares at me. I sift through the hangers and my hand brushes against silk. Cream silk. My blouse. More sifting, more disbelief as my fingers slide down the length of my navy skirt.

This cannot be happening.

Richard yanking up my skirt, tearing off my underwear. My whole body goes tense with the recollection.

I scramble to the dresser and pull the top drawer open. I need not rummage through the contents of the drawer. My favorite panties, sky blue with lace and flowers on the front panel, sit atop the rest, whole, uneffaced.

I stagger backward, away from the dresser, away from the wreckage of my consciousness. The bed meets the backs of my legs and I sit heavily upon it. I put my fist to my mouth, jam my index finger between my teeth, and bite down, hard.

I have gone insane.

NINE

Insanity does not preclude us from performing our duties and meeting our obligations, especially when those around us are oblivious to our delusions.

I walk into the kitchen fifteen minutes later to find Katie seated at the table. So rare is her appearance at breakfast these days that, for a moment, I think she is a figment of my imagination. She stares morosely at her cell phone, probably waiting for a text from *him* explaining why he didn't come for her this morning. I wonder, too, but not enough.

In appearance, my daughter favors her father, Owen, my ex-husband, whose seed was the only thing he ever gave me that was free. Her hair is red, true red, and her skin is fair with freckles. If you look at her long enough, you see the beauty she will become. If you merely glance at her, you will look away. Her boyfriend, the driveway thief, looks only at her body, with its ripe curves, ample breasts, and inviting hips. I have watched him watching her. He never meets her eyes. She is just insecure enough not to mind.

I hear Colin's and Josh's voices from the family room. The normalcy of the morning disturbs me, but I can only float on its tide. I can't fight it. If I do, I will expose my madness.

"Good morning," I say to my daughter as I cross to the counter. Perhaps, just this once, I will partake of Colin's prized espresso. Perhaps a potent shot of caffeine will help.

"Hi, Mom."

She speaks to me. My daughter is actually addressing me rather than ignoring my presence, which is her usual strategy of late.

"This is a pleasant surprise," I say, moving to the counter. "I haven't seen much of you lately."

"Yeah, well . . ." She leaves the rest unsaid. Had her boyfriend tapped on her window, she wouldn't be here. She would be with him, doing whatever it is they do. Me, Josh, Colin—*her family*—we are her consolation prize, and a dubious one at that. Again, I wonder why he didn't come but quickly push the question away. I'm glad he didn't. I don't care what the reason is.

I turn and look closely at her, something she hasn't allowed for ages due to her constant need to flee my scrutiny. Her cheeks are pale, her eyes sunken. Her hair, always lustrous and full, hangs limply around her face. I want to go to her but fear she will shrink away from my ministrations.

"Are you feeling all right, Katie?" I ask. "Are you coming down with a cold?"

"Just tired," she replies.

"Can I make you some eggs?" A paltry offering, but one I can manage.

She shakes her head. "Not hungry."

"Okay." I attempt a smile. It doesn't take. I walk to the espresso maker, pour myself a small cup.

My maternal radar hums. Kate has something on her mind, something she wants to share with me. If this were any other morning, I would be anxious to talk with her, be the listener she needs me to be, the mother she wants me to be. But this morning, my own angst outweighs my daughter's. I don't know how I can possibly connect with her when I am struggling to hold myself together, when I am desperately clinging to the last shreds of my sanity, when I am trying to discern if I have entered into early-onset dementia.

What are the signs? Wouldn't there be smaller indications of a diseased mind, doled out over time, increasing in severity until there can be no mistake that illness has struck? This is not the case. I have not once had cause to question my sanity. Often I have wondered what purpose I serve in the universe, but the soundness of my mind has never been an issue. Until now.

I take a sip of Colin's bitter brew, then peer at my daughter over the rim of the cup.

This morning, she scarcely resembles the girl she once was. Kate was such a lovely child, bright in demeanor and intelligence. Happy, precocious. She spoke at nine months and walked effortlessly before she was a year old. She wrote poetry at five and songs at eight and a novella at thirteen about a werewolf who was besotted with a shape-shifting she-lion. Katie lit up a room with her presence. All through school her teachers praised her effusively. Her grades, until six months ago, were stellar. From the time she was ten, she wanted to be a pediatric veterinarian, had plans to study at the University of Pennsylvania. Until six months ago. When she started hanging out with *him*.

Katie took the SATs last month. She should have aced the test, but her score was less than spectacular. Study time was replaced by pizzas and B movies and fondling her boyfriend. UPenn is now a fairy tale someone once told her.

"My dad wants to see me."

I set the demitasse down, then smooth my skirt. The one I wear today is dark peach, and I have complimented it with a pale-pink blouse. The navy skirt and cream blouse and my favorite underwear lie in a heap in the wastebasket in the master bathroom. Whether or not my encounter with Richard was real, I can never put any of those items on my body again.

"I know he does," I tell her. My ex-husband has been hounding me with phone calls for the past week. His messages range from sickly sweet to irritably frantic to unabashedly hostile. I suspect Owen is bipolar, but he has never been diagnosed and he only self-medicates with copious amounts of alcohol.

"I don't have to see him, Mom? Right?" Her tone is plaintive.

"Yes, you do."

"But I don't want to see him. Not like this."

"Like what?"

She sets her lips in a grim line. I know what this expression means. No further explanation will be offered.

"Well, you could wash your hair and put some makeup on . . ." As soon as the words leave my lips, I realize I've said the wrong thing.

"Oh, just forget it."

"Kate, your father wants to see you, and there's nothing I can do about it." I leave out the fact that I did try to do something about it. I don't need to burden my daughter with the truth, that Colin and I spent an ungodly amount of money—money we didn't have—petitioning the court to disallow Owen the right to see her. We hired the best lawyer we could afford. He was worth less than we paid. The judge presiding over the case was moved by Owen's boyish good looks and engaging oratory, and the false repentance he wore on the sleeve of his Hugo Boss suit, which I'm certain his girlfriend paid for. *A daughter needs her father,* Owen had said, and the judge, likely thinking of his own daughter, his eyes crinkling at the edges, concurred.

"But you said I didn't have to!" Katie cries. "You said it was all settled and that I didn't have to see him if I didn't want to, that it was up to me."

"I never told you that, Katie. I don't know where you got that from."

And yet, her words swirl around in my head. *You said I didn't have to. You said it was all settled.* Something about those words is familiar but also elusive. I don't allow my thoughts to linger.

I pick up the espresso and take another sip. "Why don't we try to make the best of the situation?" Such a stupid phrase, and one I can't adhere to in my own life, so why should I expect my daughter to do so?

"This sucks," Kate says. *This sucks* is the cornerstone of Kate's communication skills. *Everything sucks.* Most of the time, I don't disagree.

"No bad dreams last night?" Colin walks through the kitchen, his own demitasse in hand.

I swallow a breath at the memory of Richard's erection breaking me apart.

"Uh-oh." Colin sets his cup down and looks at me. "Did you have another?"

I shake my head quickly. "No. No dreams. I slept like the dead." *But I'm trapped in a nightmare now.*

"Good." He refills his cup and carries it to the table. Once seated, he withdraws his pipe and clamps down on it with his teeth. The sharp sound of enamel against plastic stabs at my ears. I hate that damn pipe, and I hate the ritual to which my husband is married.

"Josh?" I ask.

"Reading an article on the possibility of actualizing time travel."

Kate rolls her eyes. "God. What a geek."

I want to slap her. Colin reacts more appropriately, as always. "Your brother is neither a geek nor a god, Katie," he says.

She shrugs. Her cell phone chirps, and her eyes light up. She grabs the phone and reads the message, then bolts from her seat. "I'm out of here."

"Kate, you should eat something," I tell her, but she is gone. I hear the echo of her footsteps as she races up the stairs to prepare for *his* arrival.

I assemble the ingredients of Josh's protein shake while Colin riffles through his morning paper. Every so often, we hear a hoot or a squawk from the living room—lively, positive vocalizations, signals that Josh is okay and enjoying himself. He has a device on his wheelchair that connects to the laptop via Bluetooth with which he can scroll up and down on whatever web page he peruses. For the moment, he is perfectly content.

I am not. I cannot banish Richard's serpent sneer from my mind, cannot erase his grasping, thrusting fingertips, his Altoid/whiskey breath.

Make Josh's smoothie, I tell myself. One moment, one step, one chore at a time.

How can I face that man today?

You must, so you will.

"I talked to Lena last night," Colin says as I dump an assortment of berries into the blender. "About staying overnight."

Lena? I think absently. No, he means *Raina.* Maybe *he* has dementia. Not funny.

He continues without correcting himself. "You know, for a weekend. I thought we could get away. You and me. Together." My muscles tense. "Just the two of us. We haven't been away together for a long time, Em."

Six years. It's been six years since we escaped to the country, found a bed-and-breakfast in Connecticut, and spent the better part of the days making love and drinking wine and visiting antiques dealers where we bought nothing because the trip already cost too much. The sojourn ended abruptly when we received a call from Josh's caretaker, who was at the emergency room with him. He'd choked on a piece of fruit, cut small *just as instructed*, she'd said, but clearly not cut small enough.

Colin and I have not gone away together since.

"I think we need it, Em." He waits for a response.

"That would be . . ." *Horrible, awful, miserable . . .* "Lovely. Let's do it." We won't. Not if I can help it. I push the button on the blender and lose myself in the cacophony of the blades.

～

Raina arrives on schedule and immediately goes to Josh.

"Dobro jutro moj slatki," she whispers in his ear. *Good morning, my sweet.*

Raina is from Serbia. She is blonde and sturdy. She loves hydrangeas and kale chips and tennis. She forces Josh to watch any and all televised pro tennis tournaments, but he doesn't mind. Perhaps he imagines another version of himself, one who sprints along the court, swinging a racquet, diving for volleys and smashing overheads, just like the players he sees on the screen. I imagine that for him as well.

When she arrives, I take my leave, sprinting for the garage before Colin can pin me down to a date on the calendar for our weekend respite.

"Don't want to be late and inspire Richard's ire," I call out.

"Richard?" I hear the confusion in Colin's voice. He says something else, but I can't make out the exact words because I am already opening the garage door, already behind the wheel, already pulling out onto the street. Fleeing my home.

In my usual fashion, I stop and depress the button on the remote and wait to make sure the garage door closes all the way. But as I sit, watching the descent of the lumbering door, my attention is wrenched to my front yard and the anomaly that lies within its perimeter.

The tree, that wretched tree with the hazardous erupting roots, the one that has caused me such bodily harm over the last seven years . . . The tree is gone.

The car idles in park. My mouth falls open, and I am powerless to close it.

Where the fuck is the tree?

Kate alights from the front door and ambles down the walkway to the curb. She stares at me questioningly.

I roll down the passenger window and she approaches. She furtively glances to her left, then to her right, making sure her boyfriend isn't around to catch her conversing with her mother, God forbid.

"What?" Her tone is defensive. She thinks I am going to reprimand her for her short skirt or her heavy-handed eyeliner or any number of things that I couldn't care less about at this moment.

"Where is the tree?" My voice is a whisper, and she leans against the passenger door, elbows resting on the window jamb.

"What?"

I breathe. "The tree. Where the *f*—Where the *hell* is the tree?"

Adolescent ambivalence morphs into genuine curiosity. "What tree, Mom?"

"The tree in the front yard."

Her expression screws into one of mistrust. She shakes her head. "You mean the one that was here when you guys bought the house? Colin got rid of that tree as soon as we moved in, Mom. Remember?" A brief flash of concern crosses her face, only to be replaced seconds later by disgust. "Are you losing it, Mom? 'Cause if you are, let me know. I don't want another psycho parent. I already have one of those."

She jerks away from my car and heads down the street, her fingers typing out a text.

I hold my hands up in front of my face and inspect my palms, then scoot up my skirt to expose my knees. I was so focused on the lack of evidence of Richard's attack that I forgot about the wounds from my tumble yesterday morning. My hands are perfect, and although I'm wearing hose, I can see through the sheer fabric that there are no abrasions on my knees. I suffer no aftereffects of my harsh encounter with the redbrick pavers.

My earlier suspicion is correct. I'm gone.

TEN

I spend the fifteen-minute drive to my office mulling over the one question that matters more than any other. Not whether the tree was actually there yesterday, or if my boss really violated me in the ladies' room last night, or if my neighbors purchased a puppy named Charlemagne. Those things exist for me, real or imagined. The question that dominates my thoughts is this: *If a person is insane, does he know he is insane?*

At a stoplight, I close my eyes and rewind the minutes and hours to yesterday morning. I can still feel the impact of my knees hitting the pavers, my teeth clacking together, the raw burn of the skin on my palms being scraped away. And yet, when I imagine the tree, I can no longer visualize its presence in the remembered scenario.

A faint recollection emerges of a large, dented cargo truck and a Hispanic man wielding a chain saw and a half dozen laborers hauling the desiccated limbs and branches and leaves away while Colin and I watched from the window of a living room full of unopened boxes.

A horn sounds from the car behind me, pulling me from my dendrological musings. I press the accelerator and revisit my earlier conundrum. *If I think I am crazy, am I?*

I consider the possibility that I'm asleep, that the past twenty-four hours of illogical and impossible occurrences are merely an extended dream. Perhaps I'm lying in a bed in the ICU of our local hospital after suffering some sort of trauma. An accident. The Honda was T-boned at an intersection and the doctors put me into a coma to give my damaged organs an opportunity to heal. This explanation seems unlikely, but I am willing to explore it further if it means I'm sane.

But it doesn't ring true. I know I'm awake. I know I'm not dreaming, nor am I in a coma. My choices are limited. Either something inexplicable is happening, or I am truly, absolutely out of my mind.

I slide the Honda into my designated parking spot in front of my office building and stare through the windshield at the day around me. So normal, so typical is this early summer day. Shining sun, bright-blue sky, puffy white clouds. No distortion, no illusions or prisms of light or shimmering mirages, no chimera lurking in the shadows waiting to swallow me up. Only an idyllic facade of reality.

My mind is suddenly blank. I know I have to make a decision. Usually I'm good at making decisions, but now, in this moment and in this circumstance, I falter. Panic sets in.

Should I get out of the car and go into my building and pretend that my world has not turned on its axis? Or should I drive to the hospital and have myself put under observation?

I was never accomplished at meditating, but I know I need to calm down and I have no other method at my disposal. I lean back against the driver's seat and close my eyes. I concentrate on my breathing, on my heartbeat, on the blood pumping through my veins. I disallow thoughts from forming, although they try to breach the fortress, cracking, pounding, pressing in on my consciousness. The effort it takes to keep them at bay is exhausting.

When I open my eyes, fifteen minutes have slid by. I am late. Again.

I pull the key from the ignition and alight from the car.

~

Mr. Mosely is back, and his presence behind the security counter grounds me. Briefly.

"Good morning," I call to him.

He nods his white-capped head at me. "Good morning, Mrs. Davies."

"Mrs. Davies," I repeat. "So formal. I'm glad to see you back. You're feeling better?"

He cocks his head to the side and gives me a strange look, not unlike the look Katie gave me this morning when I asked her about the tree. "Feeling fine as per usual, ma'am," he says.

His stiff posture and solemn manner unnerve me. This is the man who regularly poses for me, making silly faces and often bringing with him comedic accessories so that I might coax a grin or a chuckle from my son. This is the man who pens rhyming couplets poking fun at my fellow employees without ever being truly mean and recites them to me on my way in, hoping I will be able to guess the person about whom he writes. This is the man who spent forty minutes showing me his photo album from his trip to Nepal, where he scattered his wife's ashes—upon her request—at the base of Annapurna Mountain. His polite indifference this morning is unnatural and distressing.

"Is everything all right, Mr. Mosely?" Ironic that I ask someone else this question, when, for me, everything is inarguably *not* all right.

"Right as rain." A canned response, a conversation closer.

As I move past his counter and through the lobby, I wonder if the security guard has been reprimanded for his familiarity with some of the employees, including me. Unlikely, but how else can I explain his behavior?

A couple of my colleagues stand in line at the deli, waiting for last-minute cups of coffee and possibly doughnuts or bagels or sweet treats they can hide in their desk drawers in case they are berated by their bosses and find themselves in need of confectionery solace. I used to keep a Twix bar in my desk until Richard found it and paraded around the staff meeting, holding it up for all the employees to see and casually suggesting that my hidden stash might be the reason for my expanding middle.

A ponytailed young man wearing a Grateful Dead T-shirt gives me the peace sign from his place in line. I know I should recognize him, but I don't.

Still distracted by Mr. Mosely's ambivalence, I pause at the elevator and dig into my purse for my phone. I unlock the device and touch the picture gallery icon, then spend the next minute, a precious sixty seconds that will extend my tardiness and probably draw further wrath from my boss, scrolling through the stored images. Yesterday morning I couldn't locate the picture of Charlemagne, but I passed the picture of Mr. Mosely and his rubber nose. Today I can find neither puppy nor security guard. Backward I scroll, a flurry of images popping up at me while my fingertip furiously slides along the screen. No Mr. Mosely, not anywhere in the gallery. Surely I could not have deleted every single image of the man.

I drop the phone into my purse and head to the far end of the lobby, where the glass doors of Canning and Wells are situated. I grab the distressed-nickel handle and pull. The door seems to weigh a thousand pounds, and the muscles in my arm strain with the burden.

Several employees have arrived ahead of me, and I will receive a severe lambasting because of it. But I can't bring myself to hurry. The closer I get to my desk and Richard's office, the slower my pace becomes. Dread is a living creature, clutching my blouse from behind, tugging at me. I hunch my shoulders and press forward, but I can't break free of dread's grasp. My heart pounds and bile rises to my throat. I haven't seen the man yet, but I already know that when I do, the moment I lay eyes on his vile face, I will be sick.

Blessed relief washes through me when I turn the corner. Richard's office is empty. I've been given a momentary reprieve.

Valerie Martin sits at my desk, staring at my computer monitor. I feel a stab of anger at the sight of her. She is likely going through my files, scrutinizing my work for the slightest mistake.

Valerie, an intern, freshly scrubbed, communications degree neatly folded under her arm, came to Canning and Wells just after Xander's departure. She worked hard and submitted to the misogynistic atmosphere of the company in a most gracious manner, flirting mildly, complimenting greatly, and taking the blame for her superiors' missteps with nary a complaint. She was promoted to VP of marketing last year. Above me. And from what I can glean from the water cooler conversations, she never had to perform fellatio on Richard, or any of the other partners, to garner the promotion.

I have tried to hate her, but I cannot. She reminds me of myself—the me before my life went to hell. Bright, optimistic, enthusiastic, and warm.

I near my desk and gaze down upon her. I refrain from asking her what she's doing there. She is my superior, after all. Underlings do not question their superiors lest they are prepared to forfeit their jobs. I know what I am willing to endure to keep my job. Allowing Valerie to pore over my hard drive is the least of it.

She looks up at me, and a smile unfolds across her face.

"Good morning," she says brightly.

No. Not a good morning. A terrible morning that will be made worse by the appearance of my boss—the devil.

"Where is he?" I ask, shrugging off my purse and setting it on my desk. I gesture to Richard's office.

"Where is who?" As if she doesn't know. Valerie and I have shared a few confidences regarding our boss, none of them positive.

"Richard? Is he getting coffee?"

She peers at me, then her eyes go wide with understanding. She types a command into my keyboard and peers at the monitor screen. "You mean Richard Stein with SoundStage? He's not due in until ten."

I vaguely recall the names SoundStage and Stein, and a user-friendly software program for in-home recording studios. It was an account we failed to land because of Richard's obstinacy. I had suggested he go with a modern, alternative-music vibe with his proposal, but he saw my input as a threat and went with his own archaic sensibilities, backgrounding his PowerPoint with an old Jimmy Dorsey tune. SoundStage went elsewhere with their PR business.

I'm about to tell Valerie, *No, not Richard Stein. Richard Green, our boss.* But something stops me before the words reach my lips. That not-right feeling. I glance down at my desk, at my nameplate, and my body goes cold. The nameplate, which for the last six years has had my name etched into its plasticized surface, now bears the legend VALERIE MARTIN.

"Oh, I put the revised Peters proposal on your desk. Let me know if you want any tweaks."

I don't respond. I can't. My throat is constricted, my vocal cords frozen, every fiber in my being thrums.

"Thanks for giving me a shot at it, Em," she says. "I think it's good, but I won't be offended if you make changes. You're the boss. Oh, and I booted you up."

"Okay." It's all I can think of to say. I turn away from her and trudge toward Richard's office on legs that simultaneously feel disconnected from my torso and heavy as anchors. Even before I see the nameplate affixed beside the door, I take in the office as a whole—the cheerful yellow paint, the verdant plant on the side table next to the overstuffed chocolate-brown couch, the Frida Kahlo print on the wall, the framed family photo of Colin, Josh, Kate, and me on the prized real estate of the desk.

I squeeze my eyes shut, then open them and lower my gaze to the nameplate. It reads: EMMA DAVIES, DIRECTOR OF MARKETING AND BUSINESS ACQUISITION AND RETENTION.

~

I don't faint. My knees don't buckle beneath me. I don't become hysterical and draw curious looks from my fellow employees as they make their way to their stations. Instead, I cross the threshold and enter Richard's office, *my* office.

I feel Valerie's eyes on me, so I make a concerted effort to appear as though all is well with the world, *my* world, which has suddenly become unrecognizable to me.

I make it to the desk, then collapse into the distressed black leather ergonomic chair, the one I found for Richard, the chair he refused to let me purchase because he deemed it an uneconomical expense.

A folder sits neatly atop the desk, the Peters file. I brush my fingertips across it.

At what point does mounting incomprehension cause the mind to snap?

I open the file and pretend to read the contents, even going so far as to occasionally nod my head and smile. But my thoughts are far from the proposal. My brain is puzzling over a mystery, trying to work it out, to unearth the clues that will explain what brought me to be where I am at this moment: in an ergonomic chair I never bought in an office that, until this morning, belonged to a cruel tyrant who stole my dignity and my marital fidelity.

It began with a puppy and a wish, I realize. *Charlemagne.*

The puppy, I understand now, was not a dream, even though my subconscious rewrote the story and I willingly accepted the revision and made it my own. The puppy *was* next door, barking at all hours, and I wished him away.

And then . . . and then . . . the tree.

I wish you took that damn tree out when we first moved in!

And then . . . and then . . .

I think back to yesterday morning in this office, this same office, which looked very different, when Wally Holleran stood in the doorway suffering Richard's degradation.

I wished . . . I wished . . .

I wish Richard Green had never come to work here. I wish he never existed.

"Can I get you some coffee?" Valerie asks. I flinch and the file slips from my grasp.

"You don't have to do that," I say automatically. I haven't yet caught up with the fact that I am now her superior.

"It's no trouble. You always do it for me, Em."

Do I? Am I that kind of considerate boss? I've never held a position of power, so I can't conceive of my conduct in that circumstance. We all desire to put our best selves forward, but more often the world sees us as we really are: flawed, challenged, oppressed, denied the lives we feel we deserve, and resentful for it. Valerie's one small sentence inspires hope that my demeanor as an administrator is that which I would want it to be.

"This is good," I tell her, although I haven't read a word. I know Valerie's work. I've witnessed it from the background for five years. The proposal, I'm certain, is perfect.

Her eyes light up. "You think? Then I'll go ahead and tell Roger to print and stitch."

"I think you should run the meeting, too."

Valerie beams. "Really?"

"Yes," I say. *Because I have no idea what the fuck is happening.* "You'll be great."

She practically vibrates with enthusiasm. I wonder, for a moment, when the last time was that I felt such excitement. The specific occurrence eludes me.

"I'll be back in a jiff with your coffee, yes?"

I nod. She starts to leave, but I call to her. "Val, does Richard Green still work here?"

Her forehead creases. "I don't recognize that name. There's Ritchie Fields in SoMe." Our term for social media. "Did he work here before I came aboard?"

I quickly change the subject. "Cream, no sugar."

"Like you need to tell me." She gazes at me for a moment. "Are you—you seem a little preoccupied this morning."

I almost laugh at the understatement, but I'm afraid my laughter will sound ghoulish. I force a casual smile. "Caffeine will help."

She nods. "I'm on it."

Beneath my skirt and blouse and panty hose, my skin is slick with nervous sweat.

ELEVEN

As soon as Valerie disappears down the hall, I turn to my computer and type in a command. The Google logo appears on my monitor and I type *Richard Green* into the search box. Thousands of hits, a common name. I click the box and revise my search. *Richard Green Canning and Wells.* No hits.

I rub my index finger against my upper lip, then type in another command. *Richard Green Delilah Amherst.*

Delilah is Richard's wife of twenty-seven years. She is the daughter of Henry Amherst, a real estate magnate responsible for most of Hoboken's urban renewal. I've encountered Delilah on numerous occasions in the last six years and found her to be a harpy. I could never decide whether she was always a mean-spirited nag or if serving a life sentence with Richard made her one. She gave him four children, two boys and two girls, all of whom are grown now, but still feeding off the family teat, as Richard likes to say. The eldest have children of their own, and the only time I have seen the humanity in Richard is when he talks about his grandchildren. If the man is truly capable of love, it is for them only.

The new search yields hits solely about Delilah Amherst. I quickly scan through the many articles but find no mention of Richard Green.

A Google image displays the photo of a woman I hardly recognize. Delilah Amherst, frothing with joy, has her arm hooked through the elbow of an attractive silver-haired gentleman with a twinkly eye and mischievous grin.

> Ronald Clayton and Delilah Amherst-Clayton enjoy
> the Van Gogh exhibit at the Met.

An image captured two weeks ago.

Shaking hands is my new normal. I move the mouse to the text box. My fingers hover over the keyboard. *What do I know, what do I know?*

Richard graduated from the University of Ohio. I search the alumni database at the university. No hits. I scour my memory banks. Born to Alma and Joseph Green, Cleveland, Ohio. I search the public records for Cleveland, Alma and Joseph Green. No hits. I google Joseph and Alma Green, Cleveland, Ohio. One hit.

> Proud parents Joseph and Alma Green root for
> their only child, daughter Sybill, as she leads John
> Jay High to softball victory!

Only child.

Bile rises again. Horror pulsates through me. There is no possible way, in any known reality, that I could have wished away a person's entire existence.

I lean back and force myself to breathe. My emotions are a swirling, frantic vortex.

A few cleansing inhalations and exhalations help quiet my mind. If I am honest with myself, I feel little or no remorse about stealing Richard's life. How could I? This man was a sadist, a rapist, an abhorrent human being. But what about his children? His grandchildren?

I lean forward and type furiously onto the keyboard, calling up FamilyTree.com and inputting Delilah Amherst's name. Relief floods through me as I scan her family tree. Four children with Ronald Clayton, their names matching perfectly with those of Richard's off-spring. Six grandchildren to date.

So. I have not killed off an entire clan. I backtrack to the picture of Delilah with her current (only) husband and gaze at her celluloid image. The reason I hardly recognized her is because she appears to be something she never was when I knew her. *Happy.*

Valerie steps into my (Richard's) office and sets a cup of coffee on the desk. The color is just right. I quickly close the browser and look up at her.

"So, we have SoundStage at ten. Are you ready?"

I have never been less ready for anything in my life. I should ask Valerie to cancel the meeting. I should run from this office, this build-ing, this city, and not look back. My spine is a steel rod; my jaw aches with tension. *What do I do now?* I've never run a meeting—the idea was never even considered by my boss or by me. I was always grateful to be allowed on the periphery, an invisible woman, quietly tucked in the far corner of the conference room, silently taking notes she would never share with another soul. Listening and learning and contemplating the ways in which she might do things differently.

"You're going to kill it," Valerie says and tucks a strand of blonde hair behind her ear. "I love how you use KONGOS in the presentation. Very hip." She winks at me. "I'll bet you five bucks they sign with us before they leave the building."

SoundStage. KONGOS. This is the proposal I would have presented to our would-be clients had Richard given me license. He didn't. But he's not here. It's possible he doesn't exist.

I have no choice but to navigate my way through the meeting.

And I do.

~

I am not an actress, but somehow I manage to preside over the pitch meeting with savvy and aplomb I never knew I possessed. Words, phrases, sentences pass my lips that I seem to be accessing from a new memory cache, a file on my mental hard drive that was created long before this morning, however impossible that is. For one hour and fourteen minutes, I am in command of myself and others around me, free of panic and fear and confused disorientation. I revel in it, because in the back of my mind, I know it won't last.

Richard Stein is a youngish forty-something with a stern countenance contradicted by an easy smile. He listens to me as though I am an expert, as though I know what I am talking about, and nods continuously like a devout parishioner to my portrayal of a PR priest.

Stein and his SoundStage compatriots sign with us before they take leave, just as Valerie prophesized.

"Do I have anything before Peters?" I ask her as we tuck away our papers and pretend not to be surprised by our success.

"No," she replies. "Bidwell rescheduled."

Bidwell. Chain of women's gyms. Misanthropic CEO.

I've never heard of them before.

"I'm going to run a couple of errands, then." She nods. "I'll be back before Peters."

She smiles. "Congrats. The big boys are going to be impressed. The first woman partner at Canning and Wells. I can see it now."

I shiver with delight and remorse.

"I'll be on my cell," I tell her, then stride from the conference room, and moments later, from the building.

The fresh air burns my lungs.

～

When Joshua was an infant and I had no idea how to care for a child with cerebral palsy, and I was overwhelmed to the point of utter self-destruction, Colin suggested we see a therapist. A colleague of his at the local college where he teaches creative writing and literary theorems lost a child to SIDS. This colleague recommended a psychoanalyst who helped him and his wife though their dark days. The therapist's name was (and is) Lettie Barnes. If it weren't for her, I might not have survived those first few years with Josh.

In the space between my frenzied computer search of Richard Green and the meeting with SoundStage, I reached out to her. I haven't seen Lettie for a decade, so I was relieved to hear her familiar voice on the outgoing message of the phone number I dialed. I left a frenetic voice mail that suggested I might be losing my mind, and she called me back almost immediately. After a few catching-up pleasantries, she told me to come see her at noon.

Ironically—or not—Dr. Barnes's office is downtown, in one of the second-floor apartments of a brownstone three doors from Paw-Tastic Pets. I experience a kind of déjà vu when I pull up to the curb at a meter on Main Street. I can't seem to quicken my pace when I walk down the sidewalk. My feet betray me, grinding to a halt in front of the pet store window.

There he is, Charlemagne, curled into a ball in the corner of the kennel, motionless in the midst of the merry chaos of his cellmates. He doesn't look up at me pleadingly, nor does he lift his head. His eyes remain downcast, focused on a piece of urine-soaked newspaper. My chest tightens.

Still here because of me . . .

No. It was a dream.

And the tree? Was that a dream? And the existence of a horrible, sadistic man, was that also a dream?

I take a step back, then another and bump into something soft. I whip around to see the little woman—what was her name?—from the next shop down.

But if yesterday was a dream, then how do I recognize this old woman?

"Oh, dear, excuse me." Her voice is like tinkling glass, high and light, with a trace of a British accent.

"I'm sorry, I didn't see you," I say.

"That's one of the problems with being profoundly petite." She giggles at her use of alliteration.

"Yes, well . . ." The day is warm, no breeze, yet a chill courses through me, leaving a trail of gooseflesh along my arms. I rub at them awkwardly and turn to go.

"He's an adorable little moppet, isn't he?"

I follow her gaze to the window. Her focus is unmistakably on Charlemagne.

"They're all cute," I say.

"Yes." She nods slowly. "But there's something about that little one in the corner, isn't there? Something that brings to mind Western Europe and the Middle Ages."

My head jerks so violently toward her that a spasm of pain stabs my neck. The woman watches me closely, then her lips spread into a knowing grin. She winks.

"Charlemagne," I whisper.

"Though Charlie seems more appropriate, don't you think?"

I'm suddenly struck with vertigo. The sidewalk expands and contracts beneath my feet, the brownstones seem to breathe, the air pressure shifts as though all the oxygen around me is being sucked into a vacuum.

"Oh my, are you quite well? You look as if you've seen a ghost."

She reaches out and places her palm on my hand. The warmth of her touch steadies me.

"I'm . . . I'm just not myself today."

"Why don't you come into my shop for a few minutes," she suggests. "I've just made some tea. We can have a nice chat."

I shake my head and pull my hand away from hers. "I c-can't. I have an appointment."

"Well, that's a shame. But I understand."

I move past her, forcing myself *not* to look at the puppy. The swirling patterns in the concrete dance before my eyes, making it difficult for me to walk in a straight line. I sense movement beside me. The woman has fallen in step with my strides. She stops in front of her shop.

"This is mine," she says, gesturing to the window. Again, I follow her gaze. The house, the miniature of my own, still sits in the front display.

From where I stand, I can see it clearly. Where yesterday there was only fake grass lining the yard, today a Lilliputian tree stands in the center of it.

TWELVE

Dr. Lettie Barnes takes one quick look at me and ushers me straight into her office.

The years have been kind to my former therapist. She has given up dyeing her hair auburn, and the result is a mass of lovely, silky silver locks framing her oval face. The lines around her dark-brown eyes and mouth have deepened, but they do not age her as much as they add a degree of wisdom and worldliness to her aura. Her hips and torso have widened fractionally, but she still wears her uniform of jeans and open-knit sweaters with the same confidence she did when she carried less weight.

"Please don't ask me if I'm okay," I say before I sit down.

Her inner sanctum is much the same, although she's had it painted recently. The leather couch has been traded for a newer model, as have the overstuffed chairs, for patients who prefer to sit up, but they are each in the same place as when I was last here, couch beneath the window, chairs catty-corner to Lettie's desk. I recognize quite a few of the family photos on the wall, but there are a great many additions due to the expansion of her clan—the collection now includes her children's spouses and her grandchildren.

The familiarity of the room fails to calm me or restore my sense of order.

"All right," she says. "I won't ask. Where would you like to sit?"

"I don't know." I wring my hands, then realize what I'm doing and force myself to stop.

"How about if I tell you where to sit." I nod and she points to the couch.

"I don't want to lie down."

She nods. "You don't have to lie down, Emma. I am merely suggesting the place, not the position."

Lettie Barnes's voice is low and breathy like that of a smoker, soothing as a cup of warm milk and honey. Her sentences are measured, delivered slowly and methodically, but they never come across as rehearsed. "I can see that something is upsetting you," she says.

I shake my head back and forth as a wave of panic sets in.

"I'm not upset. I. Am. Not. Upset. I'm going insane, Lettie. But not the okay kind of insane, not the way most mothers of teenagers and special-needs kids feel—overwhelmed and overwrought and distraught and delirious. I'm the bad kind of insane, the straitjacket kind." I still haven't taken a seat.

"Emma, take a breath. Please."

"I can't. I can't breathe deeply or exhale on a sound or clear my mind anymore. I've tried. All I've done for the past twenty-four hours is breathe, but it's not helping."

"Emma!" Her tone is sharp. I swallow hard and meet her eyes. "Emma." Softly this time. "Sit down." I comply. The cushion beneath me is a million miles away, but after a long moment of descent, I feel the leather against my butt and upper thighs. I fold my hands in my lap.

Lettie drags her chair around the desk and sets it next to the couch, less than a foot from me, then lowers herself into it. She reaches out and takes my hands in hers and looks at me intently.

"It's been a while since you've been here, Emma, so I'm going to remind you that whatever you share with me is strictly confidential and will never leave these walls unless you give me permission to disclose it."

Her words, slow and mellifluous, seep into me, and I feel myself, finally, unwind. I am safe here, if only for the time being. When 12:55 comes, I will be thrust out into the world, into my false life, my perpetual hallucination. But for the next fifty minutes, I'm safe.

"Okay, Emma," she says with her milk-and-honey voice. "What's going on?"

I tell her the tale, beginning with my wish the night before last and Charlemagne's subsequent disappearance; the tree and my fall against the brick pavers; Richard's attack and this morning's denial of yesterday's sins; my ascendance to an un-abdicated throne, my internet search, my meeting with SoundStage, the revised memories at war with the originals. She listens patiently without interruption, without ever donning a skeptical expression, without ever loosening her grip on my hands. When I finish, I lean back against the couch, slip my hands from her grasp and press them against my face. Hearing myself relay the events of the last thirty-six hours confirms what I already suspect. My story is a fantasy, a fiction. Madness.

Lettie's first question surprises me. "How is Joshua?"

I collect my thoughts. "Fine. The same. Good days and bad days."

"And Katie?"

"She's a typical teenager. Hates me most of the time, and the rest of the time tolerates me."

"And how are you and Colin?"

I understand what Lettie is doing. She's making simple and prosaic inquiries about my life to lure me away from my delusions. It works. I relax a trifle more when recounting the humdrum facets of my everyday existence.

"Colin and I are as always. Married."

She nods and permits herself a chuckle. Not rancorous or condescending, but an acknowledgment of all women's occasional complacency with marital life.

"Are you making love?"

I shrug. "Not lately. It's a phase, right? He wants to take me away for a weekend. Rekindle our passion."

"You don't want to go?"

I breathe, as instructed, only moments too late. "I don't want to leave Josh."

"But you are comfortable with his current caretaker?"

I sigh and feel the muscles in my shoulders contract. "Yes, but this has nothing to do with why I came here today. Lettie, I need help."

Her smile is compassionate and sympathetic, not charitable. "Emma. I am going to speak frankly with you, okay?"

I nod.

"I haven't seen you for a decade, but I know you are the same woman who came to me more than a dozen years ago. I saw no signs of mental illness then. I saw a woman overwhelmed and stressed to the very brink of breaking. That is what I see today."

"It's more than that," I say, but my voice falters.

She sits back in her chair. "Human beings are a strange lot, Emma. We are enslaved by our intelligence. Frequently, when we feel anxiety or disquiet, our minds take us places we don't want to go, create scenarios that seem unlikely if not downright impossible. Our brains are complex computers that we don't fully understand. Where do thoughts come from? How do we distinguish fantasy from reality? What is the basis for our certainty that a thing actually exists?"

She doesn't believe me. And why should she? I don't believe me, either, except that I know what I know.

"Let's do a little exercise, okay?"

I don't want to do any exercises and I don't want psychobabble. I want an explanation. I want a rationalization. I want to know that somewhere in recorded history, someone has experienced that which I am experiencing now.

I nod to her in acquiescence.

"I want you to close your eyes, Emma. Breathe deeply. Whatever images are floating through your mind, I want you to let them flow, then let them go."

So easy for her to say, so difficult for me to do. I close my eyes, and a montage of snapshots flies across my brain. Charlemagne, Richard, Colin, the tree, my discarded clothing, my ravaged cheek, the bathroom stall at Canning and Wells. I take another breath. *Let them flow and let them go.*

"Go back, Emma. Let the years fall away. Go back to that day when your boss Xander left your firm."

The renegade images recede, and I see Xander's face. I feel a smile come to my lips at the sight of him, so jolly, so ebullient and generous of spirit.

"We're having a retirement party for him," I murmur. Wally Holleran was new to the firm and desperate to get into his colleagues' good graces. He brought the champagne and played bartender, filling everyone's glass but his own.

"Tell me what Xander says to you," Lettie coaxes.

My boss approaches, a sad smile playing at the corners of his mouth. He doesn't want to retire, but Bill Canning and Edward Wells are pushing him out. And his wife is ailing. He wants to spend time with her and their grandchildren. But he will miss the daily mayhem, the battle, the sweet scent of victory when a campaign produces a client's success.

"Emma," Xander says. "Thank you. I know it was you who put this soiree together."

I don't contradict him. He has been my mentor and my champion for the past year. I'm sorry to see him go. Will his replacement treat me with the same respect that Xander has?

He puts his rough, wrinkled hand on my shoulder and gives me a warm, jowly smile. "I've put in a good word for you, Emma," he said. "I was thinking you might take my position when I leave. Bill and Ed are convinced. Beginning next week, you will be the new director of marketing and business acquisition and retention. On a trial basis, of course, but I have no doubt that you will be a formidable successor."

My eyes snap open. Lettie is staring at me. This memory is fraudulent, although it resembles the truth. I shake my head and close my eyes again, willing the proper recollection to materialize.

"I was thinking you might take my position when I leave, but Bill and Ed think you need a little bit more time. But they are aware. And so is Richard. They'll do right by you. I promise."

Both memories resonate, but I know that only one could have happened. Unless, at some point, I was sliced in half and am currently living dual lives in parallel universes. A bark of terrified laughter escapes me, and I press the heel of my hand against my mouth to mute the sound. A few seconds pass.

"How did you feel in your meeting today?" Lettie asks in front of my closed lids.

I drop my hand and let out a sigh. "I felt good." *For the first time in as long as I can remember, I felt in control, a part of something that mattered. My family, my son—they matter, of course. But the meeting in the conference room, with Richard Stein hanging on my every word and Valerie surreptitiously giving me the thumbs-up signal, was something that was solely about me.*

What a selfish woman I am.

"Open your eyes, Emma," Lettie says. The cadence of her voice suggests that our session has come to a close. "I want to see you again, at the end of the week. In the meantime, I'm going to prescribe something for you. Xanax. It will help you achieve a sense of calm without corrupting your daily life."

She stands and crosses to her desk, leans over and scribbles something onto her pad. I maintain my composure, but on the inside I'm screaming. Xanax will not help me. Medication will dull my senses and further confuse the situation. I will fill the prescription, because I know Lettie will confirm my receipt of it, but I will not take it.

"How is next Friday at noon?" she asks.

The old woman from the antiques shop—Dolores is her name—comes to mind. She knew the puppy's name. For some reason, when I recounted my ludicrous story for Lettie, I omitted any reference to Dolores. Perhaps I should seek the old woman's counsel.

No. I should stay away from her. She will only make matters worse.

How can matters be worse?

"I'll have to check my calendar," I say. I gain my feet. The world still sways on its axis, but I am more acclimated to the roller coaster now.

Lettie hands me the prescription and looks at me closely. "I don't disbelieve you, Emma."

Yes, you do, I think. *And why wouldn't you?*

I *disbelieve me.*

"Thank you for seeing me on such short notice," I say. "I feel better." A lie. I tuck the slip of paper into my purse and head for the door.

"See you Friday, then?" Lettie calls to me.

"I'll let you know," I reply, then leave the security of her office and head back out to my nightmare.

THIRTEEN

I cross the street to avoid walking past the antiques store and Paw-Tastic Pets. I can't handle the sight of Dolores or Charlemagne, not when my head is filled with conflicting accounts of my past, not while shadow images pursue me.

As soon as I get behind the wheel of my car, my cell phone rings. I check the caller ID, and my shoulders spasm in response to the name that appears. I swipe the screen to answer, because letting the call go to voice mail will only prolong the inevitable.

"You bitch." Owen. "Do you really think you can get away with this?"

"I don't know what you're talking about, Owen." And I don't, but I manage to maneuver my way through the conversation as if I do.

"You can't keep her from me, you know. She's my daughter, too."

"Only when it's convenient." My retort surprises me. I never engage with my ex because I haven't the strength. Perhaps, with my impending stay at the local sanitarium, and with nothing to lose, I've grown balls.

He hisses into the phone. "You can say what you damn well please to the judge. Oh yeah, you can charm him and wave your pay stubs to him and trash-talk me, but Katie's still mine. You can't change that, Emma. She's half of me."

"Hopefully the better half," I say, feeling a rush of giddiness at my quick thinking.

"I won't let you do this, you know. I have a right to see her. I've put in another petition."

"How can you afford a lawyer?" I ask, then let out a breath. "Never mind. I can't believe your girlfriend is willing to put up the money for another lawsuit. You must make her scream with pleasure, Owen. Too bad it won't be long before your dick shrivels to the size of a peanut from all the alcohol and drugs and she'll have to look elsewhere for satisfaction."

He is silent. I'm about to hit the "End" button when I hear him sigh. "When did you get so nasty, Em? You didn't used to be this way."

You knew me in a different time, when my life was bearable and you weren't a slave to your addictions.

"Goodbye, Owen."

"Wait!"

I hang up and drop my cell phone into my purse. Katie's words come back to me.

You said it was all settled and that I didn't have to see him if I didn't want to.

A vague recollection of a court appearance suddenly manifests itself in my memory—Owen looking disheveled in an ill-fitting suit, his girlfriend tatted up and pierced and clinging to him like an octopus devouring a mollusk; Colin and me dressed to impress in our professional best, a smart, savvy, expensive lawyer beside us; a heavyset, balding judge at whom I merely had to bat my eyes to win his partiality, and a ruling decidedly in my favor.

This memory might be false, constructed by a feverish mind. But I like it.

~

I met Owen on a slate-sky kind of day in March, when the rain fell so hard it hurt. I was in the last semester of the graduate program at Montclair State University, vying for my communications masters along with 127 other candidates. The certificate would lead nowhere for approximately two-thirds of the graduates.

I stood outside College Hall, the oldest building on campus, with a malfunctioning umbrella and a mouth full of curses. Owen rescued me with his stalwart brolly and infectious laugh. I needed humor and a lightness of the spirit after my separation from Dante. The best—and worst—thing about Owen McBride was that he was the exact opposite of my former lover. He was a guy from Jersey who didn't philosophize or aggrandize or fantasize about living a life beyond his meager skill set.

He was in graduate school because his parents could afford to send him. They clung to the hope that the business degree for which he strove would save their precious Paterson pub. His grades were less than spectacular, not because he wasn't smart but because he had no attachment to his own intellectual enrichment. During the course of our relationship, the family bar–cum–restaurant was forced to close its doors.

Owen was charming in a self-effacing manner. His good looks and guileless appeal concealed a host of neuroses I couldn't or wouldn't see at the time. Ours was a love affair that existed in my mind and his trousers. I should have ended it sooner—I knew he was not made of the stuff I needed in a lifetime partner—but his penis and his prowess with that part of himself were a constant enticer. When we made love, passionately, sometimes savagely, Dante was erased from my mind. To be able to forget the love of your life with the thrust of another's sword can be a powerful drug.

When I found myself pregnant that November—and why shouldn't I? Even the most fail-safe birth control cannot withstand constant, frenzied coupling—Owen was resigned to do the "right thing" by me. He wasn't making an honest woman out of me. Quite the contrary—he made me a liar.

We got married on a cold day in January at the county courthouse. The marriage lasted seven months. Two hundred and ten days of Owen trying to drown his resentment with booze and barbiturates and me trying to convince myself I'd made the right decision not aborting the baby. He left me the morning I went into labor, unaware that the pool of liquid on the floor of our studio apartment in the cheapest part of Montclair was the result of my water breaking.

I birthed Kate with my mother beside me instead of my husband. The nurses looked down on me with pity as I screamed and pushed and viciously propelled my daughter from my womb. But I was lucky, I told myself between blistering contractions. I was free of Owen before he could wreak more havoc on my life.

I thought that then. I know better. His havoc infects me even more now.

~

When I return to Canning and Wells, I toss a casual wave at Mr. Mosely and he gives me a curt nod in return.

Nepal. He went to Nepal with his wife's ashes. I know that about him. But how?

Wally Holleran stands beside my (Valerie's) desk. I almost don't recognize him. His glasses are missing and his skin is clear of imperfections. I can tell by his posture and his grin that he is flirting with Valerie. He sees me in his peripheral vision and immediately straightens and washes the grin from his unblemished face.

"Hi, Emma," he calls as I approach. "I heard about SoundStage. Totally g-g-great." The acne and glasses might be gone, but the stutter remains. I remember how his speech impediment tortured him, inspiring slouched shoulders and the refusal to meet another person's eyes during a direct exchange. Today he seems not the slightest bit self-conscious. "Way to g-g-go."

"Thanks"—*Golly Polly*—"Wally."

Fuck you, Richard. You're ether.

You've been teasing me for five years, Em. I know this is what you want. It didn't happen . . .

You like it rough, huh? I had a feeling.

Valerie and Wally are watching me expectantly. Did one of them just ask me a question?

"Sorry. My mind was on something else. What did you say?"

"I just asked if you want me in the meeting with P-P-Peters this afternoon," Wally says.

"I thought it might be good to have him there to help with the website pitch," Valerie adds. She looks up at him and gives him a quick smile. If I didn't know better, I'd guess that Wally's flirting has paid off. Except that Valerie has a fiancé named Erik with a *k*, a former college football star and current pool man who lives off her generous salary.

But that was before, when she was your superior. What is she making now? Enough to support the quarterback? Perhaps now she goes home to an empty apartment and drinks copious amounts of wine to obliterate her loneliness.

"It's your meeting," I remind her. "If you want Wally there, then he should be there."

"G-g-great!" Wally says again. He has trouble with his *g*'s and *p*'s. I pray he keeps his *g* and *p* words to a minimum in the pitch meeting. As if reading my mind, he says, "Oh, and don't worry about the, uh, you know." He points to his mouth. "I don't know why, but it tends to g-g-go away when I'm speaking in front of p-p-people."

"I'm not worried," I assure him. *I have a son with cerebral palsy. Who cares about a lousy stutter?*

I must have spoken aloud, because the two of them gape at me openly.

"Seriously?" Valerie's eyes are shiny green buttons.

"I'm sorry. That came out wrong. I don't mean to minimize your challenge, Wally."

"Not that," she says. "How come I never knew about your son?"

Because Richard doesn't exist, therefore he was never here to expose my secret.

"Emma has to get home to her disabled son."

"Sorry, everyone, but we'll have to cut this short. Emma's disabled son has been sent to the emergency room."

My son's disability was not a subject I wished to discuss at work. I told Xander out of necessity when I first came to work for him, and he took the news with grace and empathy, patting my hand and suggesting we come up with a code to spare me my coworkers curiosity and gossip. *Josh's babysitter canceled* was my signal that I was unable to stay late. *Josh is in trouble at school again* meant I had to leave that very minute, no matter my current task, because of an emergency. Although Xander was duty bound to pass along all pertinent information to Richard regarding the firm's employees, I have no doubt that he asked Richard to keep Josh's circumstances to himself. But Richard being Richard, he could never forgo an opportunity to degrade one of his underlings. Richard fed off other people's misery.

Not anymore.

"I'm so sorry, Emma," Valerie says, buttons glistening.

"Yeah, Emma, that's g-g-got to be tough."

"I can't believe you never told me."

Remorse is a difficult emotion to contrive. Especially since, as far as I'm concerned—and based on my old memories—Valerie has known about Josh from the day she started here. When we've had the occasion to converse, she asks after him and periodically sends him a card with a funny cartoon on it. But on this not-real day, this here and now, this alternate reality, the news of my son is a revelation to her. I bow my head.

"Well, it's not the kind of thing you just g-g-go and announce," Wally says. "Now is it?"

Valerie's expression is that of a chastised child. "I just thought I knew everything about her, that's all."

"What?" I ask. "What do you know about me?" *In this surreal place and time.*

She takes a breath. "Well . . . I know that you're kind and fair, and sometimes stern, but only when you need to be. You never make us stay late. You demand that we give our best because you give your best."

Kind? Fair? Stern? I am none of these things.

I am insecure, I am desperate, I am unfulfilled. I am resigned to play the cards I've been dealt, and I play them poorly at that.

"Your husband, Colin, writes biographies about famous literary figures."

"And he teaches literature at the JC," I interject.

"Since when?" she asks, giving me a suspicious look as though I am keeping secrets from her. "I thought he gave that up when you got your promotion."

I clamp my lips shut to stop myself from contradicting her. "I mean he *taught* literature."

She nods, mollified, then continues. "And I know that your daughter, Kate, is going into her senior year of high school and you're worried about her because you think her boyfriend is corrupting her and also that he's an ass, and your son . . . Josh . . . , well, I just thought he was a typical teenager."

I allow myself a mental tangent, a fanciful image of Josh as a typical teenager, but I cut the vision short. I will not go there, *cannot* go there.

"I apologize, Val. My son's condition is something I try to keep private. I don't want people talking about it at the water cooler. Josh deserves his anonymity."

Valerie gives me a solemn look. "I understand."

And I think she does. Despite having watched her clamber to achieve success within the Canning and Wells hierarchy for the past five years—the five years that happened before my boss-extinguishing wish—I honestly believe Valerie Martin is a good person.

I just don't know what *I* am anymore.

FOURTEEN

When I arrive home that evening, the tree is still gone. The front yard looks bare without it, empty. Even the grass looks forlorn without the companionship of the oak's overbearing roots.

I am desperately clinging to my to-do list. Whatever I'm experiencing, be it a dream, or a coma, a parallel universe, or a complete psychotic break, I need to get through it, and the only way I know how to do that is to check things off my list, one by one.

Workday completed. Check. *I won't think about non-Richard or my newly acquired position that is* not *new.* Prescription filled. Check. *I won't think about the reasons for the prescribed drug or Lettie's rote explanation for my circumstances or Dolores and her knowledge of Charlemagne, the puppy who does exist but is not barking next door.*

As I pull into the garage, I don't concentrate on the strange and inexplicable, but instead on the mundane: my to-do list and the looming tasks on it. Make dinner. Feed Josh. Pay bills online. Get Josh ready for bed. Read to Josh. Watch TV in bed with the volume low while I track Josh's breathing on the monitor until I know he's asleep. One by one, I will accomplish each task and mentally check them off.

The muted sound of Cole Porter greets me when I walk into the house. The melody line is familiar to me; my parents played Cole Porter frequently during my childhood. Every Friday night, they would put a vinyl record on the stereo, drink enough wine to get them on their feet, then proceed to cut a rug across the living room floor.

The music comes from behind Colin's closed office door. When our realtor showed us the house seven years ago, I was opposed to buying a two story. It was a fixer-upper and the only thing we could afford in the school district we wanted for Katie's education. Our options were limited, so we decided to make it work. We deliberated about whether to put Josh on the first or second floor. Colin fought for the second floor. He argued that Josh would feel isolated from the family on the first floor and we would feel more at ease with him close by. I had to agree with his reasoning, but I also knew he wanted the spare room on the ground floor for himself.

I pass by the closed door without knocking. I know what the music means. Colin only listens to music in his office when he's struggling with his manuscript. I hear the music more often lately. If Valerie is correct, and Colin no longer holds his position at the JC, he spends the entirety of his days within the walls of this room, feverishly typing on his keyboard, or, alternately, listening to music when his muse deserts him.

I wonder how long Cole Porter has been playing today.

As I walk down the hallway, the sound of jazz fades only to be replaced by some kind of techno hip-hop. The living room is flooded with light emanating from a large flat-screen television mounted on the wall above the fireplace. I have never seen the TV before, nor have I seen the raven-haired young woman standing in front of the couch, hopping back and forth on one foot and gyrating her slender hips in time with the music. She holds an Xbox remote in her hand, and I assume that the strobe lights and colored circles and left and right arrows on the TV screen represent a dance game she's playing. Josh sits in his wheelchair a few feet from her zoetic form. Panic is not unfamiliar to me—I experience it regularly with my son and the many life-threatening challenges he's faced—but today, panic has been ever present, and I feel it strike me with renewed intensity.

Who is this girl and what is she doing in my living room and what are we doing with a giant flat-screen television and an Xbox console?

The young woman whirls around and stops in her tracks. She greets me with an ice-blue-eyed gaze.

"Oh, hi, Mrs. D!" She puts a hand to her heart and takes a few gulps of air, then collapses against the side of the couch. "Thank goodness you're here. I was about to have a heart attack."

"Hi, Maah!" Josh calls, turning his wheelchair so that he can see me. But he doesn't move closer, as he usually does to accept my kiss and hug.

"Where's Raina?" I ask, but I'm not sure if I want the answer.

"She left at her usual time," the girl says. "We've been dancing up a storm, haven't we, Joshy?"

I wince at her use of the nickname. I called my son Joshy until, at nine years old, he told me in no uncertain terms—despite his near-unintelligible speech—that he no longer wanted to be called Joshy.

"Of course, I do all the work, don't I?"

She is comfortable here, at ease. Clearly, she's been a constant presence in this household for quite some time.

"Y' d' th' moo, bu' Aye pi' th' gas." *You do the moves, but I pick the games.* "Thas ha' wor', t'." *That's hard work, too.*

"Oh yeah? Well, then how about I pick the games and you do the moves, huh? Let's see that."

"I cu d' i, Leeah." *I could do it . . . Lisa? Linda?*

"Lena," she tells him, exaggerating the *N* sound. "Come on, Joshy, Lena."

"Leeah," he repeats.

She shrugs. "We've been working on his *N*s, but he's such a lazy butt."

"Am 'ot." *Am not.*

"See? Am *not*. Lazy butt."

She reaches over and chucks him on the chin, and he gazes at her with absolute adoration. My panic turns cold.

"Dinner's all ready to go, Mrs. D," she says, this Lena of the icy eyes and shapely body and disturbing familiarity with my son. My expression must reveal my confusion. "The chicken breasts. I put them in the oven at five, as per your instructions. The salad's made and the garlic bread only takes five minutes."

I nod. "Thanks."

"That's what you pay me for," she jokes, then nudges Josh. "And to take care of this lug."

"Aye 'ot a luh." *I'm not a lug.*

"Not. With an *N*."

Josh raises his chin, the cords in his neck straining, his mouth stretched into a grimace. I see the exertion, the pain such an effort causes him, and I want to go to him and place my hand on his shoulder and tell him not to worry, not to struggle, because the cost isn't worth the meager spoils. But I don't, because he isn't striving to make the sound for me, but for Lena.

"Nnnnnnah."

The young woman rewards him with a beatific smile. She leans into him so that their noses are mere inches apart. "I knew you could do it," she whispers. "Lazy butt."

They gaze at each other for a long moment, and I stand watching, an outsider, a fifth wheel, a spare prick at a wedding.

"I'm going upstairs to change," I say. This seems like something I would do. Lena nods, validating my hunch. I turn away from them and head for the stairs, absently thinking that this is the first time I can remember when I arrived home from work and didn't kiss my son hello. The subtraction of this ritual from my daily routine makes me ache like an addict in withdrawal.

I climb the stairs, thoughts racing—another new normal. We could never afford nighttime care for Josh, not with my executive-assistant salary and Colin's paltry junior-college wages. But now . . . now. EMMA DAVIES, DIRECTOR OF MARKETING AND BUSINESS ACQUISITION AND RETENTION.

Now we can afford *Lena*, siren, temptress . . . caretaker.

∼

I steer my way through dinner without betraying the fact that I am stranded in an alternate version of my life. Like the actor's nightmare, I don't know my role or my lines or my stage directions. I mostly stay quiet and observe as the play unfolds around me.

Colin emerges from his office after a swift tap-tap from Lena upon his office door. Kate enters stage left through the back door, eyes puffy and swollen and offering no explanation for them. She silently takes her seat next to Josh. Josh, who used to scrutinize each of us, who—before tonight—would have asked Kate why her eyes looked like those of an ill raccoon, barely acknowledges her. His attention is glued to Lena. Lena, who moves through the kitchen—*my* kitchen—as though she is mistress of the house, plating the food and setting it at each place while Colin compliments her on *how divine it smells*. I want to tell him that *Lena* didn't make the chicken, only reheated it, but I honestly don't know whether or not she did, I only know it's my recipe, handed down from my mother, and one of the few things I still undertake to cook on the rare occasion, so *surely* I made it. But I don't know, so I say nothing and continue to watch Josh watch *her*.

Kate pushes her food around on her plate, then suddenly stands up, hand to her mouth. A second later, she drops her arm to her side. "I'm tired," she announces and hurries out of the kitchen.

Lena takes no notice. She sits beside Josh and feeds him his mashed sweet potatoes and ignores Colin and me.

"Should I . . . go after her?"

"What's the point?" Lena replies, although the question was addressed to my husband. "I'm surprised she even came to the table in the first place."

I do not like this girl at all. How could I have invited her into my family?

Colin asks about my day as I choke down a bite of chicken.

What is the proper response? *Ho-hum? Same old, same old? Totally un-fucking-real?*

"Fine," I say. "Good, actually. We landed a new account."

"SoundStage?" I glance at him, surprised. He knows about SoundStage, but how? Our conversations about work never go beyond the superficial. *How was your day? Fine, and yours? Good. Great. Terrific, blah blah blah.* Are we now the kind of couple who discuss the minutiae of our occupations? Do I know the particulars of his manuscript? I search my mind but come up short.

"Is it SoundStage, Emma?" he repeats, and I nod. "Well, congratulations. That's wonderful. Isn't that wonderful, Josh? Your mom landed a big account at work."

Josh barely moves his head. "Yaaa, gray, Maah. Cahgras." *Yeah, great, Mom. Congrats.* Little enthusiasm. His attention never leaves Lena's face. I pretend not to notice.

"Thanks, Josh."

I set down my fork and gaze across the table at my husband. I can't remember the last time I looked at him closely and for more than a split second. For years, there has been an undercurrent of disquiet between us, almost like a secret we've been keeping, and if we allow our eyes to meet and we look too long upon each other, the secret will be revealed and we will have to acknowledge it and, consequently, deal with it. I've been an active participant in keeping this secret because I am too weary to explore the consequences of its exposure.

Colin senses my stare and looks at me. He gives me a closed-mouth smile, and I notice that the usual trace of dolor in his eyes has been replaced by contented complacency.

"What?" he asks. "You're giving me a funny look, Em."

"Sorry." I'd forgotten how attractive Colin is. Not handsome in an obvious way, he is neither movie-star glamorous nor dangerously tempting. But his features are comely—strong chin and nose, hazel eyes that run gold, dark-brown hair shaded with gray at the temples. His hairline recedes, but not markedly.

I had begun to see Colin as a stoop-shouldered old man, beaten down by tragedy and an ambivalent wife. Perhaps in this alternate reality, I am not ambivalent and he is not beaten.

My mother introduced us. Colin was a regular guest at her women's club, the good-looking young bachelor who entertained the bored divorcées with poetry readings and discussions of Steinbeck and Salinger and F. Scott Fitzgerald. He was older than me by eight years and seemed so grounded in his life, even though he'd never been married and had no children of his own. I loved Colin in a calming way, and he accepted Kate into his world with no complaint and no restraint, and I knew that I could do no better, for her or for myself.

And my mother's handprints were practically visible on my back. She would not admit, not to anyone, how much she longed to have her daughter and granddaughter at a normal distance—down the block or in the neighboring tract of houses or one town over—instead of in her own home. My mother had taken a shine to her empty nest, and although she opened her arms to Kate and me when Owen discarded us, she was more than happy to help us into our new life with my new husband.

"How is the book coming?" I ask him, and he grins, which is a good sign.

"Excellent," he says but does not expound further.

I rise and begin to clear Colin's and my plates, but Lena stops me. "I'll do that, Mrs. D. Soon as I'm done."

"Yes, hon, why don't we take a glass of wine out back? It's such a nice night."

Wine? Out back? "I shouldn't. Maybe after I take care of Josh."

"Horning in on my job, eh?" Lena says, and there is a sharpness to her tone, a possessiveness that betrays her irreverent smile.

"No, I . . ." *I what?*

I always take care of Josh after dinner. I bathe him and put him in his pajamas and read to him. Not anymore. *My to-do list has been undone.* I should be relieved. I should be grateful. I am neither.

I turn to Colin and nod. "A glass of wine sounds good."

I try not to think about the prescription in my purse upstairs.

FIFTEEN

I sit on the back patio beside my husband listening to the gentle song of the cicadas. The July night is balmy with a wisp of a breeze, the sky is the color of a lavender blossom.

The wine helps to placate me. If my consumption is unusual, Colin makes no mention of it, just fills my glass as soon as I drain it, which is frequently. At one point, he rises and goes into the kitchen, returning moments later with a fresh bottle.

Over the last several hours, I have come to a place in this not-right world where I no longer have expectations. For the first time in my life, I am adhering to the rules of Zen, living completely and fully in the moment. A Zen master would spit on me; I live in the moment not because I want to or strive to but because there is no alternative. Whatever *this* is, I have no choice but to endure it until it stops or I'm thrown into a padded cell.

I breathe deeply and let out a sigh. "This is nice. It's been a long time since we've done this."

Colin chuckles conspiratorially. "Yes. Last night was *ages* ago." I glance at him and he winks. A running joke?

It strikes me as odd that in this new *now*, with my salary that affords us Colin not teaching and full-time care for Josh, that we are still sitting on the rickety wooden chairs we've had since we moved in, in a back-yard with the same plain strip of yellowing grass, gray concrete patio, and no embellishments, horticultural or decorative.

I let the thought go.

"I'm worried about Katie," I say. A neutral subject and one that would plague me under any circumstances, new life or old.

"I know," Colin agrees. "I am, too. But you know what her school counselor said."

I have no idea. When did we meet with a counselor? A hazy vision materializes: a corner antechamber in the high school attendance office, an olive-skinned woman with adult braces and mousy brown hair seated behind her utilitarian metal desk, peering down at two report cards.

"We can't coddle her anymore," Colin says. "We have to let her sink or swim."

"We don't coddle her, Colin. I don't even know how to talk to her anymore."

"That's it. You can't talk to her. Neither can I. She's unknowable to us. She's only knowable to her friends and to—"

"Him. I do not like him at all."

"There's the understatement of the year." He smiles at me as I take another sip of the wine. I can't taste the fruity undertones or the tart, dry overtones anymore, but the pinot noir is doing its job. A numb warmth has spread through me like a subdermal electric blanket. I relax against the wooden slats.

"She'll move past him," Colin says, sliding a hand across the sleek fabric of my lounge pants.

"But how much damage will he do before then?" I ask. "Her grades are in the toilet, Colin. Her SAT scores were abysmal. She'll be lucky to get into the JC." If he is offended by this denigrating remark regarding the junior college he works at (*worked* at) he doesn't show it. "All her dreams and aspirations and plans, down the crapper because of a stupid boy."

"She still has a year before college, Em. She has a chance to pull out of this slump. She can retake the SATs, and if her grades improve . . ."

His voice trails off. These so-called improvements will only be made if she breaks up with *him*. Somehow, knowing my daughter, if even a little at this point, I don't see her letting him go just yet.

"How about we talk about something else," he suggests as I finish off my third glass. Or is it my fourth? I've lost track.

"Do you like Lena?" The question pops out of my mouth without my thinking about it.

"She's terrific. Josh positively lights up around her, doesn't he?"

"He has a crush on her."

"Of course he does. He's fifteen."

"That doesn't bother you? That he's infatuated with his caregiver? I'm afraid for him."

"Em. He has few pleasurable diversions in his life, doesn't he?"

I nod and set my glass down. I need to take a break. The wine is doing funny things to my head. Memories, both old and new, are waging a war against one another.

I see Lena on her first day, peering at me speculatively, figuring out how overbearing an employer I will be. *Did this happen?*

I see Raina, offering to stay late because I am exhausted to the point of collapse, and me thanking her profusely for granting me the respite I need, a sixty-minute nap to recharge. *Did this happen?*

"A Bitcoin for your thoughts," Colin says. I allow myself a smile. *This is our joke, his and mine, in this and every other world.*

"How long has Lena been with us now?" I ask, using a tone that suggests I merely have to think about it for a moment and the answer will come to me. It won't because I have no idea. My faux memories only take me so far.

"Two years?" Colin says. "Two and a half, right?"

"Right." *Two and a half years this woman has been in my home, watching my son grow from a prepubescent to a man-child, bathing him and changing his diaper and—God.*

"You have to admit, she's much better than Frau Gewürztraminer."

I assume that this is an ironic play on the woman's name. I should know of whom Colin speaks, but no faux or real memories come to mind.

"She was a piece of work, huh?"

I shrug.

Colin eyes me. "Look, he likes her, Em. He's comfortable with her. I know you have issues, but I think she's good for him, don't you?"

My foot taps against the concrete. The sky is darkening to amethyst. When was the last time I saw the stars blink to life in the night sky? Before Josh was born? A tremor passes through me. I should not be here, relaxing against the uncomfortable wooden chair. I should be upstairs, tending to my son, stroking his forehead, sponging his pasty-white skin, reading to him from *The Hobbit* or Harry Potter. We were three chapters into *The Goblet of Fire*.

I ache with the sudden realization that someone other than me is reading that book to him tonight. *That's my job*, I think, although God knows why I continued the ritual—he started reading well past my level ages ago. But he always loved the sound of my voice, that's what he told me. He loved hearing me procure accents for the different characters and catch my breath at the scary parts and sigh with relief at the resolutions. We giggled in unison, my son and I, at outlandish plotting and unforeseen twists and certain characters' foibles. We critiqued the stories we read and wondered aloud about the authors' motivations. A book club of sorts.

I always considered reading to Josh a chore, one more check on my to-do list, but now, in this moment, I feel the shame of an overdue epiphany.

Josh and I will never climb a mountain together or go waterskiing or paddle surfing or hiking or camping or bungee-fucking-jumping. But through the books I read to him, we shared adventures vast and wide.

I really want to know what happens to Harry in *The Goblet of Fire*.

"Wow. I guess I'll have to up it from a Bitcoin to actual money. You seem miles away tonight."

"I'm sorry," I say again. "I have a lot on my mind."

"I know."

No you don't, no you don't, NO YOU DON'T! I briefly consider confessing to Colin the craziness of the past thirty-six hours but immediately suppress the urge. I know my husband. He would pretend to understand and pat my knee and make the appropriate inquiries to assure me that he believes every word I'm saying, when in fact he has the asylum on speed dial and his bathroom-break excuse is only a cover to make that call.

"I think I know something that will help," he says, his voice low and sly. He slides his hand farther up my thigh, bringing it to rest at the border of my pubis. The antipathy I expect at my husband's touch fails to materialize. Instead, my pulse quickens.

"Colin." There is warning in my voice but no conviction.

He stands and takes my hand and gently tugs me to my feet. "Come on," he says, a lascivious grin playing at his mouth.

I allow him to lead me back into the kitchen, where the table has miraculously been cleared, the dishes washed, and the counters wiped to spotless.

"Wow." *This must be how an amnesiac feels*, I think. Everything is recognizable, but the foundation upon which the familiarity rests has been deleted.

"Wow, what?" Colin draws me closer and slips his arm around my waist.

"The kitchen is so clean," I murmur.

"Yes, Lena's good."

I bite my lip to banish the reflexive frown inspired by his praise of the young woman. She cleans my kitchen, she cooks our dinners. She tends well to my son. How can I begrudge her my husband's praise?

And here she is, emerging from the hallway, her eyes raised and her lips already open with the promise of speech even before she sees us.

"I'm taking him up," she tells Colin and me. "He seems a little tired today, so I might keep it to one chapter."

Does Josh seem tired? I was only granted limited access to him this evening, was never close enough to him to touch him or kiss him or scan his face for signs of fatigue. What else am I missing?

"Thanks, Lena," Colin says, his voice oozing appreciation.

Lena looks at me expectantly, waiting for something, but what? My thanks? Further inquiries about my son's current state? Compliments on a dinner well-cooked/served/cleaned up after? Acknowledgment that she is now the leading lady in Josh's life?

I settle for simplicity. "Thank you, Lena."

"No problem," she replies, satisfied.

"I'll be up in a minute," I tell her, and she cocks her head to the side.

"You know how long it takes, Mrs. D. We won't be to the book for another forty-five. Then give us twenty for Harry."

"Maybe I'll read to him tonight." Lena and Colin don matching expressions of puzzlement. I attempt to backpedal, but crash. "I mean, I haven't done it for a while, I know."

Colin clears his throat and Lena inspects her shoes. "He likes the way Lena reads, Em. You know that. The sound of her voice when she's doing all the characters."

"Why, thank you, gov'nah," she says in a mock London accent. It's good, I'll give her that. My heart splinters a tiny bit more.

"And anyway, Em, I wanted to show you that chapter I'm working on."

My turn for confusion. Colin never lets me read his works in progress. I glance at him and he winks, and his underlying message is perfectly clear. There is no chapter. He wants me alone in his office for far more scandalous reasons.

"Leeah!"

"Oh, well, my master calls." She shrugs good-naturedly at Colin and offers me the barest hint of a smile before she leaves the room.

We listen to the ascent of the wheelchair lift. Once we hear the snap of the chair reaching the second floor, Colin pulls me in and kisses me hard on the mouth. I would be surprised, I *should* be surprised, but my body responds to him in kind. It stands to reason that my body, my physical being, is more in tune with the constantly changing tide and the perpetually shifting memories and can roll with them more easily than my mind can.

"Let's go to my office so I can show you *that chapter.*"

"I should check on Katie."

He kisses my ear. "Check on her later. This can't wait."

He grasps my hand and slowly lowers it to the front of his slacks, then presses it against his manhood. Shadows of Richard Green and the bathroom stall seep into my mind, and I pull my hand away.

"Come on, babe. It's been over a week."

"No, it hasn't." I shake my head. *It's been three months at least.*

"One week and one day," he says, lowering his head to my neck. He bites softly, and again, I think of Richard Green's Altoid breath. I let the thought slip through the cracks of my consciousness. Richard Green doesn't exist, no matter how vivid my nightmares are. I banished him with a wish. He is but a construct.

We stride through the living room and down the hallway, passing the laundry alcove. I think of last night and my fervent removal of the offending ensemble, which seemed to be an accomplice to the horrific acts exacted upon me earlier in the evening. But now I can scarcely remember peeling the clothes from my body. *I threw them in the trash*, I tell myself. *But I didn't. There was no reason to throw the clothing away because there was no attack because Richard Green doesn't exist.*

I call upon my newly found, moment-to-moment thinking. I can't tether myself to any of my memories, otherwise I'm afraid my brain will blow apart.

We reach Colin's office and he pulls the door shut behind me, then drags me to the desk. The room is small and overloaded with books and magazines and stacks of newspapers, because Colin refuses to read anything on a tablet. The shelves are piled with fragments of old, discarded manuscripts, the pages listing toward the ground from the pull of gravity coupled with the despair of abandonment.

Colin kisses me again and half pushes, half lifts me onto the edge of the desk, disregarding the papers that are now beneath my butt. And although the ghost of the man who no longer exists (who *never* existed) tries to intrude, he/it is unsuccessful. Because I am responding to my husband in a way I haven't for (*one week and one day*) years. My arms reach up and circle his neck as I pull him closer.

Colin presses against me, the outline of his penis imprinting itself on my thigh, and I can feel the blood rushing to my loins. He yanks at my lounge pants, his hands losing traction on the slippery fabric, then firmly grasps the elastic band and shoves it to my knees. I shimmy my legs until the pants drop to my feet. I kick them away and absently watch the mound of satin slide across the floor.

Colin's face has gone magenta. The golden flecks in his hazel eyes glow with desire. He leans away from me and tugs at the waistband of his trousers as I hurriedly remove my underwear. We finish our separate tasks simultaneously and come together. I lift my knees to grant him access as he plunges his stiff erection deep within me. I cry out and absently hope that the walls of this old house are thick enough to withstand my prurient exclamations.

It takes only a handful of thrusts for me. I come, and come, and come as I haven't for as long as I can remember, the untrustworthiness of my memories notwithstanding. My resounding orgasm inspires Colin to drive himself deeper within me, and a moment later, he explodes—seizes, goes stiff, shudders, gasps, shrieks, then collapses against me.

We breathe in unison for a while, neither of us offering up a spoken word because words are useless in the aftermath of such powerful lovemaking.

"I really need to keep some towels or tissues handy," he says finally, and I offer him a low chuckle.

He withdraws from me, and I feel a trickle of moisture leak out onto his desk.

"Do you think anyone heard?" I ask, because I am still me and still concerned with proper social deportment.

"Does it matter?" Colin asks. "We're married. We have every right to copulate."

"Copulate. How romantic."

He laughs, and the carelessness of his laughter strikes a chord in me. I realize that he *wants* Lena to hear us. He wants Josh's caregiver to know we are fucking. Because maybe, just maybe, he is envious of her attention to our son. He is attracted to this obsidian-haired minx, and in some perverse scenario, devised by his own covetousness, he thinks that she'll be jealous if she is aware of our coupling and will seek him out with the intention of making me a cuckold.

I don't know this to be true. But it *feels* true.

I gather myself together and stand. Colin pulls up his trousers.

Emma Davies, director of marketing and business acquisition and retention.

I use my discarded undies to mop away the effluvium from my vagina. My husband kisses my cheek, more obligation than inclination.

"Thanks for that," he says.

I still throb from my climax, but my enthusiasm is gone. "You're welcome."

I refrain from asking to see Colin's latest chapter.

SIXTEEN

I watch carefully, discreetly, from the living room as Colin walks Lena to her car, the three-year-old Prius parked across the street that I failed to notice upon my arrival. The clock in the hallway reads eleven o'clock. Apparently, this is her usual departure time; Colin and I still have overnight duty.

My husband and Lena exchange words, but I can only guess at them. He holds the car door open for her then dawdles as she disappears behind the wheel. The engine whispers to life, and the driver's window descends. He leans down and says something to her, and the slightest hint of resentment percolates inside me at the sight of him conversing so gratuitously with her. Colin is infatuated, as is Josh, with this *Lena*.

I understand his—and Josh's—enchantment with this woman. She is young and attractive and *vigorous*. And the unassailable fact is, I have brought her into our lives through whatever conjuring powers I possess, so it is ridiculous for me to resent her. Yet I do.

When moments pass, and they are still immersed in their duologue, I make a concerted effort to move away from the window. I walk down the hall, pass through the kitchen, and enter the family room. The next item on my checklist is a task only I can accomplish.

The family room, like the rest of the house, is tired. The couches are careworn, just as they were yesterday and the day before, when everything was right in its wrongness and I knew the depth and breadth of my existence. I wonder again at the state of our home, at the cracks in the ceiling and the fading paint on the walls. Why, if we can afford luxuries such as *Lena*, can we not support a fresh coat of paint?

I sit in front of the computer and press the "Power" button, my thoughts hovering over my husband and my son's caregiver who must still be deep in conversation since I haven't heard the front door open and close.

I twist the knob of the baby monitor on the side of the desk, and the room fills with the sound of my son's loud, rhythmic breathing. I listen for a moment and match his inhalations and exhalations with my own. Then I turn my attention to the computer screen and type in a command. A second later, my QuickBooks home budget/income and expenses file opens. All our household bills are listed here with their individual due dates. In the past, I didn't put these bills on autopay because I was never sure if my checking account could cover them. I'm expecting the bills to be automatically paid now that I am a *director of marketing*, but, as before, each payment requires my permission. Strange.

I click onto my checking account, and my mouth opens in surprise at the amount displayed in the balance column. Another of my expectations—one of a flush bank account with plenty of padding—is dashed. The balance is the same as it was three days ago. Minimal.

I scroll over my account history. My salary, although more than twice what it was, is eaten away every month due to the addition of a second caregiver, the subtraction of Colin's income, and extortionate legal fees, which I can only assume are related to Owen. I bite my lower lip. *How perfect.* I thought life might be easier with the newly vaporized Richard and the lofty position at my firm. But no. The struggle remains.

And I no longer get to read to my son.

I hear the front door close, and a moment later, Colin appears in the doorway.

"Bills, huh?" he says and I nod. "Good times."

"Did you have a nice chat?" The question sounds snarkier than I meant it to be. Colin doesn't notice.

"She's a very interesting girl."

"She's not a girl, Colin," I reply, my eyes fixed on the computer screen. "She's, what, twenty-four, twenty-five?"

"That makes her a girl to me, doesn't it?"

"I suppose."

"Do you know she spent a year in São Tomé? Talk about off the map."

"Hmm." I don't want to talk about Lena. I'm poring over the list of expenses, many of which are completely foreign to me, which is no surprise since I am an accidental tourist in my own life right now.

"Colin, what is this debit payment to Staples for nineteen hundred dollars?"

He moves to the desk and leans over my shoulder to peer at the screen. "Laptop, remember? My Samsung crashed."

"Nineteen hundred dollars?" I repeat. "For a laptop?"

"It's a MacBook Pro, Em. You know that."

"Why do you need a MacBook Pro, Colin? It's not like you're doing graphics. You're word processing. A Chromebook would have cost us five hundred bucks out the door."

"This is so typical," he says. "You tell me to get what I need and I do and now you're throwing it back at me."

"You didn't *need* a MacBook," I say quietly. "What about this? Three nights at the Red River Inn?"

He squints down at me. "Are you having a senior moment, Emma? The writers' conference? You don't remember me going?"

No, I don't remember. Because yesterday you worked for the junior college and I was a lowly assistant and we never would have been able to afford three nights at the Red River Inn for either one of us.

"Right. Sorry. I forgot. The conference. Speaking of which, you said the book's coming along well."

"It's a *manuscript*, Emma, not a book. It's not a book until it gets published." This is one of Colin's favorite sayings. I've heard it dozens of times and still I make the same mistake.

"I'm thinking positively," I reply. "How soon do you think you'll finish?"

He answers with a shrug. Not a good sign.

"I imagine Lawrence is pretty anxious to get it from you." Lawrence Gibbon is Colin's agent, the man responsible for Colin's book deals and possibly the only person in the world who still believes in Colin's writing.

I glance up to find Colin giving me a sharp look. "You know I'm not with Lawrence anymore, Em. Jesus. What's the matter with you tonight? It's like you're in a fog."

"You're not with Lawrence."

I rack my brain to come up with the newly formed correlating memory. Nothing.

"I fired him after Hemingway tanked. Remember he wanted me to do a thing about Ferlinghetti instead of Frost? I mean, come on. Ferlinghetti?"

"Your book—manuscript is about Robert Frost?" Talk about overdone.

"You know, Emma, I'm a little bit worried about you. Maybe you should make an appointment with Lettie."

Too late. Already did. She can't help me.

"Colin, I know your manuscript's about Frost, I just . . . I don't know . . . I think we need to talk about how we're going to bring in more money. How do you feel about going back to teaching?"

He glares at me, then looks down and shakes his head with disgust. "Well, how pleasant this evening has turned out, eh?"

I have to choose my words carefully because I am missing too many pieces in this puzzle.

"I don't mean to upset you, Colin. It's just that I'm a little concerned. Katie is a year from college. How are we going to pay for it? We have no savings to speak of."

"You said it yourself—she'll be lucky to get into the JC. We can afford that, can't we?"

"I don't know."

He lifts his hand to his face and squeezes the bridge of his nose with his thumb and index finger. An acupuncturist taught him this trick a hundred years ago, before I met him. He uses the technique at those times when he would prefer to be screaming.

"Look, Emma. We decided when you got your promotion that your salary was big enough to *allow* me to work full-time on my manuscript. I'm sorry if my creative timeline doesn't concur with your expectations. Three years isn't that long to write a manuscript like this one."

Three years. Colin has been working on his manuscript for three years. *For God's sake.*

"You know what, Colin? Forget it. I'm sorry I brought it up."

"So am I. I was feeling so good after our . . . earlier antics. But now . . ."

The familiarity of the moment charges me. In my new reality, this is a common theme with Colin and me. We argue about finances, about my resentment that he is basically a kept man, that I am bringing home the bacon while he is listening to Cole Porter between minuscule bouts of typing. If I believed in him, if I thought this rubbish about Frost was going to be a success, we wouldn't have this repetitive skirmish. But he knows that I have no faith in his words, and I know that he knows it. We make love once or twice a week to give credence to our union, to offer proof that our connection remains intact. But the subtle undertones of our marriage have gone gray.

He waits for me to say something, but I have nothing to offer. He sighs.

"I'm going up," he says. "Unless you need me for something."

I shake my head.

He leans down and kisses my temple—a conciliatory gesture, a white flag, an olive branch. On the one hand, Colin recognizes that he is a leech and I am the body whose blood offers him sustenance. On the other hand, he knows that he saved me—and Kate—and therefore it is his right to expect recompense for his sacrifice.

"I'll be up soon," I tell him. He slinks from the room.

~

With Josh's breathing as my soundtrack, I spend the next fifteen minutes signing off on bills—the mortgage, which makes me cringe every time I pay it, gas, electric, cable. We could cut back on our cable service. What the cable company charges is akin to extortion. But Josh likes all the random stations that cost extra—the nature channels that have programs dedicated to river monsters and polar bears and the sci-fi channels that show what life would be like in space, in the future, in alternate pasts, the pay stations like HBO and Starz with their blockbusters that Josh doesn't see in movie theaters like everyone else. I can't bear to take any of these channels away from him.

I check my account balance one last time before I shut down. Alarming.

Colin has turned off most of the lights downstairs, but the ambient light from the street, the glow of the digital clock on the cable box, the LED on the hood of the kitchen fan illuminate my path. I climb the stairs slowly, my footsteps heavy and listless.

When I reach the second floor, I automatically head for Josh's room.

His night-light winds through its cycle, blue, green, red. I approach the bed and gaze down at my son. He sleeps deeply tonight, for once unimpeded by his ruined body, and I briefly wonder if Lena's attentions inspire him to sleep thoroughly, so that he might dream of her and of a self without hindrances to which she might attach herself.

I had such dreams for this boy, this almost man. I remember him in my womb. At twenty-six weeks, in a tiny cubicle of a room, the ultrasound technician measured the length of his spine and pointed out his penis and told me that all was well. *All was well.* And in that small room, with the cold gel on my stomach and the Rorschach blob of a baby on the screen, I made a million plans for him, saw a million sports events with him as the head of whichever team he played on, watched him walk to the dais of his high school graduation, college graduation, down the aisle at his wedding. None of my fantasies in that tiny room included a wheelchair and a staircase lift and a boy who couldn't pronounce consonants.

I hate the memory and how it makes me resent the person I see before me. He is my son, and I love him, but he is also a promise unfulfilled. I despise myself for thinking that, but I cannot deny the thought.

His breathing is regular. I needn't worry. Another sound presents itself, a soft mewling, like that of a kitten. I turn toward the bathroom.

The adjoining door to Kate's room is closed, and the sound is coming from behind it. I walk into the bathroom and press my head against her door. The mewling is louder. My daughter is crying. Not the volatile sobs of a fresh bout of tears, but the lethargic end to a lengthy round of weeping.

How long has Katie been shut away in her room, a prisoner to her misery? She ran from dinner hours ago, her face drawn, her expression bleak. Why didn't I, *her mother*, go to her to offer her comfort? Where was I as she lay on her bed, clutching her covers to her chest, bawling into her pillow to mask the sound?

I was fucking my husband. I was paying bills. I was avoiding this moment.

I tiptoe across the bathroom tiles and shut the door to Josh's room, then turn on the light. The mirror reflects a woman I hardly recognize, but I defend myself by ignoring my reflection.

I open the medicine cabinet and see only the expected contents. Toothpaste, floss, face cleanser, acne cream, moisturizer. What else did I expect?

Something.

I turn in a circle, avoiding contact with the me in the mirror but scanning the rest of the bathroom. I don't understand what I'm doing, but I'm compelled to do it, and because I must go with my gut on this and everything else, I continue.

My gaze comes to rest upon the toilet then shifts to the waste can beside it.

I know what I'm going to find.

Buried beneath wads of tissues and used paper cups and the crumpled packaging of Kate's new adult soft toothbrush is a long, narrow, white plastic stick.

A pregnancy test. With a plus sign in the window.

My daughter is pregnant. By *him.*

SEVENTEEN

I knock softly on her door. She doesn't answer. I don't expect her to. But I am the mother, so I can walk into any room in my house without permission.

"Katie?"

Her bedroom is dark, but I know she is awake. I move to the bed where she lies. The mewling has stopped, no doubt because of my presence.

I sit on the edge of her bed and reach for the bedside lamp, clicking it on with two fingers.

She left the test for me to find. She could have put it in the recycle bin and the sanitation truck would have come Monday and hauled it away and I wouldn't have been the wiser. She could have scheduled an abortion without my knowledge, sneaking off to the women's clinic under the guise of meeting friends at the mall, and I would have accepted her story without question.

She wanted me to know.

Kate is facedown, her arms tucked under her pillow. I stroke her hair, greasy, unwashed, but it belongs to my baby girl, my firstborn. Her hair could be riddled with lice and I would still weave my fingers through it.

"Honey?"

"Go away." There is no force behind her words.

"I can't," I tell her. "Do you know why?"

A slight shake of her head is her only response.

"Because I love you, that's why." She stiffens but says nothing. "I'm sorry I haven't been there for you, Katie. Sometimes I feel like I'm in such bad shape that I can't possibly be a good mom to you. It's like, I want to be. But I just don't know how."

Slowly, glacier paced, she rolls over onto her back. She doesn't meet my eyes, but the fact that I can now see her face is a step in the right direction, and I'll take anything at this point.

"You're a good mom." Whispered doubtfully, but she thinks she needs to say it.

"No. My mom was a good mom. I'm mediocre at best. But I do love you."

A tear erupts from the corner of her eye. I follow its path down her cheek to her ear before I block it with the tip of my index finger.

"I found the test, Katie."

She moans with agony and rolls away from me again, curling into a fetal position on her side.

"Is it *his*?"

"You hate him," she says.

"Yes, I do," I admit. "But maybe not for the reasons you think."

"I love him," she says.

That *is why I hate him.*

"Does he know about the . . . does he know about it?"

Her greasy head bobs up and down against her pillow. I'll have to wash the pillowcase tomorrow, and the rest of the sheets, for that matter. Her scent is pungent, fear coupled with pregnancy hormones, a noxious combination.

"What does he want to do?"

Another moan followed by an epic sigh. "He wants me to kill it. He doesn't even think it's his. But it is. I haven't been with anyone else. He doesn't believe me."

I bite my lip to keep from screaming. "And what do you want to do, Katie?"

She turns her head to face me, her eyes glistening with tears. "I don't know, Mom."

How ironic that our first shared confidence in years revolves around an embryo sired by a complete bastard.

I fold my hands in my lap. Another new habit. I close my eyes and see my daughter as a toddler, running around my mother's living room, her mop of red hair flying in every direction, her smile guileless and carefree.

I open my eyes and see my daughter now, her heart torn, her expectations of a life well lived already demolished.

"We'll figure this out, honey. I promise."

"But how?" she asks.

"I'm not sure yet. But we'll figure it out." I stand and lean over her, kiss her forehead, something I haven't done—something she hasn't allowed me to do—for so long. "Try to get some sleep. It will all be okay."

As I walk to the door, I hear her fractured voice call to me.

"I love you, Mom."

When was the last time I heard these words from her lips? And in which incarnation of my life? It doesn't matter.

"I love you, too, Katie."

I close the door and go to the master bedroom. Colin has already turned the monitor on. Josh's breathing comingles with my husband's snoring, creating a somnambulist symphony. I remove my lounge pants and underwear and cotton top and toss them into the hamper beside the dresser. I pull a pair of fresh undies and my nightie out of the dresser, put them on, and move to the bathroom.

Like an automaton, I go through my nighttime ablutions with no thought, no consciousness, no awareness of what I'm doing. My thoughts are cleaved to the complex group of cells multiplying within my daughter's abdomen.

What will we do about this? I promised Katie we'd figure it out, but I have no idea how. The word *abortion* echoes through my mind. I was raised in the Catholic church, but my faith has long since lapsed. I no longer believe that abortion is a deadly sin, that my daughter will burn in hell should she choose to end the pregnancy. But how will such an experience scar her? Should we consider adoption? I do the math. If she's somewhere around eight weeks now, the baby would be born at the end of spring. We would have to pull her out of school by February; she wouldn't graduate with her peers. Her life, which has already veered off course, would be irrevocably derailed.

When I finish with my night cream, I shut off the bathroom light and walk to the bed. I sit on the edge, feeling the crunchy comforter beneath my thighs, and stare into the darkness.

Charlemagne. The tree. Richard. Is it true? Is it real? Is it possible?

Without hesitation, I impart a wish to the universe.

I wish Katie never met that boy.

~

Saturday, July 9

Hungover. That's how I feel when I wake the next morning. How much wine did I drink last night? I felt completely sober when I went to bed, when I did my going-to-bed tasks and donned my nightie and sat on the comforter and . . . and . . .

Made a wish . . .

I spring out of bed. So this is the new me. Not lingering beneath the covers, praying for a reprieve from the daunting, overwhelming, miserable life I lead. But jumping up, jumping in, if only to discern whether my wish has been granted.

Colin is already up. I smell espresso. I hear the TV in the kitchen. The monitor in the bedroom is off.

What day is today? I glance at the bedside clock. Saturday. No work. But also no Raina and, I assume, no Lena, so the burden of Josh's care is left to me. Colin always claimed Saturdays as writing days, having been cleaved to his professorship Monday through Friday. I wonder if, in this new life where he has weekdays to write to his heart's content, he takes Saturdays off to help with our son.

I cross to the closet and feel a slight ache between my legs, likely the result of my time in Colin's office last night. I should shower and brush my teeth and pee, but I'm too anxious to do any of those things right now. I need to see. I need to *know*. I toss my nightie onto the bed and grab a pair of jeans and a T-shirt from the closet.

I can tell by the blinding fissure of light pushing through the notch in the curtains that today is going to be a hot one. I slip on a pair of sandals and hurry down the hall, past Josh's room to Katie's closed door. I knock softly, then wait. I realize I'm holding my breath and force myself to let it out on a silent sigh. No answer from within. I turn the knob and open the door far enough to see that the bed is made and the window is ajar and my daughter is not there.

She's with him.

My wish didn't come true.

I stand for a moment, absently gazing at the made bed. If last night's wish was ignored by whatever forces have been at play these last few days, perhaps my prior wishes have been revoked. Perhaps the ache between my legs is from Richard's attack and that vile man has reentered my life. A hard pit of dread catches in my throat.

But no. There is no barking from next door, meaning Charlemagne hasn't returned. I push the door all the way open and cross to the window, then lean down and peer down at the front lawn. The tree is still gone. I move to Katie's dresser, above which hangs a mirror. My face remains unmarked.

Charlemagne. The tree. Richard. Three wishes, like the fairy tale, only without the genie and the bottle.

Of course, a simpler explanation is that there were no wishes. There was no Charlemagne, no tree, no Richard Green. My mind has already adopted the last five years without my boss, and I can barely call upon his image—his features are blurred, obscured, as if he wears a stocking over his head. The assault in the bathroom seems more like a scene from a movie I once saw. My mind has already erased the many bouts I had with the pavers caused by the tree roots. I know I have fallen, but I can't remember any specific occurrence. And Charlemagne . . . the feel of his fur beneath my fingers, his sandpaper tongue against my cheek, both memories gone, recalled now as fantasy not reality. I can no longer remember the exact cadence of his bark.

The room around me spins, and I grasp Katie's dresser to steady myself. If the wishes weren't wishes, if reality is constant, if all that has happened has always been . . .

I tell myself it doesn't matter—*ha*—then silently scream at myself to *get a grip, get ahold of yourself, hang on, hang tight, hang tough. Stand up. Take a breath. Go downstairs and kiss your son good morning.*

I do what I must. I stand up, take a breath, and go downstairs to kiss my son.

I make my way to the first floor, continuing to coach myself, knowing that if I don't *get a grip* and take charge of my emotions, my thoughts—my *life*—some greater, possibly malevolent force is going to take charge of *me*. By the time I reach the kitchen, I'm almost convinced that I'm all right. But when I enter, I stop dead. This time, the room doesn't spin. This time the room careens beneath my feet.

Katie sits at the table, but not the Katie from yesterday, Katie from BH. *Before him.* Her hair is clean and full of body, the lustrous red curls restored. Her complexion is no longer sallow but rosy and glowing, her eyes not swollen and puffy but bright and shining. She sits beside Josh, feeding him his oatmeal, sneaking in enthusiastic bites of toast for herself. She looks up at me and smiles, the radiant, genuine smile of a happy teenager.

"Hi, Mom," she says.

"Maah!" Josh exclaims, twisting to see me.

I'm afraid to move, afraid I'll crash to the floor if I take even one step in any direction. Katie's eyes narrow. "Are you okay, Mom? You look a little pale."

I feel more than pale. I feel transparent. I quickly regroup—what choice do I have?—and take charge of my wobbly legs. "I'm fine, sweetheart," I lie. "Good morning."

"T'j'aye-es." *TGIS*.

I walk to Josh, relieved that my steps are steady, and kiss his forehead. "Yes, thank goodness it's Saturday."

I can't peel my gaze from my daughter. The not-right feeling has been replaced by utter joy at the sight of her. I want to throw my arms around her, but I know I can't, shouldn't, won't. Such a display would give me away.

"What, Mom?" she asks. "Jeez. Why are you looking at me like that?" Her expression morphs from puzzlement to panic in a split second. "Do I have a zit?" Cataclysmic fear of a skin eruption. Oh, to be a teenager with such trite concerns.

"Y' ah a zeh," Josh says. *You are a zit.* Followed by his laughter that sounds like the bray of a donkey.

"No, you don't have a zit, Katie. I'm just surprised to see you here."

She scrunches up her face. "Where else would I be? Monkey man can't feed himself, you know."

Josh attempts a monkey voice. "Ooh ooh ahh ahh." Katie laughs.

"I don't know. I thought after our conversation last night you might not be feeling up to breakfast."

"Last night?" She gives Josh a funny look. "Um, Mom, last night I was with Simone, remember? I didn't get home till after you guys were asleep."

Simone. Katie's best friend since grammar school, whom she cast aside when she met *him*.

I wish Katie never met that boy.

"Maee y' dree' i, Maah." *Maybe you dreamed it, Mom.* Then to Katie: "Sh' bi' haaey a ah' a' stay dree' laelee." *She's been having a lot of strange dreams lately.*

Oh, Josh, if you only knew the half of it.

"I forgot something," I say. "I'll be right back."

Straining to keep my footsteps even, *don't rush,* I walk out of the kitchen and head for the stairs. As soon as I'm certain my children cannot see me, I quicken my pace. I scramble up the stairs, two at a time. My foot catches before I reach the second-floor landing, and I fall, my chest and chin connecting with the carpeted riser. I right myself and continue up, one thought, one question propelling me forward.

I scurry down the hall and into the bathroom. Both bedroom doors are ajar. I move to the toilet and look down into the trash bin next to the porcelain bowl. Tissues. More tissues. I reach into the waste can and riffle through the contents, my fingers expecting to connect with plastic—a long, thin, hard harbinger of doom. They encounter nothing. I grab the waste can and overturn it onto the tile floor, then sift through the trash. There is no pregnancy test.

Three minutes later, I am back in the kitchen.

"Loo', Maah. Fuh a' Fe maee witah i' suher." *Look, Mom. Phineas and Ferb are making winter in summer.*

I glance at the TV, but the image is blurred. *Who the fuck cares about Phineas and Ferb?*

With forced composure, I walk to the fridge and pull out a Greek yogurt. I'm not hungry, but I'm hoping the yogurt will soothe my queasy stomach. The creamy tart/sweet yogurt tastes foul, not because it's out of date but because it's comingling with the taste of bile in my mouth. I swallow quickly.

"So, what's on the agenda today?" I ask. My question draws another peculiar look from Katie.

"We're taking Josh for a haircut, Mom." Said as if I should know.

But I don't know, and I would never have made this plan, not after last time. I shake my head. "No."

She rolls her eyes and gives Josh a quick sideways glance. "Yes, we are. We discussed this last week." She speaks to me as though she is the mother and I am the inattentive child. "I set it up with Mimi. He has an eleven o'clock."

"Mimi's?"

"Mom, you didn't want to take him back to Jack's, so we're trying something different this time, right, Josh?"

He nods. "Riy."

Obviously, this is a decision, a plan, we made together last week. The memory hasn't been formed yet, so I have to bunt.

"I still don't think it's a good idea," I tell them.

Kate rises from her seat and approaches me. She leans close and whispers below the sound of the cartoon on the television.

"I know what happened at the barbershop, Mom. But Josh wants to have his hair cut in a normal place like a normal person."

But he's not a normal person, I want to shout. I press my lips together to keep myself from voicing the horrible words. Because Josh *is* normal in so many ways. Just not in *enough* ways to be excluded from other people's scorn and callousness. And I am a terrible mother for thinking these things about my beloved son, weighing his normalcy against his disability and finding him wanting.

"Mimi's is going to be good," she continues. "Lola, you know her, she's the stylist we're going to. She has a special-needs daughter. She gets it. She brings her daughter in all the time and the customers are, like, used to that kind of thing. They won't make fun. I promise. I'm going to be there." She grins at me. "And I'll beat the crap out of anyone who even looks at Josh funny."

129

"Watch your mouth, young lady," I tell her, but I'm grinning, too. God, I've missed this girl.

"Wuh a' y' ta wispee a'ow?"

"Yes, what are you two whispering about?" Colin asks as he strides into the room and heads for his espresso machine.

"We were trying to decide what kind of haircut Josh should get today. I'm thinking buzz cut, but Mom is leaning toward a mohawk."

This draws another bray of laughter from my son.

"Let's keep it simple, shall we?" Colin suggests. He walks past me without stopping to kiss me. I feel the leftover chill from our argument last night as he wordlessly fills his demitasse, emptying the small carafe. He glances at me.

"Did you want some?"

"No, thank you." I take another spoonful of yogurt and feel Colin's eyes on me. I turn toward him and meet his gaze. I have been married to this man long enough to decipher his expression. He is waiting for me to apologize. And his expectation that I will fold, that I will take the blame for last night's contretemps and offer him my polite and contrite apology, irritates me. I am not to blame for our fight any more than I am to blame for the appalling state of our finances. In this new life, I am the breadwinner and he is a sycophant, keeping me satiated with his cock while freeloading off my gains.

I take a breath. The me from three days ago would never have had such ugly thoughts about her husband.

The me from three days ago wasn't supporting this family, I think. *But the me from three days ago certainly had* other *unflattering things to say about her husband, didn't she? Things that had nothing to do with money.*

"What are you doing today?" My question is a sharp arrow, which Colin deftly deflects.

"Working, of course," he replies, his tone ambivalent. "No days off for writers."

I've heard him say this before. I bite back a scathing comment about the perpetuity of his work equaling failure and that failure often needs a day off.

Although I sense that I am psychologically prepared to spar over this issue, I refuse to engage with my husband. Because I am still trying to comprehend the aftermath of my wish, if it really came true. Colin's authorial prowess, or lack thereof, seems insignificant compared to Katie's presence—her shining, lovely presence—in the kitchen this morning.

Unknowingly, my daughter offers more clues about our new actuality.

"Oh, Colin," she says, "you don't have to worry about next weekend. Simone's mom is going to take us to UPenn for a tour. I don't think Simone really wants to go there, but she says she wants to see it, too."

My reaction is reflexive and based upon yesterday's Kate. Not this morning's Kate. Because this morning's Kate is an alien to me. "Honey, I wouldn't get my hopes up for UPenn, what with your SAT scores and all."

She rolls her eyes again. "Yeah, like twenty-three hundred totally stinks, right?" She shrugs. "I think with that and my 4.9, chances are good. You're the one who said that, Mom."

I did, back before *that boy* changed everything. But *that boy* has been erased. Not from the planet, like Richard. Just from my daughter's life.

I take a moment to thank my lucky stars, God, the fates, the universe. Whoever or whatever is responsible for granting my wishes.

Thank you for giving me back my daughter.

Colin glances at me, still expectant, then shrugs and moves toward Josh and Katie. He gives Josh's hair a perfunctory ruffle, then leaves the room. A moment later, I hear the door of his office slam shut.

"We're done with breakfast," Katie announces, setting the almost-empty bowl of oatmeal on the table. I match her by setting down the half-eaten yogurt.

"I'll get Josh ready," I say.

"That's okay, Mom. I'll do it." She leans in to Josh and smiles at him. "Let's get it done fast so we'll have time to get a smoothie before your appointment."

"Who's buying?" I ask.

My son and daughter turn toward me and say in unison, "You are."

A buzz sounds from my cell phone, and I move from the counter and withdraw the charging cord. The caller is Owen, and I hesitate. But then I remember that in this new life and new world, I have the upper hand. I answer.

"This is Emma Davies."

"This is Emma Davies," he mocks. I recognize his tone. Likely my ex-husband is already on his third Bloody Mary.

I bury the impulse to be conciliatory and remind myself that I need not appease him. "What do you want?"

"You know what I want, Emma. I want to see my daughter."

Josh guides his chair out of the kitchen. Katie hangs back and gives me a questioning look.

"That's not going to happen." I smile reassuringly at her and she reluctantly follows Josh.

"I'm coming over right now," he hisses. "You can call the cops if you want, but I'm coming."

"That's fine, Owen. We're just leaving for an appointment. We won't be here. From the sound of your voice, I would suggest you take a cab."

I end the call and take a deep breath. That felt good. I go upstairs to change into something appropriate for a morning at the salon. My new power wardrobe offers me many choices.

EIGHTEEN

Irony. In a new world, in a new life, a parallel universe not yet decoded or defined, irony is an ambiguous thing. Mimi's is downtown, across the street from Lettie, the psychiatrist—*my* psychiatrist. The smoothie shop to which Katie referred at breakfast is down the block from Paw-Tastic Pets and the antiques shop. Is this irony? Coincidence? A series of unrelated circumstances connected by a scorched mind searching for threads of consistency in her newfound inconsistence? I don't know.

I pull the van into a metered space fifteen yards from Paw-Tastic Pets. I don't encounter any feelings of déjà vu, possibly because I rarely drive the van, but more likely because my sense of reality is skewed. When you aren't sure that the events you experienced the previous day actually happened, it's impossible to feel déjà vu.

Katie sits in the back seat next to Josh, who is seated in his wheelchair. They are discussing which smoothie each is going to get. Peanut butter banana chocolate? Strawberry mango? I make Josh smoothies almost every day—he is unable to eat anything that requires a great deal of chewing or that which might choke him—but he never shows me a fraction of the enthusiasm he shows for the frozen concoctions from Smoothie Palace. My kids are practically tittering with glee behind me.

I pull the key from the ignition, and the van shudders and rumbles before falling still. I gaze through the windshield at the storefronts. The smoothie shop, Paw-Tastic Pets, the antiques shop. I think about

Dolores, the old woman with the twinkly eyes and surreptitious wink and knowing grin who may or may not know something about me, although I'm not certain what that something might be, or if there is any truth to my supposition.

"Uh, Mom, are you waiting for an invitation?" Katie snipes.

"Yaaa, Maah, ah y' wayie fah ah ivitayah?"

"All right, already. Hold your horses." The phrase tumbles out of my mouth. For an instant, I am transported back in time to when my children were both under ten. We did things together back then, went places, shared time, before I went back to work and before adolescent hormones wreaked havoc on both their lives in vastly opposing ways. I didn't feel the drudgery back then, the dread about leaving the house and foraying into the world with them. They were my babies, one upright and lovely and charming, the other slouched and bent in a wheelchair, but also lovely, also charming, because his smile was as sunny as hers.

It still is, I realize, as I gaze upon them in the rearview mirror. Josh has Colin's coloring, and Katie her father's. But if you look upon them long enough, you see that they look alike, almost exactly, when they smile.

I get out of the van and circle to the curbside door. By the time I open it, Josh has turned his chair to face outward on the hydraulic lift. I depress the button on the inside of the door and the lift descends to the sidewalk. As soon as his wheels hit the concrete, Katie is out of the van and trotting beside him toward the smoothie shop.

"Something with protein," I call to them, but my words are stolen by the breeze and lifted toward the blue heavens. Katie and Josh don't even glance in my direction.

I lock the van manually—the vehicle is over ten years old and most of the mechanisms are either tired or expired. My alarm fob is useful only in that it is large enough not to be lost easily. As I follow the kids to the smoothie shop, I glance at my watch. Ten thirty. Plenty of time before Josh's appointment at Mimi's. Enough time to drink our smoothies and . . . and . . . what? Is there enough time to take a moment and peer into the window of Paw-Tastic Pets to see whether Charlemagne/Charlie still inhabits the display kennel? Enough time to sidestep from the pet store to Dolores's novelty shop to see if the miniature house—*my* house—has been sold to some overprivileged child who will love it for a fortnight then cast it aside?

What am I doing downtown?

Kate reaches the smoothie shop first. She opens the door and holds it for Josh, and my son glides through the entrance as though this is a usual event for him, a ho-hum activity in his life. When was the last time I brought my son downtown? The memory escapes me. When did I stop taking him on adventures? When did I start relying on the celluloid pictures I capture on my phone to broaden his horizons, and how could I be so foolish as to think that my cell phone images could offer him a wide view of the world and a vicariously fulfilled life?

My ruminations come to a halt the moment I enter the air-conditioned smoothie shop and my gaze lands on *him*.

I'd recognize him anywhere—the slick jet-black hair produced by shoe polish or Miss Clairol, although he would never admit to the latter; the meek concentration of stubble just below his lower lip that strives to be a soul patch but is soulless and stupid and craves the swift flick of a sharp blade to wipe it from his angular face; the watery, puppy-dog eyes of a sociopath that flash from adoration to malice in an instant. *That boy.* Just another customer in line for a smoothie on a Saturday morning.

My heart pounds. My right hand grips the van key so tightly, I fear my palm will bleed.

I wish she'd never met that boy.

Oh, I could kill myself a hundred times in a hundred different ways. I should have tailored the wish to include the past, the present, and the future. I wish, I wish. If only I could go back and re-wish, but some innate and primal part of me knows/feels/understands that the wish is what it is, and it stands as it is, and cannot be altered.

He is a few patrons ahead of Katie and Josh. He is not alone. Two unwashed, tattooed, loudmouthed compatriots flank him. They are boisterous and embarrassing. *I* am embarrassed for them and their awkwardness, which they mask with bravado and puffed-up chests and gesticulating arms.

I move in front of Katie and Josh, hoping to block my daughter's view of him. My children are staring up at the menu, even though I'm sure they have already made their decisions. But I don't care, as long as Katie's eyes don't meet his. Again with the intuition thing, which I shouldn't trust based upon my experiences these last few days, but I really believe that if Katie looks at him, meets his eyes, the cycle of destruction that began ten months ago, and was undone by my wish last night, will begin anew.

"Maybe we ought to forget about the smoothies, guys, and get over to Mimi's." My voice wavers slightly, but my kids don't notice. They are too focused on the myriad choices of icy treats at their disposal.

"No way, Mom."

"Yaaa, 'o waee," Josh mimics his sister.

"We have plenty of time." Katie withdraws her cell phone to confirm her statement. "It's only 10:32."

I lower my head in submission. "Okay. What are you getting?"

The boys, *he* and his cohorts, reach the front of the line. They spend a few minutes taunting and teasing the harried Smoothie Palace employee, asking inane questions about the freshness of the ingredients and the nutritional value of several of the smoothie options.

I'm desperate to keep my children's attention on me. "Well? What's it going to be?"

"I think I'm going to get the Caribbean Sunrise," Kate announces. She mentioned the drink in the van, so her choice is no surprise, but I ooh and ahh my agreement.

I lean down to Josh. "What about you, honey? What's it going to be?"

I don't know how long it's been since Josh has been out and about and free of the confines of our home. Kate's reemergence into his life is not a reemergence at all, except to me. Have we been here recently? I sift through my mind, but, again, the new memories, if there are any, are yet to be created. But Josh is glowing; his eyes burn with the fire of liberty. He is happy, truly, wholly happy. He is downtown with his sister and his mother, getting smoothies before a haircut, like any other kid would do. His smile is effortless.

"Muhee," he says. *Monkey.*

"That's perfect, isn't it?" says Kate with a laugh. "A monkey smoothie for monkey man."

"Yum," I say. "I hope you'll let me have a sip."

"Ah'cose, Maah." *Of course, Mom.* "Ye byee." *You're buying.*

Kate moves forward as the boys move to the right-hand counter where the finished products are administered to the waiting crowd. I catch a glimpse of him as he claps one of his friends on the back and snickers in agreement with whatever insult the other just made about the girl behind the counter. They are cruel and mean-spirited, these boys, but I recognize their charisma, *his* charisma. They suck energy from the room and draw attention to themselves because they are so present. I catch sight of my daughter as she catches sight of them. My throat constricts as I see her gaze roam across the shop toward *him*.

I brush the strap of my purse from my shoulder, covertly overturn it, and allow it to fall the floor, then yelp with feigned surprise. "Oops!"

Katie's head snaps toward me, and she looks down to see my purse and its contents littered across the vinyl tiles.

She gives me an exaggerated eye roll, then grins. Simultaneously, we drop to our knees.

"Way to go, Mom," she says as she reaches for my wallet and my cell phone. As I grab my checkbook and travel pack of tissues, I use my peripheral vision to track the boys' progress. They are at the counter, grabbing their smoothies. Katie continues to pick up the detritus from my purse, lipsticks and hand sanitizer, a package of Motrin, a stray tampon so old the paper cover is yellow and frayed.

"Jeez, Mom, I wouldn't use this if I were you." She shoves the tampon into my purse quickly before anyone can take notice of it. I couldn't care less if the entire world sees my ancient tampon. As long as their eyes don't meet.

Kate is starting to rise to her feet, but the timing is off, because *he* and his friends are heading toward the exit and if she stands up right now they will practically crash into each other and then . . . and then . . . it will all be over.

The key in my hand. I jerk my wrist and open my palm at the same time and the fob slides across the floor.

"Oh, Kate, crap! My key."

She turns back to me and I jab my finger at the floor where the key fob has come to rest, then I sigh, as though the short distance to the key is far too great for me. "Please, Katie. Can you get it?"

She shakes her head, then shrugs and moves toward the key. She bends over and retrieves it just as the electronic ping of the door sounds, signaling the boys' exit.

I've been holding my breath. My chest aches. I stand up and see that the boys—that *he*—is moving down the street. I allow myself to exhale. Katie hands me my purse.

"Thanks, honey," I tell her.

"No, problem, Mom," she says, patting my shoulder. In her eyes, I am already an old woman to be placated when I do something stupid. Okay. That's okay. *He* is down the street. Their eyes didn't meet. My daughter's categorization of me stings less than her demise would. I'll take it.

～

"Let's look at the puppies," Kate suggests.

My reaction is swift and adamant. "No." I do not want to look in that window. Will not. Cannot.

"Come on, Mom. We have time."

"Yaaa. W' af tiee," Josh agrees.

I shake my head. "It's 10:49."

"Mom, Lola's always late," Kate says.

Josh is already steering his wheelchair down the block. Kate catches up with him, and I trail behind.

"All right, fine," I tell them. "Go ahead. I'm going to check my emails."

Kate and Josh reach the pet store window. I linger at the curb next to a streetlamp. I pull my cell phone from my purse, but I have no intention of checking my email. I have every intention of keeping a close watch on the street in case *he* appears again. A wide sweep of my surroundings reveals that he is nowhere to be seen. But his possible presence infects me with unease.

"Oh my God, they're so cute!" Katie exclaims as I pretend to peruse my cell phone. "Josh, look at that one in the corner. Isn't he adorable?"

I know without looking or seeing or being remotely near the window that she is talking about Charlemagne.

"He' 'ot scahpuhee uh-ow lie' th es' a theh." *He's not scampering around like the rest of them.* "Maee he' si." *Maybe he's sick.*

"He doesn't look sick," Katie says. "Just sad."

I wish they'd never gotten that godforsaken dog!

The door to the shop on the other side of Paw-Tastic Pets opens, and Dolores emerges. My cell phone slips from my fingers, but I reflexively grasp it before it hits the concrete. Dolores, wizened, her gray curls a helmet, lifts her head, then turns it my direction, much like a coyote sniffing its prey upon the wind. I try to look away, down the block, at my feet, across the street, but some otherworldly force prevents me from doing so. Our eyes lock, and for an instant, my whole body turns to stone, then to ice. I am unable to move. A hurricane of conflicting images of all my pasts and presents and possible futures swirls above my head and below my feet, and then pulls me into itself until I am the hurricane. And, like Dorothy, I'm hurtled toward Oz with no understanding of why this is happening to me.

"Mom!" Katie's voice shatters my fugue state and the storm disintegrates around me, shards of thoughts disappearing into thin air.

Breathe, swallow, speak. "Yes, honey."

"Are you okay?"

"Yes." *Steady, Emma.* "Why?"

"You looked like you were going to pass out."

"No," I say. Certain. Authoritative. "I just got a work email that kind of threw me. It'll be fine."

She nods, but I sense her skepticism. "Bad news?"

"No, honey. Nothing I can't deal with." *If only that were true.*

"We should get to Mimi's."

"Yaah. Le's g' sss Loah." *Yeah. Let's go see Lola.*

I nod, then glance toward the antiques shop. Dolores is nowhere to be seen.

NINETEEN

We cross at the crosswalk and I see *him* immediately, standing in front of the comic book shop with a group of teenagers, smoking a cigarette and feigning importance. Katie has a smoothie in her hand and she's talking to Josh about his hair and what he wants to do with it and seems completely oblivious to *that boy* and his friends. With a pounding heart, I manage to insinuate myself between her and the sight line that would include him, and steer Katie and Josh to Mimi's without her catching eyes with him. Once we pass through the front door of the salon, I relax a fraction. But then . . .

I regret our appointment the moment we reach the waiting area.

Mimi's is well lit and bustling on this Saturday morning, filled with mothers whose weekdays are brimming with PTA activities and after-school sports and culinary and housekeeping duties that necessitate that they fulfill their grooming obligations on the weekends.

Lola's daughter is here, skipping between the salon chairs and the reception area with unknowing impertinence, white daisies looped into the strands of her mousy-brown hair. The girl has Down's Syndrome, as Katie referred to this morning. But there is a vast difference between a girl with pretty pug features and beguiling fortitude and a man-child chained to a wheelchair who cannot form intelligible sentences and whose every movement is a trial.

When Josh glides into Mimi's, accompanied by the low hum of his motorized chair, the women avert their eyes. The children, held hostage to their mothers' beauty demands, gape openly at him. Katie pretends to be oblivious. My son, so seduced by the power of normalcy, doesn't notice the aversive scrutiny.

From her station, Lola marks our arrival and greets us with effervescent grace. She is Amazonian masquerading as Polish, tall and wide with a moon-shaped face, bleached-blonde hair, and a vampire brow, well plucked but dark as night.

"Ah, Kate. Welcome." Her accent has been smoothed by her years in this country, but the way she clips the ends of her words betrays her heritage. She looks down at Josh and smiles. "And you must be Josh."

Josh nods.

"Well, I understand why you come to see Lola. Look at that mop. When was the last time you had a proper haircut?" Josh grins but doesn't answer. Probably he doesn't want to offend me, since I am the one who last took a pair of sewing shears to his head. "Come over to my station and let us discuss what kind of look you want."

Lola treats my son with such casualness, I know that Katie must have prepped her about his condition. She gestures toward a chair in the back half of the salon, and Josh slowly rolls in that direction while Katie and I follow. I force myself to keep my eyes on my son, but I feel the stares of the women in the other stations, tracking our pilgrimage to Lola's chair as their stylists snip and blow-dry and foil their tresses. I feel their pity, heavy and thick, and it creates a green haze above my head, but I try to ignore it.

"Here we are, then," Lola says. "You just pull yourself around to the other side of my chair. There is much room over here."

Josh does as he's told, steering the wheelchair into an open space between Lola's chair and the wash sink. As he comes to a stop, he peers at his reflection in the mirrored wall. A sorrowful look crosses his face. No one else would notice because his features are perpetually twisted and strange. But I gave birth to this boy, have watched him grow, have memorized his every minute expression. My heart breaks at the inner turmoil he experiences from gazing upon himself. In another life, he is handsome. In this life, he is handicapped.

Katie and I stand behind him, side by side. She glances at me and gives me a heartening smile. *This is good*, she tells me with her smile. But she didn't see the look on Josh's face, would not have recognized it if she had.

Lola moves in front of Josh and bends at the waist so that her face is only a foot or so from his.

"Okay, so? What are we going for, Josh? You want glamorous? Like that movie star in all those pictures that has his shirt off all the time? Or you want short all over, like military man? Or maybe like Beatles cut, but me personally, I don't like giving the bowl cut because it is so 1967."

"Th' Beeus se'uh ahbu wa' elea' ah th' sae dae J'Ewf'Kuh wa' sh'."

Lola tries a smile, but it doesn't take. She looks at me with subtle desperation.

"The Beatles' second album was released on the same day JFK was shot," I translate.

Lola raises her black brows, her eyes going wide. "Really? Well, that is very interesting. I did not know that."

"Josh knows everything about everything," Kate says proudly.

"Aye doe." *I don't.*

A staccato shriek across the room draws Lola's attention. I follow her gaze to the reception area. Lola's daughter has removed a flower from her hair and is batting it at another younger child while the mother waves her arms frantically.

"Hey! Devi!" Lola calls. *"Co ty robisz? Tu teraz!"*

The girl drops her arm then trots over to Lola. Lola smiles down at her.

"That's my girl, *dziekuje*. Devi, say hello to Josh. Josh, this is my daughter, Devi."

The girl turns her large, lazy eyes to Josh. Her tongue protrudes slightly between her teeth and lips. She does a half curtsy.

"Plee' to meet you," Devi says.

Josh stares at her. "Plee' t' mee y'."

"Why aw you in a wheewchair?" she asks, an innocent question from a cherub, asked without prejudice or judgment.

"Aye af sirbil pauzie." *I have cerebral palsy.* Another fracture to my heart.

Devi nods, then surprises me by translating his words. "Oh. Cerebraw pawsy. I have Downs."

Josh tries to nod. "Dow sydruh uhke we a' idividuah ha a xtruh cahee a kroahzoe twahee-wah." *Down syndrome occurs when an individual has an extra copy of chromosome twenty-one.*

Devi shrugs. "I guess. I don't know about chrozones."

The girl takes a tentative step toward my son, then reaches out and hands him the daisy, the same flower she was using as a weapon only moments ago. I want to grab it for him, knowing what it will cost Josh to take it from her without my help. But I bury the impulse because I can see that he wants to do it himself. He groans slightly as he shoves his gnarled, clawed hand in her direction. His fingers spasm, his wrist jerks, but he pushes on, frantically trying to receive the gift that is being offered to him.

Katie inhales sharply, and I turn to see her wearing an expression that mimics my own. Frustrated agony.

Finally, Josh's fingers meet Devi's. But just as she relinquishes the daisy's stem, Josh's hand spasms, and his fingers inadvertently clutch Devi's. His grip becomes viselike. Confused and afraid, Devi starts to scream. And scream. And scream.

And suddenly, Josh's body twitches, his head jerks left and right, his eyes roll over and over. His shoulders tighten, his right arm flails, and his breathing hitches in his throat. *Gulp, wheeze, hitch,* until no air is passing through his trachea and into his lungs. Josh is choking.

Lola grabs Devi and covers her mouth with a manicured hand to silence the girl's screams, but Josh continues to writhe.

"Mom!" Kate's face is white, her eyes saucers.

I am calm. "Kate," I say quietly, below the muffled screams of Devi and the roar of murmuring soccer moms. "Call nine-one-one. Now."

I move around the wheelchair to face my son. I place my hands on his and bend toward him so that our faces are inches apart. His eyes are wild, roving, scanning, searching for ground zero, something to focus on, but they can't because, for him, the room is spinning like a tornado.

"Josh. It's Mom. Josh, breathe."

He gasps for air. His cheeks are turning purple, his lips a frightening shade of powder blue.

I have successfully guided Josh through seizures before now, but this seems different. If only I could look down his throat, but that isn't possible because his head is still snapping to and fro, his alien neck stretching, stretching as he struggles to draw in oxygen. I don't dare attempt to peel his lips and teeth apart—the force of his jaw during a seizure is like a guillotine and could sever my digits in an instant.

"I called them," Katie tells me, gripping her cell phone and staring at her brother helplessly.

"Good, honey, that's good."

By now, Lola has ushered her daughter to the back of the salon, and the ladies in the neighboring stations have vacated their seats to get away from the spectacle. But they watch, those ladies, oh, how they watch, still as statues, false sympathy painted on their faces, which doesn't conceal the smugness of self-congratulation they exude. It seeps from their pores and I can smell it, can hear each of their thoughts in stereo. *My life is so much easier than hers. My children are shits, but they're* normal *shits.*

I'm doing all I can for Josh, but it is so little, and for a moment, I fear I'm going to lose him. I stand and throw my arms about his neck and hold his face against my chest and tell him over and over how much

I love him, how he is my guy and the light of my life and my pride and joy. And these things that I say aloud are lies, because I've resented him and hated him for *that thing* that happened to him that was not his fault, that was no one's fault, not even mine, *that thing* that created his disability, and I have despised all the ways I have felt like a failure because of him and *that thing* and his condition. But the love is true, so I repeat it, just in case. Just in case . . .

Sirens erupt in the background. They are familiar. They are the recurring soundtrack of my life.

~

A banana. An unblended piece of frozen banana, sucked into his mouth through the wide Smoothie Palace straw. There it was caught and cradled by his tongue and lay in wait for that moment, that instant, when a sudden inhalation drew it into the back of his throat, partially obstructing his airway. This is what the ER doctor tells me.

~

Colin arrives just as the medical staff stabilizes our son. He clutches my hand tightly as the doctor delivers the news that Josh will be okay.

"We're going to keep him overnight, just to be sure," he says, tossing his latex gloves into a nearby receptacle. I've been to the ER countless times over the course of Josh's life, but this fair-haired, gleaming-toothed doctor is a stranger to me. He looks about twelve but is probably in his thirties.

"Thank you, Doctor," Colin says, pumping the man's naked hand enthusiastically.

"We'll get him to a room in the next twenty minutes or so. Just have a seat in the waiting area and a nurse will let you know when that happens."

I nod as Colin repeats his appreciation. Katie stands sentinel by the reception desk. Colin updates her, and she crumples with relief. She wants to stay, wants to be here when Josh wakes up, but I urge her to leave, to go home, or to Simone's, or to go anywhere as long as she's not here in this place that smells of antiseptic and death and manufactures despair and grief and only the occasional victory.

Colin offers to drive her, and although he assures me he will return shortly, I know how this will play out. We've performed this scene with Josh a thousand times before today, and the series of events is always the same. Colin will leave, under the pretense of returning, but then he will call to check in and ask how Josh is doing and whether it makes sense for him to come back, and I, as I always do, will tell him that it doesn't make sense for him to come. His time is better served elsewhere, with Katie, with his fucking manuscript, with his *whatever it is he does when he's not here.*

Colin is a good father and he loves Josh deeply. But he was not prepared for the curveball that life threw at him. He was never fully invested in having a child. But I wanted another baby, a sibling for my daughter, another opportunity to feel that connection with the universe, the stirring in the womb, the creation of a human being. So Colin acquiesced, and as Josh grew within me, his father's excitement grew exponentially. *A son,* he'd say as he caressed my expanding belly. *A mini me. A reflection of myself that I can nurture and guide and tell stories to and play catch with and buy condoms for and share firsts, like driving a stick shift and drinking a beer.*

The disappointment Colin felt, and continues to feel, at Josh's actuality is a shameful secret he thinks he keeps. But there are moments of quiet contemplation, when his guard is down, when he thinks no one is looking and his frustration and dashed expectation are written on his face and read by his wife.

He cares well for Josh. He gets him up in the morning without complaint and goes to him in the middle of the night when it's his turn.

He engages Josh in conversations about politics and history and science fiction and literature. But beneath my husband's ministrations there is always a barely perceptible sense of distractedness and skepticism, as though he is still waiting for his real son to show up.

I don't resent Colin for his detachment. I envy him for it.

My blessing and my curse is that mine is the one face for which my son searches when he regains consciousness. Always my face. So I will stay. I don't consider asking Colin to stay in my stead. I will be here when Josh awakens. This is my duty. This is my life.

~

I sit in a standard hospital guest chair in the corner of room 408. Josh lies in the bed next to me, his chest rising and falling in perfect rhythm thanks to the breathing tube pushing air in and out of his lungs. He is asleep, but his vitals are strong. The steady beep of the heart monitor reassuringly disturbs the silence.

Josh stirs, and I lean over to see whether his movement is a sign of consciousness regained or a shift in his REM. When I'm certain it's the latter, I lean back in my chair and gaze at his face. In the emergency room, the medical staff administered sedatives and muscle relaxants, and the combination has loosened his limbs and rendered his face into a mask of complete serenity. For a moment, I allow myself to look upon him as though he were any other teenage boy, a boy who will wake tomorrow morning with a slight sore throat from the breathing tube, a boy who will rise from the bed without assistance and dress himself and trot down to the car, ready for a Sunday afternoon of touch football at the park with his friends followed by an Xbox marathon.

I press my hands to my eyes, then swipe away my tears before they fall.

I wonder if the drugs in Josh's system, which make him appear normal, also help him to dream his "normal" dreams. I wonder if he, too, is imagining my Sunday scenario. I hope not, for his sake.

One morning, a few years ago, I awoke to a horrific screech blaring from the monitor. I ran to Josh's room to find him halfway out of the bed, his arms and legs flapping uselessly, his joints white with strain, his face contorted with agony. His keening wails felt like jagged shards of glass digging, scraping, stabbing through my eardrums into my brain. I rushed to him and used all my strength to push him back onto his mattress.

The bed rail that prevents such an occurrence had been detached from its upright position and hung impotently along the bottom half of the bed. I remember wondering, as I whispered calming words to my son and tucked the pillows beneath his knees and under his lower back and arms, how this had happened. When you have a child with severe cerebral palsy, there are certain things you do without thought that are as essential and automatic as breathing. The guardrail on the bed is one of those things. Had I not locked it into position? Had Colin forgotten? *No and no*, I thought. Not securing the guardrail would be like accidentally pouring gasoline into your child's juice glass. You would never do it.

"Aye wa' riee a bi', Maah," Josh wheezed. *I was riding a bike, Mom.* "Aye wa' rayee w' Kaee." *I was racing with Katie.* "Aye bee huh, t'." *I beat her, too.*

I caressed his cheek and told him to go back to sleep.

The tide of slumber pulled at him, his words soft and slow. "Aye cu d' aeethee, Maah. Aye cu ru a' ju' a' das. Aye cu ge' uh ow a thi' be." *I could do anything, Mom. I could run and jump and dance. I could get up out of this bed.*

I glanced at the guardrail, then at the small lever that controls the mechanism. Was it possible that Josh lowered the rail himself? Was his dream so powerful, so real, was his imagining of himself as normal so trenchant that it enabled him to perform a task he could never perform in his real life?

I didn't ask him. Perhaps I didn't want to know the truth. Perhaps I wanted to believe that Josh did it, because if he was able to lower that guardrail with the sheer power of his mind, then what was to stop him from one day feeding himself or brushing his own hair or walking on his own two feet or riding a bike?

Tears were leaking out of the corners of his eyes and his keening had changed to low moans. His voice was a strangled whisper. "Aye wah t' d' tho' thee, Maah." *I want to do those things, Mom.*

"I know, honey," I told him, drying his cheeks with the sleeve of my nightshirt. "I do, too. I'm so sorry, Josh."

"Aye soee, t'." *I'm sorry, too.*

I didn't tell him to have sweet dreams. I never do. Sweet dreams are anathema when every day you awaken to a nightmare.

~

Hours pass. The sun moves through the sky. Colin calls, as expected and we go through our usual lines. Katie calls and asks if she can bring me anything to eat or fresh clothes. I thank her for her consideration but decline, telling her that I'll get something at the cafeteria downstairs. I never leave Josh's room. The TV remains a blank screen. The nurses come and go, asking after me. One young Asian woman brings me stale coffee and an uneaten patient meal. I thank her and set it aside.

As the moments tick by and my son sleeps peacefully, my mind sifts through the events of the past few days. I drift into a kind of twilight trance, allowing thoughts and memories to take shape and comingle. I don't fight them or push on them or analyze them in any way. But at some point, they twist and turn and fill my head with noise so deafening, I worry that irreversible damage might occur.

I straighten in my chair and reach for my purse. I withdraw a small notepad and a pen from the side pocket, then begin to take notes. The words come slowly at first, then faster and faster until my hand aches. When I'm finished, I read what I've written.

Wednesday: Charlemagne barks furiously.

Wednesday night: I wish him away.

Thursday morning: Charlemagne is gone. I wish away the tree.

Thursday: I wish away Richard Green. Richard attacks me in the bathroom.

Friday: The tree is gone. Richard Green no longer exists; the attack was erased. I am the head of marketing and new business. We have a new caregiver, Lena. Colin writes full-time. I find Katie's pregnancy test.

Friday night: I wish that boy away.

Saturday morning: Katie is not pregnant. She has never met that boy. She is a radiant, successful teenager heading for the college of her choice. She and I are taking Josh for a haircut. We stop at the smoothie shop. That boy is there, but I make sure that Katie doesn't see him. We end up in the ER.

And here we are.

Night has fallen around me. Josh is still asleep, and the nurses assure me this is normal. He will likely wake up soon, they say. Probably in the middle of the night or the early hours of the morning. He might be confused, bewildered, possibly very upset. He might need more sedation to understand the situation fully.

More confusion, more bewilderment, more upset. As if my son doesn't have enough of these emotions in his life already.

The Asian nurse helps me convert the hospital chair into a makeshift bed and brings me blankets and a pillow. I do my best to wash the day's stink off me in the small bathroom, then curl myself into the chair and pull the hospital bedding up to my chin. I stare at my son.

My wishes are coming true.

As I gaze at my son, I think about the one thing I've wanted, more than anything else, for the past fifteen years.

Be careful, Emma.

I push the thought from my mind and take a deep breath.

I wish we'd never gone to Smoothie Palace.

~

I awaken disoriented. Again.

The sun slices through the bedroom curtains. Colin sleeps beside me. Josh's steady breathing sounds from the monitor on the dresser. I hear the shower down the hall.

Sunday morning in the Davies house.

TWENTY

Even though I still don't have a rational explanation for the circumstances of the past few days, this morning I understand that I need to accept that which is happening to me as real. What is my alternative?

I get out of bed before my husband, without the expected background noises of heart monitors and overly solicitous nurses, and tiptoe down the hall to Josh's room. He sleeps soundly, albeit noisily. I approach the bed and look down upon him. His hair is cut short. I close my eyes and a memory forms of Lola snipping at his brown locks, chattering on, an endless monologue of humdrum verbal regurgitations while her scissors rhythmically *whoosh-snap*, sending clumps of my son's hair fluttering to the floor. Devi remains in the reception area, playing pass-the-daisy with two young girls. No choking. No paramedics. No hospital. No Smoothie Palace before the salon. My wish, once again, has come true.

I am rarely the first to arise, but on this Sunday morning, while my husband and children continue to sleep and dream, I descend the stairs to the quiet and empty first floor. I enter the kitchen and cross to the stove. Without thinking, I turn on the baby monitor on the far side of the counter, and Josh's gurgling snores are instantly imported into the room. I make myself a cup of green tea, sweeten it with honey, then carry it with me to the kitchen table.

I sit for a long while. Seconds pass, moments. I track them with an occasional glance at the clock on the microwave. I count my heartbeats. I breathe in and out purposefully. I sip at my tea. The tea is hot and scorches the roof of my mouth, but I welcome the pain. The searing heat is tangible, a sensation I can connect with. The pain tethers me to reality.

I think back on my childhood, my girlhood, those precious years without responsibilities, when the future, vague and hypothetical, seemed bursting with possibility. As a young girl, I wished. I sent out prayers to the night sky—for a pony, for a new best friend when my old one moved across the county, for a sibling, for a groovy birthday party. *Starlight, star bright, the first star I see tonight, I wish I may, I wish I might, have the wish I wish tonight.*

Some wishes came true. My seventh birthday party was a fete extraordinaire, engineered by my mother, which included a petting zoo, a magician, and the tallest Hello Kitty cake I'd ever seen. Some wishes did not come true. I never got a pony. Our yard, my mother explained, was not big enough for a horse of any size, and furthermore, my father snapped, the city didn't allow equine inhabitants in residential neighborhoods. I also never got a younger brother or sister. But I did get a new best friend, Mary Anne Kurtowski, a chubby, bespectacled girl from Long Island who moved in with her grandparents down the block because her parents were getting divorced.

Mary Anne was allergic to everything and was teased mercilessly by the other kids in school, and I took her under my wing as a sort of outreach program, and also because my mom made me. But she turned out to be nice and funny and incredibly smart, and she introduced me to *Family Ties* and *The Wonder Years*, shows I wasn't allowed to watch because my dad owned the TV.

We were inseparable. My mom called us the Wonder Twins, and we liked that.

Mary Anne moved away, too. The night before her father came and swept her off to a remote town in Indiana, I sat at my window and watched the azure sky, waiting for the first star to appear. And when it did, I said the chant aloud and then wished with all my might that Mary Anne wouldn't have to leave, that by some miracle she could stay with her grandparents and be my best friend forever. The next morning, her dad showed up in a beat-up '72 Chevy Nova. I never saw Mary Anne again.

I never wished upon a star again.

I finish my tea, then take my cup to the sink to wash it. As I fill the cup with soapy water, I picture Mary Anne Kurtowski's round, smiling face.

~

I make pancakes from scratch. And bacon. I can't remember the last time I did this, cannot access specific memories, but shadow recollections loom in my mind of Sunday mornings at the griddle.

On this morning, I revel in the feel of the whisk in my hand, folding the ingredients together, the sizzle of the butter on the heated iron pan, the bubbles erupting from the disks of batter as the underside of the pancakes turn golden, the aroma of crackling pork from the broiler.

The lure of bacon draws my family to the kitchen. Colin brings Josh down and Kate appears shortly thereafter, showered and fresh.

Josh can't eat bacon, but pancakes are okay, if they soak up enough syrup to be mushy. I plate a stack for him and pour maple syrup over the top and set the plate aside.

No one utters the slightest bit of surprise over my culinary undertaking. And why should they? My shadow memories have already revealed that I make a fabulous breakfast on a regular basis.

As I set the food on the table and watch my children and my husband enthusiastically dig in, shame rises from my gut. The false memories are just that—lies. I haven't been making pancakes for my family. I've been lying in bed, wallowing in self-pity, resenting my obligations, and, in turn, offering up only the barest minimum. Oatmeal. Protein shakes. Half the time I let Kate and Colin fend for themselves while I curse the fact that my son can't pour his own cereal, let alone eat it himself, or eat it at all.

This, this family breakfast, produced by my hands, is what I should have been doing all along—*would* have been doing if I weren't so busy hating myself and my life.

Dante and I cooked together. Fabulous meals—French, Italian, Russian, Chinese, Greek. We bought a map of the world and taped it to the wall in the living room. We would go to the library and peruse the cookbook section, discovering recipes from all around the globe. Then we'd find the region that corresponded to our particular culinary adventure and mark it with a thumbtack.

Dante's grandfather was a chef, and Dante taught me how to dice and mince, how to separate yolks from whites, how to reduce wine and make a roux. We paired our meals with correlating alcohol: spaghetti bolognese with chianti, ahi spring rolls with sake, Mediterranean lamb shanks with ouzo.

When Dante and I parted, my passion for the kitchen dissipated. I tried with Owen, honestly I did. But every homemade meal I proffered was met with criticism. *Too much sauce, babe.* Or, *Good thing I hit the drive-through on my way.* If the food was unrecognizable to his limited palate, it was rejected out of hand. I stopped trying.

And Colin, Colin was so happy to have a wife that he didn't care whether his meals were masterpieces made from scratch or purchased from the freezer section of the local supermarket. With Katie, I never gave much thought to how a home-cooked meal might affect her. I made uninspired stews and meat loafs and pastas with canned gravy.

Occasionally I pulled out one of Mom's recipes, but only when I had extra time and energy, and those instances were rare. Josh's dietary restrictions further distanced me from the joys of cooking.

But now, as I take my place at the table and watch Katie feed Josh his pancakes and Colin scrape his last bite around the rim of the plate to soak up the butter and maple syrup, as I absorb the contentment in the kitchen inspired by a simple mixture of flour and baking soda and buttermilk, I realize that I have been undermining my family's happiness as much as I've been undermining my own.

The pancakes are delicious. But they feel like cement in my stomach.

~

I discern from the breakfast conversation that, in this new version of my life, we have no caregivers on Sunday. The family is together without interference. Katie and Josh play Xbox or catch up on beloved TV shows or go to the park and feed the pigeons. Or all three. Colin reads the paper, then may or may not work on his manuscript. On Sundays I catch up on emails and the few blogs to which I subscribe and attack any carryover work from the office, if a deadline approaches. Occasionally, if I am free of my career obligations and Colin is suffering from writer's block, we undertake to go on an outing.

But not today.

Today I have other plans.

Keeping my voice neutral, I ask Colin about his writing schedule and if he is planning to work today.

A fleeting sneer followed by a complacent smile. "I was hoping to get some words down," he says.

"Aw, do you have to?"

"Yaaa, Daah, d' y' af t'?" *Yeah, Dad, do you have to?*

"You must take inspiration when it comes," Colin replies, then turns the spotlight on me. "What about you, Em?"

I clear my throat. "Well, I have a big meeting this week. I could sure use some time today."

Katie rolls her eyes, but I can tell that she is used to my work ethic. Her eye roll is perfunctory but not malicious.

"Your mother's job pays the bills around here," Colin says. My champion.

Katie shrugs, then turns to her brother. "I checked the weather, Josh. I think there's going to be a perfect breeze for that dragon kite of yours. How about I call Simone and the three of us can go to the park and try to fly it?"

I could cry. Tears crowd my eyes. I won't release them, because tears would give me away. But in my mind, three days ago, my daughter was off with *him* and her brother was a castoff, an embarrassment, a shirked responsibility. Today, she loves him as always.

"Te' Siowe t' we' th' pe' sher a her." *Tell Simone to wear that pink shirt of hers.*

Kate's eyes go wide with mock consternation. "You're such a perv, Josh. I know the shirt you mean, the one that shows off her . . ."

"Boo." *Boobs.*

"I am not telling her that, Josh."

"Tha' jus rog'. Aye stuh i' thi' cheh. Th lee' y' cu d' i' hep m' sss boo. Aye doe' wah t' loo' a' yos." *That's just wrong. I'm stuck in this chair. The least you could do is help me see boobs. I don't want to look at yours.*

"Thank God for that," Katie replies. "You can see boobs on the internet. You're not going to ogle my best friend."

"Aye ca' og. Aye droo t' muh." *I can't ogle. I drool too much.*

There is a moment of silence in the kitchen. Then we all burst into laughter—Colin, Katie, Josh with his donkey bray. Even me. My laughter feels foreign. It feels good.

~

Simone arrives within the hour. She is lean but curvy, with long, straight, silky black hair that cascades to the middle of her back. She is *not* wearing a pink shirt, but she is ready. Simone is Katie's best friend. Anyone who holds that office must be fully accepting of Josh. And she is. She speaks to him as though he is not imprisoned in his body. She teases him and jokes with him and even flirts with him. Not the same way that Lena flirts with him. Lena's flirtations seem calculated and cold, obligatory. Simone is a well-adjusted teenager who sees beyond the wheelchair to the heart of my son. She is not bothered by the need for Katie's translations.

As I gaze upon them sparring in the living room, I am careful to not make wishes.

Once the three teenagers have set out for the park, and Colin has barricaded himself into his office, I head for the family room. I lower myself onto the ancient, wooden, slat-backed desk chair and boot up the hard drive, then wait while the computer drags itself to life.

When the computer is ready, I click on my search engine of choice and begin to type in questions. The answers are not forthcoming. As far as I can tell, no one in the history of mankind has ever experienced what I am experiencing.

This seems far-fetched to me. I don't consider myself to be extraordinary; I am average with a capital *A*.

When my questions about wishes coming true glean no answers other than ridiculous YouTube videos about magic spells and inane opportunities to "creatively visualize my desires" and "jettison my intentions out to the universe," I expand my search. *Desires actualized*, I type. *Self-fulfilling objectives*, I add. My new search calls up several websites regarding existentialism.

My father was Catholic, my mother Episcopalian, which is like Catholicism light. When my father was present, which was about half the time, we went to Mass. When he was absent, Mom and I baked or knitted or went to the movies, reasoning that God wanted us to explore the world around us and appreciate His creation in all its aspects.

Although my religious upbringing was largely impacted by my father's presence, I never questioned the existence of God. Even through my trials with Owen and, more importantly, with Josh, God's omnipotence was a given. My residual Catholic guilt led me to believe that the punishments I received were due to some horrible sins I'd committed.

Existentialism is a word I've heard but never fully understood. This is what I read now:

Existentialism is a philosophy that emphasizes individual existence, freedom, and choice. It is the view that humans define their own meaning in life and try to make rational decisions despite existing in an irrational universe.

Something about this idea strikes a chord in me. *I am exercising choice*, I think. *I am defining my own meaning and trying to make rational decisions despite the fact that my life does not make any sense.*

"Is it possible?" I wonder aloud to the empty room. *Is it possible that we are all in charge of our own destinies? That every human being has the power to assemble or disassemble their own lives through the sheer power of their minds?*

I continue reading, article after article, several blog posts, and one research study about the effects of the existential viewpoint on the life of the typical housewife. After an hour of poring over endless paragraphs about this philosophy, I realize that my question and the answer no longer matter.

I am making wishes. They are coming true. It is what it is.

Existential? Perhaps. Unlikely? Definitely. Happening? God, yes.

~

At two o'clock on that Sunday afternoon, I shut down my computer. I am not reassured about the state of my sanity. But I have uncovered a lifeline to clutch, however desperate my grasp upon it is. I have no more definition or explication or justification for my current circumstances than when I began my search. But I now possess a philosophical supposition, a theory through which I can vindicate myself.

For the time being, that's enough.

Edith Piaf's warble sounds through the wall of the family room. I stand and walk from the room, then grab my keys from the table in the foyer and head out into the blazing sunshine.

The Krummunds' SUV is parked in the driveway, the back hatch open, the cargo bay half-full of bags and equipment. My neighbors have returned from the lake. Spencer, the twelve-year-old, comes out from the house trailed by his little brother, Steven. They each grab something from the back of the SUV and drag their booty to the house. Spencer waves at me as he goes, and I wave back. I have the crazy urge to run over to him and tell him about the little puppy in the pet store downtown, how cute the little guy is, how his family *just has* to buy him.

Instead, I walk down the path to the sidewalk and gaze down the block toward the park. From the curb in front of my house, I can see the dragon kite fluttering in the air.

TWENTY-ONE

Monday, July 11–Thursday, August 4

There are rules. Aren't there always rules?

For the next several weeks, I push aside questions about my own sanity and test the extent of my puissance. I don't think of myself as a superhero à la Marvel or DC Comics, but if I am to assume that I've been given some sort of power, I have an obligation to discern its scope and limitations.

Through trial and error, this is what I learn: my wishes cannot be undone.

At the beginning of my research, I start small, not wanting to unleash complete chaos into my world by wishing something life altering or drastic. I've already done that with Richard Green, and I still experience vertigo each time I go to work, expecting my boss to be there only to re-realize that *I* am the boss.

On that first Sunday night, perched on the edge of my bed, hands clasped, I begin with my husband's pipe.

I wish Colin didn't have that stupid pipe anymore.

The next morning, Colin comes bustling into the kitchen, his brow furrowed. He has misplaced his father's precious pipe and he is in an absolute lather over it. The pipe is nowhere to be found, he says, and has anyone seen it, and he's searched the house top to bottom twice, and how could a person lose a pipe, and are you sure you haven't seen it? He is so churlish for the next few days I am tempted to wish for a divorce. But I understand my mistake. My wording was nonspecific.

Had I said *I wish Colin never owned a pipe in the first place*, the scenario would be different. He wouldn't ransack the house for three days straight, wouldn't snap at Katie and Josh and me, wouldn't slam doors and yell for no reason and storm into his office and hide there for hours at a time with Louis Armstrong playing at full volume. He would never have had a pipe to lose.

The next night, I wish the damned thing back, but I know, just as I suspected the morning in the smoothie shop when I saw *that boy*, my original wish cannot be undone. The pipe does not magically reappear.

By the end of the week, I'm so fed up with Colin's childish tantrums that I buy him another pipe, not an exact replica of his father's, but close enough in size, shape, and color. He doesn't want it at first, tells me it isn't the same, doesn't have the same history, doesn't have the same taste or smell. But he takes it. In order to reestablish the feel and flavor of his father's pipe, Colin starts smoking again. Outside only, and only until the pipe is well cured, he claims. I don't believe he'll stick to his promise.

So this wish backfires. Clearly. But I learn a valuable lesson. My wish must be concise and specific and well worded.

The second and more important rule I learn is that I cannot wish something back that is gone. Like the pipe, yes, but also things that were already lost in the past and not lost as a result of my requests.

After my experiment with Colin's pipe, I plead for my mother's return. *I wish Mom was still alive.* This wish feels akin to some desperate appeal made by a character in a Stephen King novel, and afterward, I'm plagued by nightmares of my mother's corpse rising from the dead, her flesh eaten away, her mouth a toothless, tongueless cavern, screaming accusations at me while jabbing a finger of bones into my chest. Thankfully, the nightmare does not come true, but neither does my wish.

I try it several ways, changing the words, hoping against hope that I might stumble upon the magical combination that will unlock the chains of her demise and rewrite the past. My intention is so strong that on the morning after my final attempt, I think I hear her voice whispering into my ear. *Let me go*, she says. To which I respond, *Never.*

On that same day, I take out the notes I made in the hospital and study them closely. I reason that all the wishes I've made that have come true involve subtractions. The additions to my life—my beautiful daughter restored, my high-powered position at work—these are products of the *subtractions.*

I test the theory over the course of a week. I wish for the reappearance of a ring I misplaced two years prior, I wish for more money in my checking account, for designer furniture in my living room; I wish that Colin's second book was a huge success, that he still had his job with the JC, that our backyard had a gazebo, which I've always wanted. None of these wishes materialize.

I then begin to wish things away. Little things. *I wish there were no cracked tiles downstairs.* The next morning, I inspect every inch of the first floor but can find not a single fissure in any of the tiles. *I wish the banister wasn't broken.* The following day, I behold a sturdy railing with no loose screws. *I wish I didn't have crow's-feet or that horrible wrinkle between my brows.* Upon waking, my reflection reveals a face out of a dermatologist's pamphlet. I discover later, through my Google calendar, that in this new version of my life, I see a nurse practitioner three times a year for Botox and filler.

I wish my stupid protuberant belly, from two larger-than-normal babies, was smaller. This, I realize, is a stupid wish, because I am a size eight and have a good body and when I awake the following morning, I feel an exquisite ache in my abdomen. I find a wide swath of bandaging around my middle and discover from the conversation with Colin, as he brings a tray of food to my bedside, that I underwent liposuction the day before. Even though I know it's futile, I try to unwish the procedure. I spend a few days in bed, telecommuting to work and cursing myself for my vanity and my ill-placed priorities.

Another rule: my wishes must be about me and my life. I learn this after the lipo debacle when I attempt to be selfless and philanthropic by deleting miseries from the world at large. I try to eliminate famine, war, crime, disease. The daily news broadcasts remain unchanged.

Next, I wish something silly, just for fun. I write myself a note and set it on my nightstand, then I wish I never saw the movie *All That Jazz*.

When I was a teenager, growing up in a decidedly middle-class home, with a father who drank and disappeared regularly and a mother who desperately tried to make up for his absences, I fell in love with motion pictures and the escape they provided. I couldn't sing particularly well or dance like a gazelle, but when I saw *All That Jazz* at a girlfriend's sleepover party, I was swept away. I didn't understand the minutiae of the film, the underlying theme, or the main character's misbehavior, but the idea of total dysfunction creating greatness, the profound and eerie imagery of death as a desired beauty, the unctuousness of success—these things struck me. This was a movie I watched again and again, until I knew every line by heart, could mimic every movement of every character. I wanted to see it with fresh eyes.

The next day I find my note, and that night, after Josh is put to bed by Lena and Colin retires to his office and Katie kisses me good night and heads upstairs to read pamphlets on UPenn, I rent *All That Jazz* on demand. The experience is revelatory. I remember snippets from seeing it in my old life, but they form a trailer of sorts, and watching it anew has a dual effect on me. I feel both like a teenager witnessing something fantastic and innovative, and also like the Roy Scheider character in the film, frenzied, frantic, determined to exercise control even as his life spirals out of his grasp.

I make a wish that I never read *Gone With the Wind*, then spend three days furiously absorbing Margaret Mitchell's prolific words.

I wish that Colin didn't work all hours at home. As I say the words in my head, I'm not sure why I make this wish. Perhaps I have grown tired of being greeted nightly by Ella Fitzgerald and Cole Porter and Cab Calloway, or possibly I've come to resent how complacent my husband has become, strolling into his office in his pajamas even as I style my hair and don my appropriate ensemble and do my makeup and squeeze my feet into professional-looking, bone-crushing shoes. The next day, he ambles off to the local library for his daily writing session, inspired, he tells me, by all the books and authors around him.

I am careful at work not to make grandiose requests. None could be so catastrophic as obliterating a person's existence. But I'm wary. I wish we no longer had the decades-old Mr. Coffee machine in the break room. The next morning, I'm greeted with a shiny new Keurig. I wish Valerie didn't wear cloying perfume, and from that wish on, her scent is subtle, lovely. I wish that Golly Polly Wally Holleran didn't have such an offensive wardrobe. The next day, and for the foreseeable future, he shows up for work absent the horrible bow ties, sporting fashionable blazers and chic collared shirts instead. I wish away the furniture that decorates my office, because although the desk and the chairs and the couch were carryovers from Xander's time, they remind me of Richard Green. On that Friday morning, I enter Canning and Wells to find that the spirits have whisked away his desk and couch and chairs and replaced them with cozy, inviting pieces out of my imaginings.

During this period of time, which I have deemed my trial phase, I'm like a little girl again, filled with awe at the world around me and my own omnipotence. Children are like that. They live in egocentric universes, which is their right. I am an unfulfilled middle-aged woman with a disabled son, and for the past decade, I've been defined by my limitations and the challenges life has placed in my path. But with my new ability to delete that which I abhor, I am also eradicating that which feeds my unhappiness. And although I don't, for a single minute, trust my powers, I use them like a child would, freely and without inhibitions. Without stopping to consider the ripples. Anyway, my wishes are small and not greedy.

The greatest challenge I face is that my memories are inconsistent and incompatible; the new recollections obscure the old but do not completely erase them. And often there is a definitive lag time between the new reality and the formation of coinciding memories, so for a while I am stuck in a kind of amnesiac limbo. I'm forced to keep my mouth shut and my ears open and let the conversations around me clarify the situation.

To help with this conundrum, I'm keeping a journal. The first entry is about the beginning of this odyssey, transcribed from my hospital notes—Charlemagne, the tree, my *boss*. I write in it every night. I record my wishes as I make them, along with the events of the day and the consequences of said wish.

The journal has a lock and I keep the book tucked in the back of the drawer in my nightstand to guard against prying eyes. Anyone who reads it would instantly banish me to a psychiatric ward. But it helps me keep my thoughts straight, helps me preserve the fading memories. I often wonder whether holding on to the memories of a life that no longer exists will, at some point, cause me to have a psychotic break. How can so many memories coexist? But I'm not ready to let go of any of my lives, not completely, not yet. I'm not even certain these new realities will last. What if, suddenly, I awaken back in my old life? Without my journal, without my records, I'll be completely lost, a life raft at sea with only a sheet of blackness overhead, no stars to guide me.

On the positive side, I don't have to drag myself out of bed in the morning. I no longer have the impulse to bury myself beneath the covers and avoid my to-do list. My duties and responsibilities are still present, but I have an urgent motivation to get up, get going, get dressed, to see whether or not my wishes have come true. I now greet the day with eager expectation.

Janis Thomas

If Colin or my children have noticed a change in me, none of them have commented. If my new self is the old self to them, the mom and wife who jumps out of bed and *carpes* the *diem*, then they wouldn't know the difference. To them, this is the way I've always been. They've never seen the woman who clutched her pillow over her face, contemplating suffocation as an escape to her life. They've never heard the mother who sobbed in the shower in the morning, grieving her horrid existence.

Sometimes I wonder about *their* memories—Colin's, Kate's, Josh's, even Valerie's and Wally's. My wishes have altered and modified their lives. Do any of them have residual memories of BW (*before wishes*)? Does Colin ever wake up with the urge to enlighten a roomful of students? Does he harbor any resentment that his home office remains empty, unused, and quiet every day, his stereo silent, his computer unbooted until his return from the library? Does Katie dream of a black-haired boy with an earring sparkling from his left lobe and a cheeky swagger? Does Valerie fantasize about being my equal, or superior, as she was before my Richard wish? Does Wally cry out in the night, scraping his way out of a nightmare in which a horrid, demonic power castigates and criticizes and humiliates him? I think of Delilah Clayton, too. Does she ever jerk into consciousness with the residual panic from the shadow of a lecherous abuser?

Of all of them, I wonder about Josh the most. Occasionally he looks at me strangely, as though he's puzzling out an answer or working through a hypothesis. He doesn't ask the question. But I know it's there. Josh is intuitive and senses things other people miss. Does he know, on some fundamental level, what's happening to his mother? Does he relive BW in his mind? Is he aware of the shifts, some subtle, some cataclysmic? I push my own questions away when they surface, but on the odd morning, I find myself wanting to share all that's happened with my son, get his take, his impressions, his advice, on the paranormal and impossible occurrences. He would provide solid counsel, I think.

Ever since that night at the hospital with Josh, when I realized my wishes were coming true, I've had an ever-present urge to make the one wish I desperately want to make, the wish that would cataclysmically change the course of my life. The words of this wish sit anxiously upon my tongue in the dead of night, waiting for me to give them voice, but I resist. I keep them unsaid because I'm terrified. What would the outcome of such a wish involve? I fear the consequences would not be ripples, but rather a tsunami. Every molecule of my being wants to make this wish, but I cannot, *will not* make it. Not yet. Not. Yet.

~

In my new life, or lives—as every wish I make impacts the world around me in some way, large or small, and creates a different *me* on some level—I am a participant in social media. I have a Facebook page, a LinkedIn profile, a Twitter account. These online outlets fill in some of the gaps in my memory banks. I scan Facebook daily now, beginning with my home page.

Some of my own posts are foreign to me: my family on an outing to the shore, Colin and Josh laughing as Katie tries to wrap her mouth around the famous triple-decker lobster roll; Katie receiving an award at the end-of-the-year high school banquet, smiling into the camera as she clutches a gold trophy announcing her prowess in creative writing. Some images are familiar—cheers for a job well done, posted by Valerie when I landed the SoundStage account; a picture of my smiling son, flanked by Lola and her daughter at Mimi's after his successful haircut, posted by me. Regular updates from a page called CP Parents, on which people share stories, concerns, and questions about their lives with children who have cerebral palsy.

At some point I liked this page, although I have no recollection of doing so. I've never been the kind of woman who reaches out to strangers or discloses my personal challenges to a faceless, nodding crowd.

From the looks of things, I don't post regularly on CP Parents, but I like other parents' posts.

One night, when the house is quiet and Josh's breathing wafts through the air in the family room, I read through the timeline of CP Parents. And I become the nodding crowd, covering my mouth with my hand when certain passages hit close to home: the struggles, the conflict, the endless battles. I'm surprised by the candor of these men and women. They admit to feelings of inadequacy, of resentment, of unendurable fatigue. I relate to them, but I'm not strong enough to admit to those emotions I consider flaws, those feelings I have but despise myself for having, not even anonymously on an open forum.

On this same night, when I can't read any more war stories from faceless CP families, I do something about which I have only fantasized up till now. I move the cursor to the search bar on the top of the Facebook page and type in two words.

Dante Forgionne.

There is only one match. Of course.

I click on his timeline, and for the first time in twenty years, I am gazing at the beautiful face of my first, and perhaps only, true love.

Dante's sleek black hair, previously shaggy and unkempt, is now cropped short, but he counterbalances the lack of hair on his head with a scruffy beard, more salt than pepper. There are deep grooves at the corners of his sky-blue eyes, and I can tell these lines were etched through years of smiling and laughing. A prick of bitterness pokes at my chest. Laughter, smiles, joy, irreverence. Had Dante and I stayed together, I would not have my two children, but also, I would not carry *that thing* that happened, would not bear its burden like a sack of bricks. He has climbed mountains, Dante, and gone on safaris and helped to produce wells for peoples in third-world countries. He has jumped out of planes and cliff dived and bungee jumped and sampled exotic meals all over the globe.

How could this man, whom I loved so desperately, have gone on to live such a happy life when, all the while, unbeknownst to him, his ex-lover went on to suffer tragedy and misery? The lines carved into my brow and forehead, only recently smoothed cosmetically, were forged not by laughter but by grief and supplication.

I move the cursor to the box that indicates a friend request, for although my heart aches at the idea of our opposing outcomes, something deep within me wants to connect with this man again. And now that I have a respectable position, an enviable career (regardless of how I obtained it), I could reconnect with Dante with a sense of confidence and self-assurance. My finger hovers over the mouse, twitching and ready.

On the baby monitor, I hear Josh stir. I move the cursor away from the friend request box and close the Facebook window.

Another day. Perhaps.

"Maah?" The monitor crackles with Josh's whispered voice.

I shut down the computer and go to my son.

TWENTY-TWO

Friday, August 5

During my trial phase, I didn't think of Charlemagne at all, unless I happened to reread that first passage in my journal. And even at those times, the puppy, or the *image* of the puppy, was obscured by a gauzy film of surrealism, as though he only ever existed in my mind. And he did, didn't he? Who is to say whether that reality, in which Charlemagne inhabited my neighbor's home, is more real than the present? I've tried not to allow my thoughts to idle over this riddle.

But on this unseasonably cool August morning, I make a detour into downtown on my way to work. I pull to the curb at a meter, the very same one I stopped at so many weeks, so many lifetimes ago.

Several storefronts down, I spot Lettie Barnes unlocking the main door of her building. I crouch in my seat until she disappears inside the brownstone. I never called her back. I don't want to see her. She will only confirm my insanity, and I no longer need that confirmation. I am well beyond that.

I wait a few minutes, then I get out of my car and step onto the curb. I drop a quarter into the meter, then walk down the sidewalk toward Paw-Tastic Pets.

Four weeks. Surely that adorable little creature has been adopted by some enthusiastic and optimistic family. I can just imagine a tribe of frenetic, energetic wee ones rolling around on a carpeted floor with Charlemagne/Charlie, offering their rosy cheeks to be kissed by that sandpaper tongue. They probably have named him something pedestrian like Fluffy or Duke. But they love him, even as their mother entertains second thoughts while she scrubs his urine out of the carpet.

I approach the window of the pet shop, knowing/believing/praying that he will no longer be a prisoner in the display kennel.

My relief is palpable when I confirm my suspicions/hopes/prayers. Half a dozen furry, wiry Lab puppies scamper around the kennel. Three goldens, one blond, two black, one brown. None Charlemagne.

I stand and watch them for a few minutes, laughing at their playful antics. A dog's life, I think, must be one of the better existences on the planet.

If the dog has a true and proper owner.

I send up a quick prayer that Charlemagne has found a good home, then glance at my watch. Eight thirty. My shoulders tighten reflexively. Richard has been gone for nearly a month, but I still experience that whoosh of panic at my impending lateness.

I am the boss, I remind myself. *I will not be punished for tardiness.*

I take a deep breath and give the puppies one last look.

I turn toward my car and take a step, then another. On the third step, I hear a voice behind me.

"Oh, hi. It's you."

I recognize the voice. It belongs to the girl from the pet shop who rescued me when I fainted, the morning everything began. Pennsylvania meets South Jersey. I turn around and force a smile.

"I thought it was you," she says. She holds a fat window marker in her hand, neon pink by the looks of it.

"How are you feeling? I hope you ate a good breakfast this morning."

I nod. "I'm doing well," I tell her. "Thanks."

"Good," she replies simply, then she sidles up to the window and takes the cap off the marker.

I haven't experienced that not-right feeling for weeks. It washes over me as the girl begins to write on the glass. I stare openly, and my gaze must carry force, because the girl jerks her head sharply in my direction. Her expression is questioning. My lips, my vocal cords, all frozen.

"Do you need something?" she asks.

I shake my head. She shrugs and turns back to the window. Seconds pass. Wide-sweeping hot-pink cursive soon scrolls across the lower half of the glass. I read the legend as the girl pockets the pink marker and removes another, this one neon yellow, with which she begins to highlight the words.

LAST-CHANCE SALE! HALF OFF SHEPHERD-TERRIER MIX!

Iron fist to the gut. The air rushes from my lugs. *Charlemagne.*

"Is that the puppy I saw in the window last time?"

The yellow marker goes still. The girl looks at me and lowers her arm. She seems to be concentrating, then she remembers. "Oh, yeah, that's right. He was in the window that day. Yup, it's him. Poor little guy. I thought for sure he'd get scooped." She shakes her head sadly. "You just never know."

"Is he the only one left from that group?"

"Yeah. But, you know, with a price cut like this . . ." She gestures to the window. "We're hoping someone will take him home."

"Where is he?"

"In one of the kennels in the back," she says.

As though a string is pulling me from the center of my body, I move toward the entrance of the shop. I don't want to go inside, *do not* want to see that little fuzz ball trapped behind the bars of his tiny prison. But I can't stop myself.

The air inside the shop is thick with the scent of caged domestic animals—urine, feces, wet fur, and longing. I move on leaden legs to the back of the shop. Past aquariums rife with spectacularly colored fish, past the row of cages with frisky kittens and a show kennel filled with newly arrived Pomeranians, past stacks of feed and litter and toys. In the far back corner, away from the clamor and squawks and caterwauling of the more energetic of the would-be pets, stands a two-by-two-foot cage, and inside that cage lies a small lump of fur-covered flesh.

Charlemagne. Charlie. I kneel down, my knees protesting and my skirt stretched to the ripping point, and gaze at the puppy. His captivity hasn't kept him from growing; he's roughly a quarter larger than he was the last time I saw him. He's curled in an unmoving ball, oblivious to or ambivalent toward the shreds of soiled newspaper around him.

I find my voice beneath a sturdy pile of regret. "Hey. Hey, Charlemagne."

Seconds pass. The infinitesimal rise and fall of his chest is the only indication that he is alive.

"Charlemagne," I say again, this time with slightly more strength. An ear twitches. A paw flinches. His eyes open, they search his cage, then land on me.

On an intellectual level, I understand that dogs are a lower species, they don't possess complex reasoning skills or experience emotions the same way humans do. But this dog, this puppy, whom I may or may not have deprived of a comfortable life, who now lies in a cage, unknowingly awaiting whatever fate might befall him, looks upon me with a lugubrious expression, as though he just awoke from a dream in which he had a good home with a nice, albeit rowdy, family, who lived next door to a house with a monstrous tree in the front yard upon which he yearned to pee. The force of his despair is like a blow and propels me to stand up and back away. I sprint for the exit.

Outside, the girl has finished her task and meets me at the door.

"What will happen to him?" I ask. "The puppy. If no one buys him at the sale price?"

She lowers her head as she tucks the yellow marker into her pocket. Then she shrugs, and the pedestrian gesture is full of meaning. "We can't keep 'em. You know? We try to find a shelter, but if we can't—they're always so full . . . so, then, we have to send them to the pound."

My blood turns to ice at the word *pound*. The pound is death row for dogs.

"When?" I demand, and the girl's mouth drops open. "When will you send him, if no one buys him?"

"The max is six weeks," she tells me. "He's been here almost five. So, like, ten days."

I nod but say nothing. She gives me a final suspicious glance, then retreats into the shop.

I gaze at the front window, reading, rereading the neon legend. Movement in my peripheral vision captures my attention, and I turn to see Dolores ambling from her shop, moving in my direction. I'm not surprised. Her withered face opens in a crinkly smile as she presses her fingertips against my hand.

"Come for tea," she says, her voice like the wings of a hummingbird.

Even as I shake my head, I follow her to the antiques shop. The girl from Paw-Tastic Pets watches us pass as she pretends to clean the inside of the display kennel.

The house, *my house*, is still in the front window. I stop to inspect it, and Dolores comes up beside me. Through the reflection of the glass, I see her watching me.

"Where did you get this dollhouse?" My voice is whisper thin.

"Let me think. Isn't that strange. I can't quite remember. My memory isn't what it used to be, I fear. It must have been an estate sale or the like. Why do you ask?"

I turn to her. Her expression is nonchalant, but her eyes dance.

"Because it's my house. I mean, it *looks* like my house."

"Really." Her response is an acknowledgment, not a question.

"It looks *exactly* like my house," I tell her.

"Mmm, I see." The old woman gazes at me thoughtfully. A moment passes. "Well, isn't that wonderful?" she says. "How very lucky you are to have such a lovely home."

Her words cause me to shiver. I clasp my arms at the elbow and return my gaze to the house. "I don't have a tree in my front yard. We had it removed."

Dolores touches me gently on the sleeve, then graces me with a placating smile. "Come. Let's go inside for that tea. You look as though you could use it."

She ambles to the entrance and pushes through the front door to the tinkling of bells. I follow wordlessly.

"Chamomile, I think." She moves purposefully to the back of the shop as I take in my surroundings. The shop is heavily air-conditioned and smells of furniture polish and lavender. The large room is filled with bounteous treasures. I am not an expert in antiques. I have no idea where or when or by whom the many chairs and couches and tables were made. But every piece is in pristine condition, and I recognize their value. A long display counter acts as a barrier between the sales floor and the back room where Dolores hums a melody. Inside the display case are knickknacks, French souvenir boxes, Lalique decorative items, crystal vases and decanters, several old-fashioned hairbrush and mirror sets, costume jewelry, cameos. Atop the counter at the far end sits another dollhouse, much smaller than the house in the front window, a one-story clapboard-sided prewar home with a white picket fence.

I gaze into the display case, and a gold pendant and chain catches my eye. I lean down for a closer look. The pendant is engraved with the image of a lioness and a cub, and I think of Katie. She is a Leo—her birthday is the twenty-first of this month.

"Ah, here we are," Dolores says, crossing to the counter with a china cup and saucer in hand. She carefully places the tea set on the countertop, and the steam from the hot liquid carries the aroma of chamomile flowers to my nose.

"I added a spot of honey," she tells me, then follows my gaze to the pendant. "The lioness. I love that pendant. It dates back to 1936. So the story goes, a jeweler in New York was commissioned to make it for a young gentleman to give to his fiancée upon her return from safari. She had gone to Africa with her parents, one last trip with Mum and Dad before she was to become a wife. But alas, she never returned."

"What happened to her?" I ask, and Dolores grins enigmatically.

"I don't know that part of the story. The woman who gave it to me said she thought the girl had died—an accident, or an acute illness. But I like to imagine another scenario, whereby the girl, who was betrothed by her parents' decree to a man she didn't care for, fell madly in love with another—a guide on her safari, perhaps, some strapping young Englishman who stole her away and filled her life with joy and love."

I can't help but laugh at the old woman's fanciful tale. She takes no offense; instead, she laughs along with me. "It's a far more agreeable story, though, isn't it?"

I nod and reach for the china cup. I lift it to my lips and take a small sip. The tea is smooth and hot and slightly sweet. Dolores peers at me, a knowing smile playing at her lips.

"Wouldn't that be nice?" she says. "To eliminate the disagreeable and be left only with the good?"

Our eyes meet. My hand trembles and tea spills over the rim of the cup, splashing onto the glass counter. She knows. Somehow, *she knows*.

"I'm sorry," I stammer as I set the cup on the saucer.

"Not to worry," Dolores says. She retrieves a cloth from behind the case and deftly wipes up the spilled liquid.

But what *does she know?* I make a show of looking at my watch. My hand still trembles. "I'm late for work."

"I understand," she says quietly.

"Thank you for the tea."

"You are quite welcome, my dear. I'm sorry if it was too hot."

"It wasn't."

"Perhaps you'll come back when you have more time. I would very much like to hear *your* story, both the agreeable and the disagreeable."

A hundred questions fill my head—they butt up against one another, clamoring to be given voice. *Who is this woman? Is she a part of what's happening to me? A conspirator? The puppet master? Can she give me an explanation? Guidance? What will she say if I ask her?*

I open my mouth to speak, but another question comes to mind that obscures the ones before it. *Do I* really *want to know?* I clamp my lips together and turn to leave.

"What about the pendant?" she asks. "For your leonine daughter?"

I stop dead. She knows I have a daughter, and she knows Katie is a Leo. I look at Dolores. Her expression is placid.

"I'll give you a wonderful price. Let's say thirty dollars, shall we?"

The pendant is probably worth four times that much. I slowly return to the display counter as Dolores removes the pendant from the case. She holds it up, then lowers it into a velvet bag. I hand her two twenty-dollar bills, and her fingers brush against mine as she takes them from me.

"I do hope you will come back, Emma. I feel there is much for us to discuss. And that I might be able to offer you some assistance."

I never told her my name. Of course she knows it. Compared with all the other things she knows, my name seems the least astonishing.

She hands me my change along with the velvet bag.

Logistically it's not possible, but I feel her eyes on me all the way to my car.

TWENTY-THREE

I should have stayed with Dolores. I should have sipped her tea and confessed to her and listened to her counsel. I realize my mistake as soon as I reach my office. Had I stayed in the antiques shop, I would have missed him. But there he sits, in one of my new/old chairs, facing my desk, looking angry and smug at the same time.

My ex-husband. Owen. Tension grips my neck and shoulders.

When Valerie sees me, she springs from her seat and approaches. "I tried to get him to leave, I really did, Emma, but he wouldn't go," she says in a rush. "I didn't want to call security without your say-so."

"It's okay, Val. I'll talk to him." I hand her my purse. "But keep an eye out. If I give you a signal, make the call."

She nods solemnly.

Owen doesn't bother to stand up when I enter. He never did, not when we were married, nor when we were courting. He explained his lack of chivalry by telling me that he didn't want to offend my feminist sensibilities, of which I had none. It was an inept excuse for his laziness. The only time he stood upon my arrival was in court, but that was for show and prompted by a swift elbow nudge from his lawyer.

I walk past his chair and glance down at him. My ex-husband looks almost decent this morning, shaved and dressed in pressed slacks and a collared shirt. He reminds me a little of the man I married. Just like Richard Green, that man never existed. Not really.

My hands clench and unclench, but I can't stop them. I pray that things won't get ugly, that he won't berate and belittle me, as he is given to do, at which he excels.

He turns toward me, and the instant our eyes meet, during that briefest passage of time, a world of information is transferred to me. The *new* me.

I always cowered around Owen because he is a bully and his energy and life force—although negative and destructive—are overpowering. When I couldn't avoid him, I kowtowed to him and tried to appease him just to avoid any unnecessary conflict.

But in this new reality, I have the upper hand, the power, the control. I catch the fleeting flash of deference in his expression, followed by resentment. This knowledge emboldens me.

"Good morning," I say coolly. "To what do I owe the pleasure of this visit?"

He shakes his head with disgust then mimics me. "'To what do I owe the pleasure of this visit?' You're such a poser, Em."

"And you're an ass," I reply. I expect him to explode with anger, and I'm almost disappointed when he remains calm.

His response is a seething whisper. "Fuck you."

"Keep it civil, Owen, or I'll have you removed."

He clenches his jaw to stop his retort. "You know why I'm here."

"Actually, I don't." I circle my desk and take a seat.

Again with the mimicry. "Actually, *you do*. I want to see my daughter. I don't care what the judge said. Katie is my flesh and blood, and I have a right to be a part of her life."

"You lost that right."

Crimson splotches appear on his cheeks. "Just because you have an expensive lawyer and a great job and a *respectable* husband doesn't make the situation right. You can't buy the truth."

"The truth?" I allow my ire to rise and inspire me in a way I never could before. "The truth, Owen, is that you are an alcoholic and a drug abuser and the farther you stay away from Katie, the better."

He jumps out of his chair, but not in the way I anticipate. He doesn't look furious, but instead imploring. "I've been sober for a year, and you know it."

"I don't know any such thing." Or do I? A shred of a memory passes through my gray matter—a tall, middle-aged man with a short salt-and-pepper afro standing on my doorstep, Owen's sponsor, pleading Owen's case and swearing by all that was holy that Owen had been clean for the better part of a year. Another fragment assembles in my head—the same man seated beside Owen in court, in place of his tattooed girlfriend, futilely testifying on my ex-husband's behalf.

Three months ago, before Charlemagne, before the wishing, Owen crashed his car into the concrete divider of an overpass, high as a hot-air balloon. His lawyer claimed Owen was having a negative reaction to prescribed antibiotics. I knew it was bullshit, but my lawyer (the lawyer in that reality) couldn't argue the point, and the judge sided with my ex-husband.

Is it possible, in this new reality, that Owen is clean? Is it possible that my having a steady job and a steady income and a happy home life in some way motivated him to get his own life together so that he could be a part of our daughter's?

Valerie appears at the door to my office, brow furrowed.

"Is everything all right?"

I stand. Owen's gaze is aimed daggers. "Everything's fine, Valerie. My ex-husband was just leaving."

"I wasn't," he says.

I steel myself and meet his gaze. "Yes, you were."

He shakes his head slowly. "This isn't over."

"For now it is, Owen." I break eye contact and return to my seat, a pointedly dismissive gesture. Rage radiates off his body in waves, but he keeps himself in check. He withdraws from my office, and I track his retreat through the glass window. I want him to look defeated, shoulders slouched, eyes on the floor, but he doesn't. His posture is straight, sure. He is not the same man I knew three months ago.

"We have a slight problem," Val says, drawing my attention away from Owen. I turn to her. She looks worried.

"What?"

"Mr. Canning and Mr. Wells want to see you. It's about SoundStage."

I shrug my shoulders. After Owen, Bill and Edward will be a piece of cake.

~

Again, I've miscalculated.

Twenty minutes later, I'm seated in a chair across from Bill Canning's desk. He and Edward Wells perch on the near side of the mahogany desktop like twin statues, arms crossed over their chests.

"But they signed the contracts," I hear myself saying.

"We gave them a ninety-day out," Canning says. "They're taking it."

"But they loved the presentation . . . and everything we've given them so far." My voice is tissue-paper thin.

Canning and Wells exchange a look. Wells rubs at his chin with a leathery hand. "They liked it, at first," he says. "But they've decided to go in a different direction."

"They want a more old-timey feel," Canning says. "Jimmy Dorsey, Benny Goodman, that kind of thing."

Goose pimples erupt on the flesh of my arms. *Jimmy Dorsey.* I think of Richard Green, ex-boss, ex-person, a man who never was. His presentation for SoundStage was backgrounded by Jimmy Dorsey's "Amapola."

"Stein liked the modern spin, but apparently the CEO is a second cousin once or twice removed to Ol' Blue Eyes and has a penchant for the big-band era. It's a shame you didn't have that information."

Meaning, if I'd done my homework, I would have known not to use KONGOS's music during my proposal. I now understand Richard's obstinacy when I suggested going modern. He wasn't simply dismissing me. He knew what he was doing, although he would never lower himself enough to offer me an explanation for his choices. My boss was a bastard, but he did his job well. He did his homework. I've been faking it.

"Richard Stein also implied that he is more comfortable working with a man."

"Excuse me?"

Edward Wells shakes his head. "I know, Emma. It's difficult to imagine that such sexism is still prevalent." This from a man who asks that his female employees call him Mr. Wells, while his male employees are free to address him as Ed. "We've come across this several times before, as you know."

I don't know, but I can guess. I need no memories to understand the direction of this conversation. Our business is male dominated. If Richard Green had lost a new client, the onus would be placed on the client's capriciousness. But because I am a woman, the blame lands squarely upon my shoulders. I may have banished him from the face of the earth, but Richard Green exists somewhere, on some plane, and he's laughing at me.

"Look," Canning says, "times are tough. The economy isn't what it was a few years back. Businesses are reluctant to part with their money unless they feel completely confident in their partners."

"I understand." Despite the cool air being pumped in through the vents, I'm sweating.

"Xander made a good choice in you, Emma. You've been a great addition to management around here. But we need to focus on the bottom line."

"I know."

"Sometimes it's good to shake things up and move people around."

I swallow hard. Losing SoundStage is a blow from which I might not recover.

Five weeks ago, I was an executive assistant. I took no responsibility for the success or failure of Canning and Wells. I now see what a luxury that was. I wouldn't wish Richard back, the sadistic prick. But if I'd made a more specific wish, perhaps I wouldn't be facing the firing squad. What will I do if I lose my job? Colin isn't working. We have no other income. How will we survive? How will I, a middle-aged woman who just got fired for inferior performance, land another position elsewhere? I'll have to start over. I'll end up as an assistant again, only without the fancy "executive" title.

"Emma, you look worried. We're not firing you."

I let out a breath I didn't know I was holding. Bill Canning smiles kindly, but his eyes are black as a shark's.

"We're just having a conversation at this point," Edward Wells agrees. "Why don't we take a few weeks and let the SoundStage dust settle. See what you can bring in. Make sure you keep everyone happy. Then we can meet again and talk about how everything's going."

I nod mutely, then stand and leave the office. I head down the hall. I wish I were heading for my old desk, but I know it doesn't work that way. Unless I wish Valerie Martin away.

And I won't do that.

~

When I was six, I dreamed of growing up to be a fairy princess, with a dress and crown like those of Glinda the Good Witch. When I was eight, I wanted to be an astronaut. Weightlessness appealed to me even then. In third grade, I did a report on the first moon walk, complete with a bulky, silver spray-painted costume and a recreation of Neil Armstrong's famous declaration. During the Q&A that followed my report, Kevin McCleary informed me and the rest of the class that the entire moon landing was a fake. I punched him in the face with my helmet and had to sit in the principal's office for the rest of the day.

When I was twelve, I decided I wanted to be an Olympic figure skater à la Katarina Witt, Debi Thomas, and Jayne Torvill, if I could find an appropriate partner. I implored my mother to take me to the salon to get a haircut just like Jayne's. At the time, my lustrous chestnut hair spilled down my back almost to my bottom. Even though Mom would no longer have to brush through my tangled locks, she cried with every snip of the stylist's scissors.

When I was sixteen, I wanted to be a movie star. Doesn't every girl at some point dream of stardom, walking the red carpet in stiletto heels and a Valentino couture gown, arm intertwined with a fetching tuxedoed gentleman who happens to be her leading man? I learned, after a disastrous debut in the junior play, that I had no gift for drama. I spoke my lines with less emotion than the automated voice of the time-telling phone operator.

By the time I entered university, I had realigned my goals. My stoic and dispassionate delivery would be perfect for television news reporting. I practiced in the mirror of the dorm bathroom, earning titters and eye rolls and the occasional insult from classmates. But I was not deterred. Not until Dante, who unintentionally stole all my focus, energy, and enthusiasm.

Of all the things I dreamed of becoming, I never had in mind "executive assistant." I'd never even heard the term.

But now, as I collapse behind my desk, with Valerie nervously watching from the other side of the glass, I dream of being an executive assistant again.

I could wish my own job away. Before I lie down tonight, I could say the words aloud. But I am afraid. What would the outcome of such a wish be? Can I make the words specific enough to ensure that I am still employed in some capacity tomorrow morning? I don't know. I don't know.

And will such a wish undo what I have gained from this prosperous position—full custody of my daughter and full-time care of my son? If I wake up as a clerk in the post office, surely those precious rewards will be lost.

If I am fired from Canning and Wells, I will likely lose both anyway. Owen will pounce immediately, a lion striking an injured antelope, claws extended. We will have to cut back on the caregivers, return to Raina solely. I don't care for Lena, but I appreciate the respite she provides me.

According to Bill Canning and Edward Wells, I am safe for at least two weeks. I will not wish away my job tonight. Who knows what reality I'll be living two weeks from now.

TWENTY-FOUR

I'm not myself when I arrive home that night. I've spent the day prostrating myself to clients, deferring, placating, prostituting myself in exchange for their acknowledgment that they are happy with our firm. I've done research on every prospective client we have in the hopper, reading blogs and wikis and news articles and press releases until my eyes felt like they were bleeding. I met with Valerie and Wally and several people from the other departments in what was to become an equal parts brainstorming and browbeating session.

I called home to let my family know that I would be late and not to hold dinner. Colin, usually so in tune with my moods, dismissed me quickly, told me not to worry, not to hurry, and everything was fine.

Lena's car is in the driveway. This has happened frequently over the last few weeks, and I've been given the same explanation each time: that Lena has brought groceries and needs easy access to the refrigerator in the garage. Tonight the excuse doesn't dispel my irritation. I park at the curb and stomp up the herringbone path to the front door.

Kate and Josh are together in the living room. Kate is seated on the couch with a large book open in her lap while Josh looks on from his wheelchair beside her. Ella Fitzgerald quietly croons from Colin's office.

"Hi, Mom," Kate says as she turns a page.

"H', Maah," Josh echoes.

I cross to the couch and kiss both of my children on the tops of their heads, then peer down at the book they're reading. The lush full-color image of the African savannah nearly bursts from the page.

Two years ago, Katie declared that she wanted to go on safari and planned to do so after graduating from high school. Colin and I saw this as a momentary fancy, but she was not to be swayed. She said she would pay for it herself, that she would work through her junior and senior years of high school and all through college if she had to. Colin and I made a deal with her. If she waited until after she finished college, Colin and I would finance the trip. God knows why we made the offer—at the time, a trip to Africa for our daughter was not something we could afford. But she accepted, and we figured we could somehow find a way to produce the funds by then.

To show our support and commitment, we gave her this book for her sixteenth birthday. She stopped looking at it and talking about going on safari when she started with *that boy*. But now that she's never met him, I see that the pages of the book are tired and worn from her constant perusal.

"Maah. Aye wa' t' g' ah safa w' Kae," Josh says. *Mom. I want to go on safari with Kate.*

I don't say that will never happen. I *never* say that. "Wouldn't that be great?" I say instead.

It doesn't matter that I never say it. He knows. He looks up at me, his expression pained. *I'll never go on safari,* his eyes tell me. I have to look away.

"You know, they have special safaris for people with disabilities," Kate says matter-of-factly. She turns the page to reveal a pack of cheetahs loping across a grassy plain. "I read about it online. Josh could totally come with me."

This conversation coupled with the pressure of my day feels like a vise grip on my skull.

Do you know how much those special safaris cost? Do you have any idea what it would take to get your brother to Africa? Do you?

Behind the couch, I clench my hands into fists, then force myself to relax my fingers. "Where's Lena?"

"She was in the kitchen before, doing dishes. Oh, look at the baby hippos, Josh. Aren't they cute? They're called calves, like cows."

He turns his attention back to the book. "Th' uhlee."

"They are not ugly. They're darling," Katie says as Josh starts to snort.

I back away from them and head for the kitchen. As soon as I reach the archway, I realize I'm famished. I skipped lunch to get more work done and subsisted only on coffee (from the new/old Keurig) and a PowerBar Valerie gave me when she saw I was beginning to lag.

There is no sign of Lena. The dish drain is full and the countertops are sparkling. A lone plate sits in the middle of the granite counter, loosely covered with foil. I peel away the foil and sneak a rosemary red potato. Even cold, it tastes good.

Where is Lena?

I tuck the foil back around the edge of the plate and walk to the family room. The room is dark and empty. I cross to my desk, then rummage through my purse for the lion pendant I bought from Dolores. I tuck the package into the top right drawer of the desk, then retrace my steps to the living room, where Kate and Josh are still arguing about the adorability of baby hippos. I glance toward Colin's office and see that the door is slightly ajar. Without contemplating the reason, I slip off my pumps and kick them aside, then walk on bare feet down the hall.

I stop at the open door and peer into the office. Colin is seated at his desk wearing an undershirt, head lolling against his chest, eyes closed. His collared button-down is carelessly draped across the back of his desk chair. Lena stands directly behind him, her hands on his shoulders, her fingers kneading his flesh. Ella sings. Colin moans. My body goes rigid.

I push the door all the way open. It bangs against the inside wall of the office with a *thwack*.

Colin straightens immediately. Lena looks up. The kneading ceases, but she doesn't remove her hands from my husband's shoulders. She doesn't blink or recoil, doesn't bat an eye, just looks at me with her usual expectant expression.

"Hi, Em," Colin croaks. He stands up, forcing Lena's fingers off him.

"Hi, Mrs. D." Not the slightest hint of contrition.

"Tough day at the library, *dear*?" I ask.

"Hours in front of the computer puts me in knots. You know that. Lena was being kind to an old man."

"You're not old, Colin," the girl says, and I bristle at her use of his first name. So casual. So familiar. I am not a violent person, save for the whole astronaut helmet/Kevin McCleary incident in third grade. But I would very much like to throttle Lena. She moves around the desk and approaches me.

"You look like you had a rough day, too, Mrs. D. I could do some work on your neck, if you want." She smirks at me.

I know what I'm going to wish tonight.

"Thanks anyway, Lena."

I could simply fire her and be done with her the old-fashioned way. But that method involves forms and phone calls and explanations and the protracted search for a replacement and arguments with Colin and Josh. A wish will circumvent the red tape.

"Did you know that Lena is a licensed masseuse?" Another item for her résumé. I shake my head.

"It's good for my patients," she says, still smirking.

"You should let her have at you, Em."

"Leeah!"

We all turn toward the door at the sound of Josh's voice.

"Oh, well. Duty calls. Maybe some other time, eh, Mrs. D.?"

"Yes." *When hell freezes over.*

Lena passes me and heads down the hall. I glare at Colin as he dons his collared shirt and starts to button it. He looks at me.

"What?" he asks as though he doesn't know. I say nothing. I see his Adam's apple bob up and down as he swallows.

I turn and leave the room, pausing only long enough to grab the doorknob and slam the office door shut behind me.

~

I watch her. I don't intrude. This will be Josh's last night with her. Tomorrow she will be gone—not erased, just absent from our lives as though she's never been here—working in another household with another special-needs person, possibly seducing another husband and alienating another wife. Josh will not know what he has missed. So I will grant him this night. Perhaps the feel of her hands on him will leave an indelible imprint upon his subconscious, create a memory he can access as a dream or a fantasy. I hope so, in a way, for his sake.

Kate is downstairs watching something on the big-screen TV while chatting with Simone. I stand in her darkened bedroom and peer through the crack in the bathroom door, a peeping Tom. What I'm doing is reprehensible, perverse, but I do it anyway.

Tonight is bath night. Lena has Josh situated on the heavy-duty medical shower bench. When we moved in, one of the few improvements we made was to gut the entire upstairs bathroom and put in an enormous stall to accommodate the bench and my son.

Josh is naked. For modesty's sake, his genitals are hidden beneath a folded towel.

My son's limbs are long. Fate is cruel. Colin and I are average height. Were Josh able to stand, he would tower over us. If his limbs were equal to his parents', as they should be due to genetics, they would be far easier to cope with. But, no, they are elongated and gawky. Fate is a bastard.

I watch as Lena massages soap into the cramped muscles of his calves and thighs.

Josh flinches and color creeps up his cheeks.

"It's okay, Joshy," she coos to him, her hands whispering up and down his legs. "It's totally normal and natural. We've talked about this before. There's no reason to be embarrassed."

My son has an erection. Of course he does. An attractive woman is massaging his legs. Apparently this is not the first time the issue has presented itself.

I've read the books and been counseled by professionals, and on an intellectual level, I understand that my son's disorder does not preclude him from experiencing sensations of a sexual nature. But the idea of Josh's sexuality has always been an abstract.

Here, in this moment of purposeful voyeurism, the concept is no longer hypothetical. It is reality.

I wonder about the future and how his needs will be met. Will Josh marry and procreate? Will Colin and I have to procure prostitutes for him? Will I stand outside his bedroom door, much like I'm doing now, to make sure that the woman is not abusing him but delivering him the satisfaction he craves? I make a mental note to reach out to the Facebook page with these questions, where my anonymity will guard against my humiliation.

Josh moans, not with pleasure, but with shame. I know him well enough to know the difference.

"I love you, Josh, you know that," she says. "But not that way. I can't." She reaches for his hand and begins to lather his fingers, one at a time. She moves to his palm, his wrist, all the way up to his biceps.

"Plee," he whispers. I have never known one syllable to contain such misery.

"I can't, Joshy," she tells him.

A tear squeezes from the corner of his eye. "Plee, Lee-nnaah." The magnitude of his distress inspires him to pronounce the N. My son is not capable of satisfying himself. The pressure he feels must be intolerable.

Lena stops and gazes at him. I carefully, silently, step back and allow myself to be swallowed up by the darkness of Kate's room just as Lena turns and looks around to make sure no one is watching.

I should leave. I should tiptoe out of Kate's room and go downstairs and sit on the couch and watch the rest of whatever crap show she's watching. But I cannot. I step forward. Through the crack of the door, I see Lena slide her fingers up Josh's thigh, up under the towel.

"Just this once, okay, Joshy? Just one time and never again. Okay?"

His nod is almost imperceptible. I catch it and so does Lena. "Okay," she says.

The terry cloth twitches with the movement of her hand, slow at first, then gaining speed. His head jerks back, and he moans again. Although his face is twisted into a grimace, there is no mistaking the nature of this moan.

My son is having his first sexual experience. I am a witness, lurking in the shadows, knowing full well that I am also the executioner of this memory. I will kill it before it takes hold. It will linger in my mind for a while before time obscures it. Josh will not remember it at all.

I think of Colin in his office, Lena's hands on his neck.

My guilt is tempered by my hostility.

I'm sorry, Joshy.

But not sorry enough.

~

Saturday, August 6

She's gone. I know as soon as I walk into the kitchen for breakfast. The energy in the room is different somehow. Josh listlessly eats the oatmeal offered to him by Colin. Colin barely acknowledges my entrance. He absently feeds Josh while silently poring over his newspaper. I see a middle-aged man and a man-child, both deflated by a void they don't even realize exists.

Today is Saturday. No caregivers. I'll have to wait two days to see her replacement, but whoever she might be, she is nothing like Lena. I can tell by the way Colin and Josh hold themselves. Whoever she is, she does not charge the air with her sexuality and charisma. Her spirit does not carry over from her presence the night before, as Lena's did.

"Maah," Josh says, but without enthusiasm. He turns to face me as I kneel before him, and there is a sharp edge to his gaze. He looks as though he's lost something, something precious, but he can't figure out what it is. His eyes implore me for an answer he knows I don't possess. I do, but it's a secret I must keep.

"Morning, honey," I say. Regret oozes from my pores. I smell the stink of it. "How did you sleep?"

"Aye h' th' weedis dre lah nie." *I had the weirdest dream last night.*

"So what else is new?" Katie says as she bustles into the kitchen. "You're always having weird dreams, loser."

Usually Josh brays with laughter at his sister's derogatory comments. He knows that love underlies them. But this morning he doesn't even grin. "Y' w' the," he tells me solemnly. *You were there.*

I don't want to hear the dream. I suspect it mirrors the image burned into my brain of Lena and my son in the upstairs bathroom. I didn't record last night's wish in my journal because I desperately want the memory to fade. But the edges of this particular memory haven't even begun to blur, and I suspect they never will.

"The wa' suwuh e' the', t'," he says. *There was someone else there, too.*

"Was it me?" Kate asks as she drops a piece of bread in the toaster. Josh jerks his head no.

"Who was it?"

"Aye doe 'o," Josh says. *I don't know.*

"So, what's on deck?" I interject, trying to change the subject.

Josh stares at me past the spoon Colin is holding up to him. He knows something. Not in the way Dolores knows, but on some primal level. Josh senses that not-right feeling. I avoid his eyes by addressing Katie directly.

"Are we still going to the outlets today for school clothes?"

Kate nods. Her bread pops from the toaster, and she grabs it with two fingers. "I was planning on it."

"What's this now?" Colin folds his newspaper and pushes it to the center of the table, then looks up at Kate and me.

"There's a sale at the outlets, this weekend only. I'm taking her for school clothes." Colin narrows his eyes at me. For a split second, I see Lena standing behind him, hands on his shoulders. I blink and she is gone.

"What about Josh?" he asks. "Are you taking him?"

I smile at my husband through clenched teeth. "No. I'm leaving him with you. We discussed this earlier in the week."

Josh is no longer looking at me. His head hangs against his chest, his eyes are closed. But he is not asleep. I can tell by his posture. I sense the struggle going on inside his brain, the tug-of-war he plays with his elusive dream, with the memory I stole from him.

A mother's job is made up of a tireless barrage of decisions, most of which we question, all of which we make based on what we think is best for our child. Occasionally, although we don't admit it and possibly don't even realize it ourselves, we make decisions based on what's best for us. I know I wished Lena away for myself. But last night I had no doubt I was also doing the right thing for my son. This morning, I'm not so sure.

"Is there a problem, Colin?"

Colin shakes his head. "No . . . I just . . . I wanted to go to the library."

"Why don't you take Josh with you?" I suggest. Our library has a multimedia room that is outfitted for handicapable persons. Josh always enjoys himself there.

"Aye doe wah t' g' t' th libree," he says. *I don't want to go to the library.* His eyes remain closed. Colin sighs with resignation, and I have the urge to rebuke my husband for making his disappointment so obvious to our son. Josh's life is a series of disappointments.

A month ago, I was weighed down by my own disappointments, by the ways in which I felt life had let me down. But now, as I gaze at my son, knowing I have imparted another blow, created another defeat for him, I realize that ours, Colin's and my disappointments, have no meaning compared to his.

"Oh, well, that's okay, buddy," Colin says, his voice full of false earnestness. "We'll just do something else. Maybe we can rent a couple of movies on demand or look up some cool stuff online."

"Wuevuh," Josh replies. *Whatever.*

My heart breaks for Josh. I can't unwish. That's the rule. Even if I could, I probably wouldn't. But Lena's departure has affected him in a way I didn't anticipate. I only hope I can find some way to make it up to him.

TWENTY-FIVE

The outlets are just off the highway at the edge of town. We arrive a full fifteen minutes before the stores open at ten, but the parking lot is already full.

"We should have brought the van," Katie jokes, gesturing to the many available handicapped spaces.

After a lengthy search, I locate a slot at the far end of the lot. Waves of August heat shimmer up from the macadam. Women, children, and men trudge toward the long row of outlets like a herd of cattle. Minivans disgorge strollers and infants and fussing toddlers and bored grade schoolers. Mothers struggle to organize their broods in the most timely and efficient manner possible, motivated by the possibility of skinny jeans at 50 percent off.

Kate and I enjoy the air-conditioned car for a few moments, leisurely finishing up our Starbucks as we go over her list of clothing needs for her senior year. The list is long. Finally, we emerge from the car and step out into the hot sun, both of us gasping at the radical change in temperature. We walk toward the beige stucco buildings without haste. She skips ahead a few feet and I gaze at her from behind, seeing her as if for the first time. She has grown taller, and the slight plumpness she always carried has melted away, leaving a lithe, nubile young woman. Her hair bounces across her back, catching the light of the sun. She turns and bestows upon me a beatific smile. Katie is beautiful. But more than that. She is happy.

We bypass Katie's former fashion alma mater, Juicy Couture, and head for 7 For All Mankind. My daughter knows what she wants.

I was never a slave to designer labels. My grandmother was a seam-stress and taught my mother the skill. Many a night I fell asleep to the rhythmic sound of the sewing machine. That sound was better than a nighttime story or counting sheep. It represented safety and security to me. I knew exactly where my mother was, a room away, a mere call of her name away, a heartbeat away.

Growing up, I had a closet filled with homemade clothing, all of which fit me like a glove. Peer pressure existed, although not to the degree it does today, but my contemporaries in grade school and middle school and high school never found my ensembles wanting. In fact, I was approached regularly by eager girls desiring skirts and beaded jack-ets and slacks just like mine.

My mother tried to teach me how to sew, but her tutelage was lost on me. In the simplest terms, I wasn't interested in learning, but even if I had been, I would never have achieved her skill level. I am not a cre-ative person, in that crafty kind of way. I never have been. I was skilled at puzzles and word games and algebra. I memorized the entirety of the periodic table in one night. I could right a wronged Rubik's Cube faster than most. I'm great with a marketing plan and I can arrange words cleverly, seductively, even. But creating something where before there was nothing . . . I did not possess that gift. I didn't mind back then. I had a mother who made me beautiful ensembles that made me feel fine. That was more than enough for me.

When Kate was a baby, that fearful time during which every hitch in her breath suggested SIDS, I castigated myself for not being able to knit booties or sew together a frock for my precious child. But as time passed, my guilt was assuaged by the realization that even had I learned to sew, my daughter would never have been content with that which I could produce. As a child, she was influenced by the images put forth in magazines and on the TV. She had a keen sense of fashion from the time she was three.

Katie is a savvy consumer of the latest trends. I don't mind that she wants her appearance to reflect her personality. Even in lean times, I have always budgeted for my daughter's clothing, knowing that a certain amount of a teenager's self-esteem is related to his or her outward representation to the world. And I rationalize that Josh, with his limited capacity and correlating limited wardrobe, has saved me a fortune in clothing costs. The fact that his care has been an exorbitant expense remains an extraneous and rarely acknowledged counterargument.

We reach the building, and as soon as we pass through the glass door of 7 For All Mankind, Katie immerses herself in the offerings. She darts from rack to rack, oohing and ahhing and grabbing at hangers with abandon. I stand well away from her, allowing her the freedom to make her own choices, but occasionally she holds an article of clothing up and gives me a questioning look to get my opinion. Each time she shows me something, I nod with approval, and not because I am yessing her but because she has impeccable taste.

She heads for the back of the store, in a race with three other girls for the sacred try-on rooms, of which there are only two. She manages to elbow a competitor out of the way and secure a cubicle.

"Mom," she calls. "Can you come here?"

I do as requested and stand outside the fitting room. Should she need a different size, a different color, a different ensemble altogether, she doesn't want to relinquish her cubicle to an awaiting party.

Because she has a plethora of items to try on, and because I know my daughter well enough to know that she will look at herself in each item at varying angles, and likely try the same item on three or four times before she makes a preliminary judgment, I have time to kill. I withdraw my cell phone and swish it to life. I peruse my email in-box, searching for a communication that is not there.

Yesterday evening, before I left Canning and Wells, and after a brief huddle with Valerie, I reached out to Richard Stein and the CEO of SoundStage, imploring them to reconsider their decision to go elsewhere for their PR needs. Today is Saturday, a universally agreed-upon day of rest, but SoundStage is a start-up, a fledgling business, and its administration might consider working weekends mandatory at this point.

Regardless of their stance on Saturday labor, neither Richard Stein nor the CEO of SoundStage has replied to my email. I scroll through spam and a few interoffice memos, most of which can either be deleted or dealt with on Monday.

"Mom, I want to know what you think. I'm coming out, okay?"

Immediately, I tuck my cell phone away. Heat rises to my face as though I've been caught doing something untoward.

I think back to BW. *Before wishes.* When I was home at night, or on weekends with my family, I never checked my office email, and why should I? A lowly executive assistant never brought her work home with her. She needn't. After all, her boss reminded her ad nauseam that she was dispensable, replaceable. Not the most flattering assessment. But outside that dull-gray building, the lowly executive assistant was free.

Then again, *before wishes* I likely would not be spending a Saturday with my lovely daughter, buying her clothes. She would be in absentia or barricaded in her room, moaning over her latest contretemps with her boyfriend. And I would be catching up on housework and chores, knowing full well that my daughter was in crisis but not knowing how to approach her or deal with the issue without alienating her completely, so I would choose avoidance.

I owe an inconceivable debt to my new superpower for bringing my daughter and me back together again, but I wonder about my own efficacy in my daughter's life BW. *Before wishes.* This last month I have been present in my life, more so than I have been for a long time, if for no other reason than to ascertain the consequences of my wishes. Had

I been present before, like I am now, would my daughter have spun out of control in the first place? Would she have sought comfort in the arms of that abhorrent boy if her mother were giving her the attention and nurturing she needed?

Katie emerges from the fitting room and brings my musing to a halt. She wears navy slacks that gather at the waist and flare at the bottom with a sleeveless white turtleneck embroidered at the bottom hem. She looks lovely and mature, and I resist the impulse to throw my arms around her and wish for her not to grow up any more than she already has.

"I love it," I say simply.

"I don't know," she replies. "I think the flared leg will be a problem. I don't want to trip down the hall at school."

I consider her words. "True. But you can wear the top with anything. Jeans. A navy skirt."

"I'll put the top in the 'yes' pile," she agrees, "and the slacks in the maybe pile."

I nod. "Good idea."

"Okay. I'm going to try on the slim cigarette now."

"The what?" I ask, but she has already disappeared into her cubicle.

"They're jeans." I turn to see a bored-looking young woman leaning against the archway between the cubicles and the showroom. She holds a wad of tagged clothing in her arms, and I realize that she is one of the girls Katie beat to the try-on rooms. "You have to be pretty skinny to look good in them," she says doubtfully, as though she thinks my daughter is too heavy to wear them. I turn away from her and withdraw my cell phone again.

I press the speed dial for Colin. He answers on the fourth ring.

"How's it going there?" I ask.

"Fine," he says, slightly annoyed. "I'm working on the manuscript."

"What about Josh?"

"He's playing video games."

"I thought you guys were going to do something together?"

His irritation rises. "I tried, Emma. I suggested several things to Josh. But he wasn't interested in any of them."

"Couldn't you at least play *with* him?"

Colin lets out an angry breath. "I suggested that, too," he tells me. "He wanted to play the machine instead of his dad. I tried not to be offended." I say nothing. "What do you want me to do, huh? Sit in the living room and stare at him while he plays? I thought I could get some work done, try to make some sense of this new chapter. The monitor's on. I'll hear him if he needs me."

"He seems like he's in a funk," I say.

"Yes, well, aren't we all."

"Why are you in a funk, Colin?"

He doesn't respond.

"Okay, Mom, I'm coming out," Katie calls to me.

"I have to go," I say, then hang up without saying goodbye. Kate walks out into the open wearing dark-blue formfitting jeans. They look fabulous on her. I nod.

"Definitely a yes."

She smiles her agreement, then returns to the fitting room. I glance at the young woman and give her a smug grin. She rolls her eyes.

"They really should have a limit on how many things you can try on."

I shrug with false empathy. "Yes. It's too bad they don't."

~

We move to the Roxy store. After a short wait for a fitting room, Katie disappears behind another closed door with a bevy of items in her arms. I stand guard outside, three sizable bags from 7 For All Mankind at my feet.

I resist the urge to check my emails and busy myself with searching my purse for a stick of gum or a breath mint. A moment later, I hear Katie's voice.

"I love this, Mom. I don't know where I'll wear it, but I love it."

"Well? Come on, let me see it."

She opens the door of the fitting room slowly, as if to make an entrance, then steps out of the cubicle wearing a thigh-length dress with spaghetti straps, a sleek gray bodice, and a diaphanous pale-pink skirt. Her Cinderella smile is contagious. I put my hand on my chest and am about to compliment her when I see her expression change from euphoric to pained.

"God, you look gorgeous" comes a voice from behind me. I whirl around to see my ex-husband standing beside the return rack, looking past me as though I'm not there. His thumbs are looped into the front pockets of his jeans, and he wears a tattered short-sleeved shirt emblazoned with the legend DON'T WORRY, BE HAPPY.

I clench my jaw. "What the hell are you doing here?"

He doesn't look at me when he responds. His gaze is glued to Katie. "I'm seeing my daughter."

"How did you know we were here?" The answer comes to me as soon as the question leaves my lips. "You followed us?" His jaw twitches. A giveaway. Bad enough he followed us from our home, but he spied on us in 7 For All Mankind without making his presence known. "You need help, Owen. Seriously."

He ignores me and takes a step forward. I turn to Katie. Her eyes are round with alarm, and I force myself to speak calmly and casually. "Go back into the fitting room, Katie. Lock the door, okay, honey? Everything's fine, I promise." She nods quickly and does as she's told.

"Wait, no!" Owen says, rushing toward the cubicle. I step into his path and he nearly knocks me down. "Katie! Katie! I just want to talk to you. You look so grown-up."

"For God's sake, are you drunk?"

He wheels on me, his eyes full of venom. "I told you I've been sober for a year!"

"And I don't believe you!" I retort. Some of the doors to the other fitting rooms have opened a crack, and I can guess that several patrons of the store are equally horrified and entertained by the impromptu matinee unfolding before them.

A Roxy employee hurries toward us from the floor. She is young, stick thin, and aggravated by the disturbance. "Is there a problem here?"

I give her a look—*What do you think?*—then grab Owen's arm. He jerks it out of my grasp.

"I have to insist that you take this outside," the woman says sternly, as though she will bodily remove us from the premises. She couldn't bodily remove a *toddler* from the premises.

Owen pounds on the fitting room door.

"Mom?" Katie cries from within.

"Get away from her, Owen. I'm going to call the police."

"Go ahead," he rails. "Just go ahead and call the fucking cops, Emma. She's my daughter, you bitch!" He draws his hand back and swings at me. I see his palm come toward me as if in slow motion, but I can't move fast enough to evade the hit. An instant later, fiery pain explodes in my head as his palm connects with my cheekbone.

I'm down, my legs splayed awkwardly on the floor. Through a soupy haze I hear the employee's voice. "Yes, nine-one-one, I have an emergency."

"I'm going," Owen says. His shadowy figure crosses my line of sight. "I love you, Katie," he calls out. "Please remember that. I just want to be a part of your life."

The employee hovers over me, a shadowy gray blob, then her features slowly come back into focus. She reaches down and I grab her hand, and she lifts me to my feet with surprising strength.

"Are you okay?" she asks, still holding her cell phone against her ear.

I nod. "Hang up," I instruct her. "Cancel nine-one-one."

She shakes her head, and I squeeze her hand in response. Hard. My voice is quiet. "I don't want to put my daughter through a police report. Please cancel nine-one-one."

The woman speaks into her phone, then hangs up.

"Mom?" comes Katie's frightened voice.

"It's okay, honey. He's gone."

The woman gives me a meaningful look. "I'll get you some ice."

"Thank you."

Katie comes out of the fitting room and falls into my arms without noticing my burning cheek. I hold her close, desperately trying to stop her tremors along with my own.

TWENTY-SIX

I manage to salvage the shopping expedition. My first instinct is to undo the damage, subtract Owen's appearance from the equation. *Make a wish.* I might. But I still have to get through the rest of the day and turn things around for Katie. If I don't, she'll withdraw from me, relive the scene in Roxy repeatedly, blame herself, blame me. Who knows how her father's invasion of our day will affect her psyche?

I also consider that if I erase Owen from today, tomorrow morning I will awaken with the same conundrum I've faced for the last month. Katie's memory will be safe. She will have enjoyed the day shopping with her mom. My memory will not be pure. A new made-up memory will bloom, but it will be blemished by the old reality.

I've been deleting from my life things I find objectionable, unfulfilling, things that make me unhappy. Do I really want to avoid communicating with my daughter, even if the subject matter is difficult and the reason for the communication is a jackass I detest?

I resolve to confront the situation head-on with Katie. I'll decide whether to delete my ex-husband's intrusion later.

She no longer wants the dress she was wearing when Owen showed up. In fact, she doesn't want anything from Roxy. We carry our 7 For All Mankind bags to the food court in the center plaza of the outlets and splurge on fried food. At first, she only plays with her french fries, dipping them in the ketchup and making patterns on the wax container.

I apologize to her for her father's behavior and tell her that it's not her fault. She is disbelieving. How could it not be her fault when she is at the center of the conflict, the golden prize being vied for? Her eyes dart to my cheek, which is red, but, thanks to the Roxy employee's ice pack, not swollen.

I touch my fingertip to my cheekbone and experience a phantom flashback. I no longer have palpable memories of my former boss's attack. I remember only because I wrote about it in my journal, back when it was yet to be obscured by overlapping memories of Richard's nonexistence. I now recall the attack as one might recall a passage in a book she read a very long time ago. No substance, no emotional impact. Owen's slap, although far less potent than my boss's assault, seems far more intense.

"He hit you," Katie says. Her bottom lip trembles.

I drop my hand to the table and snag an onion ring, roll it between my fingers.

"I think it was a reflex, honey. I don't think he meant to hit me. He never hit me when we were married. He was very upset." It feels strange to defend Owen, but better to defend him than to further distress Katie.

"Upset because of me."

I shake my head. "No, Katie. *About* you, not *because* of you. He wants to be a part of your life. I don't think it's a good idea for your sake, but I understand why he wants it. You are beauty and light and joy, all the things he doesn't have. All the things he isn't. He thinks that contact with you will give him those things and make his life better. And it would." I smile at her. "How could it not? But it won't make *your* life better. And that's all I care about."

I think back to the days of shared custody, when I was forced to relinquish my daughter to Owen's care. His rights included two weekends a month, every other holiday, and a week of summer vacation. He was not reliable then. More than half the time, when his weekend approached, I would receive a phone call that included some ridiculous excuse for why he couldn't take her. She never stayed a full week with him during summer. He always had someplace to be or a friend coming into town or a job offer he couldn't refuse because he "needed the bread." Stories, all. He was unable to stay sober for an entire seven days.

The last time he took her for a weekend, a little over a year ago, he picked her up on Friday after school. She wasn't supposed to return until Sunday, but on Saturday morning his truck appeared at the curb without warning. I reached the front porch just in time to see her bolt from the front seat, her eyes swollen with tears, her face a mask of anguish.

She rushed past me without a word and locked herself in her room, wouldn't come out until Sunday night and refused to tell me what happened. I tried to talk to her, I tried to coax her, bribe her, bully her into confiding in me. She wouldn't. I could only ascertain from her sparse words that Owen hadn't touched her inappropriately, but that was as much as she would allow. When I confronted Owen about it, he feigned ignorance, blamed her menstrual cycle and told me to go to hell.

Colin and I retained a lawyer that Monday.

I have a faint recollection of losing my bid for full custody, but that was BW. *Before wishes.*

At last, Katie takes a bite of a fry, then chews thoughtfully. "Why did you marry him, Mom?"

Two months ago, when Katie and I were for all intents and purposes estranged, I would have dismissed the question. She never would have asked in the first place. But even before *that boy*, when we were playing the role of mother and daughter well enough to fool everyone including ourselves, I realize that I would still have avoided her inquiry. Sidestepped. Changed the subject rather than confide in her the truth.

"I thought he was what I needed," I confess. "I was very much in love with another man who broke my heart. Your father was as different from him as two people could be. I took that as a good sign and talked myself into loving him. Your dad was different, too. He didn't drink too much or use back then. That business started after we got married. I'm not sure why. The pressures of marriage, fatherhood. Some people buckle under the strain. But your dad was a good guy before. And I don't regret him. I have you because of him."

She nods thoughtfully. "What was his name? The man you were in love with."

My reflex is to say it doesn't matter, that he's in the past, that I never think of him. "Dante," I tell her.

"Do you know where he is now? What he's doing?" She doesn't wait for an answer. "Have you looked him up on Facebook? Is he on it?"

"Katie, it doesn't matter what Dante is doing or where he is. I'm married to Colin."

To a teenager, everything is high drama. Her eyes shine with the idea of intrigue and lost love and being reunited. "I'm just saying, you should look him up. Not to run away with him or anything. Just to, you know . . ."

"Life is complicated enough," I tell her. *Especially now.*

She takes another fry, dabs it in ketchup, then sets it down. "He says he's been sober for a year. My dad, I mean."

"He does say that."

"You don't believe him."

I shrug noncommittally. "I don't know, honey."

Her voice is quiet. "Do you think it would help him if I had contact with him?"

I try to squash the bubble of resentment that rises within me. I want to give her an unbiased answer, not one that's akin to the roar of a lioness protecting her cub. I buy myself a moment by taking a bite of onion ring.

"Help him stay sober?" I ask. "That's what you're talking about?" She nods. I take a deep breath and let out a sigh. "I don't know. Again, I don't know. Your father loves you, Katie. He does. But if he thinks of you as a talisman, a good-luck charm that will keep him from drinking or using . . . that's a lot of pressure to put on you, don't you think?"

"He loves me."

"Yes. He loved me, too. But not enough. Not more than he loved drinking or using. He loves that most of all."

"I don't love him." She bites her lower lip as tears threaten, and I realize that this declaration is a guilty secret she's been keeping. She looks at me for absolution. I smile gently and take her hand across the scarred Formica table.

"It's okay. You don't have to love him. It's not mandatory, just because he's your biological father. He's an ass."

A slow grin spreads across her face and she giggles. "You said *ass*."

I open my mouth in mock surprise. "So did you!"

We laugh together. It feels good.

A moment passes, and I glance at my cell phone to check the time. "What do you say we hit Justice, just for fun?"

"Okay. Sounds good. But let's finish the fries and onion rings first." She pops a fry into her mouth even though they are long cold. "Thanks, Mom."

Two words filled with meaning. A connection born of that terrible incident with Owen in Roxy.

Before we leave the table, my decision is made. I will be making no wishes tonight.

~

But I still don't know what to do about Josh.

At the dinner table, he hangs his head as though he's lost his best friend.

He has. You took her from him.

After spending the rest of the day at the outlets, Katie and I decided to pick up Chinese takeout as a special treat. On the way home, we stopped at a local restaurant that makes a special egg foo yong (with no chokeables) for Josh. Several open cartons of steaming, aromatic Asian food sit in the center of the kitchen table.

Katie offers to feed Josh, but I want to do it myself. Penance. The mere act of spooning egg foo yong into my son's mouth is hardly enough to atone for my sins.

"You two had a successful day," Colin comments as he piles shrimp lo mein onto his plate. "I'm surprised you didn't have to hire a moving van for all your bags."

"It was great," Katie says. "Except for the Owen thing, it was perfect."

I should have instructed her not to bring up my ex-husband, but following such an open and honest dialogue, I felt it would be inappropriate to ask my daughter to lie.

Colin straightens in his chair. "What's this now?"

Katie gives me a worried glance. I smile to reassure her.

"Owen showed up at the outlets," I say calmly.

"Showed up?" Colin repeats, his mouth set in a thin line. "What exactly does that mean? How did he know you were there?"

"Why don't we talk about this after dinner?" I suggest. I bring the spoon to Josh's lips, but he refuses to open his mouth.

"Emma, tell me what happened," Colin demands.

"Come on, Josh," I entreat my son. "Take a bite. You've hardly eaten anything."

"Aye 'ot h'gee." *I'm not hungry.*

"But you love egg foo yong."

He shakes his head.

"Emma . . ."

I glare at Colin. "Owen showed up at the outlets, made a scene, then left. That's it. End of story."

"How did he know you were there?"

"I guess he followed us."

"How can you be so calm about this? First he shows up at your office, then he *follows* you and Katie? We have to do something. We need to take out a restraining order against him."

"I don't think that's necessary." I absently swipe at my cheek. The red outline of Owen's hand has faded, thankfully, but the skin is still tender.

"Mom handled it great, Colin."

Colin snaps his head toward Katie. "That's not the point. The man is pernicious."

"Pernicious," Katie says. "Total SAT word."

"Cawee isideuh hah, eei, wikeh," Josh says quietly. *Causing insidious harm, evil, wicked.* I turn toward him. His head is down, but he's looking at me. When our eyes meet, he quickly drops his gaze.

"Owen isn't evil, Colin."

"No, he's just an addict and an alcoholic." Colin's tone is full of disdain and superiority. In his mind, my ex-husband has never been a threat. Colin may be a failed author, now supported by his wife, but by comparison, he is a champion and Owen is a loser. Colin exists in the gray area—he himself is a study in shades of gray. But when it comes to Owen, there is only black and white.

"Enough," I say. "Let's enjoy dinner, okay? We can talk about this later."

Colin harrumphs, then starts to shovel food into his mouth.

Katie regales Colin with her clothing purchases, and he pretends to be interested. I turn my attention to Josh and prepare him a fresh spoonful of the egg foo yong. Again, he refuses it. I set the spoon down and lean into him.

"What is it? What's wrong, my sweet boy?"

Josh's cheeks go red. "Aye 'ot a booe!" he explodes. "Kay? Aye 'ot a booe!" *I'm not a boy, okay? I'm not a boy!*

I sit back, stunned. Katie falls silent, and Colin stops chewing. We're unaccustomed to such an outburst from my son.

The thought comes to me again. *He knows. He knows something.*

"I'm sorry, honey. I know you're not a boy." I reach out to touch his cheek. He recoils from my touch. I pull my hand away, stung by his rejection.

"Someone had a little too much Xbox today," Colin says, and I want to yell at him to shut up. He has no idea what his son is going through. Neither do I, really. But I can guess because I have more information.

"I think that fighting game makes him irritable. It does."

"I' doe't," Josh counters. *It doesn't.*

"You could have fooled me, the way you just spoke to your mom."

"Soee." *Sorry.*

"It's okay, honey."

"Em, it's not okay," Colin corrects me. "Josh, do as your mother says. Eat some more of your food. And no video games after dinner."

"Wyee?" Josh asks.

Ironic that Colin is taking away the Xbox as punishment when he allowed Josh to play the damn machine all day.

"You've had enough. Plus, it's shower night tonight."

"Josh had a shower last night," I say. Colin gives me a confused look.

"No, he didn't."

I turn to Josh. He stares at me accusingly. I look away.

"He didn't? I thought he did."

"Alice only bathes him Wednesdays, as per her contract." Colin rolls his eyes as though my mental capacity is in question. "Remember?"

I've never met Alice. How could I remember? "Right. Sorry. I got my days mixed up."

"Again," Colin says pointedly. I've used that excuse many times in the last two months.

"Aye doe wah a showeh." *I don't want a shower.*

"You have to have a shower. You smell."

"Colin."

Colin tsks. "He's fifteen. He smells. Just like every other fifteen-year-old boy."

"I'll make it quick, okay?" I tell Josh.

"Aye doe wah y' t' d' i, Maah." *I don't want you to do it, Mom.* Angry. I clench my teeth to keep my emotions in check.

"Okay."

Colin sighs dramatically. "I want to get some more work done."

"You had the whole day."

"And I'm at a critical part. I would think you'd want me to strike while the iron's hot. You do want me to finish, right? Aren't you always nagging at me to finish?"

I lean in to Josh. "We'll make it quick tonight. No shower. Just washcloth."

Josh is not mollified. He stretches his head back, his usual grimace twisted farther into an ugly frown. "I wah mo' ecksbah." *I want more Xbox.*

"And I said no," Colin says.

"Maybe a few minutes before bath."

"Emma," Colin says sharply. "I said no."

Katie pushes her chair back and stands up. She senses the tension in the kitchen and tries to defuse it. "How about I show you my new clothes, Josh," she suggests.

Josh shakes his head. "Yuck." No translation necessary.

Katie thinks for a moment. "Okay. How about we look at my safari book?"

"Aye doe wah t'," he says. *I don't want to.*

"Come on. All those cute little baby hippos will cheer you up."

"The' cawd cafs." *They're called calves.* The barest hint of enthusiasm.

She takes her empty plate to the sink. "I'll go get the book while you eat a little more egg foo yong, okay? And you can tell me all the names of the baby animals and make yourself feel like Stephen Hawking with your brilliance."

Josh wrinkles his nose. "Seeveh Hawee i' a fisisi a' a cosmulju, 'ot a zoolois," Josh announces, sounding like his old self. *Stephen Hawking is a physicist and a cosmologist, not a zoologist.*

Katie comes over and bends down, wrinkling her nose back at him. "Yeah, whatever. Meet you on the couch in five."

Thank God for my daughter.

For the next few minutes, Josh acquiesces to be fed. But he doesn't say a word, doesn't look me in the eye. Not once.

TWENTY-SEVEN

After dinner, Colin retreats to his office and closes the door. I gather and wash the dishes, marry the leftovers and tuck the remaining Chinese cartons in the fridge. I move slowly to allow Katie and Josh more time with the safari book. When I finish, I stand in the archway between the kitchen and the living room, watching the two of them pore over the book, experiencing déjà vu.

In this new reality, in which Lena is absent, I don't know if they looked at the safari book last night. Judging from the fact that Katie had to search her room for the book, I'm guessing they didn't. But their evident enjoyment is the same as it was BW.

My children. They are fortunate to have each other, especially since I have not been the mother they deserve. Yes, I have fulfilled every obligation and duty. Yes, I have provided the unimaginable care that someone with cerebral palsy requires. But I've been so preoccupied with my own unhappiness that I've rarely allowed myself the pleasure of sitting between them looking at pictures of wild animals. Such a simple and small thing.

Tears threaten at the loss of all those small and simple things. In this new reality, I know I've experienced day trips and fun times, but those outings are only real to the kids. Not to me. No matter how vivid the new memories become, they will never be real to me.

After a while, I alert them to my presence and tell them it's time for Josh to go upstairs. Josh says nothing, just maneuvers his wheelchair to the stairs. Katie asks if she can watch TV and I nod absently, my attention on my son. He still won't look at me.

I flank him as the lift ascends to the second floor, my footsteps muted thuds on the carpeted stairs. My heartbeat quickens the closer we get to the top. I am nervous—like a fledgling firewalker about to step onto hot coals for the first time, a grade-schooler speaking in front of the entire school, a novice skydiver staring through the gaping open door of the airplane, readying to dive into the vast blue.

I hear the voice in my head, the questions. *Why should I be nervous? Why should my hands be clammy and my forehead damp? I've bathed Josh a thousand times; why should tonight be different?*

But this voice belongs to the Emma who exists in the new reality, the reality without Lena. She doesn't understand what I stole from Josh. She doesn't know what I saw last night—that image is more vivid now than it was when I lay my head upon my pillow and wished Lena away. Tonight is different, because the old Emma of the old reality knows. She knows—*I* know that my son is no longer a little boy. He said it himself at dinner tonight. Even though he has been robbed of the memory, somewhere inside him, he knows it, too. He has become a man.

I follow Josh to his room, the hum of his wheelchair echoing in my ears. He stops beside his bed, then pivots his chair so that he faces me. After a long moment, he raises his eyes to me. They shine with hurt.

"Aye doe wah y' t' ba' m'," he says. *I don't want you to bathe me.*

I cross to him and kneel down. "Why are you upset with me, Josh? What have I done?"

I know what I've done, but I want to understand how *he* knows.

"Aye 'ot uh-se wi' y'." *I'm not upset with you.*

"I don't believe you. I can tell. We've been together a long time, you and me, Josh. You're my guy. I know you're upset. I'm just trying to figure out why."

He looks at me for a couple of beats, then throws his head back. He pulls his curled hands up to his chest and lets out a low moan.

Tears escape the corners of his eyes. I reach out and place a hand on his knee.

"What is it? Tell me. I'm sorry, for whatever it is." A smooth liar, I am. How can I ask such a question of my son when I'm fully aware of my misdeed?

"I' 'ot y'," he says. *It's not you.* "Aye doe 'o wuh i i." *I don't know what it is.* "Aye fe' ba' bu' Aye ehbaras 'ow wi' y'." *I feel bad but I'm embarrassed now with you.* "Y' thi' a m' a' a lee' boi, bu' Aye 'ot aeemo." *You think of me as a little boy, but I'm not anymore.* "Aye doe wah t' hu' y'." *I don't want to hurt you.*

I lower my head, ashamed. I have loved him and protected him and imprisoned him, rationalizing that it was for his own good. I've wanted to keep him a child because it's easier to think of him that way. But I have been doing my son a disservice. With or without Lena, he is growing into a man. Her removal from our lives is not the issue.

"It's okay, honey," I assure him. I place my hands on his wrists and gently pull them down, then interlock my fingers with his—not an easy task. "You *are* growing up, Josh. You're almost a man. Everything you're feeling is totally normal. And I'm not hurt. I promise."

He looks at me and manages a crooked grin. "Reee?" *Really?*

"Really. I'm so sorry if I made you feel badly. I never meant to do that, you know?"

He nods his head. "Aye 'o."

I smile at him. Wetness on my cheeks. "I'm going to get your dad now, okay? He can give you a bath."

He nods again. "Tha', Maah." *Thanks, Mom.*

I withdraw my hands from his grasp, then gently stroke his cheek. "No problem, my man."

His donkey bray of a laugh is welcome music to my ears. He has absolved me.

But I still bear the weight of guilt. Because I know that somewhere, buried in his subconscious, Josh is aware of my betrayal. I don't know why I am so certain of this, or how it might be possible. I only know that it is. And I resolve to make it up to him.

~

Colin accepts his task grudgingly. He slams his laptop shut with venom, as though I've interrupted something of great importance. I follow him out of his office and watch as he climbs the stairs, shoulders slouched. His defeated posture, to which I became accustomed before wishes, has returned.

Katie is immersed in a reality show based on fashion dos and don'ts. I kiss the top of her head, then move to the family room, where I boot up my computer. I don't check my email. SoundStage and their decision to leave my company mean little to me at this moment. My mind is full, old and new memories competing for valuable real estate in my gray matter.

I plan to do a Google search, but first I call up Facebook. My conversation with Katie in the food court swirls through my brain. I type in Dante's name. I've done this a lot over the past month, although I'm not sure exactly why. As before, his smiling face greets me. And as before, I move the mouse over the "Friend Request" button. My finger hovers over the mouse for an obscene amount of time before I close the page. As I told Katie earlier, my life is complicated enough.

I go to Google and enter the words *safari petting zoo* into the search bar.

~

Sunday, August 7

I wake up Sunday full of energy and enthusiasm, but not because I am eager to see the results of my wish. I made none last night. I'm anxious to get the day started. I have plans. For the first time in as long as I can remember, I have plans that fill me with excited anticipation.

The rest of my family is still asleep. Josh's heavy breathing comes through the monitor. Colin snores. Katie's door is closed.

I pad downstairs barefoot, head for the garage. On one of the storage shelves, I locate a cooler bag and two small backpacks, and I carry them with me to the kitchen. Careful not to make noise, I set an ice pack in the cooler bag then fill the bag with water bottles, juices, some string cheese for Katie, a yogurt squeezer for Josh. I fill one of the backpacks with pouches of trail mix, chips, napkins, plastic straws, then take the second backpack to the downstairs bathroom, where I load it with sunscreen, hand sanitizer, hand cream, moist towelettes, and lip balm. From beneath the sink, I withdraw one of Josh's spare urine bottles, fill it with water to check the integrity of the cap, then empty it and stuff it into the backpack.

I bypass the kitchen and walk into the family room. The tickets I printed last night lie in the output tray of the printer. I fold the sheets in half and stuff them into the backpack.

By the time I hear Josh's breathing change on the kitchen monitor, I'm all ready to go.

I hurry up the stairs and into Josh's room. He's awake, one hand grasping at the metal bed railing, his bedsheets a tangled mess between his legs.

Because of the warm summer nights, he wears shorts and a tank top. I've been trying not to see it, to keep him a child in my mind's eye, but in the morning light, I can't help but notice how much darker his leg hair has become in the past few months. The hair under his arms is still sparse but markedly thicker than it was only weeks ago. He is yet to grow noticeable facial hair. It's coming. Soon we will have to add "shave Josh" to our list of duties. I assume Colin will take that task.

"Good morning," I call to him as I approach the bed. "I'm so glad you're up. We've got a big day to—"

Josh's lips are two tight white lines; his eyes are squeezed shut. I recognize one of his many expressions of pain. I bend down over him.

"What's wrong, honey?"

"Craa," he says with much effort. *Cramp.*

I nod. "Okay. Where is it?"

"Le' ca." *Left calf.*

Reflexively, I reach for his leg, but immediately stop myself.

"Do you want me to get Dad?" I ask.

"No. Plee, Maah, i' hurs." *No. Please, Mom, it hurts.*

I place my hand on his left calf, then dig my fingertips into the straining muscle. Josh jerks with anguish, then mewls softly. How many hundreds of times have I done this over the course of his life? I hate that I'm causing him further pain, but I know what I do is for a good cause—to calm the seizing muscle and bring him relief.

I release my grasp on his leg, then rub my hands together quickly, feverishly, bringing heat to my palms. Then I place them on his calf again and begin to knead. After a moment, I feel the pop. Josh's body goes rigid then instantly relaxes. He lets go of the rail and falls onto his back, breathing heavily. I gently lay his leg on the bed, then straighten up.

"Better?"

"Yaaa," he says. "Tha', Maah."

"At your service."

He manages a smile. "Aye 'o." *I know.* His brow furrows. "Wuh w' y' sayee a'ow uh bi' dae?" *What were you saying about a big day?*

I smile back at him. "Let's get you dressed. Family meeting in the kitchen over breakfast. I'll tell you then."

~

"A what?" from Colin.

"That is so cool!" from Katie.

"Reee?" from Josh.

"Yes, really. I got the tickets online last night. Everything's set."

Colin, Kate, and I stand around the kitchen counter. Josh sits in his chair, looking up at me excitedly. When I dressed him, I chose khaki shorts, thinking them appropriate for our adventure.

Colin frowns at me, a stark contrast to Josh's enthusiasm. "Do you think this is such a good idea?"

"Actually, I do."

"I mean for Josh."

"Colin, they have wheelchair access, I checked. And trainers who work specifically with handicapable kids. It's going to be great. We're taking the kids on safari, right here in New Jersey."

"I'm still totally going to go to Africa," Katie says. "This isn't in place of that, right?"

"Of course not," I reply. "But that trip is years away, honey. I thought we might consider this a test run."

She nods vigorously and pats her brother on the shoulder. Josh donkey laughs with sheer joy, and for a moment, my heart is so full I almost can't bear the tightness in my chest.

One glance at Colin deflates me. He is shaking his head. "Emma, I think you and I should have discussed this first."

"It's Sunday, Colin. Family day. This is a fun family outing. I don't know why you're so opposed to it."

"I'm not opposed, necessarily," he retorts. "Just surprised."

I manage to smile at him. "That was the point. I meant to surprise you. All of you."

"Come on, Colin, it'll be fun," Katie says.

"Yaaa, Daah. I'uh b' asuh." *Yeah, Dad. It'll be aces.*

My breath catches. *It'll be aces.* Josh learned the expression from my mom.

"It's just, I was hoping to get some work done today." He shrugs at the kids. "Your mother keeps reminding me of my self-imposed deadlines. 'You can't sell a book if you don't have a book to sell.'"

I've never said that to Colin. His old agent said that to him. I resent my husband for making me the heavy, but I keep the smile glued to my face. This day isn't about Colin or his failures or our marriage, which may or may not be a sham.

"Well," I say, "I'm taking the kids. I bought you a ticket. You can come if you want to, and if you don't, fine." I turn my attention to Josh and Kate. "GPS says ninety minutes," I announce. "We have to get a move on. I'll make some protein smoothies to go."

~

Twenty minutes later, the kids and I are flying down the highway in the van. Josh's wheelchair is situated in the bay behind the passenger seat, secured with thick cords that attach to the door frame on one side and the underside of the bucket seat on the other side. Katie has opted to sit in the bucket seat next to him, even though the front passenger seat is empty.

I thought Colin would fold under the pressure of the children's entreaties, but he refused to come. He watched stoically from the porch, arms folded across his chest, as we pulled out of the driveway, gave a curt wave—which I did not return—then retreated into his lair.

The Best of Eric Clapton sounds from the tired speakers. Katie and Josh sing along to "Lay Down Sally." I ponder my marriage.

Before wishes, Colin and I were both miserable. Me because of the heavy burden life seemed to pile upon me, and Colin because he was married to a woman tethered to her own self-pity. Now neither of us is miserable. But he is dissatisfied and I am disillusioned.

The song comes to an end, and Katie leans forward so that I can hear her.

"What's the name of this thing, Mom?"

"Zimbabwe Zeke's Traveling Safari," I tell her. "The owner lived in Africa for a decade. He was a guide for one of the more popular safaris down there."

"Coo," Josh says. *Cool.*

"Totally, right?" Katie agrees.

"I read about him on his website. So the story goes, one of his nephews was badly injured in a car accident. His family was planning to come to Africa, and Zeke was going to take them on safari, but the kid couldn't make the trip. So Zeke decided to bring Africa to his nephew. That's why he started the whole thing."

"Reee coo." *Really cool.*

"They travel all over the country, like the circus," I tell them. "I printed up some info about it if you want to read it."

I glance in the rearview mirror. Kate and Josh look at each other and simultaneously scrunch up their faces. Obviously, neither has the slightest interest in reading about the safari petting zoo.

"I get carsick when I read," Katie declares, although she's never been so much as nauseous in any moving vehicle. "Besides, I just want to see it in person."

"M', t'," Josh agrees. *Me, too.*

"Fine," I say, smiling to myself. "Let's just crank up the tunes, shall we?"

My kids make sounds of approval. I turn the volume up, and we all join Eric for a lively rendition of "Layla."

I can't remember the last time I felt so good.

TWENTY-EIGHT

Zimbabwe Zeke's Traveling Safari has raised its tent in Asbury Park, a place eulogized in many Bruce Springsteen tunes. The doors open at noon. Because today is the last day of the safari, and also the middle of summer, we hit gridlock as soon as we reach the Garden State Parkway. It takes nearly forty-five minutes to travel three and a half miles to the downtown district.

Bored attendants wearing Day-Glo orange vests and wide-brimmed hats that do little to block the August sun direct the masses toward parking spaces. I stop, as instructed, and point to the handicapped card hanging on the rearview mirror. The attendant, a young Asian guy, nods and gestures toward a row of spaces abutting the boardwalk. I follow his wordless directions and maneuver the van into one of the few remaining empty slots.

Josh is giddy as the van lift lowers his chair to the street. Katie climbs out behind him. I glance at the massive number of people already crowding the boardwalk, tourists and locals alike, pushing and shoving and weaving right and left, a tidal wave of humanity with the power to drown my son. A young boy standing by a kiosk glances curiously at Josh, then elbows the boy next to him and starts laughing. An older couple slowly moves past us, and the woman gazes pityingly at me. Two teenage girls dressed in butt-revealing denim shorts and halter tops stare unabashedly at my son from the boardwalk railing.

A stab of uncertainty jabs at my gut, and I suddenly wonder if Colin was right, if this was a bad idea. But Josh is unaware of the scrutiny and unmoved by the crowd. He and Kate are excited, smiling exuberantly and pointing at the many shops and kiosks and sights and sounds around them. I force myself to think positively.

As I try to redirect the course of my thoughts, I realize that positive thinking does not come naturally to me anymore. Yes, I am a mother, so I am always analyzing the situation and figuring out the worst-case scenario, just like any other parent. But for a long time now, my analysis has paralyzed me, shackling me to the safe and complacent. I have allowed my fears and the drudgery that has become my life to keep me from living it, and in turn, I have kept my children from experiencing all the wonders around them.

We are here, on the Jersey Shore, on the boardwalk, about to see wild animals. A host of tragedies could occur. But it dawns on me, as Katie and I walk—and Josh rolls—across the pitted wooden slats of the boardwalk headed for the convention hall, that a host of tragedies could occur anywhere, even in the most banal and *safe* of places.

We approach the majestic, old, brick building and I scan the facade for the wheelchair-accessible entrance. I find it on the far left side of the hall. Due to the nature of the event, only small groups are allowed in at a time. The line at the main entrance is backed up almost to the sand, and I smile to myself as we bypass the enormous crowd of people, many of whom are fanning themselves with flyers, brochures, or their hands. The proximity of the ocean ensures a steady breeze, but the temperature is no less than sweltering. One of the few perks of Josh's disability is easy access to most events, attractions, and amusement parks, although we seldom visit any of those—at least we didn't BW. Hazy recollections stir in the back of my mind of our family outings, but I know that these are false memories. I am glad to be creating a real memory with my children, one that will not be obscured or erased or overwritten.

I present our tickets to the usher, a dark-skinned, middle-aged man with an easy smile and a slight accent I can't place. He refers to his clipboard and scribbles a check mark halfway down the page. Because of Josh's situation, we will be receiving special accommodations, although I'm not certain what those entail.

"Welcome to Zimbabwe Zeke's. It says here there are four in your party."

Katie glances at me. I clear my throat. "My husband couldn't make it."

"That is unfortunate. He is missing something truly unique."

I shrug and lower my eyes. Katie reaches out and gives my hand a squeeze. The man catches the gesture.

"Ordinarily, we don't give refunds on the day of the event, but I might be able to get you some food vouchers. I see that you already signed the waivers online. Just one moment while I contact your guide." He pulls a handy talkie from his belt and speaks into it. "Yes, we have the Davies party here at Gate 4. There will be three guests." He returns the device to his belt and smiles down at Josh. "Well, sir, you are about to have an extraordinary adventure. Are you prepared to be amazed?"

Josh nods, then stretches his head back and gazes up at me. "Tha', Maah."

"You are so welcome," I say. I'm thrilled that the old Josh is back, and not only because it tempers my guilt, but because he deserves these moments of happiness. For him, they are too few and too far between.

The usher gestures for us to enter the lobby.

"Kenneth will be with you momentarily."

Katie loops her arm through mine, and the three of us enter the convention hall. A guide greets us, dressed much like Josh, in khaki shorts, a short-sleeved shirt, and a vest. He wears a safari hat on his head.

"Well, hello there," he says. "I'm Kenneth, and I will be your chaperone today." He bends down to face Josh. "And what is your name?"

"Jo'," Josh says.

Before Katie and I have a chance to translate, Kenneth says, "Welcome, Josh." He chucks Josh under the chin and receives a throaty chuckle in return. I'm taken aback that this young man can understand my son, but then I realize he must have read Josh's name on a list. Still, Josh is pleased he didn't need a translator. His smile is full of teeth.

Kenneth stands up straight and looks at Katie and me. "And ladies? Names, please?"

"I'm Katie, and this is my mom, Emma."

Kenneth nods cheerfully. "Wonderful. You are in for a real treat." He herds us toward a set of double doors on the far side of the lobby. "Now, I just want to tell you a few things before we go inside. I've been with Zimbabwe Zeke's for four years. Before that, I worked as an EMT and a caregiver for special-needs individuals. That's just a little about me. All of our trainers and animal handlers have over a decade's worth of experience . . . that's more than a decade *each*, not cumulative." He winks at us. "They know their stuff, so be sure and listen closely to them and follow their instructions to the T.

"Also, we don't allow photography of any kind. I know that's frustrating, but the rule is to ensure your safety as well as that of the animals. Zimbabwe Zeke's isn't like other safari petting zoos. I don't want to say too much, because I don't want to spoil it for you." He kneels in front of Josh. "So, listen. It can be a little overwhelming. How about you and me come up with a signal. A way for you to let me know if you have any feelings of unease, discomfort, or distress."

Josh looks concerned, and Kenneth pats him on his bony knee. "I'm not saying that's going to happen, Josh. I just like to be prepared for all eventualities. Understood?"

"Uhdestoo," Josh replies solemnly. "H' a'ow thi'?" He raises his right hand to his forehead, pressing his curled thumb into the space between his eyebrows.

Kenneth nods. "That's a good one. I'll be on the lookout, but like I said, I don't expect any trouble. I only expect you to be amazed." He gains his feet and places his palm on the door, then turns back to us, a mischievous smile on his face. "Are you ready?"

Josh emits a squeal of anticipation. Kenneth pushes the door open.

Last night, it felt like kismet when I found the safari online. Not only was it happening so close to us—their next venue is New Hampshire—but today is their last day in New Jersey. I knew I had to bring Josh. And Katie. But when I read that the safari took place *inside* the convention hall, I was skeptical. Despite the size of the space, I wondered how they could simulate such a vast and boundless experience as a safari within four gray walls.

When we pass through the double doors and enter the great hall, my doubts instantly vanish.

Moving images of the African plain have been projected on all four walls of the building, creating an endless panorama. The ceiling is no longer a ceiling, but a blue sky peppered with rolling, fluffy white clouds. A warm breeze caresses my face, carrying with it the scent of earth and grass and violets.

The ground is not concrete flooring but sandy earth dotted with savannah trees, brush, and vibrant flowers of gold and orange and magenta.

The images on each of the walls contain a different view of the plains and different groups of animals: elephants drinking from a watering hole surrounded by oxpeckers, lions sunning themselves on an outcropping of rocks while cubs play nearby, zebras grazing on shrubs and twigs, giraffes chomping on acacia leaves, hippos bathing, a herd of antelope bounding across the plain, leopards perched in a tree, Cape buffalo, hyenas. In front of each projected image are enormous pens with the same groups of animals within them, overseen by animal handlers dressed in camouflage jumpsuits. The pens are made of glass or some other durable transparent material, giving the illusion that the animals are not confined.

A wide footpath lines the perimeter of the hall, and small clusters of visitors move from pen to pen, led by guides. For an additional charge, guests can gain access to certain pens, guarded closely by handlers. Across the great hall, a young woman is being led into the antelope pen by a burly camouflaged man. Even from this distance, I can see the excited apprehension on her face. A low hum of energy fills the entire space, and echoes of oohs and ahhs are underscored by the faint sound of a tribal drum.

Running through the center of the hall is a dusty winding path. A few zebras and giraffes and emus roam freely, while small vehicles carrying groups of visitors slowly wend through them.

I gaze at my children. Josh's eyes are shiny and round as twin moons. Kate wears a look of utter astonishment. Kenneth smiles knowingly.

"I've never seen anything like it."

"Yes, ma'am. I'm sure that's true." He looks down at Josh. "So, what's it to be first? A walking tour of the animal areas or a ride through the plains? We have special vehicles for special guests like you, Master Josh."

"A rie, a rie. Plee."

Kenneth nods. He withdraws his own walkie-talkie and speaks a few words into it, then leads us to the main entrance, where an open-air jeep awaits. One side has a lift similar to the one in our van. The driver, a rosy-skinned woman with short auburn hair, tips her safari hat to us, then depresses a button that releases the lift. As soon as it reaches the floor, Kenneth helps Josh maneuver his chair onto it. The lift ascends, jolts to a stop, and Kenneth secures the chair and straps Josh in. Katie and I climb onto the other side of the jeep behind the driver, and Kenneth steps onto the running board next to Josh. I sit on the left side, and Kate sits between me and her brother.

"This is Mickey," Kenneth says, jerking his thumb toward the driver. "She's got something for you."

Mickey hands us a small pail full of dry pellets. "We only allow you to feed this to the animals," she tells us. She sounds Irish. "It's all organic and made completely with grass and vegetation. Sometimes the animals want to eat, and sometimes they don't. It's early hours now, so they might be a bit peckish. I suggest you remove any earrings or necklaces and place your pocketbooks at your feet."

Katie giggles nervously, then removes her jewelry. I am wearing none, but I take off the bandanna I threw around my neck. We deposit the items into our purses, then stuff them under our seat. The jeep moves forward slowly, and Josh donkey brays with enthusiasm.

As soon as we pass the initial barrier, a zebra wanders over to my side of the jeep. Mickey brings the vehicle to a stop and the zebra flaps its ears at us.

I've never seen a zebra in person. The black-and-white zigzag patterns of its coat are almost vertiginous. The creature is stunning.

"Well, hello, Dolly," Mickey says, turning to us with a smile. "This is Dolly. She's a very lovely lady. You may touch her if you like, just remember to keep your movements slow and measured. No sudden jerks or jabs, right?"

I move my hand toward Dolly's long snout and gently brush my fingers along the top of her nose. She blinks at me and flaps her ears again. Her lips curl back to reveal a set of enormous teeth. Katie follows my lead, leans over and touches Dolly on the jaw.

"This is so cool," she whispers, her voice thick with reverence.

Dolly takes a step back and bobs her head up and down. She trots around the back of the jeep and comes up next to Josh. I sense his trepidation, but he doesn't flinch. Kenneth reaches over and takes a few pellets from the pail in Katie's lap. He grasps Josh's hand and carefully turns it palm up. Josh's fingers are curled tightly, but there is ample room on his palm for a few pellets. Kenneth guides Josh's hand toward Dolly. A moment passes during which Dolly seems to be considering things. Then she jounces toward Josh and gobbles the pellets from his hand.

Josh shrieks, and I can't tell if the sound is one of delight or abject terror until he follows it with a bray of laughter.

Mickey pulls the jeep forward, and we are next met by a giraffe who must be twelve feet tall. Its majestic neck stretches toward the faux blue sky.

"This is Fabian," Mickey says. "He's not yet full grown. He'll be seventeen feet tall when he reaches adulthood."

Fabian bows his head at us, but he isn't interested in food and won't come near enough for us to pet him. Another giraffe, smaller than Fabian, wanders over.

"Oh, Cherise. She'll be wanting some of that food. She's a beggar, she is."

"Ah th' bruth' a' sisuh? O' twi?" Josh asks. *Are they brother and sister? Or twins?*

Again, before I can translate, Kenneth answers. He must have worked with CPs before. "No, Josh, they're not. Twins are extremely rare. Giraffes generally only have one calf at a time. The gestational period is fifteen months."

"Wow," I say. "I suddenly feel lucky to be human."

"Right, Mom?" Kenneth says with a wink. "Female giraffes can have up to ten calves in a lifetime, but these two here aren't related."

As Kenneth suspected, Cherise dips her head into the jeep and grabs at the pail. Kenneth laughs and shoves her away. Josh turns to face me.

"Sh' byufuh, i' sh', Maah?"

"Yes, she is beautiful."

"Aye wah' wuh' fah a' pe," he says, and Katie laughs. *I want one for a pet.*

"I'm not sure your city ordinance would allow that, eh, Josh?" Kenneth says, then winks.

By the time we reach the far corner of the hall, our pail is empty. Ironically, the emus were the most gluttonous of the animals on our short journey. Kenneth helps Josh from the jeep, and Katie and I grab our purses and step to the ground. We thank Mickey and she gives us a cheerful wave, then begins her return trip to the entrance.

Visitors move down the footpath toward the next pen, and we insert ourselves into the group. Kenneth is giving us information about hippos, which we're about to see, regaling the kids with fun and little-known facts about the species. I listen with only half an ear, as my attention is drawn to a little girl of about seven in the group ahead of us. She holds tightly to her mother's hand and continually looks back at Josh with alarm. I can't help but think of the hairstylist's daughter and the ensuing debacle, which I chose to delete. Suddenly, I'm gripped with dread. I glance at Josh, who is animatedly explaining something to Kenneth. Kenneth smiles and nods while Katie giggles. I take a deep breath and will myself to relax. Everything is going to be fine.

We come to a stop in front of a large pen. Josh rolls his chair as close to the barrier as possible. Katie and Kenneth flank him. I stand behind him and place my hands protectively on his shoulders. He stiffens at my touch, then relaxes.

The hippopotamus pen, like all the others, has been designed to seamlessly connect with the projected image on the wall behind it. A large wading pool has been created in the center of the pen, and two of the enormous animals lounge in the water, only their heads and backs visible. Two other hippos meander outside the pool, one of them close enough to touch if it weren't for the glass.

"Tha cyu," Josh says.

Kenneth chuckles. "I'm not sure how cute they are, Josh. But I'll tell you, hippos are unpredictable creatures. They can be very aggressive and are considered highly dangerous." Kate takes a step away from the glass, but Kenneth is quick to reassure her. "Not to worry, Katie. This pen is stronger than steel. And these animals, all the animals in our safari, are pretty tame. They're used to the circus life. That's not to say that any of them are domesticated. There's no way to domesticate wild animals, not really. But you're safe."

The hippo nearest to us stretches its mouth open to reveal large canine tusks. I'm mesmerized by this strange and comical-looking mammal, with his leathery skin, enormous snout, and portly gray body. I find myself laughing for no particular reason.

"What is it, Mom?" Katie asks.

I shake my head and shrug. "It's just . . . pretty neat."

She nods in agreement.

"The Greeks called hippos river horses," Kenneth tells us. "Hippos are the third largest land mammal. Funnily enough, their closest relatives are whales and porpoises."

Once again, my eyes are drawn to the little girl. She stands a few feet from Kenneth. She stares not at the hippos, but at Josh. I watch as she tugs hard on her mother's arm. The woman gives her daughter an exasperated look.

"What, Penny?"

"What's wrong with that boy?" the girl asks, her voice at full volume. Everyone standing in front of the hippo pen goes silent. Josh and Kate turn toward the girl, and I feel myself tense.

"Penny!"

"I don't like him," the girl wails.

"Penny, shut your mouth," the mother hisses.

"He scares me."

The mother drops to her knees and grabs the girl by the shoulders, gives her a shake. "I told you to be quiet."

"What's the matter with him? He looks weird."

Primal maternal rage courses through me. I want to throttle this stupid child. My rational brain knows she is not being mean on purpose, but the urge to strike, my compulsion toward violence on behalf of my son is so intense, I have to grab the handles of Josh's wheelchair to steady myself. This, this exact occurrence, is the very thing that compels me to keep my son behind closed doors.

The wish I have been ignoring, suppressing, fleeing from, presses against the inside of my skull, throbbing, demanding to be given voice.

"Kenneth." My voice is a hoarse whisper. "Maybe we should move to the next pen." Kenneth narrows his eyes at me, and I can tell he doesn't think my suggestion is the best way to handle the situation. I do. I clench my teeth. "Now."

Finally he nods. "All right," he says. "Lots to see. Best to keep going."

As we pass the groups in front of us, Josh opens his mouth as though he wants to say something to the girl. She cringes, then ducks behind her mother. Josh closes his mouth. The mother looks at me apologetically. And although I know that kids are curious and callous without meaning to be, and that her daughter's behavior is not her fault, I can't help but glare at her.

"Ki," Josh says as we reach the lion pen.

"Yeah, kids," Kenneth agrees. "They don't have a filter."

"I' happeh a' ah," Josh says. *It happens a lot.* "I' ki'ah hurs m' feee." *It kind of hurts my feelings.*

Something inside me tears, an aching fissure of regret opens in my chest. My poor son.

"Well, I've got just the thing to cheer you up, Master Josh," Kenneth says. "How would you like to hold a lion?"

"Wa?"

"Really?" Kate asks. "Can I, too?"

I interject before my kids can get too excited. "I didn't pay the extra charge for that, Kenneth."

"Well, it's my gift to you. Is that okay, Mom? I'm not talking about a full-grown lion, by the way. Just a cub. What do you say?"

Josh looks at me expectantly, his lips curled into a grin, the little girl's cruelty forgotten.

I nod to Kenneth. Words cannot convey my appreciation. "I say . . . okay."

I'm about to learn how quickly a gift can become a disaster.

TWENTY-NINE

The lion pen is vast. A large rock formation has been erected on one side. On the other side is a roomy alcove where guests are allowed to play with the cubs. A long, thick slab of glass partitions the alcove from the main pen so that the adult lions can see their offspring.

We wait just outside the alcove while Kenneth talks to the handlers in the pen. One of the handlers is a large man with mocha-colored skin and a shaved head, the other a shorter balding man with ruddy cheeks. Both of their belts are equipped with walkie-talkies and tranquilizer guns. The sight of the guns gives me pause, but I don't mention them to my kids, who are shaking with anticipation.

After a few minutes of conversation, Kenneth approaches. He opens the wide glass gate and gestures for us to move into the alcove. As soon as we're clear, he closes the gate and locks it behind us. A sudden rush of claustrophobia passes through me.

"Okay, now, a few instructions. These cubs are about five months old. They're still nursing, but they've started on meat. They're playful but powerful. Be gentle and be wary. You can pet them, but again, no sudden movements, no loud noises. You don't want to alarm them or their moms."

The handlers are gathering two of the lion cubs. The adult lions are watchful. Although there is a tall, thick sheet of impenetrable material between us and the animals, their proximity is mind-boggling.

The cubs are the size of Labrador retrievers, covered with taupe fur. The first handler carries his cub, while the second handler leads his cub into the alcove on a makeshift leash. I look down at Josh. He is spellbound. Kate nervously fidgets with her hands.

The first handler's name tag reads Maurice. In his huge arms, the cub looks like a house cat—a house cat with a very long tongue and very large teeth.

"This here is Kimba," he says, scratching the cub under the chin. His voice is deep and reminds me of an actor's. "That"—he nods to the cub on the leash—"is Maya. They're brother and sister. Their mom is the lovely lady over there watching you."

We look past Maurice to see the lioness in question. She perches on the nearest rock, muscles tense, ready to pounce, her golden eyes never wavering from her offspring. Behind her, a large male with a dazzling mane feigns indifference.

Maya is reluctant to enter the alcove and the balding handler tugs on the leash, coaxing her forward. "Come on, girl." His name is Matt, and he speaks with an Aussie accent. "Here we go, then. That's it." As soon as Maya steps into the alcove, Kenneth closes the interior gate and locks it.

Katie drops to her knees as Matt brings the cub to her.

"Oh my God, oh my God," she cries.

"'O low' sows," Josh reminds her quietly. *No loud sounds.*

She nods, chagrined, and reaches out to touch the cub. The cub bats at her hand playfully. Matt lowers himself next to my daughter and eases the leash over Maya's head. The cub rolls over onto her back, and Kate giggles. The cub rights herself, then dashes at Katie. Surprised, Katie falls back onto her butt and Maya immediately hops into her lap, then starts swiping at the air with her paws. My daughter looks up at me, too overcome with emotion to speak.

"Katie's going to be a pediatric vet," I tell Kenneth.

"She's clearly got the knack," he replies.

Maurice brings the male cub over to Josh.

"Maah?" I hear the apprehension in his voice. I move around the wheelchair so that he can see me.

"I'm right here."

Kenneth kneels in front of Josh. He places his hands on Josh's forearms, which are curled up against his chest, and gently moves them outward, setting them down on the armrests.

"Maurice is going to place Kimba on your lap, okay, Josh? I'm going to hold your arms here, okay? And then I'll help you move them, just to keep them steady, so you can pet him. Is that all right with you?"

Josh nods, then gives me a worried look. My heart pounds, but I keep my expression neutral. If I were to smile cheerfully, Josh would know I was faking it, would sense how fearful I am. But I will not sabotage this experience for my son.

"It's okay, Josh. Everyone knows what they're doing."

"Sep' m'," he says. *Except me.*

"Just do what Kenneth and Maurice tell you to do."

A muscle twitches in Josh's cheek. The slightest motion, the barest flutter, but a portent nonetheless. Suddenly, the voice in my head roars at me to stop this, to keep the cub from my son's grasp, to escape the alcove while we still can. I open my mouth to speak, but I am too late. Maurice is already setting the young lion down on Josh's lap.

Time freezes. All the air rushes from my lungs. I hang, suspended in that ghastly limbo in which I know something awful is about to happen, but I'm powerless to do anything about it.

And then—nothing happens.

The cub settles himself on Josh's lap. Maurice straightens up and takes a small step back but remains close enough to give assistance if needed. Kenneth guides Josh's hands over Kimba's fur.

"I' sah' b' coa', t'," Josh says quietly. *It's soft but coarse, too.* "I' tikuh." *It tickles.*

Josh laughs, but with caution so as not to upset the cub. My son is rarely able to control the volume of the sounds that come out of his mouth, so I know how important and special this is to him. I sigh with relief on dual counts—one, that I didn't stop it, and two, that everything is fine.

"Aye thi' th' i' th' be' moeh a' m' eti' liey," Josh says. *I think this is the best moment of my entire life.*

My eyes fill with tears, not of pain but of joy. The fissure closes a fraction, healing ever so slightly.

And then. Something happens.

The cub is small compared with his parents, which weigh hundreds of pounds each, but he is still a sizable creature. He bats at Josh's hands, and although the action is playful, it causes the cub to shift. He scoots his hindquarters against Josh's upper thighs, then slaps his paws down on Josh's knees.

Suddenly Josh's eyes go wide with panic. With great effort, he lifts his right hand to his forehead and presses his curled thumb into the space between his eyebrows—his signal to Kenneth that something is wrong. But everything happens too quickly. Josh's right calf jerks, sending his foot forward off the bottom of the wheelchair. His head spasms backward and a strangled moan erupts from his vocal cords. This is not a seizure. It's a—

"Craa!" Josh cries. *Cramp.* He tries to squelch his actions, but the force of his agony is too great.

Before anyone can react, Josh's arms break free of Kenneth's grasp and fly together, smashing the cub and trapping him against Josh's chest. The cub snarls and struggles to break free. His claws extended, he swipes at Josh's legs. Beads of blood appear on Josh's skin, and he shrieks with surprise. I turn toward the pen to see the lioness poised to strike. I recognize the look in her eyes, the primal instinct to protect her offspring that I experienced only moments ago with the little girl. But she is a lion with no civility, no constraints, no ability to control her animal urges. She springs from the rock and lopes toward the alcove, and her frenzied attack alerts the male. He too charges the alcove.

The glass barrier deflects both lions, but their aggression is petrifying. They raise themselves on their powerful haunches and smash their weight against the gate. The gate vibrates. Hollers of alarm rise throughout the convention center, and in my peripheral vision, I see people both hurrying toward and rushing away from the lion pen. Matt is yelling into his walkie-talkie, eyeing the adult lions, one hand on his gun. Katie has shrunk into the corner of the alcove, her back pressed against the glass. Impossibly, she manages to keep Maya calm.

Maurice and Kenneth flank Josh, battling him to free the lion. Josh writhes, his arms and legs spasm violently, and his chair tips precariously to the left. Kenneth makes a grab for it, but misses. The next instant, the wheelchair tumbles over backward, taking my son and the cub with it.

The lions are snarling, hissing, pounding against the glass. *Thud, thwack, thud, thwack.* Josh lies on the ground, his limbs flailing in every direction, his head wrenching back and forth. Maurice grabs Kimba and scoots away from him. I rush to Josh and drop to the ground. Tears pour from his eyes, rivers of snot stream from his nostrils, spittle flies from his mouth as he gasps and wheezes, laboring to breathe. His eyes roll back and forth in their sockets.

"Josh. Josh! I'm right here." I try to grab his arm, but he is thrashing too much for me to get a hold of it.

"Maah," he screams. "Maah! Aye ca' d' thi! Aye hae' thi. Aye hae m'se." *Mom! I can't do this! I hate this. I hate myself.*

The fissure cracks open, a wide, dark crevasse of heartache. I no longer stand on the ledge. I am falling in.

Josh starts to seize; his entire body convulses.

"Katie! I need the stick."

Matt takes Maya from Katie, and she scrambles over to me with my purse. I dig for the tongue depressor I keep in the side pocket. I withdraw it. It's covered with tissue scraps and chewing gum. Kenneth is beside me, doing his best to hold Josh down.

My shoulders rise and fall with my own sobs and I can barely see through the tears gushing from my eyes. "I'm so sorry, Josh," I tell him, choking on the words. "This is my fault. This isn't your fault. This is mine. Stay with me, honey."

I manage to get the stick between his teeth, to keep him from biting or swallowing his tongue.

"I'm calling nine-one-one," Katie says. My brave daughter; there is no tremor in her voice, but she grips her cell phone so tightly her knuckles look like they are about to burst through her skin.

Josh rolls his head back and forth and wails, a high-pitched keening sound that echoes through the great hall.

Maah. I hate myself.

The wish slams into me like a sledgehammer. *I will. No, I can't. You can. You must.*

Suddenly, Josh goes still. His eyes meet mine. The world around us goes dark; the safari, the great hall, the guides and handlers, the animals—they disappear as though they no longer exist. Only my son. Only Josh. And me.

"What, honey?"

Something in his expression tells me he knows.

"Maah," he murmurs. I don't know whether this single whispered word is an entreaty for me to go forward with what I am about to do or a plea against it. I'll never know. It doesn't matter. The world slams back into focus around me as Josh begins to convulse. His eyes roll back in their sockets until only the whites are showing. I hold the stick between his teeth with one hand and place my other hand on his chest, over his heart. The beat is erratic.

My own heart slams against my rib cage. My pulse is a deafening roar in my ears. I close my eyes.

I wish that thing never happened.

THIRTY

Monday, August 8

I bolt upright in my bed. Predawn darkness surrounds me. That not-right feeling is a living thing, lurking in the shadows.

My bedroom is quiet. But not quiet in the way that marks the absence of a barking dog next door. Deathly silent.

Josh isn't breathing.

I spring from the bed and rush to the hallway, where the darkness swallows me. The night-light from Josh's room has gone out. I feel my way down the hall, and my hands slide across my son's closed door. Odd. His bedroom door is never closed. Perhaps I'm still asleep and this is a dream.

I turn the knob and push the door open, and the yellow glow of the night-light in the far corner of Josh's room greets me. I pad across the floor to the bed.

Josh is curled in a fetal position facing the wall. I can't see his face, only the back of his head. He doesn't move, doesn't snore. My breath catches in my throat, and my body stills. Seconds pass.

Then. Josh shifts in his sleep and emits a low wheeze.

I let out my breath, reach down and gently run my fingers through his hair. I turn and walk back to the hall, back to the bedroom, and climb into bed. Colin's side is empty. I absently wonder where my husband could be at four o'clock in the morning, then sleep overtakes me.

~

The next time I open my eyes, the sun is up and shining into the bedroom.

I glance at the bedside clock and see that I've overslept. I'll have to hurry if I want to get to work on time.

As I move to the bathroom, snippets of images come to mind from my predawn awakening. The darkness in the hall, Josh's closed door, his quiet slumber. I stop before I reach the sink.

There was no bed rail on his bed.

No. There had to be.

But it wasn't there.

I take a few steps back and gaze disbelievingly at my dresser.

The baby monitor is gone.

Wearing only my nightshirt, I race from the bedroom and down the hall to Josh's room. His bed is empty, the bedding a deformed lump shoved next to the wall.

There is no bed rail.

I back away from the open door, then stagger to the top of the stairs. I blink a couple of times. My jaw goes slack.

The wheelchair lift has disappeared.

Lions and cubs and a wish.

I take the stairs two at a time, lose my balance halfway down and bump-slide on my ass until my bare feet hit the tile landing. My chest feels as though an anvil sits upon it, and I gulp at the air, desperate for oxygen. Bright spots skew my vision and I realize I'm hyperventilating, but I can't slow down, can't stop, must keep moving until I get there.

I reach the kitchen. The sight before me is more than my fragile mind can handle.

Josh stands at the counter holding a cell phone to his ear while he takes a huge bite out of a shiny golden delicious apple. He looks up at me and grins.

"Hi, Mom. Nice ensemble."

H' Maah. Ice' ahsahb.

I stand frozen, watching as he finishes his mouthful and returns his attention to his call. He speaks animatedly into the cell phone. He's talking, his lips are moving, but the words aren't registering. I can't understand him because he is speaking normally, not in the Josh language I know.

"Morning, Mom," Katie says. She sits at the kitchen table, a half-eaten English muffin on a plate in front of her. She looks up at me, her brow furrowed. "Are you okay?"

I swallow. I can't form words. I can't move. I can only stare at Josh. My son. Who is standing on his own two feet, feeding himself—an *apple*, no less, holding a cell phone with his own hand, *talking* to someone.

I remember my wish, of course I do. But all the wishes I've made before now seem insignificant by comparison, even the extradition from the world of my former boss. When I made the wish on the floor of the alcove of the lion pen, as Josh sputtered and flailed and howled with anguish, I didn't really believe it would come true. It was too big to come true. But it has.

Pain explodes in my head as a flood of (new) memories assaults my brain. *Josh rolling over in his crib, Josh crawling, Josh taking his first step, Josh pumping his legs on a swing, reaching higher and higher until I thought he would take off.*

I press my hands against my temples, hoping to bring a stop to the onslaught of images. They are false. But more importantly, they are the past. Right here, right now, my son is *normal*. I hate myself for having that thought, but it's the truth, and I want to stay in the present. I still don't know how this wish business works. There might be a time limit.

Like Cinderella, if the clock runs out, the pumpkin and the wheelchair might return.

I have an excruciating impulse to run to him and throw my arms around him and caress and kiss every formerly useless limb.

I remain where I am.

"Don't you have to get ready for work? Mom?"

I turn to Katie. "Yes. I do. I just . . ."

"Okay, so I'll see you in twenty."

My head snaps back toward Josh. As he walks around the counter and approaches me, I look down at his legs. Even encased in thick denim, I can see how strong and muscular they are. His feet, wrapped in Nike sneakers, are long, like twin boats. This is the first time I've ever heard the soles of his feet slap against the tile floor. The sound is like a symphony. I close my eyes and listen until the sound stops. When I open my eyes, Josh stands in front of me, less than two feet away. He is much taller than me, and I have to look up to see his face. Without the usual tension and strain of his facial muscles, he is handsome. Truly handsome, not just a mother's projection. His jaw is strong and square, his nose aquiline, his eyes a deep blue, his hair dark brown, wavy and thick and longer than it used to be.

"Yo, Mom. Morning."

"Good morning, my guy," I say. The floodgates crash open. I'm crying and laughing as I pull him in for a hug.

"Whoa," he says, patting me on the back. "Heavy dose of emotion this a.m., huh?"

"Typical," I hear Katie say. "I don't even get so much as a hello and you get hugs and *good morning, my guy*." This last is said with sarcastic malice.

I pull away from Josh, even though it pains me to do so, and turn to Kate. "Sorry, honey. Good morning, my girl."

"Oh, please, Mom. Gag." She rolls her eyes, and I turn back to Josh. "Like you ever call me *your girl*."

"If you weren't such a butt, she might," Josh counters.

"You're the butt, Josh."

This dialogue between my children is not their typical banter. It contains a sharp edge. It occurs to me that without Josh's disorder, their relationship has grown and evolved differently; the dynamic has shifted. They no longer like each other. Kate is no longer his caregiver and companion; she is simply an older sibling whose thunder was stolen by the arrival of a newborn when she was not even two years old. I have taken their mutual admiration away from them, but I consider it a small price to pay for that which we have received.

"What's with the eyes?" Josh asks me.

"Seriously, Mom," Kate says. "What's your damage?"

Keep it together, I warn myself.

"It's probably the change," Katie snipes.

"I wish *you'd* change," Josh says.

"Bite me."

Josh ignores her comment. "You okay, Mom?"

I reach up and brush a strand of hair from his face. "I'm fine. I just had a terrible dream about you."

His eyes flash, and a ghost of a frown flits across his face. "That's weird. I had a bad dream, too. I can't remember it too well, but it was like . . . I couldn't move."

My shoulders stiffen. *What is a dream and what is real?*

"That sounds like a nightmare," I tell him. His life before my wish *was* a nightmare.

He shrugs. "It didn't feel terrible. I mean, I wasn't scared or upset or anything." He gazes at me intensely, as though he just asked a question and he's waiting for a response. When I give him none, he shrugs again. "Anyways, I gotta get moving." He kisses me on the forehead and brushes past me.

"No, wait!" My voice is high and shrill. I take a breath. "What . . . uh . . . what's on the agenda today?"

"We talked about this last night."

"Remind me. I'm getting old and senile."

"Parker and I are going to ride over to Jesse's house. Maybe go to the park and shoot some hoops."

Shoot some hoops. My son is going to shoot some hoops. I have no idea who Jesse and Parker are—the memories have yet to materialize, but I couldn't care less. Josh has friends. *Friends.* Kids his age with whom he hangs out. I bite the inside of my cheek to stop a fresh batch of tears.

"The new Marvel movie is out, so we might head to the Cineplex later."

"That's a long way on your bike, Josh." I nearly choke on the words *on your bike.* "Why don't I give you guys a ride?"

"Chill, Mom. We've done it before. Plus, you have to work today. Monday, remember?"

There is no way on God's green earth I am going to work today.

"I'm going to the mall with Simone, if anyone's interested," Katie says. She drops the uneaten portion of her English muffin on her plate and pushes away from the table, then takes her plate to the sink.

"That sounds like fun," I say, although my focus is firmly on Josh. I can't take my eyes off him. So tall, so long and lean. A teenager, just like any other teenager.

"You and Simone could come to the movies with us if you want," Josh says, and I'm surprised by his suggestion until I hear Katie's response.

"Forget about it, Josh. Simone is never going to go for you. And not just because you're younger. She has higher standards. Like guys who can actually pass algebra."

"I passed algebra," Josh says.

"D minus? That shouldn't even count as passing."

I can't control myself in time. "You got a D minus in algebra?"

"Mom," Josh says, his tone full of complaint.

"Did you totally hit your head when you got up this morning, Mom? Josh got a D in every subject."

"I got a C in shop," he counters.

"Oh, wow, call the newspaper. Any moron can get a C in shop."

This doesn't track. My son's IQ is in the superior category, brushing up against genius. How could he have gotten mostly Ds and one C?

Doesn't matter, Emma. He has working legs and arms and everything.

"Katie, that's enough," I say, because I think I'm supposed to reprimand her for her insulting remark. Since I'm doing my best to block the new memories so that I can stay in the moment, I have to rely on my instincts.

"Your brother is doing his best."

"Oh, please. I got one A minus in calculus and you'd think I was doing heroin with the lecture I got."

"That's enough," I repeat. Josh and Katie glare at each other, which I assume is their (new) normal. I glance around the kitchen, and for the first time, I realize that Colin is nowhere to be seen. I turn to Josh.

"Where's your dad?"

He turns to Katie and a curious look passes between them. I swivel to face Katie.

"Where's Colin?"

She cocks her head to the side, then marches over to me and places her hand on my forehead. "Do you have a fever? Are you having an acid flashback?"

"He's at his apartment," Josh says quietly.

This just isn't working, Emma. You don't love me anymore. I don't know if you ever did. I think you needed me, at first, but you don't now. You've got your job and your kids and I'm superfluous. Maybe if I were the successful author you thought I would be, things would be different. I'm trying to be that for you . . . killing myself to be that, but I don't know if I ever will. I need to be with someone who loves me for who I am, not what they want me to be. Someone who lets me in. Someone who opens up to me. Someone who cares that I'm here.

I shudder with the sudden recollection. I know my kids are watching me closely, wondering what the hell is going on with their mom. I raise my eyes to the ceiling and pretend nonchalance.

"I know he's at his apartment. I thought he was coming over with some papers to sign." How quickly I've become an accomplished deceiver.

"You're going to be late for work," Katie says. She strides past me and heads for the living room. Josh moves to follow her from the kitchen.

"Hey," I call. "Family dinner tonight."

They both stop and turn back to face me, wearing dual expressions of puzzlement.

"Family dinner?" Josh repeats.

"That's right. Family dinner."

"Why tonight?" he asks.

Because I want to sit with you and watch your lips move and hear you speak. I want you to tell me all kinds of fascinating things that I won't have to translate.

"Are you going to invite Colin and Eliza?" Katie says with a sneer.

Eliza, young, looks just like me, has lots of money and a daddy complex.

I stiffen. "No. Just the three of us."

"I'm supposed to go to Simone's."

"Yeah, Mom, and I'm hanging with Parker and Jesse."

I will not be swayed. "You can *hang* with them afterward. You guys are spending the whole day with your friends. You can take a break for family dinner. I'll make your favorite. Spaghetti."

Katie rolls her eyes. "Whatever." She turns on her heel and heads for the stairs. *The stairs with no lift.*

"You sure you're okay, Mom?" Josh asks.

I smile at my son. My smile feels neither strained nor false.

"I'm good, honey." *I am. I've never been better.*

He smiles back. "Okay. Parker's going to be here in a few minutes. I'll see you later?"

I nod then watch as he walks (*walks!*) to the living room, phone in hand. He plops down on the couch and starts to text. *Text! Josh is texting!*

My heart bangs a strident rhythm. I trot to the stairs and take them two at a time.

In the master bedroom, I peruse Colin's closet. My clothes line the rack. I stare briefly at the absence of my husband's wardrobe, waiting for some feeling of anger or resentment or heartache. It doesn't come.

While a small part of me grieves for the loss of my marriage, I would be lying—again—if I didn't admit that another part of me celebrates. Nothing—not Josh's poor performance in school, not the overt antipathy between him and Katie, not even the dissolution of my marriage—can impede the joy I feel right now. Josh is walking! Josh is speaking! Who cares about the rest of it?

Truth be told, in the rare, small spaces of quiet I was granted in my former life, I often wondered whether Colin and I would have stayed together if that *thing* hadn't happened. I would lie awake, listening to Josh's breathing and my husband's snoring, and I would think, *what if?* I needed Colin, because to raise a CP child alone was inconceivable. But *what if?*

On the day of our wedding, when I cleaved myself to him and promised to love, honor, and cherish him, I stood at the altar knowing myself to be an impostor. Because although I did love Colin, and because he was saving me from single motherhood, I knew we were doomed. Because I did not want him, not as I had wanted before. Did not love him as I had loved before.

I cross to the bed and sit, then reach for my cell phone and yank it from its charger. I make the call.

"Hi, Val," I say when she answers. "I'm not coming in today. I'm feeling (*euphoric, ecstatic, elated*) under the weather."

"Emma, no, Em, you have to come in. Richard Stein just called. He got your email. He wants to meet with you this morning."

"I can't." I am not conflicted.

"You have to." Her tone is imploring, and I know why. She's my executive assistant. If I get sacked, her job is in jeopardy.

"I can't," I repeat. "I have a fever and I just puked all over my comforter. I don't think we'll get SoundStage back if I puke all over Mr. Stein, do you?"

A beat. "I'm just worried," Val says.

"I'm not, Val. Reschedule."

"And if he won't?"

Then fuck him.

THIRTY-ONE

Timing is crucial.

I hurry through my morning ablutions, then don a pair of jeans, a light cotton shirt, and my Crocs. I step into the hall at the exact moment Kate alights from her room. She looks at my outfit and narrows her eyes.

"You're wearing that to work?"

"Casual Mondays," I reply. "New thing."

She follows me down the stairs, and I can feel her eyes boring into the back of my head. She knows something is going on with me, but not exactly what. And how could she?

Just as I reach the landing, the garage door slams. I grab my purse and rush to the front door. The pictures on the breakfront catch my eye, and I pause. All of Josh's pictures have changed. The wheelchair is gone. The photos depict a different life: Josh standing in the driveway palming a basketball, running though the waves at the beach, sitting on a rock, lying on a hammock, and always sporting a Cheshire smile.

The pictures of Colin and me are gone.

Outside, adolescent voices call out greetings. I hurry to the front door.

"Oh, sure, don't say goodbye to me," Katie says sarcastically. I ball my fists. I don't have time for this.

"Goodbye, honey." I reach for the doorknob. "Have fun with Simone."

"Um, Mom, I need the keys to the Civic." I turn around to see Katie tapping her foot impatiently and holding her hand out to me.

"What am I supposed to drive? The van?" My brain catches up too late. *We don't need a van because Josh is no longer disabled.*

"The what? Mom, you're totally freaking me out this morning. What the heck is going on?"

"I'm sorry, Katie," I say, shoving my hand into my purse. "I haven't had my coffee yet and I'm still in a daze." I pull out a key ring with an inordinate number of keys attached to it. The Civic key is connected to the ring by way of a carabiner. I detach it and give it to Katie. The voices outside have quieted, and I struggle to stay calm. Katie stares at me, her jaw tight, but she says nothing.

"Be careful driving, okay, Katie? See you tonight."

I pull open the front door and rush to the porch. Halfway down the steps I realize Josh's ramp is gone. *Of course it's gone.*

I stop at the herringbone pathway and gasp. Not because there is a C Class Mercedes sitting in the driveway next to the Civic. But because at this moment, my son is slinging his leg over the seat of a bicycle. *A bicycle.*

Another teenage boy—Parker?—with too-long sandy-blond hair wearing tattered cargo pants and a Nirvana T-shirt, is already astride his bike. He urges Josh on. "Come on, man. Let's go."

I feel my mouth drop open again—*my* new normal—as Josh effortlessly glides down the driveway and into the street.

Miracles do happen. Wonders never cease. My amazement is profound and unsettling, and suddenly my legs are beset with tremors so violent, I'm afraid I'll collapse onto the bricks. I steel myself. If I fall down, will I get up? And if I am unable to get up, how will I follow Josh? He'll disappear from view, and I'll lose track of him. No, I can't collapse, cannot falter in any way.

When I'm certain my legs will not give way, I hustle to the Mercedes. Although I've never seen this car before wishes, I know it like the back of my hand. I depress the button on the fob, and the doors unlock. I slide behind the wheel and turn on the ignition.

As I shift into reverse, I see Louise Krummund approaching the fence between our properties. She looks as though she wants to talk. Too bad, Louise. Not today. I cast her a curt wave, then pull into the street. By the time I shift into drive, Josh and Parker are at the end of the block, making a right-hand turn. I realize that Josh isn't wearing a helmet, and a surge of fear grips me. He should be wearing a helmet.

This isn't his first day on a bicycle, Emma. He's been riding since he was four.

Guys don't wear helmets, Mom. It looks gay.

You are gay.

Shut up, Katie.

Make me, Josh.

Enough!

I take a deep breath and gently place my foot on the gas pedal, slowly easing the silent automobile down the street. I mustn't let Josh see me. I want to observe him in his environment. I feel akin to a spy or a secret agent or a cop on deep cover. Or a scientist peering at a new life form on the slide of a microscope. I watch the road, make appropriate stops, pull over when a car threatens to tap my bumper, and stay aware as a driver, all the while keeping constant watch on Josh. And every time my eyes find him again, I experience that same exhilaration I felt when I first beheld him in the kitchen.

Tears flow, ebb, flow again, cycling through to laughter, full-blown, belly-aching laughter. The radio plays softly, an old Aerosmith tune. I haven't listened to Aerosmith since college. I crank up the volume and sing along, surprised that I know the words.

Josh rides his bike effortlessly, sometimes carelessly, and my heart stops more than a few times as he weaves into traffic then cuts back into the bike lane.

I watch and watch and watch, soaking in the sight of my son on two wheels. Two very different wheels than those that have carried him until now. My cell phone rings. I ignore it.

Ten minutes later—an eon, a millisecond—Josh and his friend come to a stop in front of a ranch-style house. I pull to the curb several houses down. The boys hop off their bikes and drop them onto the lawn, then head for the front door where another teenager—Jesse?—awaits. Fist bumps, back slaps, cheerful greetings, and they disappear into the house.

I move forward, stopping in front of the neighboring yard, shift into park, and gaze at the ranch-style house. Gauzy curtains hang in the window; shadowy shapes move behind them, then disintegrate. I wonder what they're doing in there, but not with any real concern. They are kids doing what kids do. *Josh* is doing what kids do.

I realize that I might be here for a while and shut off the engine. My stomach growls. I root around in my purse and come up with a PowerBar. I don't remember putting it there, I just know it's there. I peel back the wrapper and take a bite, then reach for my cell phone. One missed call: Wells. He's probably furious with me. *I don't care.* I should call him back. *Not now.*

The phone rings in my hand, surprising me. It slips from my grasp and falls to the passenger bay. I bend over to retrieve it, assuming it must be Canning or Wells again. It is neither. The LCD reads "Colin." My estranged husband. I'm not sure why I answer, but I do. Perhaps it's because I've never spoken to Colin while enjoying the reality of having a normal teenage son.

"Hello?"

"Hello, Emma." Formal, removed.

"Hello, Colin."

"Are you on your way to work?"

No. "Yes. Why?"

"I just got off the phone with Katie. She called me. She's worried about you."

"I'm fine, Colin. But thanks for the interest."

"She said you're acting strangely, saying crazy things."

The little Judas.

"She's sixteen, Colin. Everything her mother says sounds crazy."

"Kate is very perceptive, Emma. How many times have you told me that?"

"I had a lousy night's sleep, that's all. I was just a little tired and out of it this morning."

"Look, I know you're stressed with work. If you need me to take the kids, just for a few days—"

"No!" I draw a shallow breath. "No, Colin."

"I have them this weekend anyway. I could take them, say, Wednesday."

"I said no." I will not lose one minute of time with Josh. I quickly change the subject with a reflexive question. Reflexive, I assume, in this new reality, as it springs from my mouth without prior thought or scrutiny. "How's Eliza?"

He sighs. "She's fine."

"How wonderful for you."

"Why do you do this?"

"Is she helping you with your manuscript, Colin? She's probably a terrific typist."

"I finished the manuscript."

I try to keep the astonishment from my voice. "Wow."

"Yeah. I don't know if it's any good, but Lawrence seems to think he can sell it."

"You're back with Lawrence?"

"I was never *not* with Lawrence," he says, irritated.

I make a conscious decision not to sift through the new memories in my head. I don't need to get up to speed with Colin and his life right now. But I can be happy for him.

"Congratulations, Colin. I mean it."

"Thanks." He is silent for a beat, then says, "Maybe you can read it sometime. Give me your notes."

"You have Eliza for that."

He snickers. "Novels about twentieth-century literary figures aren't really her thing. She's more of a chick-lit kind of girl."

"Lucky you."

"Anyway, let me know if you need anything, okay, Em? I know we're separated, but I still care about you."

The front door of the house opens, and I sit up at attention.

"I have to go. I'm at work. 'Bye."

The boys emerge from the house, laughing raucously at something. Another teenager is part of the group, bringing their sum to four.

I end the call and toss the cell into my purse, then make myself completely still. If Josh looks this way, I will be caught. He knows this car. If I don't move or flinch or breathe, he might not notice me. I should have parked farther down the street.

A few seconds pass as Josh and his friends gather up their bikes. He glances in my direction but doesn't spot me. I exhale as he jumps onto his bike and follows his friends down the block.

∼

They ride all the way downtown, a posse of teenagers. Their riding is more erratic than before, as though they are emboldened by their greater number. It takes strategic driving on my part to stay behind them, and several times I'm forced to veer into an alley or a parking lot to give them time to pull ahead.

I can't hear them, but I see their enthusiastic repartee. At one point, Josh throws his head back and laughs. A donkey bray of laughter echoes in my mind and I smack at my forehead, forcefully enough to smart. I loved his laughter, I did, but he doesn't laugh that way anymore. I struggle to access a memory of his (new) laughter, but none comes. I hope to get close enough without being seen so that I can hear what he sounds like now.

I'm not surprised by their destination, only unnerved. The four boys guide their bikes up to the sidewalk in front of the comic book store next door to Mimi's Hair Salon and across the street from Paw-Tastic Pets, Dolores's antiques shop, and Lettie's second-floor psychiatric practice.

I pull to the curb at a meter directly in front of the pet store, as I've done on numerous occasions in the last several weeks. I try not to think of Charlemagne, or the dollhouse, or the strange little woman who sold me a lion necklace that I hid in the drawer of my desk, or the therapist who doesn't think I'm insane. Instead, I concentrate on Josh and his friends.

They've joined an even larger group, and I recognize some of the boys from the day we came for a haircut. If my faded recollection of that (altered) day can be trusted, the group of teenagers was there before we went into Mimi's and remained there until well after the paramedics left with my son. This is their hangout. Josh could be here for hours, shooting the breeze, riffling through comics from the outside racks.

I squint across the street. Two of the teenagers, dressed in black jeans and flannel shirts despite the August heat, greet Josh. One of them looks familiar. He says something, and Josh bursts into laughter. Parker joins in.

I feel confined by the Mercedes. I can't see my son well enough from my car and I can't hear him at all. I need to get closer.

A few doors down from the comic book store is a street café with potted ficus trees lining the perimeter of an outdoor seating area. If I were to get a table in just the right spot, I'd have a perfect, and perfectly hidden, view. But I'll have to cross the street at the very end of the block to escape detection. Which means I'll have to pass by the pet store and Dolores's antiques.

I get out of the car and shove some quarters into the meter, then trot over to the nearest building. I stay close to the storefronts, hoping they'll camouflage my approach should Josh glance my way. I stride quickly past Paw-Tastic Pets without looking in the window. I know Charlemagne won't be there. I don't know if he's still in that cage in the back corner of the store, but I tell myself I don't care. Josh can walk. Josh can bike. Josh can joke with his friends and type on his cell phone and laugh without constraints. Josh can do *anything*. There is no comparison between that and the fate of a little dog.

My pace slows as I pass Dolores's store. Try as I might to keep my attention on the sidewalk in front of me, I can't help but glance into the front display. Mistake. The dollhouse is still there, and although I don't stop or slow my pace, I see it. And I know, as I continue toward the end of the block, that what I saw was neither a figment of my imagination, nor a hallucination. It was there. On the first floor of the dollhouse, next to the kitchen table. An empty wheelchair.

Gooseflesh rises on my arms. I want to turn around and run back to the shop and look in the window and ask that strange little woman what the hell is going on. But I force myself to stay the course, because I'm not sure I really want to know.

I don't want to know.

If this is all a dream and I'll wake up at any moment, if this is an extended hallucination or lunacy or if I've died and I'm experiencing one final delusion of consciousness before I depart this earthly realm, then so be it. I don't care. If any of those are true, I will wring out as many moments of seeing my son as a physically whole person as I possibly can.

I stay the course. But I feel Dolores's eyes on me.

I reach the café without being seen, buy myself a latte and a ready-made sandwich, then step out onto the patio and choose a table that affords me a slightly obscured view of the comic book store.

Josh is leafing through a comic book. One of the black-clad kids saunters over to Josh. I flinch with sudden recognition. It is *that boy*. He procures a pack of cigarettes and offers one to my son. To my horror, Josh takes it.

"Thanks, dude."

Josh walks and talks and smokes.

The mother in me, the lioness protecting her young, is compelled to march over to him and yank the cigarette from his lips. *What then? Give him a spanking? Send him home? Forget the cigarette. He's a teenager. A normal teenager trying out stupid things like all his friends. He has* friends. *Let him be, let him do this, just today. If this isn't a dream and he's still* normal *tomorrow and the next day and the day after that, then you can reprimand him, punish him, ground him. But today, let him be and be thankful that he* is.

I sip at my latte. And watch.

A moment later, the proprietor of the comic book store comes out and glares at the group of teens.

"Come on, guys, I've told you before. No smoking out here."

"It's a free country, dude," *that boy* tells him.

"Yes, it is," the man says. "You're free to smoke elsewhere."

That boy puffs up his chest. "You gonna make us leave? We spend a lot of coin at your store."

The man takes a breath. "I know," he says calmly. "And I appreciate it. But I have the right to ban smoking within a twenty-five-foot radius of my store."

"Fuck that." Josh. My throat tightens. "You gonna call the cops?"

"If I have to."

"Come on, bro," Parker says. "Let's get out of here."

"No, wait," Josh says. "Look here, dude. One, two, three . . ." Josh counts out loud, taking a step away from the store with each number. By the time he reaches twenty-five, he stands in the middle of the street.

A car horn blares, and my heart jackhammers as a Prius screeches to a halt inches from Josh's knees.

"You're gonna make me stand in the street?" he calls to the man. "That's, like, putting a minor in harm's way. Isn't that against the law?"

The other teenagers laugh, but I am aghast. My son is behaving abhorrently.

Just like any other teenager, I remind myself.

"Get out of the street," the man yells. The driver of the Prius lays on the horn again. Josh smirks then ambles back to the sidewalk.

Josh. My sweet little boy.

"Put it out or get out," the man says.

"I'm done anyway," Josh says. He drops the butt to the ground and smashes it with his sneaker. His friends follow suit. *That boy* takes one last long drag on his cigarette then makes a show of putting it out against his left palm. The other boys hoot and cheer him on.

"Teenagers can be troublesome, can't they?"

I look up to see Dolores standing beside my table. My neck spasms with tension.

"Do you mind if I sit with you for a moment?"

I don't answer. "What is it you want?"

Without an invitation, the old woman pulls out the chair next to mine and lowers herself onto it. "Well, I saw you walk by and thought I should say hello and see if there's anything you'd like to discuss."

Like why there's an empty wheelchair in your dollhouse. I don't respond.

"It's good to see you, Emma," she says. "How are you?"

"Fine." I don't want to get into a dialogue with her. I just want to watch my son. I turn away from her and return my focus to Josh.

A flash of sunlight assaults my eyes as the glass door to Mimi's Hair Salon opens. Devi, Lola's daughter, walks out of the salon, clutching her mother's hand. The hairstylist turns toward the teenagers and frowns. The group of boys goes silent as each of them sees the mother and daughter.

A ripple of laughter threads its way through the boys, and soon, they are all laughing, including Josh.

"Wha' are they laughing a'?" Devi asks her mom as they move in the opposite direction down the sidewalk.

"Wha' are they laughing a'?" Josh mimics unkindly, and his compatriots go into fits of hysterics. Bile rises from deep within me. I'm going to vomit.

"Troublesome and cruel," Dolores says quietly. "That's a *normal teenager* for you."

I stand so quickly I almost overturn my chair. I leave my latte and the sandwich on the table and scurry from the patio without saying a word.

~

I hide in my car for an interminable amount of time. It's better from here. Safer. I can't read too much into Josh's body language, nor can I hear what he says. I can merely appreciate how he moves with such ease and speaks with such vitality. Even after witnessing his unthinking cruelty, seeing him like this is a wonder.

An hour passes during which time I *miss* six calls from work. Three from Val, one from Bill Canning, one from Edward Wells, and one from Wally. I don't listen to the voice mails.

Just before noon, the four boys trade fist bumps with the rest of the group, then grab their bikes and hit the street. I follow them for several blocks to the Cineplex, then watch as they buy their tickets and head inside.

I debate whether I should buy a ticket and follow them, but I know the odds of my getting caught are greater within the walls of the theater.

I gaze at my son until he is completely out of sight, then pull away from the curb and make my way home.

The Civic is gone when I arrive, and I'm grateful that I don't have to face my daughter. I need some time alone to sort through my thoughts and my memories, both old and new.

The first thing on my checklist: look at my journal to see if I made an entry for last night. I have no memory of writing down that wish. In fact, there exists in my mind a black hole between Josh's seizure at the safari exhibit and my predawn somnambulist trek to his room. I know the rest of yesterday happened—I can contrive the events that transpired: the ambulance transporting us to the nearest hospital, Colin arriving and taking Katie home, me staying by Josh's side, listening to the drones and beeps of the machines attached to him, falling asleep in the bedside chair. The scenario is a repeat. But while I know what occurred, when I think of the specifics, the time, the place, there is only nothingness where an image should be.

I should probably be worried. But I don't have time.

Upstairs in the master bedroom, I sit on my bed and pull out the drawer of my nightstand. I withdraw my journal and flip to the last page. There is no mention of the wish.

I uncap the pen and make an entry: *Yesterday, I wished that that thing had never happened, that Josh would no longer be disabled. It came true. Josh had cerebral palsy. Don't forget, Emma. He used a wheelchair. Don't forget.*

I close the book and set it back in the nightstand.

The second thing on my checklist: I go to the family room. On the far wall are built-in shelves containing books and trophies. Before wishes, the trophies belonged only to Katie—cheer camp winner, girls' softball league, creative writing competition, coed soccer. Now Josh's name is etched into many of them—Little League baseball, boys' basketball, regional freestyle swimming bronze medal, intramural tennis. I run my fingers along the engraved letters that spell JOSHUA DAVIES.

Above the trophy shelf is a row of photo albums. I withdraw a large brown album and carry it with me to the couch. My hand shakes as I open the cover. I know what I will see—the false memories are crowding my brain, demanding attention—but the photos are real, tangible.

There he is. Josh, a baby, gorgeous. Inquisitive eyes, hands reaching up up up. Josh and Katie when we first brought him home, big sis giving the newborn a suspicious glare as if to say, *Is he really staying?* Josh, a toddler, grasping the edge of the coffee table, already standing at eight months. Josh, on the move, waddling away from a laughing Colin.

I pore over every image on every page, laughing, crying, breathing, arguing with myself. I tell myself these photos, these images and memories are not real, but I believe in them anyway. Isn't it true that manufactured memories are more real than lies? Human beings lie to themselves all the time. *I'm happy, I'm healthy, I'm fine, I'm doing what I always wanted to do, I love him, I love her, it's not cheating, it's not stealing, it's not coveting.* Just because we talk ourselves into believing the lies doesn't make them truer than a memory constructed by a hope, a prayer, a *wish*.

I push the debate aside so that I can appreciate what I see. The photos tell a tale so disparate to the one I know, of a boy, confident, egotistical even, sometimes mean, sometimes caring. A boy who plays basketball and tennis and baseball. A boy who doesn't appreciate what he has because he's a kid and doesn't need to.

When I reach the end of the very last album, shadows have engulfed the family room. I glance at the clock and see that afternoon has turned to evening.

I put the albums back on the shelves and go to the kitchen, turn on the lights, and head for the fridge. I pull out the sausage and peppers, then go to the cupboard and grab a jar of sauce and some pasta.

I cook with fervor, my movements manic. I keep picturing Josh as he was BW and as he is now. I cannot question my wish. I cannot undo my wish. I can only move forward.

When he walks into the kitchen a short time later on his sturdy legs, and hugs me with his muscular arms, and smiles down at me with that extraordinary mouth, I am exhilarated anew. Until.

"So, Mom, can I take a rain check on the whole family dinner thing?"

I realize the hug was a bribe.

"How was the movie?" If I ignore the question, will it go away?

"Totally awesome. So about dinner?"

"Josh, no. No rain check."

His tone shifts in an instant. "Come on, Mom! Seriously. We can do it another night."

"No, Josh. Tonight. I want to hear all about the movie and your day." *And why on earth you were smoking and how you could possibly make fun of a child with Down syndrome.*

He stamps his foot. "Family dinner is bullshit, Mom."

"Josh," I warn, even though I've already heard him use the F word today.

"It is!" he says. "Family dinner. *Right.* You and Dad are getting a divorce, he's with Eliza, Katie hates me. You work all the time. What family? It's total BS. It's like you suddenly get a bug up your ass and want to do the whole mom thing. And that's cool. But I already have plans." He stops his tirade and looks at me. His expression hardens. "Look, I'm spending the night at Jesse's. Parker is going to the lake with his family tomorrow, so this is like the last time we can all hang out before summer's over."

I'm taken aback by his tirade, his manner, and the way he speaks to me. What kind of son have I raised? "And what if I say no?"

"Are you? Are you saying no? That would totally suck, Mom."

I stare at him. My tall, handsome, *cruel* son. I take a breath. "Why don't you stay for a little while, Josh. We don't have to have dinner. But let's just sit down at the table and talk. Just for a few minutes."

He gives me a pained look. "About what?"

The stars, the universe, time travel, Greek mythology, all the things you used to talk about. "Whatever you want."

"Gee, Mom, that sounds really fun," he says, his voice rife with sarcasm. "But the guys are waiting for me outside."

"You could invite them in."

"No way. Ew. I'm going."

"Josh, wait. Just stay a little longer." I'm pleading with my son.

"Can't, Mom. I'm out. We'll do the whole BS family dinner tomorrow night. Okay? Thanks."

He trots out of the kitchen and heads up the stairs. I stand, hands on hips, staring after him. A few minutes pass. He reappears carrying a backpack. He doesn't bother to kiss me goodbye, just tosses a wave over his shoulder. I hear the front door slam shut behind him.

My cell phone rings. I grab it from the counter. The LCD screen displays Katie's name.

"Hi, Mom. So, Simone's dad is taking their family to Magritte's for dinner. You know Magritte's, right? Totally swag, and they invited me along. Is that okay?"

"Yes," I tell her. "Family dinner's been rescheduled anyway."

"Thanks, Mom. You're the best."

I set the phone down and begin to put away the spaghetti dinner. It will keep until tomorrow, although I suspect something else will come up that will interfere with those plans.

I think about Josh's words. *What family?* It's difficult to accept the fact that Josh's disorder created and solidified our family unit. Without the wheelchair, my husband is gone and my children and I are merely individuals sharing the same space.

Instead of eating, I pour myself a healthy glass of red wine and carry it to my computer. I don't pay bills or read emails. I don't surf. I log on to Facebook. I read some posts of anonymous Facebook friends.

Out of habit, I click on the CP Parents page, then remember that Josh doesn't have CP.

Halfway through the wine, I click on Dante's page. Before I can change my mind, I move the cursor to the "Friend Request" button and tap my mouse. *Request sent.* I quickly close the browser and shut down the computer.

~

Without Colin, Kate, and Josh, the house is eerily quiet. I lie in bed, a novel open in my lap. I don't read. I don't wish. I listen to the silence.

THIRTY-TWO

Tuesday, August 9

When I arise the next morning, I half expect to see the stair lift, the bed rail, the ramp on the porch, and my disabled son in his wheelchair. How could a wish of such magnitude come true and *stay* true?

But there is no lift, no bed rail, and no Josh, and I remember that he spent last night at his friend Jesse's.

There is also no Colin, no CNN or espresso aroma wafting up from downstairs.

I check my cell phone. No text or call from Josh. I shouldn't expect my fifteen-year-old son to be up at this hour, but for some reason, his lack of communication needles at me. It's not just concern for his safety and well-being, which is a typical feeling for a mother. More than that. I've only had one day with him as he is now. I want to see my son again, standing up, walking, talking to me. I don't care if he's angry or mean or rude or disrespectful or bad in school. All of these are vagaries of youth, trademarks of adolescence. He will outgrow them as he grows older. If he remains in this form, as an adult he will be able to do anything he wants, be anything he wants to be. I know he's a good person at his core. I *know* it.

As a mother, as a parent, I have spent the entirety of his life grieving for what he was not and secretly longing for a normal child. Today, he is. I just want to see him as he is *today*. To revel in his normalcy as I did yesterday and as I hope to do tomorrow.

I shoot him a quick text asking him to call when he can, then head for the bathroom. I can't avoid work again, much as I'd like to. I didn't check our finances last night, so I don't know whether Colin contributes financially to the household, but I am clearly still the main provider. I need my job.

By the time I shower and dress and go downstairs, Katie is already in the kitchen.

"I prepped the coffee for you," she says from the table. "So you wouldn't be as out of it this morning as you were yesterday."

"I'm sorry about that," I say. I press the button on the Mr. Coffee machine. The espresso machine is gone. "How was dinner last night?"

"OMG, amazing. You have to go there. I had the seared salmon with shiitake mushrooms. It was to die for."

I cross to the table and sit opposite my daughter.

She looks beautiful this morning in a pale-peach cap-sleeve blouse that brings out the green of her eyes.

"And the dessert? Molten chocolate cake with shaved white chocolate and a raspberry something sauce."

"Was it coulis?"

"That's it. How'd you know that?"

Because Dante made it for me. I shrug.

Katie looks at me. "You're better today, huh?"

"I was fine yesterday, too." Lie. "But yes. I feel better today."

"This is kind of nice," she says, her voice barely above a whisper. "Just you and me."

"It is nice," I agree.

"Simone and Lisa and Erica and I are going to that volleyball day camp today, but I'll be home for family dinner."

"Great, honey. And thanks for prepping the coffee. That was very thoughtful of you." *And I'm going to need it to face the music at work today.*

~

It happens as soon as I reach the office. Val rushes at me like a linebacker and grabs my arm at the elbow.

"Mr. Canning wants to see you in his office immediately."

"Can I put my purse down?"

"You didn't return any of our calls," she says, grabbing my purse from my hands. "Mr. Wells even went by your house at lunch. You weren't there."

"I was at the doctor."

She gives me a skeptical look. "I'll put your purse on your desk. You should go. Now."

I yank my purse out of her grasp, withdraw my cell phone, and hand it back. "Thank you."

I move past her and walk down the hall, dialing Josh's number as I go. I still haven't heard from him, and a prickle of unease has taken root at the base of my spine. My call goes straight to voice mail.

"Hi, honey. It's Mom. I know you're probably still sleeping, but can you call me as soon as you wake up?"

I end the call and square my shoulders as I reach Bill Canning's office. I knock softly and hear one of my bosses say, "Come."

This is a repeat of my meeting with them on Friday. They stand in front of Canning's desk, arms crossed over their chests. I take a seat and face them. For a split second, I close my eyes and imagine Josh riding his bicycle down the street. I open my eyes and find my bosses glaring at me.

"Well, Emma," Edward Wells begins. "How are you feeling?"

I manage a faint smile. "Better, thanks."

"You must have been feeling awful," Canning says. "I mean, I can only imagine, since you were unable to answer our repeated calls."

"I think it was a twenty-four-hour stomach flu. Very difficult to answer the phone when you're vomiting. I even had to go to urgent care."

"Really." Wells's turn. "How were you able to drive yourself?"

"At some point there's nothing left to throw up."

"Emma." Canning. "We're very concerned about the SoundStage ordeal. Apparently, you sent an email to Richard Stein and the CEO that moved them to reconsider their decision. But then, when it came to crunch time, you were nowhere to be found."

Josh walking to me, kissing my head. "Hi, Mom."

"I was sick."

"Be that as it may. Since you were unable to meet with them, they have solidified their agreement with another company."

"I'm sorry to hear that," I say. "I'm sorry they couldn't wait one more day to meet with me."

"Yes. So are we," Wells says. "On Friday we talked about giving your situation a few weeks. But in light of this setback—"

A knock on the door interrupts the old man. He scowls. "Come."

Valerie opens the door a crack and peers in. Her expression is grave. "I apologize for the interruption . . ."

"Yes, yes, get on with it," Canning says impatiently.

"I need Emma . . . Ms. Davies. There are some people here to see her, and it's important."

My breath catches in my throat. "Who?"

Val looks at the floor, at my bosses, at the stupid landscape watercolor on the wall. Anywhere but at me. "You should come."

Bill Canning and Edward Wells seem to intuit that something is very wrong. "Go," Canning says.

I push myself out of my seat. Never have I felt so heavy as I do now, as though I am covered in a thick layer of tar. My legs are lead. I give Val a questioning look, but she continues to avoid my eyes. She turns and walks down the hall, and I follow. Every step is a torturous challenge.

When I reach the end of the hallway, I see them. They stand inside my office, both awkwardly shifting their weight from foot to foot, speaking to each other in low tones.

I do not want to talk to them. Don't make me talk to them.

"Emma?" Val's voice is far away.

As I approach my office, the two men turn and see me through the glass. One is older, gray haired and heavyset. One is in his late twenties or so with a crew cut. Their uniforms are black and starched and stiff, their badges polished to a shine. I move through the door and force myself to stand up straight.

"Emma Davies?" the older officer says.

I nod.

"We're sorry to have to tell you this, Ms. Davies. But there's been an accident involving your son. He was struck by a vehicle while riding his bike . . ."

The rest of his recitation is lost. My ears no longer hear. My eyes no longer see. My brain no longer possesses the capacity for rational thought.

I crumple to the floor.

~

The drive to Mercy Hospital is surreal. I sit in the back seat of the police cruiser, clinging to the three words I heard before the blackness took me.

"He's still alive."

I stare at the metal grate that separates the front seat from the back. The grate shimmers, swirls, morphs, the crisscrossing patterns expanding and contracting before my eyes. I reach out and touch the cool metal, and it liquefies and envelops my hand.

I yank my hand back.

"I need to call his father." I can't feel my lips, nor any vibration in my throat, so I don't know if I've spoken the words aloud until the young cop answers me.

"Another unit was dispatched to Mr. Davies. They're already en route. Should be to the hospital a few minutes after us."

I lean back against the cool vinyl seat. I close my eyes and pray. Not to God. He wouldn't listen to me. I don't deserve Him to listen. I pray to whatever forces have been at work in my life of late. *Please change the rules. Please let me go back. Please please please . . .*

~

Harsh white fluorescent bulbs assault me as I enter the ER. I pass the waiting area where a lone woman sits, dressed in a business suit, pressing an ice pack against her cheek. I have a flash of a memory—seeing myself in the mirror after Richard's attack, my cheek angry and swollen and purple. The woman looks up at me. *The woman is me.* I squeeze my eyes shut and open them to see a stranger seated on the yellow foam bench. She holds the ice pack on her forearm, not her cheek.

The reception desk is deserted. The older cop knocks on the glass partition and calls out for assistance. A moment later, a harried clerk appears. The cop says something to him and he replies, but I can't make out their words, as if I've lost command of the English language. Perhaps if their conversation were in Joshspeak, I would understand them. The clerk presses a button on the underside of his desk, and the inner door to the ER unlatches.

The cop touches my elbow. I flinch and he withdraws his hand. He escorts me past several curtained areas, another long reception counter where many green-scrubbed staff members chat or talk on the phone or type commands into their keyboards. I am deaf to the commotion around me, to the moans of agony, the beeping of monitors, the medical orders called out by white-coated doctors. I am in a vacuum. There is no sound but the pumping of my heart and the oxygen moving in and out of my lungs.

We stop at the end of the hall, at a closed door with a window over which a white curtain has been drawn. The cop says something to me.

I stand mute. He reaches for the doorknob, turns it, pushes the door open, then steps aside to allow me entrance.

I am in quicksand. I can't move my feet. The cop reaches out to touch me again. I put up my hand to block him. Finally, with herculean effort, I manage to take a step, then another. And another. Into the room.

A nurse wearing scrubs, her red hair scraped into a tight ponytail, stands across the room next to a bed with starched white linens. She blocks my view of the bed's occupant. She hears us enter, turns and gives me a sympathetic look, then moves toward us. I gaze past her.

And there he is. I know him instantly. The broken figure on the hospital bed seems more like my son than the teenager who walked out of my house last night, or loitered in front of the comic book store yesterday afternoon, or rode his bike down our street yesterday morning. His arms are curled up against his chest and his mouth yawns open. His head is swaddled in bandages and a breathing tube erupts from the middle of his throat, held in place with surgical tape.

In this supine position he looks like *my Josh*.

"Are you his mother?" the nurse asks quietly. I nod.

"The doctor will be in to see you in a few minutes." She reaches out and squeezes my biceps. I can't feel it.

I glance at the cop. I still can't hear him, but I read his lips. He says *I'm sorry*, then lowers his head and follows the nurse out of the room.

I'm alone with my son. My eyes are drawn to the yellow plastic accordion pump that rises and falls inside the transparent shaft of the ventilator. The rhythmic motion of the pump is hypnotic. I don't know how long I stand there staring at the familiar machine. A moment. An eon. Doesn't matter.

"Emma."

Colin's voice behind me cuts through my trance. I can hear now, but I can't move. My husband says my name again, and I feel him close the gap between us. His shoulder brushes against mine as he tries to grasp my hand. My fingers remain inert.

The intermittent beep of the heart monitor echoes through the room. The whoosh of the ventilator is like a cacophony.

"Oh my God," he breathes when he sees our son. "Oh my God, Josh!"

He rushes past me and stumbles to the bed, crying out Josh's name. He grasps the bed rail and leans over it to get a terrible closer look, then begs God to give him strength. Somewhere in the back of my mind I wonder if God can hear him. He turns back to me. Anguish and horror command his every facial muscle. I can't bear to look at him.

"Oh, Em. Our boy. Our son. Oh dear God, help me, please help me. Josh!"

I suddenly long for the deafness of my arrival. Colin's cries and divine entreaties are like nails being driven through my eardrums. I press the heels of my hands against my ears, hoping to block the sound of his misery.

He is still looking at me, but his expression has shifted to one of incredulity. "What are you doing, Emma? Why are you just standing there?"

I have no answer that will satisfy him or that he will understand. My horror is tempered by the fact that I have seen Josh in a hospital bed many times before. I've beheld countless seizures, spasms, ambulances, ERs, ventilators. This Colin in this new reality has not. He only knows Josh as a normal boy.

And yet, I know that my anguish over Josh goes far deeper and is much more insidious than my husband's. It cripples me. It robs me of my limbs, my voice, my senses. Because this, this hideous circumstance, this broken boy on the bed before me, is completely my fault.

I did this. With a wish.

The door opens, and a slight man with short dark hair enters. He wears a doctor's coat and a nametag I can't read. Black-rimmed glasses perch on the bridge of his nose, and his eyes look distorted and small behind them. He glances at the smart watch on his wrist every few seconds. His hands are hairless and dainty. He nods at me and walks toward the bed. Colin straightens and looks at him with dreaded expectation. I force myself to take a few slow steps forward as the doctor plants himself between Colin and me.

"Mr. and Mrs. Davies, your son's situation is very grave." His voice is gentle, but his delivery is matter-of-fact. We are not the first parents to receive bad news. We will not be the last. "Your son has suffered several catastrophic injuries, and I'm going to be candid with you. The prognosis is bleak."

Colin cries out, then buries his face in his hands and starts shaking his head and moaning. "No. No. No."

I am a statue.

The doctor looks back and forth between Colin and me. He seems to conclude that out of the two of us, I will not fall apart. He directs the rest of his report to me while my husband whimpers and weeps.

"The impact from the vehicle caused fractures to his C3, C4, and C5 vertebrae—those are in the neck—and the spinal cord has been severely traumatized. It is unlikely your son will ever regain the use of his limbs."

Colin wails in response to the doctor's prognosis. I stiffen at the sound but say nothing. The doctor is not finished yet.

"Also, the injury is at such a place as to affect his breathing, which is why we had to give him a tracheotomy." He pauses and checks his watch. "Apparently, your son hit the asphalt with great velocity, and because he wasn't wearing a helmet . . ." His voice trails off as he watches me closely for a reaction. When I give him none, he continues. "His skull was crushed. The brain damage is extensive, most notably in the frontal lobe, including Broca's area, which controls speech production."

"Goo' mo'ee', Maah." Good morning, Mom.

I should have made him wear a helmet. I should have made him stay home for dinner.

I shouldn't have made the wish.

"We've been monitoring his EKG since we stabilized him. So far, there is no sign of brain function. Once the swelling goes down, we'll have a better picture, but . . . If your son survives, which is unlikely, he may never regain consciousness. And if he does, he will have little or no quality of life. I know how difficult this must be for you, but you need to think very carefully about what to do next."

He pauses again but has the good grace not to check his watch.

He sighs, then reaches out as if to touch me, decides against it and drops his hand to his side. "Take a little time, Mrs. Davies. Might I suggest . . . it might be helpful . . . Perhaps you might consider what *your* wishes would be if you were in your son's situation."

I flinch at his suggestion. *My wishes.* I don't know what my wishes *would be.* I know what my wishes *have been.* They've been based on my own selfishness, my greed, my covetousness.

I don't need time to decide. I know what I must do.

THIRTY-THREE

Colin pulls himself together slowly. I wait. He thinks I'm in shock. How else can he explain my behavior? I have not once gone to my son's bedside. I haven't touched Josh or spoken to him or gazed upon him for any stretch of time. I stand on the far side of the room near the door, watching Colin mourn, watching the nurses as they check my son's vital signs, watching the ventilator rise and fall, watching the glowing green line of the heart monitor sail across the screen, creating upside-down Vs, watching the clouds move through the sky beyond the window.

His eyes red rimmed and puffy, Colin finally drags himself away from Josh and comes to me. He speaks to me as though I am a very small child.

"Emma. Do you need something? What can I do for you? Shall I get another chair? You can sit over here if you like."

"I don't want a chair, Colin. Thank you."

He is surprised by my steady tone, the calm in my voice. "Okay. We should talk. When you're ready."

"We don't need to talk. You and I both know what we have to do."

A sigh of relief. My husband is glad that I'm the first to say it.

"Dr. Sadal said his . . ." He stops, clears his throat. "Josh's organs could help a lot of people."

"I don't care about other people," I say.

Colin looks confused. "But we agree about what to do."

I nod.

"Because we can't let him go on like this."

I nod.

"It's the right thing to do, isn't it, Em?"

"You need to call Simone's mother and have her go to the rec center to get Katie. I don't want her driving. But she needs to be here to say goodbye."

Colin's tenuous hold on his emotions loosens, and a sob escapes him.

"You have to be strong, Colin." *For possibly the first time in your life.*

He sucks in a few breaths then sets his jaw. "I'll make the call now."

When the door closes behind him, I turn back to Josh. On legs that feel disconnected from my body, I approach the bed. I gaze down at my son, my beautiful, brilliant, lovely baby boy. He is no longer who he was yesterday, nor is he who he was the day before that, before my wish. Even though his eyes are closed, I can see that the spark, the energy, the intangible remarkable essence that made him who he was—in both incarnations—is gone.

As I watch his chest rise and fall, rise and fall, false memories of new Josh encroach upon my thoughts. I block them.

In my mind, I see him as he was: an infant struggling to orient himself in his crib, unable to roll over, unable to crawl; a toddler who could not walk, whose arms and hands could not grasp the stuffed animals and building blocks, who couldn't feed himself or potty train; the child stuck in a wheelchair, watching the kids play ball in the street; the adolescent who busied his mind by learning as much as he could about a world with which he would never be able to fully connect. A boy whose smile lit up a room, whose humor surprised and enchanted everyone he met, whose ability to forgive other people's cruelty was immeasurable, who loved me desperately and trusted me implicitly.

The boy I betrayed.

I sit down hard upon the chair beside the bed. I ease my hand over the bed rail, then close my fingers over Josh's left hand. A small part of me hopes for a reaction, a twitch, a flinch, a slight hitch in his breath. Nothing. His skin is cool to the touch.

I have the power to wish this away. I could delete the accident, remove the car from my son's path. But within me lies a cold certainty that no matter what I wish, my son will be taken from me. I can erase a bicycle accident, an overpowering riptide, a stray bullet, an overdose. The dark specter will come for Josh. Again and again. And I will have to replay this scene. Again and again. How many times can I endure his loss? Once is already too many.

"I'm sorry, Joshy," I whisper. "I'm so sorry."

I know this boy in this bed in this hospital room can no longer hear me. But perhaps my words will be carried to wherever he is now. I pray.

I feel the threat of tears. They burn like acid in my eyes. I force them back.

With my free hand, I reach for the ventilator. My fingertips brush against plastic. I lay the pad of my index finger over the small black button on the bottom of the machine. I squeeze Josh's hand, then press the button until I hear the click.

The ventilator pump rises and falls. The heart monitor beeps. For a moment, nothing changes.

And then.

The space between the beeps lengthens. The pump rises and falls lethargically.

My own heartbeat quickens as Josh's heartbeat slows, slows, and finally stops. The pump deflates to the bottom of the shaft and stays there. The heart monitor blares angrily.

I stare at my son as his last breath leaves his body.

Aye luh y', Maah.

"I love you, too, Josh."

~

Josh is gone.

Colin walks into the room, and his face goes white at the sound of the alarm. I remove my hand from Josh's lifeless fingers and gain my feet as my husband rushes to the bed.

"Emma, no!" Colin cries. "What have you done?" He grabs me by the shoulders and shakes me, his bloodshot eyes boring into mine. "How could you do this? How? Why?"

I cannot find the words to explain it to him. He wouldn't understand.

I had to do it, Colin. It was my punishment. It was my privilege.

The auburn-haired nurse enters and hurries to Josh. "Oh, dear," she says, stricken. She shuts off the heart monitor, and the sudden quiet is as loud as thunder.

"He was my son, too, goddamn it! I wanted to say goodbye. And Katie. What about his sister? You stole our goodbyes, Emma."

His anger finds nothing in my expression upon which to feed. I step out of his grasp.

"He was already gone," I say.

Colin looks at me for a long moment, clinging to his indignation for as long as he can, perhaps hoping to stave off his grief. It doesn't last. His shoulders drop in defeat and his chest spasms as he tries to hold back his sobs. He pushes me aside, then throws himself over Josh.

"Josh, Josh, I love you. I love you so much. You were a great kid. You *are* a great kid. I'm so proud of you. So proud."

The door to the room opens again. Dr. Sadal walks in, and the auburn-haired nurse immediately crosses to him.

"Mrs. Davies turned off the ventilator," she tells him in a hushed whisper.

He looks at the floor. "We weren't able to alert the transplant team."

The nurse nods and leaves the room. I walk over to the doctor. He is trying to conceal his disappointment. He can't bring himself to look at me.

"I'm sorry for your loss, Mrs. Davies," he says quietly.

I don't respond. The walls are breathing. The ceiling is pulsating. I have to get out of here. I move past the doctor, out the door and down the hall, gaining speed with each stride. Past the long counter, past the doctors and nurses and orderlies, the curtained areas, past reception and through the wide double doors of the ER entrance. Out into the open I go, finally free of that treacherous place.

On the other side of the parking lot is a wide green belt, lush and bucolic and so at odds with the stark hospital interior that it almost seems like a mirage. I run toward it, stagger, lose one shoe, kick off the other, the soles of my feet scraping across the pebbly macadam. The pain is an abstract. I reach the sidewalk and keep going until I am in the middle of the grass. I stand, my feet throbbing and bleeding, my head pounding. I look up at the sky, at the blinding sun that burns my pupils to pinpoints. Anguish rises from my belly and escapes my mouth as a scream and goes on and on until my vocal cords are raw.

"Please!" I rage at the universe. "Change the rules. Let me take back my wish. I take it back. I take them all back. Please!"

Suddenly, what's left of my strength, my sheer force of will to remain in control, abandons me. I drop to my knees, then fall face forward onto the grass. Wrenching convulsions rack my body. I submit to them, allowing the hurricane of grief to take me.

~

Colin and Kate are given time to say their goodbyes. My husband has chosen not to tell Katie that I turned off the ventilator before she could arrive, and although I should be grateful, I'm ambivalent.

Katie is distraught and disbelieving, in turn. She doesn't know what to do with her hands. Her mouth opens and closes like a guppy's. She blinks rapidly and repeats the phrase *Oh my God* over and over again. She hiccups in order to breathe. Her grief is like a branding iron fresh from the fire stamped upon my flesh. To temper the searing heat of guilt, I fill my head with questions. *How would Katie be acting if she were confronted with the death of old Josh? The same? Would she collapse with utter despair? Would she be screaming like a banshee? Or would her pain be so excruciating that she could only survive it by containing, suppressing, and compartmentalizing it?*

I have no answers, and when I run out of questions, I excuse myself from the room. I can't bear to listen to Katie's last words to Josh. I want to tell Colin to give her some privacy, but he denies me his attention, averting his eyes whenever his gaze lands too close to me.

I stand sentinel outside the door. Hospital staff members come and go. Some grace me with expressions of sympathy. Others glare at me accusingly. I am the woman who let others, *strangers*, die by letting go of her son. I don't care. It doesn't matter. Josh is gone. Old Josh. New Josh. Both gone.

I stare at my bare feet and think back to that first morning when I fell on the uneven bricks of the cobblestone path in front of my house. The memory is washed out, faded, with a layer of new memories obscuring it, but when I concentrate, I can clearly see the path and the tree and the roots and the abrasions on my knees.

I want this to be a dream. I don't care whether I'm crazy or sane. If I've lost my mind, so be it. I don't mind being insane if the trade-off is a living son.

There was a movie many years ago about a Vietnam vet who came back from the war and his life was filled with lunacy and horror as he struggled to make sense of it. But none of it really happened. The whole of his coming home was only in his mind as he lay on his deathbed in a medical tent in Vietnam. Deep down, I cradle the hope that this is my story as well. I wouldn't mind dying. Especially now.

But lunacy or dream or deathbed vision, I can do nothing but go forward. Now without Josh.

I hear a familiar voice and glance down the hallway. There she is, pushing an older man in a wheelchair toward a curtained area. The image of her hasn't faded since I eliminated her from our lives. *Lena.*

My feet move toward the young woman of their own volition.

"Lena," I cry. "Josh is gone."

She turns her head sharply in my direction, then narrows her eyes at me. "I'm sorry. Do I know you?" The man in the wheelchair moans.

I shake my head, then look at the floor, the walls, the man in the wheelchair. He moans again. Lena looks at me as though I am a problem to be solved. A hint of recognition passes over her features, then is gone. She averts her eyes and continues into the cubby. A nurse tears the curtain closed behind her with a squawk.

I fall back against the wall and take a few deep breaths to steady myself. A moment passes. I withdraw my cell phone from my purse and bring up my search engine. I type in my zip code, then *funeral home.* I force myself to disassociate, to pretend I'm playing a role in some black comedy, to pretend that this isn't really happening.

Then I make the call.

~

Colin decides that he will stay at the house. This isn't a suggestion, and I don't bother to object. It wouldn't do any good. He says he'll sleep on the couch, and I nod.

Simone's mother, a reserved Asian American woman with worried eyes and jet-black hair, offers to take Katie, Colin, and me home. She doesn't speak a word the entire ride. Her skin is blanched from her cheeks to her chest, and she bites her bottom lip to keep from crying. She didn't know Josh, but she is a mother, and this death is too close to home. Who knows when the dark specter might come for one of her own? She pulls away from the curb a split second after we alight from her car, as though having a dead child might be contagious if she were to linger too long at our house. I don't have a chance to thank her, but I probably wouldn't have. My voice has abandoned me again.

Katie walks sluggishly to the porch. She is not speaking, either. Her tears are silent but copious, two steady streams that cut across her cheekbones and drip from her chin. She swipes at them absently. I open the front door and watch her move to the stairs and climb them, slowly, painstakingly, as if every step is a monumental feat. I realize how very alike my daughter and I are in grief. Every cell in my body weighs a hundred pounds. But I have to keep moving. I am the fish at the bottom of the ocean. If I stop moving, the leviathan will swallow me whole.

I go to the kitchen. Colin follows me. The house looks different. Not different in the way in which my wishes affected it. The light is different. Everything—the walls, the furniture, the countertops—looks gray. A veil of sorrow skews my vision.

Colin falls into a chair at the kitchen table as I move to the coffee-maker. I feel his eyes on me as I go through the motions of filling the carafe and measuring the grounds. I hear him sigh and shift in his seat.

"We have to decide whether we want an open casket or closed," he says. His words taste like chalk in my mouth. "When do we need to get his clothes to the funeral home?"

I depress the button on the coffeemaker and think of the ventilator. "Friday."

"Should we give them his suit? He didn't wear it very often."

Josh never owned a suit. Old Josh never owned a suit.

"Maybe we should take his favorite Dockers and that flannel shirt he always wore."

I intuit that Colin is trying to make a joke, but I'm not in on it because I have no idea which clothes he's talking about. A correlating memory presses against the corners of my mind, but I push it away. I want to remember *my* Josh.

"The suit is more appropriate," I say.

I stand at the counter, waiting for the coffee to brew, waiting for the nightmare to end, knowing it won't.

"I forgive you, Em," Colin says.

I tear my eyes away from the filling carafe and gaze at my husband. He stares at me, almost tenderly.

"I know why you did it. I'm not saying I'm happy about it or that I wouldn't change it if I could. But I understand and I forgive you."

I shake my head. "Don't forgive me, Colin. I don't deserve it."

I push away from the counter and head for the stairs, leaving Colin alone with a pot of coffee and his forgiveness.

I stop at the top of the stairs and listen for my daughter. Soft mewling comes from behind her closed door. I go to the master bedroom and sit down on the bed, then open the nightstand drawer and pull out my journal. I open the book to the last entry, then grab my pen and begin to write. About Josh. *My* Josh. I may have lost him, but I refuse to lose the *memory* of him.

When I finish, the bedroom is almost dark. I gently place the journal back in the nightstand, then curl up into a fetal position and close my eyes. I don't make any wishes.

Josh comes to me in my dream, as he was, a beautiful boy burdened by a terrible disorder and a wheelchair, but little else. He smiles his crooked smile at me and reaches out to me with his clawed hand, but says nothing.

I awaken to the sound of steady breathing on the other side of the bed. I roll over to see Katie lying next to me, facing the far wall. I scoot over to her and lace my arm though hers, clenching her middle tightly. She stirs but doesn't wake up. My breathing soon slows to match hers, and a short while later, I fall asleep. This time, I don't dream.

THIRTY-FOUR

Wednesday, August 10–Friday, August 12

Over the course of the next three days, I am more camera than person. I take snapshots of the events around me, but I do not connect to them emotionally in any way. If I do, I will completely unravel. I can't let that happen. I made a wish that killed my son. It is my duty to see that he is properly laid to rest.

Louise Krummund is the first to appear at our door Wednesday morning. Spencer and Steven trail behind her, and between the three of them, they carry two casseroles of indeterminate nature, two loaves of bread, and a large plastic container of salad. I don't know how she found out about Josh. I don't ask. It doesn't matter. I summon as much grace as I can and allow her to bring the food into the kitchen. She titters nervously, looking to and fro like a frightened squirrel and talking incessantly. I understand her unease. What does one say to a grieving mother? The cliché bears truth. We are not meant to bury our children. She has three. She can't imagine one being taken.

On some level, I recognize that Louise is a good person, that she has a big heart, that her simple mind and simple beliefs about the world around her do not preclude her from caring. I think we might have been friends, not best friends or bosom buddies, but companions. Another sailing ship.

I thank her for the food, then gently dismiss her. She takes no offense.

Val and Wally come together. They bring no food, thankfully, but they hand me an envelope full of gift cards from several nearby eateries, the local market, Trader Joe's. They tell me the office staff at Canning and Wells pooled funds to purchase the cards. There is a goodly amount represented. I thank them and invite them to the service on Saturday. I don't invite them in. I don't inquire about my status at the firm. I don't inquire about anything. They take the hint and graciously leave.

Colin and I make the arrangements together, but with as little interaction as possible. Neither of us can believe this is really happening, that we are hosting an event that is neither birthday party nor graduation, but instead the burying of our son. We go to the funeral home and discuss with a somber gentleman our desires for the service. He assures us that the chapel can take care of everything we need. Casket, flowers, memory cards, programs, guest book, boutonnieres for the pallbearers. My marketing brain seizes upon an ad line: *One-stop shopping for all your funereal needs.*

We choose the words we want spoken by a pastor who has never met Josh. Generic, complimentary, full of elegiac verbiage about the tragedy of a promising life cut so short. *Josh was a terrific young man* (questionable), *a good student* (lie), *excelled in sports* (did he? The trophies prove it), *had wonderful friends* (were they wonderful, or were they shits?).

As the somber man and Colin go over the minutiae of the service, my mind wanders. I think about the eulogy that might have been, the eulogy for old Josh. *Josh had cerebral palsy. He couldn't walk or control his limbs well. He could barely speak. He sat in his wheelchair and stared at a computer screen because his mother was too fearful on his behalf to allow him to have real experiences. Josh had no quality of life. His mother deprived him of one. She loved him, but not in the right way. God has taken him to be an angel that he might soar through the clouds. It's for the best that he's gone.*

We sign the papers and I write a fat check to the funeral home. I hand over the suit I don't remember purchasing and never saw my son wear.

~

Colin regularly retreats to his office, just as he did when he lived here—three days ago or a year ago, depending on which timeline I go by. He removed most of his music, but a few CDs remain, those that we both enjoyed and he had the generosity to leave behind. He tells me he is polishing his manuscript—he has his laptop with him—but I suspect he gets little work done. How can a father worry about words on a screen when his progeny has been stolen from him? Still, when he retreats to that room, I let him be. It's easier for me to have walls and doors between us.

I don't ask him about Eliza, but I hear his muffled voice occasionally as he speaks into his phone, the soft reassurances of his affection and the tight reprimands that this is what he has to do and she should understand. He sleeps on the couch in the living room with the bedding I provided for him and complains not at all, even though I catch the expressions of pain when he appears in the kitchen each morning, the hand on the small of his back, the squinty eyes as he stretches from side to side. Several times I've almost suggested he sleep in Josh's bed, but the sentence never leaves my lips because I know Colin would shudder at the thought.

Katie spends time with her friends, Simone mostly. I want her to stay with me, to tether me to this reality, but I can't deny her her escape. She moves in and out of the house like a ghost, transient, not really here. I know she cries with her friends; I see the proof in her swollen eyes when she returns, but I know she also laughs and allows herself to feel normal in a different household, a household in which tragedy has yet to strike.

She sleeps with me in my bed each night, and we spoon, entwine ourselves, as though we are each other's life float and will keep each other from drowning in our grief. As much as I can feel during this time, I cherish our bond. Katie slept in my bed as an infant and a toddler and was exiled to her own bed and her own room as soon as Colin rescued us. Her presence now buoys me and also assuages me of my guilt at her earlier banishment.

For my part, I spend my time performing mundane tasks, formerly resented chores. I dust and vacuum every day, although the dust doesn't accumulate fast enough to necessitate daily eradication. I polish silver that I haven't touched for half a decade. I wander through the rooms of my house like a visitor, as though I'm seeing the pictures and knickknacks and curtains and furniture and appliances for the first time. I sit in front of my computer and pay bills. I endeavor not to think, not to *remember*. For the first time in my life, I operate completely in the moment, because to look back would only cause confusion, discombobulation, debilitating anxiety, and to look ahead (to my son's funeral) would likely cause me to lose my delicate hold on the ledge from which I dangle.

Friday, the night before Josh's service, I click out of my banking and bill pay and call up Facebook. And there, on the top of the screen, is an icon telling me that Dante has accepted my friend request. With Josh's death, I'd forgotten about it. Dante has sent me a message. I open the window, and his words reach out to me through cyberspace.

> My Em. I have longed to get in touch but was afraid
> I might reopen wounds that were better left healed.
> So pleased to receive your request. Not a day goes
> by when I don't think about you. I am in New York.
> Not far. Let me know if and when I can see you.

I read the message three times, but I don't respond. I click onto the CP Parents page and spend the remainder of the evening reading about the trials and tribulations of parents with whom I shared a connection less than a week ago. Their posts move me to tears, not only because I recognize how great their challenges are, but because I am no longer a part of their community. My self-imposed exile hits home.

~

Saturday, August 13

And finally, Saturday comes.

Before wishes, before my high-powered job and sleek wardrobe, I owned a simple black sheath, unglamorous, unassuming. My mother made it for me twenty years ago and I kept it because it always fit, whether I was carrying an extra five pounds or had lost ten. I wore it to my rehearsal dinner the night before I married Colin. I wore it to a company party several Christmases back. I wore it to my mother's funeral.

The dress is nowhere to be found in my closet. I stand in front of the racks and stacks of clothing, gazing at the many designer-labeled ensembles hanging from padded hangers. Nothing is appropriate.

All I want is that simple black sheath.

Katie wanders in and sits on the bed. She is wearing an ankle-length charcoal skirt, a white blouse, and flat black sandals. Her hair is braided loosely down her back. Her eyes are puffy. Her face is pale. She is beautiful.

"I don't know what to wear," I tell her.

Katie says nothing. She stands and walks to the closet then sifts through the hangers. She withdraws a black skirt, a short-sleeved button-up blouse, and a peach-and-gray scarf, hands the ensemble to me, then returns to the bed.

She watches me as I dress. Something needs to be said, but she cannot bring herself to speak. I pull a pair of panty hose from the dresser drawer and think of my boss Richard who doesn't exist. I stuff the hose back into the drawer. It's too hot for them anyway.

As I stand in front of the mirror and button my blouse, Katie shifts behind me on the bed. She sighs in the manner of a teenager—a monologue sigh, a thousand words conveyed in a single exhalation of breath. I wait.

"I . . . I loved him, Mom."

I turn to her and smile. "I know you did, Katie." She is new to this reality, so she doesn't know that she was Josh's caregiver, that she fed him and wiped his mouth and played games with him and read to him and was his favorite companion—after me. She doesn't remember the many ways in which she showed her love. But I remember.

"We bagged on each other," she says. "And he was kind of a jerk sometimes, but he was my brother. I loved him."

My throat is too tight to speak.

"He was my little brother, you know?"

I nod.

"It totally sucks."

I'm sorry, Katie. I stole your brother from you. I stole your place in his heart and your connection with him, all the laughter you shared and the things you did for him that made both of you better people.

I clear my throat to loosen my vocal cords. "It does suck. But I know that Josh knew how much you loved him."

She looks up at me, her expression twisted with hope and disbelief. "Really? You think he knew?"

"Yes, honey. He knew. Boys are funny and weird and stupid sometimes. But they know. He knew."

"Do you believe in heaven, Mom?"

My shoulders tighten. I don't know what I believe. I'm not even sure I'm sane. How can I offer her wisdom from the place at which I now exist? All I can give her is my current truth.

"I want to believe in heaven."

She nods, but I can tell she is dissatisfied.

~

The service goes as predicted. Too long.

I sit in the front row of the chapel, between Katie and Colin. My gaze never leaves the casket. We chose to keep the lid closed, but I feel that decision was a mistake. I imagine Josh inside, clawing to get out, pressing against the lid with his curled fingers, the plush, satin-covered padding closing in on him as he struggles to draw breath. If the casket were open, I would see a dead boy. That would be horrific but far better that the scenario I've created in my mind.

Many of my work colleagues are present: Val and Wally, Bill Canning and Edward Wells, several employees from each department. The Krummunds are here. Josh's (new) friends, looking uncomfortable in the formal clothes their parents made them wear. Katie's friends and their families have come. Colin's girlfriend, Eliza, sits a few rows behind me. I saw her come in and was struck by how much she looks like me, albeit younger and less burdened by life's disappointments.

The pastor drones on about a teenager I didn't know. Colin reads his well-written eulogy depicting a life to which I never bore witness. Katie recites a short poem she wrote about a little brother whom she loved despite their sibling rivalry. The pastor invites others to share. A few people stand and deliver unrehearsed and painfully halting stories about the Josh they knew.

I block everything out as best I can by calling up memories of the Josh I knew. *My* Josh. I think about his laughter and his inquisitiveness. His sense of humor and sideways grin. I think about the safari and the one thing he said that made my heart expand in my chest.

"Aye thi' th' i' th' be' moeh a' m' eti' liey," Josh says. *I think this is the best moment of my entire life.*

I gave that to him. At least I could give that to him.

At the close of the service, the pastor invites the assembled to the grave. There is to be a reception at my house. I didn't want to have one, didn't want to play hostess on the day of my son's burial, but Colin was adamant. I left the arrangements to him. He chose a small catering company for which Canning and Wells did some ad work. I know the owner, Doug Craven. He and his team are at my house now, wandering through my kitchen and living room and family room, seeing the pictures of Josh on the breakfront. They are loosely connected to this tragedy but immune from the grief of it. They are going about their business of preparing trays of food and drink stations and congratulating themselves on the fact that this is not their son or their family or their loved one. I envy them. I try not to think about them.

I try not to think about anything.

THIRTY-FIVE

A shiny black limousine transfers Katie and me from the funeral home to the cemetery, three short (long) miles away. Colin has opted to drive with Eliza, likely because she is feeling insecure, unappreciated, untended. He tells me of his decision and waits a beat for some sign that I might be jealous or disappointed or disdainful. I give him no reaction, and he slinks over to her Nissan and folds himself into the passenger seat.

The air-conditioning in the limo is on the blink. The driver apologizes profusely, but his words of contrition fall upon deaf ears. August sweat drips down my back. I barely feel it. I pull the scarf from my neck and bunch it in my lap, but I don't know if it helps to be free of the fabric. Katie fans herself with the program from the service. Her face is beet red, and a thin sheen of perspiration decorates her forehead and upper lip.

The cemetery is welcome after the inferno of the limo. A slight breeze stirs the leaves of the nearby trees. My brain registers that the temperature is in the upper eighties, but at this point I am immune to all sensations. I'm operating according to a predetermined plan. Feel nothing, say nothing, follow instructions, get through this.

The pallbearers, Colin; Louise Krummund's oldest, Jett; Parker; Jesse; the other boy from the house whose name I kept forgetting; and Simone's brother Michael; all beautifully boutonniered, thanks to the somber man at the funeral home, carry the coffin from the black hearse to the awaiting hole in the earth.

As the coffin descends, I feel something deep within me loosen, uncoil. I made wishes, about a puppy, a tree, a horrible boss, my daughter, my disabled son. But I know that wishes don't come true, not really, not now in the real world. They *don't*. And if I close my eyes and shut all of this out, this figment of my worst imaginings, then *all of this* will cease to exist in reality. Josh will be as he was, imprisoned in his wheelchair, and Charlemagne will be barking furiously, incessantly, next door, and Richard, my boss, will be contriving new ways to torture and belittle and grope me, and that, all of that will be just fine, because the alternative is unacceptable and because wishes *don't come true.*

I squeeze my eyes shut and cling to my disbelief, but the squeak of the pulleys and chains lowering Josh's coffin into the ground echoes in my ears, reverberates through my head, and when I open my eyes, all is as it was before I closed them.

And then. And then, the unthinkable occurs. I see Owen walk toward us, Katie and me, as the last of the mourners throws dirt upon the wood box that holds the remains of my son.

He looks slick and pleased with himself, but perhaps I'm projecting my disgust onto him because he should not be here and his presence is like acid in my stomach. Colin is too busy catering to Eliza's dysfunctional needs to notice his approach. But Katie sees him and recoils, burrowing herself into my side.

"What are you doing here, Owen?"

He cocks his head to the side, a habit I am familiar with, then assembles his features into an expression of sympathy. The emotion doesn't reach his eyes.

"I'm so sorry about Josh, Emma," he says.

I don't thank him, as I have done in response to everyone else's condolences. Owen doesn't deserve my thanks. In the back of my mind, I realize I should have gotten that restraining order.

"Look, I didn't come here to make trouble. I just came to support my daughter."

"*Our* daughter."

He ignores me and turns his attention to Katie, moving closer to her with each word. She trembles against me.

"How are you doing, honey?"

Katie follows my lead and doesn't respond to him. "I know how hard this must be for you," he continues, unruffled. "I just want you to know that I'm here for you. I know what you're going through. My brother died when I was fifteen."

"Of an overdose."

"That's uncalled for, Emma."

"It's the truth," I say, my voice tight. "I don't want to make a scene, Owen. But you need to leave. You don't belong here. I'll call the police if I have to." *Like I should have done at the outlets.*

His eyes narrow at me. I see a flicker of rage hiding just beneath the surface of his restraint, coupled with a hint of skepticism. He knows me well enough to know I won't call the police. Not here. Not at Josh's funeral. I wrap my arm around Katie and pull her away from him.

"Katie," he calls out, following us as we move toward the limo. "I'm your dad. I'm here for you. Your mom wants to keep you from me, but she can't, not forever. You need me, just like I need you."

I hear it then. The slight slur in his words. I didn't catch it before, I was too angry and too surprised to pay close attention. But there it is—the drawn out *s*'s, the omission of hard consonants, the way his volume increases and decreases rapidly.

I glance over my shoulder. Owen's footsteps are erratic and fore-shortened. "You're drunk," I spit at him. "Get the hell out of here."

By now, Colin has noticed what's going on. He rushes toward us, leaving Eliza standing alone beside Josh's grave.

"What the hell are you doing here?"

"Stay away from me, man," Owen shouts.

The remaining mourners stop their hushed conversations and their migration to their cars. They look in our direction, an audience of sheep, unconcerned, unconnected, unsure of what to do. Eliza stands frozen next to the hole in the ground.

"Emma, what's going on?" Colin asks. "What is he doing here?"

"This is none of your business. This is between me and my daughter!"

"She's more my daughter than yours," Colin says. The cords in his neck are rigid. He puts his hand on Owen's shoulder, and Owen shoves him away. He stumbles backward as Owen reaches out and grabs Katie's arm and yanks her from my embrace.

"Leave her alone!" I cry.

"I just want to talk to you, Katie. I just want us to be together."

Colin comes up behind Owen as I move in to claim Katie. Her face is ghostly white and her mouth is open, as though she is trying to say something but unable to get it out. Colin grasps Owen by the back of the neck as I pull Katie away from him. Owen bats at Colin's hand, twists around and shoves him again, this time with more force, and Colin goes down hard. I take two steps forward and slap Owen across the face as hard as I can. White-hot pain shoots all the way up my arm. Owen starts to retaliate by raising his fist. My anger erupts.

"Go ahead. Hit me! I'll see you rot in jail before I let you get near my daughter again. How dare you come to this place on this day, drunk, high? What did you expect was going to happen? You are pathetic."

He drops his arm to his side, but his face has gone crimson.

"I am pathetic. But you're worse. You used to be . . . amazing . . . beautiful . . . happy. But now all you are is a cold, selfish, hateful woman. I may be a drunk, and I might fall, but I'll get back up again. I'll do anything to make myself worthy of that girl. And you can't erase me, Emma. You can't. Someday I'm going to get to know my daughter, and she's gonna resent you for keeping her from me all this time."

He sneers at me. "Then you'll be all alone. *Alone, Emma!* A miserable woman with a daughter who hates her and a dead son."

My whole body is shaking with rage. "You fucking bastard. I wish I'd never met you!"

Oh God. No.

My hands jerk forward, my fingers clawing the air as though I can grab the words and shove them back down inside me. I slam my fists against my mouth as my heart jackhammers in my chest.

How could I let that wish out? How could I let it out?

I turn around to see Katie staring at me, her eyes filled with tears.

"I didn't mean it, Katie. You know that." I lumber over to her and gather her in my arms. "I didn't mean it. I would never take any of it back. I have *you* because of him. I would never do anything differently. I promise."

She slides her arms around my waist and holds me tightly. "It's okay, Mom. I understand."

"I love you so much, Katie."

"I love you, too, Mom."

Jesse and Parker have made their way to Colin, and the three of them flank Owen. The teenagers look like they're itching for a brawl. Owen senses it.

"Leave me alone. I'm going," he says.

Colin puffs out his chest. "We're getting a restraining order against you, Owen. Stay the hell away from my family."

Owen smirks snidely, then glances meaningfully over at Eliza. "It's not really your family anymore, is it, *Colin*?"

Colin looks at me. I turn and lead Katie to the limo.

~

The reception is a blur. I don't talk to anyone. I don't sit down. I wander from room to room, stalking Katie. I can't let her out of my sight. The only times I lose track of her are when I have to excuse myself to the upstairs bathroom to vomit, three times in total.

The wish replays in my head. Each time I hear the echo of those awful words, my heart contracts and my stomach spasms. I try to tell myself that the wishes are over. That Josh was the ultimate punishment for my sins. How could the fates be so cruel as to deprive me of my daughter, too? It won't happen. It can't happen. I won't allow it.

I begin to pinch myself with my fingernails every time that terrible wish comes to mind. Within an hour welts cover my left forearm from wrist to elbow. I pull at my hair to stop the words. Enough strands come loose in my hand to make a wig.

By the time the guests and the caterers leave, I'm in such a frenzy, I'm afraid I will terrify Katie and Colin by going completely mad. I change into jeans and a long-sleeved sweater to hide the welts. I pull my hair into a ponytail. I force myself to take one of the Xanax that Lettie prescribed. One doesn't help. I take another.

Katie wants to go to Simone's and I forbid her. I need her, I say. I need her close to me. I don't think I can get through this horrible day without her. She can go to Simone's tomorrow.

Please, Katie. Please stay with me. We can talk about Josh. We can look at pictures and share stories. I don't have any stories you'll recognize. Let's talk about you instead. Let's talk about your birthday. It's only a week away.

She looks at me then like I *have* gone mad. She doesn't want to talk about her birthday on the same day we buried her brother. That's okay, I tell her. We can talk about anything she wants. *We don't have to talk at all. Just please stay.*

She understands and acquiesces. We agree to spend the remainder of the evening watching Josh's favorite movies: *Die Hard*, the original *Point Break*, *The Fast and the Furious*. Katie offers to go to his room to find the DVDs. I'm grateful. I don't think I'm capable of entering his room. Not yet. I know I will have to eventually, to sort through his things and pack them away. I imagine I will uncover many mysteries about the Josh I never knew, the Josh with whom I was only given one short day. But that can wait.

Colin decides to stay through the weekend, if that's okay with me. I nod mutely then watch him walk Eliza to her car. I have a sudden recollection of the night he walked Lena to her car. The memory surprises me, as I thought it had faded. When he returns, he checks to see that Katie isn't downstairs then faces me. I have the irrational notion that if I reach out to touch him, my hand will pass right through his chest. He speaks just above a whisper, and his words come to me as if from the far end of a long tunnel.

"I'll call the lawyer on Monday about the restraining order. We need to do it. The man is unstable."

Owen is a thousand times saner than me at this moment.

"It's not true what he said, you know," Colin says. "You and Katie are my family. No matter what, you always will be."

The Xanax, my terror at the possibility of losing Kate, my grief over Josh, the fact that Colin seems as insubstantial as ether—whatever the reason, I don't have a reply. Colin gazes at me for a moment.

"I think I'll pass on the movies." He touches me softly on the cheek. I feel his fingertips. They are like ice. He pulls his hand away, then walks down the hall to his office. He goes in but doesn't close the door all the way.

Katie and I sit side by side on the couch. The screen looms large before us.

I make sure that a part of me is touching her. By nine o'clock, neither of us can keep our eyes open. I grab the flesh of my upper thigh and squeeze violently. I can't go to sleep. *I can't let myself fall asleep.*

I tell my daughter I'll meet her upstairs.

"Should I sleep in my own bed tonight, Mom?" she asks.

"No!"

She flinches. "I just thought maybe you'd sleep better without me there?"

I don't want to sleep better. I don't want to sleep at all.

"I sleep just fine with you there," I assure her.

She nods, then pushes herself off the couch and shuffles to the stairs. I go into the kitchen and make myself a quick cup of instant coffee, drink it down like a shot; the liquid scalds my mouth, my throat, but I don't care. I go upstairs and into the master bedroom. Katie is already half-asleep. She mumbles a good night as I discard my clothes and don a nightshirt. By the time I pull back the covers and climb in next to her, she is snoring softly.

I write in my journal. Not about my wish, but about my Katie. I stop when I can no longer see the page through my tears.

I hide the journal then lie down, put my arm around Katie, and pull her close.

I won't let you have her, I think. *She's mine. Haven't you taken enough from me?*

But it's my fault. I'm the one who took everything away. How could I have been so careless with my wishes? I was given powers and I abused them. I didn't need them in the first place. I didn't have to wish a dog or a tree away. Not even a horrible boss. I could have reported Richard. I could have quit. I could have gotten a job anywhere. And Josh? My darling love. What was I thinking? He was perfect as he was.

I could have dealt with my life, faced it, embraced it instead of wishing it away.

If Katie is gone when I wake . . . No. *No! I won't let you have her!*

I pull her closer. She stirs but doesn't wake up. The coffee swirls around in my stomach, but the caffeine is doing nothing to stave off the heaviness of my eyelids. Twice, I get up to splash cold water on my face. I try to think of stimulating subject matter to keep my brain sharp and awake. Nothing is working.

I cry again, my tears dampening my pillowcase, as I cling to Katie for dear life.

~

Sunday, August 14

I jerk awake. I don't have to open my eyes. I already know. Colin's side of the bed is empty.

No. No. No.

I scramble out from under the covers and run out of the bedroom, down the hall toward Katie's closed door. I turn the knob and push the door open. And a part of me dies.

There are no posters on the walls, no twin bed with the pink floral duvet, no white desk with teenage clutter and jewelry boxes and books, no clothing poking out of the dresser drawers, because there is no longer a dresser. As I look around at the unfamiliar room, with the small beige convertible couch and IKEA side tables and small flat-screen TV, I hear a loud keening wail. I realize the sound is coming from me, and I slap my hand over my mouth.

No.

I slam the door shut, as though closing off the sight of the room will make it cease to be what it has become.

"Katie!" I backtrack to Josh's room, peer in. "Katie!" I know she isn't there. She isn't anywhere. I *know* it, but I can't help myself, can't stop screaming out her name.

"Katie!" I take the stairs two at a time. "Katie!"

No. No. No!

I don't go into the living room. Her pictures will be gone, and I can't bear to face the actuality of their absence. Instead, I go to the kitchen. *That's where she is. That's where she'll be. It's breakfast time. She's eating her toast or an English muffin or cereal. Please, God, she must be there. People don't suddenly cease to exist. Wishes don't come true.*

But she isn't there. "Katie, Katie!"

Colin rushes from the living room, where he's been camping out. His hair is askew and his pajamas are disheveled.

"Emma, what's wrong?"

"No, no, no." I wrap my arms around my middle to keep myself from blowing apart. "This isn't happening. This can't be happening. Where is she? Where is Katie?" I can't breathe. My heart beats too fast. Black-and-red-and-white spots appear in my vision.

Colin hurries over to me and grabs my shoulders. His expression remains calm, but his eyes belie his concern.

"Who is Katie, Em?"

"Katie!" I'm laughing now, a strangled wheeze. "My daughter, Katie. Where is she?"

"Emma, you don't have a daughter."

"I do, I do, I do." My body shakes violently with my hysterical laughter. The laughter turns to sobs then back to laughter again. The madness has finally come for me. I scream, a bloodcurdling, throat-shredding shriek that fetters me to reality. Colin's concern turns to alarm.

"Emma! We had a son. His name was Josh. We buried him yesterday."

I swing my head from side to side and pull away from him. I stagger to the family room and stumble to my desk, bang my knee hard against the chair. I yank open the top right drawer then tear through the contents. My hand closes around the small package I hid there . . . when? When was that? I can't recall. I reach into the bag and withdraw the necklace, then hold it up in front of me. The lion pendant sparkles.

"Katie, Katie!" *Breathe.* "I had a daughter." *Breathe.* "Her name was Katie."

Colin has followed me and approaches me as one might approach a wild animal. I shrink away from him until my back hits the wall. I double over, hiccupping, laughing, sobbing, retching. I vomit bile onto the floor.

Images, pictures of Katie flash before my eyes, from her first wailing breath through every stage of her life. One by one, each image, each precious recollection is plucked from my memory, like a virus destroying a hard drive.

"Noooooooooooooooooooooo!"

"You have to get ahold of yourself!" Colin is shouting. He is genuinely frightened now. "This is grief, Em. You're out of your mind with grief over Josh. You had a dream, honey. Listen to me! This is about Josh. I'm going to call the doctor, okay?" He reaches for my hand and I lash out, punching him with my fists until he backs away.

"Go away, Colin. Just go away. I wish you would go away. I wish I was anywhere but here."

I squeeze my eyes shut and slide down the wall to the floor. My bare calves land on the puddle of bile. It doesn't matter. Nothing matters.

Clutching the pendant to my chest, I fall onto the tile and weep.

THIRTY-SIX

I wake up in a state of complete disorientation. I have no idea where I am, nor who I am. I only know I have come undone.

I raise myself into a seated position and look around. My stomach yawns with hunger or nausea, I can't decide which. My eyes feel like I have crushed glass beneath my lids.

I have never seen this place before, but it feels familiar, as though, in this new incarnation of my life, I've been here for a while. The bed is smaller than my bed at home, a full with a puffy white comforter and starched white sheets. The room is tiny with bare walls. The double window is half the size of my old bedroom window. Half of the window is covered by an air-conditioning unit, cranked to high. The other side has thick black bars crisscrossing over the glass. There are no blinds or curtains, but the sun is blocked by the redbrick siding of the building next door. The floors are scuffed hardwood. Boxes are piled in the corners of the white walls.

I wear white cotton pajamas and socks on my feet. I test my legs before standing. An open door leads to another room, and I walk through it into a den and dining room combo. There is a couch on one side with a coffee table and side table in front of and next to it. Beyond the den area is an alcove with a small round table for eating with two matching chairs. My computer sits on the tabletop. Beyond the dining area is a galley kitchen with white Formica countertops and aged appliances.

More windows with bars. More boxes. Little decor. No pictures of a family or a boy or a girl on any surface. No art hanging on the walls. No splash of color. This is a railroad apartment, but it feels more like a way station.

I cross to the window and look out and am not surprised when I see Main Street beyond the fire escape. This is one of the second-floor brownstones downtown. Across the street is Paw-Tastic Pets and the smoothie shop and the antiques store and a therapist's office, which means I am either above Mimi's or the comic book shop.

I walk into the kitchen, dragging my feet, stoop shouldered, like an old woman. An open box of crackers lies on its side on the counter. A glass of water, half-drunk, sits by the sink. Bread and water. Staples of a prison.

My cell phone is plugged into a charger. I swipe the screen and see a text from Val. I don't open it.

I move slowly back down the invisible railroad tracks to the bedroom and sit on the white comforter. I gaze at the windows, at the thick black bars that disallow entrance to intruders. I feel nothing. I cannot call up a single emotion. I have been wrung dry. I am an empty shell.

For a long while, I stare into space. How strange to be sitting alone in an empty apartment. No one needs me. I have no duties to fulfill, no obligations, no cries for my attention, no demands on my time. No noise, laughter, tears. No touch.

Fragments of memories like puzzle pieces assemble and disassemble in my head.

I don't know which pieces are real. I only know I had a life. I had love. I had a husband and two children, each of them flawed, but no more so than I. *Less* flawed than I. But instead of accepting them for the gifts they were, instead of letting them in and allowing them to love me, I saw them as challenges to endure, hardships to survive, encumbrances that dragged me under. I wanted a life with no burdens, no conflicts, no struggles. And now I see the cost. Too high.

Now I have nothing.

And now the feelings come. A tide of shame rises up. A wave of remorse crashes over me.

I am drowning.

~

To exist is all I know. And yet. I've learned.

I rise to the surface of my regret, dry my eyes, breathe, straighten my shoulders. I find jeans and a T-shirt in one of the boxes in the bedroom and pull them on. The jeans are loose and the T-shirt hangs limply on my frame. I throw on some sneakers I wore in another life then find my purse in a heap by the front door and leave the apartment.

The sun almost blinds me. I reach into my purse for sunglasses but find none.

Mimi's is open for business. Through the front window, I see Devi skipping across the floor of the waiting area, passing ladies skimming through fashion magazines or glancing at their watches or twirling locks of hair that may soon be on the floor. The comic book store isn't open yet, but a couple of teenagers hang out at the curb, talking and laughing and fist bumping.

I cross the street and head for Paw-Tastic Pets, gaining speed the nearer I get to the store. A part of me wants to stop at the window of the antiques shop, but I suppress the urge. I know my mission this morning. The antiques shop and Dolores and the miniature house are for another time. I don't know when. Perhaps today, perhaps next week or next year. I only know that I am not yet ready for the reckoning. And I have something else I need to do.

The door of the pet store is heavier than I remember, or I've become less effectual. I bypass the counter, my pace quickening as I move through the aisles, the shelves of pet food and dog toys and urine pads and kitty litter. The girl, the employee I know—what is her name? Did I ever know it?—restocks a shelf with fish food. She sees me and starts to say hello, but I pretend not to notice her.

My heart pounds. What if he isn't here? What if he's been sent away already, sent to the needle? I pray that I haven't erased another being with my greed. If he is gone, I, too, will be gone. One final wish will be easy to make.

I reach the back of the store and scan the kennels. I don't see him. My throat tightens as I continue to search. Lab puppies, spaniels, a bull-dog, two Chihuahuas, calico kittens, an albino bunny, and . . . there! There he is in the corner kennel, curled up against the side of the cage, unmoving. My breath whooshes from my chest.

The girl comes up next to me. "Can I help you?" she asks.

"I want him," I say, my eyes never leaving Charlemagne.

"I knew you'd come back," she says.

~

Charlemagne isn't sick. And as with most dogs, his broken heart heals quickly in my care. I don't believe that this little ball of fur can mend my broken heart. Nothing can. I broke it myself. But I do allow him to rule my thoughts, and this keeps me from thinking about everything else—how horribly I went wrong, how I threw away my life, how I erased people, both beloved and despised. He saves me from being suf-focated by the weight of my sins.

Images, thoughts, reprimands, recriminations press against my mind, but Charlemagne obscures them. He is here and now. He is my present tense. His demands on my time and attention are welcome distractions. I give over to him fully.

The apartment is like a wonderland for a creature that has spent his life in a two-by-two-foot cell. He romps around and barks furiously at the pigeons on the fire escape and chews on the couch cushions. I don't stop him.

He pees on the urine pads, as he has been trained to do, but I take him out for bowel movements, as he refuses to do that inside. The constant walks are good for me. The fresh air revives me. After the first day of walking him, I experience hunger and know it for what it is. I satiate my hunger with the crackers because I have no other food. It only takes a few of the salty squares to fill me. I can't taste them.

By nine o'clock, Charlemagne is exhausted. He curls up by my feet as I sit at the kitchen table in the minuscule alcove off the tiny den. I wait as my computer boots. As soon as the cursor stops spinning, I click onto Facebook. I don't know what to expect in this new reality. I don't know if former communications still apply. But when I click on the tab at the top of the page, Dante's message is still there, awaiting a reply.

I type a few sentences in the message box, hit "Send," then shut the computer down. I stand and stretch. My jeans fall down to my upper thighs. I hike them up and walk to the bedroom, shutting off lights as I go. I climb into bed without changing into my pajamas, without brushing my teeth or washing my face, because, really, who cares at this point?

I stare at the dark ceiling. After a few seconds, I hear the soft click of puppy nails on the hardwood. A soft yelp sounds from next to the bed. I turn to see Charlemagne gazing up at me from the floor. I reach over and grab him, then raise him to the bed. He sniffs the air, walks around in a few circles, paws the comforter, then plops down against my chest.

He is just a dog. He isn't a husband or a daughter or a son. But he is here. I wrap my arms around him.

THIRTY-SEVEN

The next morning begins the same way, except that my disorientation is cut short by the presence of Charlemagne. He sleeps in the crook of my arm.

The employee at Paw-Tastic Pets—I found out her name, Tammy—told me that puppies generally pee several times a night until their bladders mature. But there is no way Charlemagne could have gotten himself back up onto the bed after a visit to his urine pad. I check the bedding. It's dry. He felt my need, I decide. He knew I needed the warmth of him, the constancy of his heartbeat, the softness of his fur. He held himself for me. I snuggle against him and kiss him on the top of his head.

As soon as I shift, he jumps to his feet, hops off the bed, and makes a beeline for his urine pad. I laugh, and the sound is strange to my ears. I don't dislike it, but it hurts.

I push back the covers to see that I'm still wearing my clothes from yesterday. One less thing to do. One more check mark on my short list.

The nightstand beside me is not the one from my house, but I know the journal will be in the drawer, next to a necklace with a lion pendant. I pull the necklace out and gaze at the pendant, then clasp it around my neck. The pendant feels heavier than it should. I withdraw the journal and run my fingers across the cover, but I don't open it. I carry it with me into the main room and stow it in my purse, then head to the kitchen, where I fill Charlemagne's bowls with kibble and water. I grab a cracker and pop it in my mouth. It's dry and stale. I wash it down with water.

As Charlemagne munches loudly on his food, I backtrack to the dining alcove and boot up my computer. A horn blares from the street below, muted by the triple-paned glass. I realize my jeans are falling off, so I head to the bedroom and search through the boxes until I find another pair. I put them on. They are even roomier than the last pair, so I grab a belt from the same box and loop it around my waist. I'm forced to use the very last hole.

I return to my computer and sit and push away thoughts about my diminishing middle. I log on to Facebook and see that Dante has responded to my message. I read his reply, then leave the site. I glance at the clock on the lower corner of the computer. I have an hour. Plenty of time. I go to my banking website and pay the few bills I have: rent, which is a pittance compared to my mortgage and includes my utilities; cell phone; basic cable.

I open my email provider and click on a correspondence from Val.

> Hi, Emma. Hope you are doing as well as possible under the circumstances. Mr. Canning and Mr. Wells asked me to reach out to you to let you know that you can take as much or as little time as you need. I should tell you, also, that they are making some changes, but they want you to know that there will always be a place for you here. Call me if you want to get together. I miss you and am sending you love and prayers.

Val. She is a lovely woman with whom I could have been friends, but I was unwilling to let her in. I worked with her for years and never told her about Josh's disability. I never confided in her at all. And yet she was one of the first people to offer help when my son died. Perhaps we can still be friends. I won't return to Canning and Wells—I know what she means by "changes"—but I can seek her out apart from work. If I'm still here.

As I reread her email, I realize that I have been given a kind of do-over. I don't want it. I'm forty-one years old and alone. But if this is my fate, if I am relegated to this new reality, I have to forge on. I have to make different choices than the ones I made in my old life. I must do it right this time. Or end it. Or. End. It.

The new wish, the one that has been lingering in the back of my mind since I awoke yesterday morning in this apartment, expands in my brain, pushes against the inside of my skull. I hear the words at full volume. I want to say them. Because I don't want to start over. I don't want this new life. I want my old life. If I can't have it, I don't want anything.

All I have to do is give the wish the gift of my voice.

A soft tap on my foot breaks through my thoughts. Charlemagne sits beside the table leg, one paw resting on my toes, looking up at me curiously. I bend down and pick him up, then place him in my lap and stroke his fur. He licks my fingers, my hand, straightens up and presses his forepaws on my chest and attempts to lick my face.

The wish is still there, hovering. But the volume has decreased.

~

Twenty minutes later, with Charlemagne leashed, my pockets full of dog treats and poop bags, my purse holstered over my shoulder, I leave the apartment. The day is warm, but a soft breeze cuts through the August heat and cools my face as I walk.

My destination is two miles from downtown. My stride is leisurely because I have the time and also because I need to pace myself. My strength and endurance are lower than they were before. I'm going to have to start nourishing myself with more than crackers and water if I am to keep up with Charlemagne. If I am going to go on.

I reach the gates of the park five minutes before ten. He is already there, sitting on a green wood-slatted bench a stone's throw from the playground. Although we are a hundred yards apart, he recognizes me immediately and raises himself off the bench. My heart beats faster, like it did every time I saw him, every time I was in his presence, all those years ago.

Dante.

I walk toward him down a path that cuts through an expansive grassy lawn. Charlemagne pulls at his leash, wanting to have at the grass, and I kneel down to release him from his leash. He bounds across the lawn, rolls over, cuts back toward me. I withdraw a small red ball from my purse and toss it for him. Enchanted, he races after the ball, then plops down and starts to gnaw on it voraciously.

Dante doesn't move, just stands there watching me, waiting for me to reach him. Just as it used to be. He was the light and I was the moth. Even now we play those roles.

All the questions one might ask just before a reunion such as this—*What is he like now? What will he think of me? What will we say to each other?*—none of those questions matter. I release them into the air.

So tall, still so tall and so broad, like a bear. He wears jeans and a T-shirt with the legend **NAMASTE** emblazoned across the front. How like him. I reach the concrete perimeter of the playground a few feet from where he stands and I stop. I gaze at him for a moment, taking in the whole of him, the gray in his short hair and his beard, the deep grooves around his eyes and mouth, the grin, the sparkle in his eyes. He opens his arms to me. I rush into them. He smells the same, deodorant soap and sweat and faded musky cologne. My tears are sudden and fierce.

"Em," he says in his round baritone. "Emma, my Em." He strokes my hair with one hand while holding me tightly with the other. "God, it's been a long time. I'm so glad to see you."

I feel the same, but I can't access the words.

He grabs me around the waist. "My God, you're so thin."

"I had liposuction" is all I can think of to say. I don't remember the procedure specifically, but my stomach still bears the tiny incision scars.

"Well, I daresay they took too much out of you. You need some of my bolognese to fatten you up." He laughs his hearty laugh and pulls away so that he can look at me. His eyes find mine and he stares down at me intently. I realize the passage of time hasn't diminished the connection we shared. This man knew me better than anyone. He knows me still. We are not in love anymore, but we know each other.

Looking at Dante makes me think of another man. A man with a receding hairline, a strong nose, and hazel eyes. Colin. My husband. He knew me also, even though I didn't want him to, even though I never really let him in. He took me as I was, the good and the bad, and I resented him for it because I didn't like who I was. Colin never made me tremble with lust or tingle with anticipation; he didn't make my heart flutter, not the way Dante did. But he made me feel safe and warm when I allowed him to. Those times became less frequent, but that was my fault, not his.

I swallow the lump in my throat as thoughts of Colin fade. He's gone. I wished him away.

"What is it, Em? What's wrong?"

I don't answer. Where to begin?

He covers my hand with his enormous mitt of a hand and draws me to the bench. We sit, side by side. I glance over at the grass, where Charlemagne is still at work on his ball. Dante follows my gaze.

"Cute little guy."

I nod. We are both quiet for a moment.

"You know, I was so happy when you reached out to me. After all these years, I thought I'd never hear from you. I wanted to get in touch so many times, but I didn't want to hurt you. I hurt you enough. So when you sent me that friend request . . . I . . . it was a wonderful surprise. But now, I see that you didn't get in touch so that we could catch up. You need something from me."

I turn toward him. He smiles knowingly.

"If it's an apology you need, you have it. I'm so sorry, Em, for leaving like I did."

I shake my head. "It's not that, Dante. That was another life. Another me."

"Then what?"

I take a deep breath and blow it out slowly. "I didn't know who else to turn to. Something happened to me. Something unbelievable, inconceivable. No one would believe me if I told them, that's how crazy it is. If I shared it with anyone, they'd think I'm insane. I might be. I don't know. I don't know anything anymore. Except that I needed to share it with you, this story of mine. You, because you know me. And because you've been all over the world and seen amazing things, uncovered mysteries, witnessed miracles. You're a Renaissance man."

He grins. "I'm a plumber, Em. Didn't you read my Facebook page?"

"That's what you do, not what you are."

"What I am is a lonely man who lives in a studio apartment in Queens. I have no wife, no kids, no real home. I have a thousand life experiences and no life." He places his hand on my knee, pats it. "But I do know you, Em. Even now. And I'll listen to your story."

I reach into my purse and pull out the journal, then give it to him. "It's all there. It shouldn't take you too long."

He nods then says, "Okay."

I stand and stretch my back, then walk to the grass where Charlemagne lies. He jumps up at my arrival and starts growling at me playfully, then bats the ball over to my feet. I grab it and toss it and Charlemagne makes chase.

Every so often, I glance back at Dante. His eyes are glued to the page. I wonder what he will make of my words. Perhaps he will suggest I seek therapy. Maybe he'll call the police. Possibly, he'll simply put the journal down on the bench and walk away. It doesn't matter. As much as I can feel, I feel good to have let someone in on my secret.

Seconds become minutes and minutes become a half an hour. Charlemagne entertains me. Finally, in my peripheral vision, I see Dante close the journal. He doesn't set it aside; instead, he holds it in his lap. I wander over to him slowly, hesitantly. He looks up at me. His expression is inscrutable.

"Well," he says.

"Well," I agree.

"You do realize how absolutely nuts this is."

"Yes," I say. My spirits, which are already low, bottom out. Dante doesn't believe me. He won't kidnap me and put me under psychiatric hold. He loves me too much for that. At least, he did a long time ago. I lower my gaze to the rough concrete.

He averts his eyes, shakes his head. "I've never heard of anything like this happening, ever."

I laugh mirthlessly. "Neither have I."

The wish, my final wish, whispers in my ear.

"Of course, that doesn't mean it didn't happen."

Relief floods through me. I look at him, and he gives me that mischievous smile, the one that made me fall in love with him the first time I saw it.

"So, what do I do now?" I ask, even though I suspect he doesn't have the answer. I suspect no one has the answer.

"The way I see it, there's only one thing you can do."

I let out a sigh. I already know what he's about to say. *Move on. Let go of this. Live your life. Live it better.*

"We need to go down to that antiques shop and talk to Dolores."

I stare at him dumbly. "What?"

He shrugs. "It's just a suggestion."

I'm about to ask him why, how he came to that conclusion, but the question sticks to my tongue and stays behind my teeth. I don't need to ask. I knew yesterday that I would have to face Dolores, but I didn't know when. I didn't foresee our rendezvous happening so soon. I thought I might be granted some time to get my bearings, to adjust to my new circumstances, accept my new life. Or not accept it. But Dante read my journal. And this is what he suggests. I know how his mind works. I was in love with the inner workings of his brain as much as the man himself. The sponge that could soak up, sift through, analyze and interpret information and come out on the other side with the answer. The only answer. His knowing me was only half of why I invited him here. The other half was his mind.

I reach out to him, and he hands me my journal. I take it and tuck it in my purse, then reach out to him again. "Let's go."

THIRTY-EIGHT

The light of the day has changed. The sky resembles dusk, a deep indigo, although it can't yet be noon. I glance at my watch as Dante weaves his Fiat toward downtown. The digital screen has gone dead. Charlemagne sleeps in the back seat, his head resting on his front paws. Dante concentrates on the road and hums "La Vie en Rose."

Main Street is deserted. We have entered a ghost town. The buildings along the block sag with fatigue. Storefronts are closed, shuttered, boarded up. I glance at Dante for his reaction, but his expression is indifferent, relaxed. I mimic him and pretend that nothing is amiss.

If my life over the course of the last several weeks had been normal, if none of the bizarre, implausible, *impossible* events had transpired, I might be afraid, terrified even. But of all the things that have occurred, a shift in daylight and the sudden abandonment of a city street are the least concerning.

I point to the antiques store but realize I needn't have bothered. Dante already seems to know where he's going, and the little shop is the only business on Main Street that shows any signs of life. The display window glows, and within the display case, the miniature house, *my house*, is bathed in amber light.

Dante pulls to the curb in front of the shop. I reach over and grab Charlemagne, and for the first time, I notice how thin my arms are. My wrist bone is a protruding knob that leads down to skeletal fingers.

You wanted to escape. To disappear. Wishes come true.

Charlemagne protests, yawns, then allows me to pull him into my lap. I attach his leash, open the car door, and set him on the ground. Dante gets out of the car and comes around to my side, offering me a gentle assist. I'm so frail a gust of wind could blow me away.

Dante, Charlemagne, and I walk to the storefront and stand before the display window. The glass is opaque; I can only discern the outline of the house.

The sky above has gone a starless purple. The streetlamps are dark.

"Well?" Dante says. His voice is a thousand miles away. "This is it, Emma. Go in."

I turn to him to protest, but he has vanished into thin air. The scent of him lingers for a moment, then evaporates as though he were never here at all. Was he? Perhaps not. I look down at my feet. Charlemagne is also gone. I am alone. Again.

My legs feel like they are made of straw. I limp to the front door and use the little strength I have left to shove it open. The shop is dark save for the display window and a single recessed ceiling light toward the back of the showroom.

Dolores stands in the center of the shower of light. She doesn't look old. She looks ancient. Her face is a road map of furrows and grooves and skin as insubstantial as cellophane. But her eyes are ageless and very much alive. Her irises dance.

"I knew you'd come back," she says.

"What's happening to me?"

She smiles, amused. "The necklace is lovely, isn't it?"

I touch the pendant. My fingers slide over it, then rest on the middle of my chest. I can feel my clavicles through my skin.

"Do you remember the day you bought it?"

I open my mouth to speak. My voice is friable, my words sounding more like the croaking of a bullfrog. "Not specifically. I know it happened, but I can't quite call up the memory."

"Memories are funny things, aren't they? We silly humans have a strange relationship with them. We change our memories all the time, shape them, twist them, mold them so that we can live with them. When, really, all we ought to do is cherish them and learn from them."

"How can I cherish them if I've lost them?" I ask. My throat is sandpaper. My mouth is parched.

"You could always make a wish," she says, then gives me a puckish grin. "No, wait. That's what got you into trouble in the first place, isn't it?"

I feel my lower lip tremble, but I have no tears to shed. My cheeks feel sunken and hollow. My guts feel as though they are digesting themselves.

"I have one wish left," I tell her.

"First things first," she replies. She gestures to the small dollhouse on the display counter, the one-story prewar with the picket fence. "That was my life. Until I wished it away." She looks around the shop, at the antiques and knickknacks and furniture, suddenly covered with a thick layer of dust and cobwebs. "Now I'm surrounded by ghosts."

Dolores locks her gaze on mine, then stretches out her arm. It reaches past me from where she stands, twenty feet away. I'm hallucinating, but I keep my eyes open.

"Why don't you take a look inside?" She stands beside me. She is twenty years old and looks like Greta Garbo. She moves to the front window display, within which sits the dollhouse, *my* house. She unlatches the back door of the display window, and points to the step stool on the floor beneath it. Inside the display case, there is a small area behind the house, just wide enough to accommodate a very small person.

"Go on," she urges. She is my mother. I want to hug her. I want to yell at her for leaving me. "You better hurry, honey. They're almost gone."

I stagger to the display window, grab the sides of the door frame to steady myself, then climb up the step stool. I am small enough to fit in the space behind the house. There's room to spare. The house looms before me. It looks larger than it did, but then, I'm smaller, and growing smaller still.

The back of the house is cut away, and I stare inside. My house. I see the cracked tile on the floor, the broken banister, the smallish, fat television on the stand in the living room. Through the front window I see the gnarly tree, the crooked unlevel pavers, the Civic, the van.

Inside the house, on the second floor, in the room at the end of the hall, the figure of a girl with red hair lies on a pink floral duvet, talking on a miniature cell phone. In the kitchen, the figure of a man stands at the counter, a demitasse in one hand, a pipe in the other. In the family room, the figure of a boy with dark hair sits in a wheelchair, staring at a computer screen, his expression thoughtful, delighted.

My breathing is labored; my lungs have shrunk. I don't have much time. The muscles in my arms have shriveled. I dig down to the deepest part of myself, to my core, and raise my trembling arms up, up, up. I lower them around the house, grasping the eaves on either side with my bony fingers. I press myself against the jagged wood of the cutaway, lay my head against the roof tiles.

I close my eyes. Darkness engulfs me. I submit. I go.

I wish. I wish. I wish. I wish I wish I wish I wish I wish I wish . . .

EPILOGUE

Monday, August 15

I awaken to a ray of sunlight slicing across my comforter through the curtains in the window. Glorious sunlight washing over the flowers of the precious quilt my mother made. The quilt is not tired, just well used, loved because it was made with loving hands. The room around me hums with energy, as though it has come alive with my presence, as though it has been waiting for me. The many imperfections—the scuffed furniture, the tired landscapes, the beige walls, those things I resented—are all meaningless now. I am home.

The aroma of espresso wafts up from downstairs, the strong, bitter scent arousing my senses. I hear the soft voices of CNN from the TV in the kitchen and the sound of the shower from the bathroom down the hall. I hear the loud, rhythmic breathing from the monitor on the dresser, and I think there has never been a sweeter sound in all the world. And above that, high and insistent, is the furious, incessant bark of the neighbors' puppy.

I sit up in bed as that not-right feeling comes over me.

I wait a moment, listening to the house around me.

Then I smile to myself as I throw back the covers. Because I realize that the not-quite-right thing about this morning is that everything is *just right.*

I pull open the nightstand drawer and root around for my journal. There it is, under a magazine and a worn copy of *Gone With the Wind*. My fingers tremble as I unlock the clasp and open the journal and gaze down at the pages. All blank, not a single word written upon them.

These last several weeks, disorientation has been my constant companion, and it visits me again, although only for a moment. I don't know what happened to me, whether I am waking from one long horrible, wonderful dream, or if I actually possessed the power of wishes for a short time. But as the disorientation lifts, and the world around me returns to its usualness, I realize it doesn't matter.

What I do know is that my checklist still exists, although it has altered. I grab a pen from the nightstand and place the tip against the top of the first page of the journal.

To do:
1) Report my boss no matter the consequences
2) Look for a new job that makes me proud of myself
3) Counsel my daughter and connect with her
4) Open my heart to my husband and let him in, allow him to know me.

I look up to see Colin standing at the bedroom door. My breath hitches at the sight of him.

"Good morning," he says. His voice is apprehensive. Why wouldn't it be? He fears my mood because I've given him every reason to. I smile at him as tears slide down my cheeks. He looks at me with concern and crosses to the bed. "Are you okay?"

"I'm fine. I just had a terrible dream."

He sits beside me on the end of the bed. "What was it about?"

"It doesn't matter," I tell him. His shoulders slouch. I think about my new checklist—*let him in*—and reconsider my answer. "You were gone. You and Josh and Katie. You were all gone. And I was alone."

His expression saddens, and he gazes down at his lap. "Sometimes I think that's what you want," he says quietly.

It's difficult for me to admit, but I do it anyway, because this is what my husband needs. This is what *I* need. I reach out and take his hand. "Sometimes I did, too. But I don't anymore. You guys are my life. And what a great life it is."

Slowly, his lips curve into a smile. "That must have been one hell of a dream."

I nod. "It was."

He kisses my cheek, then gives my hand a squeeze. He glances at the monitor. "Want me to get him up?"

"No. I'll do it," I tell him. "I want to take him next door to meet Charlemagne."

Colin chuckles. I like the sound. "The yapper?" he asks with a mock frown.

I match his laughter. "He's just a puppy. He'll outgrow it. Anyway, I'm finally going to taste Louise's Peruvian coffee. I think I might like it."

ACKNOWLEDGMENTS

The idea for *All That's Left of Me* came to me after my mom died, and it bounced around in my head for a long while. Her passing inspired me to ask those universal questions we all ask at some point: *What's it all about? Why are we here? Am I living the life I should be?*

I still don't have the answers to the first two questions, but as for the third, the answer is definitely yes. My life is perfect as it is. Well, imperfectly perfect. I don't always do the right thing or make the right choices—tragedy strikes, losses occur, and challenges confront me—but I am richly blessed with an amazing family, friends, loved ones (you know who you are), and countless gifts, and I wouldn't change a thing. (Except, perhaps, my waistline!)

As always, I must give praise and thanks to the many people who made this book possible.

First and foremost, thank you to my fantastic agent, Wendy Sherman. Her feedback, guidance, and unwavering support are the reasons you are holding this book (or e-reader) in your hands.

Thanks to my developmental editor, the wonderful Melody Guy, whose insightful questions, comments, notes, and suggestions—once again—made this a better book.

Thank you to Kelli Martin, who championed this book to Lake Union. Thanks to Danielle Marshall, Alicia Clancy, and the entire Lake Union team. My experience with your imprint has been unparalleled.

Thank you for your meticulousness, and your commitment to publishing the best books possible.

Thank you to my writing family: Michael Steven Gregory and Wes Albers and the entire Southern California Writers Conference community; Maddie Margarita and Larry Poriccelli and the Southern California Writers Association; my Novel Intensive teaching partner, Ara Grigorian—I've listened to your lessons how many times and I still learn new things; my online writing friends, including Melissa Amster, Julie Valerie, and Samantha Stroh Bailey.

I would not have been able to write about Josh's medical issues without the help and expertise of Linda Sanfillipo. Thank you, Linda, for your invaluable input. If there are any mistakes or misrepresentations regarding Josh's condition or care, they are mine, not hers.

To my readers, I know there are a great many choices out there. Thank you for choosing this book. I hope my stories touch you in some way and that you'll keep reading them, because I write them for you.

Finally, while creating a character challenged with cerebral palsy, I learned a great many things and gained tremendous respect—and awe—for those persons challenged by this disorder. You and your families, and the courage you display on a daily basis, are an inspiration to me.

ABOUT THE AUTHOR

Janis Thomas is the author of *What Remains True* and three critically acclaimed humorous works of women's fiction—*Something New, Sweet Nothings*, and *Say Never*—as well as the mystery *Murder in A-Minor*. She has written more than fifty songs and two children's books, which she created with her dad. Janis is a writing advocate, editor, workshop leader, and speaker. When she isn't writing or fulfilling her PTA duties, Janis likes to play tennis, sing with her sister, and throw lavish dinner parties with outrageous menus for friends and loved ones. Janis lives in Southern California with her husband, their two beautiful children, and two crazy dogs.